THE WRATH OF GOD

BY VERNE R. ALBRIGHT

To: Wendy
Enjoy!
Verne R. Albright

Hellgate Press   Ashland, OR

Playing Chess with God
©2018 Verne R. Albright

Published by Hellgate Press
(An imprint of L&R Publishing, LLC)

Hellgate Press
PO Box 3531
Ashland, OR 97520
email: info@hellgatepress.com

Interior Design: Sasha Kincaid
Cover Design: L. Redding
Cover Illustrations: (Front) "Storm at Sea" by Willem van de Velde the Younger (1633-1707); (Back) "Ships Running Aground in a Storm" by Ludolf Bakhuizen (1690)

Cataloging In Publication Data is available from the publisher upon request.
ISBN: 978-1-55571-919-7 (paperback)
ISBN: 978-1-55571-920-3 (ebook)

Printed and bound in the United States of America
First edition 10 9 8 7 6 5 4 3 2 1

OTHER VERNE R. ALBRIGHT BOOKS AVAILABLE THROUGH HELLGATE PRESS:
PLAYING CHESS WITH GOD (PREQUEL TO _THE WRATH OF GOD_)

IV   THE WRATH OF GOD

CHAPTER ONE
GONE

1859. All day, Henning Dietzel had helped victims scattered across what remained of Iquique, Peru. Despite his efforts and those of others, the moaning and screaming had too often been silenced by death. At first, dealing with so many injured had seemed impossible. But by nightfall there were no more wounds to stitch, bones to set, limbs to amputate, or tourniquets to loosen so body parts wouldn't wither.

During seemingly endless pushing, pulling, twisting, and lifting, Henning's back spasms had gone from painful to immobilizing. When there was nothing more to do, he'd finally let himself collapse. An hour later he was staring at the darkening sky, still embedded in clinging mud that had molded itself to his shape.

When the twenty-foot-high wall of water crushed Iquique he'd been miles away on a behind-schedule train. Had he arrived on time, he too would've been dead. While rummaging through the ruins of the quaint, English-style town looking for survivors, he suffered the guilt typical of those who escape death when friends don't.

Had he deserved to live more than those who died? He'd been absent years before when Domingo and Isabel Santa María lost their California *rancho*. They'd welcomed him into their family and made him one of them. Their daughter fell in love with him. He could have saved their home and livelihood. But busy chasing success, he'd lost track of them.

Maybe the tidal wave had been retribution. Or perhaps his punishment was that life went on and would now be infinitely more difficult.

Yesterday, Iquique had been the only port where Peru's nitrate was loaded on freighters to satisfy the world's demand for fertilizer and explosives. Now the town called Queen of the Coast was a scar on a ravaged beach—little more than splintered wood tangled with seaweed, wagon wheels, and debris from houses, businesses, and gardens. Already the town's doctors had ordered volunteers to burn the bloated corpses before their rotting spread disease.

Henning's businesses were gone. His savings would be depleted before Iquique was rebuilt. When he could no longer pay the banks, they'd repossess his flourishing mine, the beach where his loading dock had stood, and the downtown lot where his water hauling business had been reduced to debris.

"Obstacles are those pesky things you see when you lower your eyes from your goal." When Henning was sixteen, his grandfather's saying had inspired him. But now his future was bleak and full of difficulties beyond solution.

With mud sucking away his body heat, he felt suddenly chilly. Another effort to stand was stopped by excruciating pain. Nearby, Encinas Peralta was fast asleep. Once the madam of Chile's most successful bordello, she was now a dear friend who managed his water business and sometimes shared his bed. She would gladly help him get to his feet if he could bear to wake her. But he couldn't—not after her draining hours of helping the injured. He'd sleep where he was.

Maybe things would look better in the morning. Finding a position where the mud supported his back more comfortably, Henning cleared his exhausted mind. Concern for his uncertain future gave way to memories of Encinas telling him how different he was from Latin men and how much she loved his height, blond hair, and blue eyes. Next came random images of his mother the day she died and the Prussian farm where he'd become a man.

The screams of the injured faded.

******

With the sun barely above the horizon, stampeding men jolted Henning awake. Rolling onto his stomach he tried to stand, but stabbing pain stopped him again. Through the legs of men rushing toward the beach, he saw a newly arrived clipper ship lowering a lifeboat.

"Bring food, water, and medical supplies," a nearby man yelled between cupped hands.

"We're loading everything we can spare," a distant voice answered.

Near shore, the launch plowed onto a sandbar and wouldn't come loose. *Sea Witch*, the name of its mother ship, was painted on the prow. Instantly Henning detected something he often saw before others did, opportunity—a chance to get back where he'd been before the tidal wave—if this was the once-legendary *Sea Witch*.

Amidst floating corpses and debris, men waded into the water and freed the craft, then dragged it ashore. The disaster's scale hit Henning again as *Sea Witch's* ruddy-faced captain exclaimed, "Dearest God in 'eaven. This must have been the mother of all killer waves."

Still half asleep Encinas Peralta struggled to her feet.

"Can you spare rum to quiet the pain of the injured?" she asked, practical and efficient though her bloodshot eyes were rimmed with dark exhaustion.

"Bring every rum keg in the galley," the captain boomed, "and look for bottles hidden in the crew's quarters."

"Yes, sir, Captain Jeffers."

Henning raised his head and called out, "Captain."

Jeffers slowly turned in a circle, then looked down.

"There y'are," he said. "What can I do for ya?"

"Is your *Sea Witch* the one that used to bring tea from China to England?"

"Twice she set the record from Foochow to London," Jeffers said proudly.

"I need to get to England, fast."

"I can take you. But before I 'ead 'ome, I 'ave to find another cargo."

"Do you have authority to arrange one on your own?"

"Of course. Do I look like a eunuch?"

"Then I'll hire your entire ship." Wincing, Henning struggled to his hands and knees. His voice etched with pain, he continued. "With the world's nitrate cut off, the best substitute is guano, and I have plenty on Altamira Island, north of here. If the tidal wave didn't wreck the facilities, my men can load your ship in a day."

"A day to do what usually takes weeks?" Jeffers asked. "I'd leave myself some leeway if I were you."

"I don't have any," Henning managed between clenched teeth. Halfway to his feet, he collapsed, face down.

"Wait for the rum," Encinas implored.

"I'll be fine if you'll walk on my back like you did last time this happened."

Encinas removed her shoes and balanced with a foot on each side of his backbone. Slowly sliding them, she traveled the length of his spine and reversed course.

"Can you concentrate on my lower back, gently please," he gasped as her weight forced air from his lungs.

He cried out as his spine popped loudly.

"You okay?" Encinas asked, stepping into the mud.

"Much better," he grunted, struggling to his knees.

Standing and in obvious pain, he told Jeffers, "If we make London in sixty-five days or less, you'll get a thousand dollar bonus plus a thousand for your crew."

"Not that I want to change your mind, but why the big 'urry?"

"I have to get there fast. Even hours could make a difference."

"*Sea Witch* was demoted to nitrate scow," Jeffers said, "and forced to carry 'eavier loads than she was designed for, but 'er spirit is unbroken. Don't overload 'er with yur guano, Mizder Dietzel, and I'll prove she's still the fastest ship afloat."

"We'll load ballast weight—no more."

"What if I get you to London in sixty-two days?"

"I'll double your bonus and the crew's."

"Ya got a deal," Jeffers replied.

As they sealed their agreement with a handshake Henning asked, "When can we leave?"

"As soon as my launch brings the ship's rum and doctor. I'm going to leave him here to help the injured and pick him up after we load your guano. By the bye, I admire your quick thinking. The price of your guano will go sky-high when it reaches England along with news that there'll be no nitrate for a while. But why are you taking only enough fer ballast?"

"Will you need help in England?" Encinas asked, deflecting Jeffers' prying. Henning never revealed his plans and didn't like to be questioned about them.

"No," Henning replied gratefully. "But I promised to spend more time with you and taking you along will be a perfect start." As her sensuous mouth widened into a smile, he turned back to Jeffers. "Is that okay with you? I'll pay her fare and mine."

"I may be an old-timer but unlike most captains I'm not superstitious." Jeffers tapped his temple with an air of superiority. "I welcome women on my ship, and I have an empty cabin that should suit you two nicely."

"The clothes I'm wearing," Encinas said when she and Henning were alone, "are the only possessions I have left."

"We'll buy what you need as soon as *Sea Witch* makes port."

She didn't ask what they'd do in England. Henning would tell her when ready. And having his undivided attention would be a welcome pleasure. They'd known each other fourteen years, but life had repeatedly conspired to keep them apart.

******

While waiting for *Sea Witch's* lifeboat to return, Henning took Eduardo Vásquez, his manager, aside and quietly said, "You'll be in charge while I'm gone. Captains bringing freighters to Iquique have no way to know it's out of commission. When they get here, try to talk them into loading guano at Altamira Island. And keep the water business going. The schooners were at sea and the wagons were at the mines when the wave hit."

"Isn't that Encinas's job?" Eduardo asked with his usual gruffness. Nearly as tall as Henning and equally handsome, he had an eye for the ladies. But even though Encinas was pretty and shapely, he'd never forgiven her for having been a prostitute.

"Encinas is going to London with me. You'll have to handle things here."

"Aye, aye, sir." Eduardo saluted and clicked his heels.

"Use the profits from our guano and water sales to start rebuilding my dock."

"Exactly as it was?"

"If you think of improvements we can afford, make them. We have enough in the bank to finance my trip and make the next few payments on the mine. Before you run out of money I should be back with enough to tide us over until Iquique is back in operation."

"That'll take fifty times as much as you'll get for a load of guano," Eduardo said. "I know better than to pry into your private plans, but what if the wave hit Altamira Island? We'll soon be broke if your guano diggings are shut down."

"I'll let you know for sure when we come back to pick up *Sea Witch's* physician."

"You're the boss." His voice losing its edge, Eduardo added, "Sorry you lost everything."

"I didn't," Henning replied. "I still have my greatest asset, you."

******

Sea Witch's launch cleared the surf under a pink and orange sky. Oars shattered the reflections of seagulls gliding above as the coxswain called a double-time rhythm. Soon after his demanding voice went silent, the launch thumped against a streamlined hull.

"Let's go boys," Jeffers shouted as his men climbed rope ladders. "Breaking a record requires more enthusiasm."

After her anchors were raised, *Sea Witch* accelerated to fifteen knots. Wanting more, Jeffers had his crew adjust the sails.

"For too long we've plodded along with more weight than we should carry," he exhorted his men. "It's time to relive the glory days."

In Peru's fastest ships the voyage to Altamira Island took twelve hours. Hoping Jeffers could cut that time by half, Henning collapsed beside Encinas on the bed in their cabin.

"I wonder if *Sea Witch* is still as fast as she once was," he said before falling asleep.

Startled by a knock on the door, Henning vaguely heard Jeffers' voice announce, "Just sighted your island, Mizder Dietzel We got 'ere in four hours."

Suddenly wide awake, Henning sat bolt upright. That was unbelievably good time.

From *Sea Witch's* rail, he saw the familiar mound of yellowish guano above dark cliffs where incoming waves exploded into spray. Rounding the east cape, he saw ships waiting offshore, a good sign. They'd have been sunk if the tidal wave had hit there.

Sails lowered, *Sea Witch* coasted to a stop between the anchored ships and a launch bringing the island's pilot.

Through cupped hands, Henning shouted, "Dock this one at the new loading facility immediately and get every available man ready to load her as fast as possible."

As the pilot's launch turned toward *Sea Witch*, he pointed his speaking trumpet at the dock and shouted, "Suspend all loading immediately. Have every wagon bring guano to the mongaries above number four."

Coming aboard, the pilot gruffly commanded the crew, "Drop your ballast overboard. Come on. Let's go. Double time."

His back still painfully delicate, Henning could only watch as heavy rocks were brought on deck and dropped over the rail. After the last one burst through the ocean's glassy surface, two launches with sixteen rowers each towed *Sea Witch* toward the base of a cliff where British engineers had blasted underwater rocks to create a berth.

Chains on the starboard bow and stern were unhooked from anchors and shackled to iron rings on the cliff. Then the portside anchor chains were attached to buoys. Tethered, the ship rose and fell with the water's surges.

"I've never seen a ship put in position that fast," Jeffers told Henning admiringly. "Ya must've spiked the pilot's hand."

"He gets a bonus for every ship he ties up in less than an hour," Henning said. "What's the ideal weight for maximum speed?"

"A thousand tons if we balance the load properly."

Henning hid his disappointment. Windjammers carried four times as much but were slow.

"I don't care what your names used to be," the pilot barked to four crewmen. "They're now number one, two, three, and four." He pointed to ropes dangling from a canvas chute being lowered from the cliff top. "Grab those, and keep that chute lined up with the hatch until we fasten it down. When I call your number, do as I say and be quick about it."

Once chutes had been secured to all three hatches, the pilot yanked a string that jingled a bell high above. Trap doors on three mongary storage boxes were slid part-way open and guano from their sloping floors poured into *Sea Witch's* hold.

"Chutes are holding steady," the pilot shouted. "Open the doors all the way."

As the sun went down, loading continued under huge lanterns that lit the diggings and loading area.

After dinner, Jeffers told Henning, "We left most of our food and water in Iquique. After we pick up my physician, we'll have to re-provision in Talcahuano. Don't worry, that will gain more time than it loses. The girls at the 'Ouse of Smiles will raise my men's spirits to where they can get ten knots in wind that wouldn't put out a candle."

Henning didn't look forward to stopping in Talcahuano, and not just because he hated losing the time. Encinas had once been the madam at the House of Smiles.

******

"Unbelievable," Jeffers said at breakfast, tearing off a chunk of bread from the island's kitchen. "We're already 'alf full."

"The other half will be aboard by dinnertime," Henning promised.

"Loading a guano ship used to take months."

"This will be our record."

"Then it will be my turn to set one." Jeffers grinned.

Twenty-three hours after the first chute was attached, *Sea Witch* had taken on a thousand tons. As the crew unchained her, Alcalino Valdivia—the island's diminutive, shy, half-breed manager—came aboard.

"With nitrate unavailable, guano's price will skyrocket," Henning concluded his final instructions. "Raise ours every time the trading companies raise theirs."

Henning needed maximum profits from the coming guano boom to rebuild his other businesses. But he'd be gone for months and Alcalino was prone to mistakes. Leaving the young manager unsupervised was an invitation to disaster, but there was no choice. Henning's future depended on someone who wasn't dependable.

CHAPTER TWO
FASTER THAN DISASTER

Sea Witch cast off with trimmers still leveling guano in the hold. Normally she wouldn't have sailed before the cargo was balanced, but no one complained. After months at sea, every man aboard was eager to reach Chile's finest bordello.

Stopping briefly in Iquique—where the situation was much improved—Jeffers delivered the food and supplies Henning had brought from Altamira Island. Then with the ship's doctor again on board, *Sea Witch* continued on.

After docking in Talcahuano, Jeffers told the crew, "You're free to enjoy the House of Smiles, but only for an hour." Then he warned, "I can easily find replacements in a port this busy. Anyone who drinks too much or isn't back here in an hour will be left behind."

Jeffers selected six men to restock the larders. As the rest of the crew stampeded across the dock, Encinas asked Henning to go shopping without her.

"If someone recognizes me in front of a crewmember, this voyage will be extremely uncomfortable for both of us," she explained.

Henning soon returned with Encinas's new wardrobe across both arms. Stepping from the gangplank to the deck, he overheard the bosun's mate, who clearly hadn't seen him arrive.

"It's strange Dietzel's lady didn't go ashore."

"She's probably making up for lost sleep," the ship's carpenter responded. "From what I hear, she worked as long and hard as any man after that wave hit Iquique."

Good. They hadn't recognized her. She'd no doubt welcomed them to the House of Smiles many times. But she looked different—prettier in his opinion—without her former tight dresses, overflowing bosom, face powder, rouge, and lip wax.

******

Sea Witch's sails hung limply from her yardarms, framed in blinding sunlight. Henning stopped his agitated pacing and looked down at the ocean's flat, mirror-like surface. Captain Jeffers' speedy clipper was at a standstill. Becalmed for hours, she could remain so for days.

For Henning to succeed, he had to reach London at least a week before ships brought word that there'd be no nitrate for a year. Otherwise, his goal wouldn't simply be difficult. It would be unachievable.

For an hour after Sea Witch was becalmed, he and Encinas had paced the deck together.

"This isn't helping," she'd finally said. "I'm going below. Keep me company."

He'd been too agitated to relax, but should have gone—especially after his promise to spend more time with her.

A shapely, wavy-haired combination of competence and allure, Encinas had been his first love when they were eighteen. Her answers to his letters had gone astray while he was in California's gold fields. Thinking she'd lost interest he'd stopped writing. Years later she'd left the only life she'd ever known to run his water business. And enrich his life. She was entitled to more than his leftover time.

Late that afternoon a welcome breeze cooled Henning's brow. Gradually it gained speed until it filled *Sea Witch's* drooping sails and slowly pushed her forward. As if to compensate for its long absence, the wind surged into gusts that whipped the grayish-blue ocean into froth and spray.

The crew drew straws to see who'd stay on deck and risk being swept overboard. Clutching the rail and peering over the stern, Henning saw the rudder come out of the water. Time to go below.

Encinas was halfway up the stairs.

"Oh good," she said, reversing course with a meaningful backward glance. "I want you with me in case this storm affects me the way that other one did." Years ago during their first cruise, Encinas had found rough seas sexually arousing.

One hand on each wall, they rushed down the narrow passageway. As they hurried into their cabin, the ship rose and fell, catapulting them past the door Henning had opened, then slamming it behind them.

"This is getting bad enough to have excellent results," he joked.

The bucking and rearing grew violent. They'd ridden out that first storm on a sofa bolted to the passenger ship's floor. But there were no such amenities on freighters. Henning wrapped his arms around Encinas from behind and sat them down on the bed. Then wedged himself, back against the headboard, feet pressed to the wall.

"Good thing you're tall," Encinas said.

Uncertainty was the worst part of storms. Even after years at sea, Henning couldn't tell how bad they'd get or how long they'd last.

After breaking fast, this one ended suddenly. Until certain it was over, Henning kept Encinas securely in his arms.

"Waltz with me when it's safe," she invited, seductively.

"Dancing with me will never be safe," he said. "I don't know how."

"Does this give you incentive to learn?" Getting off the bed, she removed her blouse and the garment beneath.

"That's not fair," he said, standing up.

"Come on, handsome." She crossed her arms, plumping up her breasts. "This is *quid pro quo* and it's your turn."

Suspenders dangling, Henning undid his shirt buttons, revealing the chest hair that had distressed him when it first appeared, and still did.

Encinas ran her fingers through it and asked, "When will you finally believe I find this exciting?"

With a flash of translucent black stockings, she stepped out of her skirt then tapped her foot with mock impatience.

"I know. I know. *Quid pro quo.*" Undressed now, Henning turned toward the bed.

"Oh no you don't," Encinas protested with a playful pout. "I've always wanted to dance naked with you."

"Even though I'll go the wrong way every time?"

"Especially then. Unexpected contact is more delicious when we're undressed."

The fleeting brushes of skin were indeed arousing. Again and again Henning pressed against her, maintaining contact as long as he could before she coquettishly escaped with a change of direction or speed.

Listening to her tuneful humming, he lost track of time. The rush to reach his goal became enjoyment of the journey. He hoped she hadn't done this with anyone else...that teasing like this was as special for her as for him.

"Where did you learn to dance so well?" he asked quietly.

"My former profession could be cruel," she replied with her usual candor. "Too often, I met interesting men and never saw them again. I was however, blessed with some romantic moments. But ladies don't discuss such things. And if you and I make love now, every nerve in my body will explode."

******

In their cabin the next morning, Encinas woke to see Henning squeezed between the bed and wall at the tiny desk Captain Jeffers had provided. Shivering, he stopped covering a sheet of paper with numbers and adjusted the blanket draped over his shoulders.

"It can't be morning. I feel like I just fell asleep," she said. On her feet in the satin robe he'd bought in Talcahuano, Encinas looked over his shoulder and added, "Desks are meant for work and beds are for sleeping and certain other activities. The bad thing about having one next to the other is that you're an early riser and by the time I'm awake, your mind is elsewhere. What are you doing now?"

"Trying to figure out how to do something that may not be possible," he said, putting his pen down. "Like your bookkeeping at the House of Smiles, numbers help me predict the future."

"Numbers told me what I'd already done, nothing more. What do those tell you?"

"How to proceed once we get to England."

"You're going to do more than sell your guano, aren't you?"

"Yes." The blanket slipped off his shoulders as he slid his chair back.

Straddling his legs Encinas sat on his thighs and said, "I know you don't like being interrupted when working, but don't worry. After last night—

which was delicious by the way—I'm satisfied for a while. So give me a kiss and finish your work."

"I'll spend more time with you soon. I promise," he said after their lips parted.

After breakfast, Henning went on deck to offer the captain encouragement. Instead he found himself silently admiring Jeffers' almost supernatural ability to squeeze more speed from his legendary vessel. Not to mention the energy he put into tasks that should have bored him after decades at sea.

"Look at him," the first mate whispered. "He really wants that bonus."

"Money isn't his principal motivation," Henning replied. "He wants to reestablish *Sea Witch* as the fastest ship afloat."

"So you've already figured out that *Sea Witch* is his mistress? Very impressive. What's yours? Making money? Or that woman you're traveling with? You may not have realized this yet, but one day you'll have to choose between them."

******

No matter when Henning came on deck Jeffers was there, his strong jaw covered with stubble because he hadn't taken time to shave. He even ate topside rather than have subordinates fail to make immediate adjustments as conditions varied. He could smell the slightest variations in wind and water currents. And when he did, he was equally driven to order small modifications that saved minutes or major changes that gained hours.

Every time he turned the hourglass beside the wheel, he ordered the first mate to throw out the logline, a wooden wedge tied to a rope with knots at regular intervals. As the wedge bit into the water and pulled the rope from its spool, the mate counted the knots passing over the stern board. After he announced their speed, the men studied Jeffers. If he smiled, they returned to their duties. When he scowled, they prepared to climb the rigging and adjust the sails.

During his rare quiet moments Jeffers would catnap or suck on his pipe and watch Sea Witch's bow plow its furrow as if willing her to give everything she had.

One day after lunch Encinas tempted Henning to their room, hugged him, and fell back on the bed with him on top.

When she finally subsided and went limp, he teased, "You done? I don't want to stop before you're satisfied."

She grinned and flushed prettily. "I'm not a circus performer. Five was quite enough, thank you."

"You keep count?"

"Not usually, but I knew this time would be special." A long silence then, "Do you see yourself in Captain Jeffers? I do."

"Is that a criticism?" he asked good-naturedly.

"No, simply an observation."

Lying on her back, rising and falling with the ship, she drifted into sleep.

A shaft of golden sunlight came through the porthole and glided up and down the opposite wall like a giant paintbrush. Watching it, Henning wondered if his grandfather in Germany was still alive.

Full of resentment when he'd left the old man's farm, he now saw *Opa* Dietzel through older, wiser eyes. His grandfather too had hated farming's routines and drudgery, but had accepted them.

"Farmers and mind-numbing work—like badly matched husbands and wives—are parted only by death," he'd once told Henning. "Make the best of your fate. Trying to escape it will make you miserable as surely as it killed your father when it drove him into the military."

Intended to help Henning accept his lot in life, those words worked in reverse. At fifteen he announced his intention to go to sea. Under local law, Grandpa Dietzel could have kept him on the farm until he came of age. No doubt tempted to do so rather than pay a hired hand, the old man had let him go.

"You would have made an excellent farmer," he'd said as Henning packed his bag. "Be an outstanding sailor. No one is as ignorant as seafaring men. With the world at their fingertips, they waste their lives misbehaving. Don't follow their example. Learn everything you can."

Angry after their years of conflict, Henning left without saying *auf Wiedersehen* but remembered his grandfather's advice. At sea, he studied tides, currents, and prevailing winds. While his crewmates frequented bars and brothels, he befriended merchants who taught him what they did and why. He also learned Spanish…improved his English…bought books instead of drinking or gambling…and was truly happy for the first time.

******

When Henning came in, Captain Jeffers was at his desk, backlit by the windows across *Sea Witch's* stern. As he looked up, a nervous twitch pulled his mouth to one side. Then again. The stress of a two-month effort to constantly be at his best was taking its toll.

"Good news," Jeffers said, offering Henning a glass of champagne. "We're two days ahead of the record and only a day from London. Even a teetotaler can drink to that."

"I'll celebrate when we're at the dock," Henning replied. "But right now, I need a huge favor. Will you please assemble your men so I can offer them another bonus?"

"Fer what?"

"Signing and honoring a pledge to keep quiet about Iquique's destruction for two weeks."

"That kinda guarantee should be prepared by an attorney. Why doncha wait 'til we get to London?"

"If I do, the crew will spread the word long before I can hire a lawyer," Henning replied.

"In that case, I'll witness their signatures. It'll be pure theater but should make an impression."

Wearing his dress uniform—white breeches and a blue coat with fringed shoulder epaulettes—Jeffers addressed his men from the bridge.

"Each of you will take a verbal oath and sign 'is name or put 'is mark on a legal document," he concluded with a stern glare. "You'll receive a bonus if you honor your pledge, and go to jail if you don't."

Jeffers came down the stairs and stood beside a table. One-by-one, crewmembers stepped forward and recited a pledge, one hand on a Bible, the other raised. Carrying the hand-lettered parchment they'd signed, Henning followed Jeffers to his cabin.

"It'll be a miracle if summa those donkeys don't drink too much and blab everything," Jeffers said, closing the door behind them."

"With any luck," Henning said, "their companions will be too drunk to remember what they heard."

"I'da thought ya'd want us to spread the news and drive up the price of yur guano."

"Don't worry. The price will go up in good time, all by itself."

******

Sixty days after leaving Altamira Island *Sea Witch* reached London, a new record if only she'd left from a port where a certified dockmaster recorded departures. But even if their accomplishment wasn't official, the crew had earned a celebration. While the men secured the lines, Henning hurried ashore and hired a pub owner to deliver ale and plates heaped with bully beef, potatoes, and cabbage.

"This is how food oughta taste," the first mate needled the cook, theatrically smacking his lips. "The crew and I will gladly pay for you to take lessons from whoever prepared it."

The cook scowled as the men cheered lustily.

"Don't let anyone leave," Henning told the mate. "I'll pay the first bonus as soon as I return from the bank."

Henning arranged storage for his guano, then hired a cabriolet carriage—a cab as people in New York and London called them. Back after making a withdrawal from his bank's London branch, he stood at the top of *Sea Witch's* gangplank and paid each crewmember's bonus as they left on shore leave.

"Remember," he told each man, "no one gets another penny if even one of you violates his pledge."

With only a skeleton crew still aboard, Henning hurried to his cabin.

"We leave for Hamburg in three hours," he told Encinas.

"Did I miss something?" she asked. "Or is this the first time you've mentioned Hamburg?"

"I've adjusted my plan because it requires absolute secrecy. Being Prussian I won't attract as much attention in Germany. Besides, I know Hamburg because I grew up there."

****

After taking Encinas to a downtown hotel, Henning explored Hamburg's docks amidst huge brick warehouses, wide canals, and squawking seagulls. His long strides sped him past dock workers as he went from freighter to freighter.

Finally he asked the dockmaster who pointed out a ship that had brought nitrate. A windjammer, it would have taken at least four months to get there, meaning it had left Iquique long before the tidal wave.

He called to the captain on its deck. "Permission to come aboard please."

"Granted." After Henning came up the gangplank, the captain added, "Either you've got a twin or you had a sudden change of plans. Remember me? I loaded at your dock in Iquique. At the time you told me your grandfather lives near Hamburg, but you didn't say anything about visiting him."

"I'm as surprised to be here as you are to see me," Henning said as they shook hands, "and I'm in the market for nitrate. Who owns this shipment?"

"You'd be buying back your own nitrate for far more than you were paid."

"Yes, but after it's been transported halfway around the world."

"You could've shipped it for a lot less than the difference you'll pay."

"I would have if I'd known I was going to need it."

"Is the price of nitrate about to go up fer some reason?" the captain asked suspiciously. "If so, I should tell the owner before giving you his name."

"If I knew the price of nitrate was going up, why didn't I just bring it from my mine?"

After considering this, the captain said, "The owner is Jaeger & Sons and their office is on Deichstraße."

****

By the time Henning joined Encinas in their hotel room, he had bought Jaeger & Sons' shipload along with the nitrate in their warehouse, all at the normal wholesale price.

"I won't be able to spend much time with you for a while," he said as she turned down their bedding. "But I'll make it up to you."

"We arrived before news of the tidal wave, didn't we?" she asked, feline eyes gleaming. "You're going to buy nitrate at the regular price and when the Germans find out Iquique is shut down, you'll sell it for more."

"A lot more. But to recuperate what the tidal wave cost me, I have to purchase an enormous amount. And quietly. If dealers find out how much I'm buying, they'll raise the price."

"How much do you need?"

"All I can find."

"Can you afford that much?"

"Only by financing it with small down payments."

"Sounds risky."

"You have no idea." He loosened his tie and unbuttoned his collar. "I could wind up in debtor's prison."

Next morning Henning arranged for Encinas to take a guided tour while he continued his search. Wednesday and Thursday, Encinas explored Hamburg and its French boutiques while his mission continued in secrecy as absolute as he could make it. Morning and afternoon he changed cabs to keep any one driver from knowing too much.

When he picked up his room key at the reception desk Friday night, the clerk had unsettling news. A man waiting in the lobby had asked for him by name.

Mirrored walls made the brightly lit lobby seem larger. Henning looked from face to face until a shifty looking man sidled up, then furtively led the way to an isolated corner table.

"My name is Werner Schmidt," he began innocently. "I'm a newspaper reporter and would like an interview for my article about your attempt to corner the nitrate market."

Hiding his astonishment Henning asked, "What are you talking about?"

"You're wasting your time," Schmidt snarled with a predatory grin. "I know everything that happens in Hamburg because I reward hotel doormen and cab drivers for telling me when they see potentially interesting stories. And yours turned out to be fascinating."

"This story has twists and turns you'll never uncover," Henning said. "Hold your article for two weeks and I'll give you an exclusive interview well worth the wait."

"News has more impact if it appears while events are still in progress. In this particular case, for example, nitrate merchants will realize they're selling their product far too cheaply."

Henning had seen Schmidt's column in the *Hamburgischer Correspondent*. The man was definitely a writer but obviously a blackmailer as well.

"By some auspicious coincidence," Schmidt said, "I know your grandfather. Being unschooled, he hired me to read him the letters you sent during California's gold rush."

Henning wasn't sure his grandfather was illiterate but couldn't remember having ever seen the old man with a book or newspaper.

"I'm planning to visit *Opa* while I'm here," he said. "Is he still farming Lord Marcus Becker's land near Maximilian Academy?"

"You haven't heard? He and Herr Becker both passed away."

Stricken, Henning glanced away and was chilled by a younger version of his *Opa* reflected from the mirror beside him.

"I also write biographies," Schmidt continued, "and group them in commemorative volumes. Your grandfather wanted yours included in the one I was working on when he died."

"As poor as *Opa* was, I don't see how he could have paid you."

"Paid?" Looking hurt, Schmidt cleaned his glasses with an expensive silk handkerchief. "These biographies are a labor I perform to preserve history that would otherwise be lost. There is, mind you, the little matter of the engraving needed to reproduce your likeness. You'll also have to reimburse me for my expenses while doing research. Then there's your share of the printing costs. And you'll want a hundred copies—at a discount, of course—for friends and family. That adds up to…" He wrote an amount on his business card and slid it across the table.

"You're wise to demand your hush-money in words that won't incriminate you if I go to the authorities," Henning said, taking out his wallet. "But I'll pay only half that much."

"My price is firm," Schmidt growled.

"I was hoping you'd say that. I'll feel like I'm getting more for my money if I have you kidnapped." Henning's eyes narrowed and his mouth tightened as he snapped his wallet shut.

Schmidt looked away and said, "Okay, you win. But you have to pay now."

"Half now and half in two weeks," Henning snapped, folding the money inside his newspaper and offering it. When Schmidt reached, Henning pulled it back and coldly threatened, "If you don't keep your side of the bargain, you'll spend months in a cage."

After Schmidt left, Henning sat for a while—too angry to be good company for Encinas. And plagued by guilt. He'd stopped writing his *Opa* after getting no answers. But if what he'd just heard was true, the old man had treasured those letters and undoubtedly been saddened when they stopped.

In their room Henning hugged Encinas as if he hadn't seen her for a long time.

"I felt useless touring Hamburg while you worked," she said after he let go. "So I made inquiries and found four warehouses full of nitrate in Oststeinbek. Thanks to a Spaniard who translated, I charmed a postal clerk into drawing a map that shows their location."

Holding Encinas's face between his hands, Henning kissed her and said, "This was a perfect time to remind me that there are people like you."

The next morning he showed her map to his new driver. By noon, he'd made his largest purchase yet.

******

When Henning stopped hurrying through Hamburg's streets and took time to look around, he experienced surprisingly sweet nostalgia. The arch-shaped passageways, gothic spires, columns, vaulted ceilings, and castles reminded him of his hometown's glorious history as a powerful, independent city-state.

He found an almost sensual pleasure in speaking his mother tongue again. And felt blessed to have come from a place with such high standards and to have attended a school as excellent as the Maximilian Academy for Boys. He'd enrolled there as a poor sharecropper and graduated as a potential capitalist.

"I'm seeing a new side of you," Encinas told him one night in their room. "When you speak German, you're not the same."

Her tone said she preferred the Spanish-speaking Henning.

On his eleventh day in Hamburg, a ship brought word of Iquique's destruction. The news raced across Germany via chains of telegraph towers with semaphores that relayed coded messages between operators equipped with telescopes. Newspapers picked up the story, expanding it as ships brought more details.

By then Henning had a significant stockpile of nitrate. After speculators bid prices as high as he thought they'd go, he sold out for an amount that would go a long way toward putting his businesses back on a strong footing.

Celebrating, Henning and Encinas dined on caviar and lobster under crystal chandeliers in Hamburg's finest restaurant. As they savored paper-thin pancakes in orange sauce for dessert, Henning said, "Tomorrow I'll take you to Hammaburgh Castle and Ahrensburg Palace."

"I saw them while you were buying nitrate. Do you have family we can visit?"

"No. I was the only son of an only son. My father's resting place is in Hamburg's military cemetery. My mother and grandfather are in paupers' cemeteries. Tomorrow I'll visit papa's grave and try to find out where *Opa* and my mother are buried."

"May I go with you?"

"Of course."

He was glad she wanted to come along. She'd distanced herself during his sixteen-hour days, making him doubt she'd be interested in his highly personal mission.

******

Among rows of white crosses on a lush, clipped lawn, Henning and Encinas placed flowers on Colonel Dietzel's grave. It was precisely where a sergeant in a starched and ironed uniform had said after consulting a wall map.

Later an attendant at the downtown Hall of Records informed Henning, "Your mother and grandfather were buried in pauper's graves outside the city limits."

"Which ones?" Henning asked. "I want to mark them with headstones."

"I'm afraid that's not possible. These are mass graves, and there's no record of exactly where anyone is. Sorry."

"I feel like I just became an orphan all over again," Henning told Encinas outside.

For days he'd known it was too late to thank his *Opa* for taking in a lonely child, teaching him the value of hard work, and granting him the freedom to follow his dreams earlier than the law required. But marking the old man's grave would have provided some consolation.

A makeshift funeral was underway in the pauper's cemetery, a vast field of waist-high weeds. With a withered old couple looking on, Encinas and Henning watched workers shovel dirt into a trench, covering thirty-six wooden boxes stacked nine wide and four deep.

After the burial, Henning hired a crew. While they cleared and burned the cemetery's weeds, he and Encinas visited Hamburg's sculptors. From one, Henning bought a half-size bronze statue of a peasant couple wiping their brows on tattered sleeves. The next day he hired craftsmen to install it at the cemetery's entrance.

"My father's remains are here," one of the craftsmen said. "Wish I could do something like this for him."

"You are." Henning patted the man's shoulder. "This is for everyone here."

The following afternoon, the statue's pedestal was surrounded by a fresh concrete slab with imbedded bricks spelling out:

Those Resting Here are Remembered

"This will please a great many people," Encinas said.

"Me included," Henning replied. "Not only are my grandfather and mother buried here. When I went to visit *Fräulein* Lange at Maximilian Academy's library I was told she's here too."

"Why didn't you take me when you went to see her?"

"I did it during your nap because I didn't think you'd be interested."

"Why? Because you don't care about *my* past?"

"I care. We often talk about your life."

"But never about how or why I became a prostitute. Is that a sensitive subject? Are you ashamed of me?"

"What makes you think that?" Henning asked.

But she had a point. Lately he often found himself thinking about her past, uncomfortably and against his will.

A crowd entered the cemetery. Apparently people who'd happened by during the monument's construction had spread the word. Judging by their clothes, those who'd come to see it were poor. Admiring the statue and talking excitedly, they stood at a respectful distance rather than scuff the still-uncured concrete.

Among such poor people, Henning was self-conscious in his knee-length, black frock coat, matching trousers, and linen shirt with standing collar. Encinas also looked overdressed. Her high-waisted ivory-colored dress was closely fitted down to beneath the bust then fell to her ankles. The crown and floppy brim of her bonnet were adorned with feathers and ribbons.

"People as well dressed as you seldom come here," a man told Henning. "Who's the lovely lady and why did you put up this monument?"

"The lady is my business partner, Encinas Peralta," Henning said a trifle stiffly. "And the monument is to honor everyone buried here, including my *Opa*, my mother, and a dear friend."

Long isolated by the language barrier, Encinas enjoyed the gathering crowd's attention. Her dark beauty—exotic in Germany—brought compliments, then questions. Henning translated the inquiries and her responses until besieged by side conversations. Without his help, she could no longer follow what was being said.

Silently she felt bored, then discarded, and finally upset.

"Why did you introduce me as your business partner?" she asked Henning as they walked to their cab. "I'm not your wife, but couldn't you call me something more personal and special…your friend, perhaps, or companion?"

"I'm sorry," he replied. "The question caught me off guard."

Twice in an hour Encinas had raised awkward topics that cried out for discussion. But Henning's feelings were in turmoil. He still found her physically attractive, and greatly respected her competence. But in the years they'd known each other, they'd spent relatively little time together and quite naturally had been on their best behavior. During the voyage from Iquique, however, they'd seldom been apart—never more than an hour—which had been too much for him but not enough for her.

His long days hunting for nitrate had provided a respite, but she was clearly determined to have more of his time from now on. Henning sympathized and didn't want to hurt her. But it was increasingly obvious that their expectations were radically different. Was it wise to stay in a relationship where she wasn't getting what she needed and he was giving all he could?

They both deserved better. But he wasn't ready to say goodbye.

******

The deadline for paying the rest of Werner Schmidt's blackmail came and went with no sign of the opportunistic reporter. He still hadn't appeared by the time Henning and Encinas sailed for England.

"Why do you suppose he didn't come for the rest of his money?" Encinas asked as their ship cleared Hamburg's harbor.

"Perhaps because I discouraged him by mentioning the possibility of having him kidnapped," Henning speculated, grinning slyly.

In London, Henning found that Jeffers' men had kept their pledges until news of the tidal wave arrived on *British Miss*. He paid their second bonuses, then sold his guano for ten times the normal price and booked a stateroom on *Deutschland*, a passenger liner. The accommodation struck him as decadently luxurious, but Encinas reacted as he'd hoped.

"I love it," she breathed, flopping down on the overstuffed mattress.

"I know I'm a day early," Henning said, "but happy birthday. I've arranged for the kitchen to prepare your favorite dinner tomorrow night."

"I hope you didn't order a cake with candles," she said impishly. "I don't want the whole dining room to know my age."

"No candles, but I taught the head waiter a German birthday song. Don't worry. Dinner will be in the privacy of our room. No one else will hear."

Late next afternoon, Encinas changed into a French corset that lifted her breasts and pushed them together. Then she put on the strapless blue evening gown she'd picked out when Henning took her shopping. Sitting at the dressing table she tilted its oval mirror until it showed cleavage that would've been unacceptable in *Deutschland's* dining room.

She knew Henning would enjoy the display as much as she appreciated his romantic gestures. But she found it troubling that her appeal to him was mostly physical. And that his mind and heart weren't completely available, even after their many years together.

******

After waiters brought Encinas's birthday dinner, Henning pulled out Encinas's chair.

"Are you and I compatible?" she asked, sitting down.

Henning sat, draped a napkin across his lap, and said, "I often ask myself that question."

"How do you answer?"

"Well, we've never had the slightest unpleasantness between us."

"Compatibility is more than that, don't you think?"

Stirring his iced tea Henning watched the lemon slice revolve. Only days ago he'd cradled Encinas's face in his hands and professed his joy that there were people like her in the world. Now he felt like nothing he said or did pleased her.

"During our last days in Hamburg," he said, "the light in your eyes went out and you stopped saying you love me. Were you upset because I was working such long hours?"

"I'm a hard worker too, but I make room in my life for other things. The only other thing that seems to interest you is fucking. I want to be more than your whore."

Henning hid his reaction. Encinas's often vulgar language was a painful reminder of her time at the House of Smiles.

"My life won't always be so hectic," he said. "Lately I've had more than my share of emergencies."

"Your days will always be an endless succession of emergencies."

"There will be times when my work comes first—"

"Will there ever be a time when it doesn't? For you, the urgent always takes precedence over the truly important."

"Would you like to stop running the water business and move in with me at Salamanca?"

"I'm afraid I'd be lonelier there than in Iquique," she declared, chewing a bite of asparagus. "Being alone with someone you love is worse than having no one."

"I can't change who I am—not even for you."

"Do you love me or are you simply reluctant to part?"

Henning wasn't sure. Maybe what he felt was friendship and respect—important but no substitute for love. And as painful as losing her would be, it would also be a relief.

His decision to sleep on the couch that night didn't surprise Encinas but made her feel desolate and adrift. Years at the House of Smiles had convinced her that men not interested in her body weren't interested at all. Resigned to losing Henning's love, she didn't want to also lose his friendship.

Or her job. Short of the unthinkable—returning to the House of Smiles—she'd never find work that paid as well. Or offered the freedom and challenges she'd come to enjoy.

******

Nine weeks later, Encinas joined Henning at the rail as *Deutschland* passed Iquique's octagonal wooden lighthouse, rebuilt after the tidal wave.

"Welcome home," he greeted her.

Onshore, new structures sprawled across the flatland behind the beach. Already bigger than before, Iquique was still growing amidst carpenters, lumber piles, and frantic activity. It had reached the distant cliffs and was spreading north and south along the coastal shelf.

The crew lowered *Deutschland's* sails and she coasted toward an empty berth at Henning's partially reconstructed wharf. Carpenters there were framing a warehouse with raw new wood. Nearby, stevedores backed down a ship's ramp, their hands slowing the descent of rolling water barrels.

Swirling a scarf above her head, Encinas returned his greeting.

At the foot of the gangplank Eduardo and Henning exchanged their usual *abrazo*. Then Henning took Encinas's arm and helped her board a carriage while the ship's porter filled its cargo compartment with their luggage.

On the way downtown, Henning's most burning questions were answered before he asked them.

"With all these construction crews in town, the water business is flourishing," Eduardo began. "Iquique's reconstruction is ahead of schedule, and we're almost ready to load ships again. With no nitrate available, guano's price went sky-high. I sent dozens of ships to Altamira Island and went there twice to check on Alcalino. He did a surprisingly good job."

Hotel Estrella had been rebuilt and carpenters were adding another wing. When Henning requested a separate room for Encinas, Eduardo politely wandered away.

When he was beyond earshot, Encinas looked up and asked Henning, "Has anything changed since our last conversation?"

"Not as far as I'm concerned," Henning replied, touching her cheek. "Unless you quit, you'll be in charge of my water business as long as I have it. And from my side at least, our friendship is as strong as ever."

"From my side, too." Obeying an urge to wrap her arms around him, Encinas received a tender hug in return.

Eduardo rejoined Henning as the bellboy carried Encinas's luggage up the stairs with her close behind.

"Doesn't look like either of us will ever marry, does it?" Henning asked sadly.

"In my case that's because I don't want to." Eduardo elbowed Henning's ribs. "What's your excuse?"

******

The following day, Henning sailed to Altamira Island on *Intrepido*, the ship that delivered its supplies. Stepping from her gangplank to the dock, he was apprehensive. It had been five months since he'd left Alcalino Valdivia unsupervised. His young mistake-prone manager had done well according to Eduardo. And during their voyage, Captain Gustavo Medina had passed along encouraging news. Alcalino had used him to monitor trading company prices.

"He increased yours every time theirs went up," Medina had reported.

Good news. If the sometimes careless Alcalino hadn't taken advantage of rising prices, desperately needed profits would have been lost.

But coming ashore, Henning saw warning signs. On the dock's far corner, birds were pecking the eyes of a dead dog. And though it was crucial to make certain *Intrepido* unloaded enough food for the island's thousand workers, Alcalino was nowhere to be seen.

"I'd have been here sooner," Alcalino called out from an approaching one-horse, two-wheeled vehicle. "But knowing you'd want to look around, I took the time to hook up your buggy." He sent a worker to bury the dog, then explained, "He wasn't there earlier when I made my rounds or he'd already be in the ground." Turning to Captain Medina, he asked, "How long before you start unloading?"

"A couple of hours," Medina replied. "My ramp needs repairs."

"I'll be back by then," Alcalino said.

After Henning climbed aboard, the young half-breed didn't hand over the reins as usual. Instead he proudly took Henning around the island—first the diggings, next the loading platform, finally the warehouses and office. Everything was running smoothly.

Alcalino monitored *Intrepido's* unloading while Henning went over the books and found them in good order. He closed the ledger and went outside. Having made sure all the ordered food was delivered, Alcalino was lowering his bicycle from Henning's buggy.

"No one could have done a better job," Henning told his beaming manager. "As your reward, I'm doubling your salary and giving you a month off. I'll look after things while you're gone. You should consider visiting your father. He'll be proud of the man you've become."

"After you left, I wrote asking for his help," Alcalino replied. "To my surprise he came and stayed a month. I learned a lot and enjoyed him more than I thought possible."

"Did he admit you're his son?"

"Not in so many words, but yes," Alcalino called over his shoulder as he peddled away. "I'll be back after I oversee some repairs at the loading platform."

Henning shook his head in amazement. He'd read about unpromising men who suddenly blossomed, but Alcalino was the first he'd ever seen.

CHAPTER THREE
BLACKBIRDING

Stepping onto the dock at Cortéz in northern Peru, Henning was surprised when he didn't see Belisario Lorca. Years ago he'd loaned the old aristocrat money to build a sugar mill. Since then their mutual love of conversation—and Henning's enjoyment of Belisario's quick wit—had made them friends.

Near the parking area, Henning swept leaves and twigs from a weathered bench with one hand and sat down. No doubt Belisario would arrive soon.

Henning's letter had explained this visit as a vacation, and it was. But the end of his romance with Encinas had refocused him on one of the Chiriaco Valley's other residents, Martine Prado. He'd been enchanted by her in Lima when she was young, beautiful, and pursued by men whose attentions would have flattered most women.

Years later he'd met Martine while visiting Belisario. By then her looks and polish no longer blinded him to her intelligence, spirit, and enticing self-confidence. These however were counterbalanced by a seeming dislike for men and a sometimes brutal frankness. He'd decided she was beyond his reach or that of any man.

Now she was back in his thoughts and—

Henning saw a blond, blue-eyed, older man hurrying toward him. Today as always, Belisario's perpetually twinkling eyes made him look amused. Coming together, they greeted with a back-slapping hug, interrupted when a wind gust forced both to grab their hats.

"Where's Marco Venicio?" Henning asked.

"As you'll learn when you have children," Belisario replied, "they follow you everywhere while they're young. But when they get older they want to be with their friends."

Beyond the wharf, Belisario sped up his two black carriage horses and said, "The Chiriaco Valley's landowners have always been too independent to band together for the common good. But tonight we're meeting to consider a joint approach to the labor shortage. You should come. Emiliano Cabrera will be there, and that alone is worth the price of admission. Have you met him?"

"No."

"He lives like a hermit in a castle-like palace on a towering manmade hill. I call it Mount Olympus because from there its godlike owner can look down on us ordinary mortals. He's been a pariah since Martine Prado convinced the local gentry that he murdered her brother, Pietro."

Henning's attention sharpened at the mention of Martine.

"Cabrera murdered her brother?" he asked.

"At the time, Pietro ran the Prado's hacienda and Cabrera was trying to put them out of business. Pietro was always a step ahead or close behind. No one had ever successfully matched wits with Cabrera, and Martine thinks he had Pietro murdered to force her father to sell."

"You don't agree?" Henning asked.

"He's capable, but who knows. Seriously, you should come tonight. You've never met anyone as delightfully sinister. Only God has more land, yet Cabrera continues to underhandedly drive competitors out of business and buy their farms for pittances. Everyone hates the bastard. He was invited because he always has plenty of workers and some naïve souls hope he'll help us. But the only thing he helps people do is go broke."

"I'm worn out. I think I'll relax tonight if you don't mind."

"You sure? The meeting will be at *Don* Manuel Prado's hacienda, and he—in case you've forgotten—is Martine's father."

"Am I that easy to read?"

"Not at all. But I'm exceptionally perceptive, and if you don't believe it just ask me."

After a bath at Belisario's Hacienda Valencia, Henning put on his custom-made gray alpaca suit. Years ago, he'd worn it at Lima's docks, watching

Martine and her father sail for Argentina, where *Don* Manuel was Peru's ambassador. She hadn't seen him or his suit that day.

The jacket and trousers still fit perfectly. And had come back in style.

******

After a quick trip to Manuel Prado's Hacienda Toledo, Belisario's carriage horses were dripping sweat. A groom took charge of them in the driveway. First to arrive, Belisario and Henning were shown to the living room. Inside dark wood paneled walls under a high ceiling and chandeliers, the furniture had been removed to make space for a podium and rows of chairs. They sat in the third row.

Half an hour later the room was crowded and Henning still hadn't seen Martine. Women weren't welcome when men did business, but in her home he'd expected at least a glimpse. Responding to a touch on his shoulder he stood to greet José Geldres, the labor agent who supplied workers for his Altamira Island guano concession.

As Henning sat back down, two men made a grand entry. Taller and more slender, one matched Belisario's description of Emiliano Cabrera. His body vibrated with energy and his face was as expressive as an actor's. Every utterance ended with an exclamation point. But his mood changes were too drastic to be genuine. He was performing for the small group that had surrounded him—clearly hoping for his help—when everyone else turned their backs.

Belisario leaned close and whispered, "His emotions appear to vary as often as a chameleon changes color on a Scottish tartan. Inside however, he's calm, never loses sight of his goals, and always has a plan to reach them. If he had morals he'd be the most admirable man I've ever met."

Henning instantly disliked the man beside Cabrera. Barrel-chested with gorilla-like arms, he was ugly in almost every way and had gaps between his protruding teeth. His ruddy complexion suggested that drinking was his preferred amusement. Henning usually sympathized with unattractive people, but this man's eyes made compassion difficult. He glared at people with the intensity of a coyote immobilizing a cornered rabbit.

"Who's the gentleman next to Cabrera?" Henning asked.

"Gentleman?" Belisario scoffed. "He's Cabrera's so-called administrator, Federico García, and he's every bit as sinister as he appears."

"He doesn't look like an administrator."

"That's because his knuckles have barely had time to heal since he started walking erect."

"You're in a rare mood." Grinning, Henning slapped Belisario's shoulder.

"No one knows García's background except that he led blackbirding expeditions." Seeing Henning's puzzlement, Belisario explained, "Blackbirding refers to kidnapping and enslaving Polynesian Kanakas. García used to bring boatloads of the poor devils. He'd laugh about how his crew lured them below deck and trapped them there. After agreeing to sell his Kanakas exclusively to Cabrera, García became his administrator. I suspect Cabrera will offer to have him bring us Kanakas…for an outrageous price, of course."

After the meeting started, it wandered aimlessly and seemed doomed to fail until Cabrera strutted to the podium and took control. In an authoritative, hypnotic voice he proposed to single handedly solve the worker shortage by bringing workers from Polynesia.

"If he's anxious to run competitors out of business, why would he help them?" Henning whispered to Belisario.

"Wait until you hear how much he charges," came the muffled reply.

"Kanakas are bigger and stronger than *cholos* and *serranos*," Cabrera concluded, comparing them to Peru's Indians. "And because they come from distant islands, they can't run away and go home like our Indians can."

"You talk as if they were cattle," a familiar female voice said.

Over his shoulder Henning saw Martine Prado standing in front of a chair several rows back. Older now, she still had bright-green eyes, full pink lips, and the sparkle that had once made her Peru's most pursued woman.

"I wouldn't call them cattle," Cabrera replied calmly, "though they're not far above it."

"Even if that were true," Martine drowned out the scattered chuckles, "it wouldn't justify stealing them from their families and enslaving them."

"With all due respect—"

"When a man says that to another man, he's being diplomatic," Martine broke in. "But when he says it to a woman, he wants her to defer to him no matter what she really thinks."

"My Kanakas aren't slaves." Cabrera flashed a counterfeit smile. "I pay them wages."

"Despite which," José Geldres boomed, rising to his feet beside Martine, "they owe you money because you charge them for housing and food."

"Any other half-breed," Belisario whispered, "would be ordered to leave for speaking like that. But Geldres is the Valley's best source of workers, and landowners curry his favor by addressing him as *Don*, a title normally reserved for highborn Caucasian men."

Geldres directed his next words to everyone present, "I won't bring workers for anyone who orders Kanakas."

"Federico García can deliver a thousand men by Christmas," Cabrera said smoothly. "You couldn't bring that many of your beloved *serranos* in a month of Sundays."

Two men stood. Unwilling to let the other go first, both spoke at once. Another man jumped up and tried to silence them. With the meeting spinning out of control, Cabrera banged a gavel on the podium.

The room went silent as *Don* Manuel Prado entered, still dignified at his advanced age.

"Anyone wishing to take advantage of *Señor* Cabrera's offer can make arrangements in private," he said in a rich baritone. "In the meantime, please enjoy the refreshments."

While a few servants cleared away the chairs and podium, others brought trays of beverages and hors d'oeuvres. Martine Prado went from group to group, avoiding the men gathered around Cabrera and García.

She wore no makeup and was dressed in a simple skirt and blouse. Henning felt certain she'd been granted last-minute permission to attend. Any other highborn woman would have stayed away rather than appear in public without elegant clothes and hours of preparation.

"She's campaigning against Cabrera's proposal," Belisario said as Martine came toward them. "Sorry to leave you to face her alone, but I've had my fill of her self-righteous lectures."

Martine stumbled as she reached Henning, and a small jade hand on a neck chain popped from inside her modest neckline. Based on the Roman Catholic *mano poderosa*—powerful hand of God—it was a fist-shaped amulet available in Lima's Witches' Market and reputed to protect against the evil eye.

Martine's was a version regarded as indecent because it had the thumb tucked inside curled fingers, mimicking sexual intercourse. It was supposedly more effective than the accepted style with the thumb extended. Modesty demanded it be kept inside the wearer's upper garment, discreetly concealed in a tiny cloth sack.

"Sorry, but putting it in a bag limits its power," Martine explained, dropping the talisman back inside her blouse and releasing the pleasant scent of lavender.

She and Henning hadn't seen one other for a long time, but she didn't greet him or ask how he was. Or seem to remember how closely their last conversation had drawn them together.

"A few of our neighbors are actually ordering Kanakas," she stated, eyes smoldering, "which I find despicable. I told them Cabrera murdered my twin brother. I guess he'll have to kill one of their loved ones before they'll believe it."

"Cabrera killed your brother?"

"In those days, Pietro ran our hacienda and Cabrera was trying to put us out of business."

"If he's a murderer, why isn't he in jail?"

"You'd have to live here to understand the extent of his influence." She caught and held Henning's gaze. "I hope you and Belisario won't have García bring Kanakas for Valencia."

"That's Belisario's decision."

"If he asks your opinion, what will you recommend?"

"He never asks my opinion."

"I'm asking."

"I agree with what you said earlier, but I don't know why you bothered. Those who decide against bringing Kanakas will do so because they dislike Cabrera or don't want to pay his price—not because they think it's wrong."

"Did your grandfather use slave labor on his farm?"

"I was pretty much a slave," Henning joked. "Our farm wasn't as grand as your hacienda. Grandpa and I did all the chores."

Collecting her skirt Martine turned to go with fluid movements that showed her figure wasn't sculpted by tight undergarments.

"Nice suit," she said. "You should wear it more often."

CHAPTER FOUR
A WAGER OF CONSEQUENCE

Three of the Valley's haciendas had ordered a boatload of Kanakas each. And Federico García was organizing his expedition in Callao, Lima's port, when a blackbirder who had an empty eye socket arrived with nine Kanakas on a ship that normally carried over a hundred.

"The only males left in Easter Island's vicinity are too old, too young, crippled, or diseased," the man told García, spitting for emphasis. "And the islands farther away are protected by the British navy."

Never having had difficulty finding Kanakas, García dismissed this as exaggeration and tracked down Raul Argumosa, captain of a vessel that had returned from blackbirding the previous day. A *cholo* with reddish-brown skin, Argumosa was partway through a meal at the Black Swan Restaurant.

"The dockmaster said you got back from Polynesia yesterday," García said.

Argumosa poured steaming tea from his cup to its saucer and blew on it. After a cautious sip, he said, "I looked for weeks, but found only women, children, and invalids."

"The men must have been hiding."

"No, we looked everywhere and even tortured some of their women. Obviously too many of us have fished in the same pond for too long."

"You didn't find even one?"

"After a month, I had nineteen barely acceptable specimens, but a British man-of-war stopped me with a shot across my bow and freed them."

Later García discovered that ship owners—fearing British confiscation of their vessels—were no longer renting to slavers. And the boats for sale were too small or otherwise unsuitable.

******

Belisario and Henning sat among the shade trees where they often talked.

"Did you order Kanakas from Cabrera?" Henning asked.

"No," Belisario replied. "As much as I hate to admit it, Martine is right. Kidnapping them is unchristian."

"Maybe I can convince José Geldres to bring you more workers."

"Don't count on it." Belisario let out a sarcastic laugh. "He never brings as many as anyone needs because he thinks they're better treated when in short supply."

"Why don't you offer to pay extra?"

"It wouldn't do any good. He doesn't need money. For years he's been selling ancient gold artifacts. Rumor is, he discovered an important Inca's tomb and is selling its contents slowly to keep prices up. Sometimes his house gets ransacked while he's away. But no new jewelry or relics ever come on the market. He must have left the rest of his treasure hidden where he found it. Every now and then grave robbers try to follow him into the Andes, but their horses can't keep up with his gray."

"They don't have to keep up—just follow his tracks."

"Easier said than done. They say an antique dealer once brought an Apache tracker from Arizona. Supposedly they stayed on *Don* José's trail for fourteen hours before turning back rather than cross a deep canyon on a flimsy-looking rope and plank bridge."

"Importing a tracker sounds far-fetched."

"Not to me. You can't imagine how much collectors and museums pay for Inca artifacts."

"I'll talk to Geldres anyhow. Perhaps I can get him to bring you more *serranos*. How do I get to his place?"

"He lives on Dos Palos, an isolated farm four hours from here. I'll draw you a map."

******

That afternoon was particularly hot by the time Henning rode Sultán—a chestnut stallion Belisario had given him—into a narrow passageway through a stone escarpment. According to Belisario, the deep channel had been carved by an ancient river—centimeters per decade—and was the only entrance to José Geldres's ranch.

Listening to the echo of his horse's hooves and relishing the cool shade, Henning alternately watched the path ahead and the ribbon of sky above. Refreshed, he reached a natural amphitheater surrounded by cliffs. Overheated as soon as he emerged into direct sunlight, he turned toward an adobe shack.

When he arrived, *Don* José rose from a high back chair on his covered front porch and asked, "Does Belisario Lorca need workers or did you hear about my treasure?" Abruptly he added, "Please forgive me. A man suspects the worst when his house is regularly ransacked and he's followed everywhere he goes."

"I came because one of my other friends needs your help."

Again *Don* José's face clouded over. "I thought I made it clear I won't bring workers for anyone who ordered Kanakas."

"Belisario didn't and wouldn't have even without your threat."

"It doesn't matter. After forty-three years, I've made up my mind to do something more interesting than bring workers."

"And what's that?"

"I'm still trying to decide. Maybe you can help. Why don't you stay a while?"

While Henning unsaddled, *Don* José's eyes made two sweeps of Sultán. One started at the little chestnut's hooves and traveled upward. The other began at his hindquarters, ending at his head. That was how Henning's father had evaluated horses, starting with the most important parts and finishing with the least.

"Nice horse," *Don* José said.

Henning touched Sultán's flank. Finding it warm, he led the little chestnut back and forth to cool him.

"That's enough," *Don* José said after a while, opening a corral gate. "Your horse will be fine. Put him in here."

"I'll cool him just a bit longer," Henning said.

"I shouldn't be surprised," Geldres grumped. "You overdo everything."

Later Henning freed Sultán in the corral and Geldres set a pail of water inside its fence. Sultán started toward it. Henning didn't want his horse to drink so soon after a hard ride on a hot day. He was about to reach for the bucket when the little chestnut stopped to watch a gray stallion running the fence in a nearby corral.

"As hot as it is," *Don* José said, turning toward his front door, "you must have emptied your canteen long ago. I hope you like lemonade."

With his host out of sight, Henning set the bucket outside the corral and hurried back to the porch. He was blocking the view of the corral when *Don* José brought him a brimming glass.

Henning drained it without pause, then said, "Best lemonade I ever drank."

"You would have thought so even if you weren't so thirsty. I passed the water through my special filter." *Don* José pointed at an egg-shaped boulder near the door.

Tall as a man, it rested on a three sided rock and mortar pedestal. The basin chiseled into its top was full of water. Drops formed on its underside until they lost their grip and fell into a pitcher.

"Going through that much granite does wonders for water," *Don* José said.

They sat in facing chairs, searching without success for a new activity to fill *Don* José's time. When the old man went inside for more lemonade, Henning put the bucket of water back inside Sultán's corral.

"What do you think of my horse?" he asked as his host brought their drinks.

"When it comes to Peruvian Pasos, there are more important opinions than mine," *Don* José replied.

"Yours is the one I want. We appreciate the same things in horses."

"How can I evaluate an animal I've never ridden?"

"I'd be honored to have you try him."

Once Sultán was saddled, *Don* José rode him back and forth near withered corn stalks being knocked down and eaten by skinny pigs.

Geldres's riding showed horsemanship Henning hadn't expected from a man who'd made water available to an overheated horse.

"Take him out on the trail if you want," he called out.

Long after entering the passageway through the cliffs, *Don* José returned and dismounted.

"Few horses," he said, "would still have such vigor after carrying a man your size in this heat. I won't fill your ears with praise, but I'll pay handsomely for him."

"I can't sell him. He was a gift from Belisario Lorca."

Again Henning cooled Sultán and watered him in small increments. When he returned to the porch, *Don* José had his chair tipped back on two legs and was staring at the porch ceiling, lost in thought.

"You came here to get workers for *Don* Belisario," the old man said after a while. "Let's make it interesting. Why don't we have a horse race across the Wrath of God Desert? If Goliat wins, Sultán will be mine. If Sultán wins, I'll bring Belisario as many *serranos* as he wants. I've never done that for anyone."

"I'll return Sultán to Belisario so you two can trade," Henning responded. "That way you'll both get what you want."

"Getting what I want will be sweeter if done at the risk of not getting it at all," *Don* José said with a peculiar smirk. "A five-hundred-mile race with a white man will provide some of the juice I need from life."

"May I bring Belisario tomorrow so you two can discuss this further?"

"Why? I won't have to convince Belisario. He'll find the challenge irresistible."

That might be true, but Henning wanted to involve Belisario for another reason entirely.

******

Near the Prado's Hacienda Toledo, Henning saw Martine riding toward him. He'd never seen a woman astride or dressed in pants. They emphasized her long legs and contours—the reason—no doubt—that guardians of public decency didn't want women to wear them. They stopped side-by-side, facing opposite directions.

When Henning told Martine where he'd been, she said, "Most men go to Dos Palos for one of two reasons…to beg for workers or to find *Don* José's treasure."

"What do you think I was doing?"

"I don't know. You're different from other men."

"In what way?" he asked, heartened.

"The ones I know are overly civilized, lazy, and old-fashioned. They live in leisure made possible by workers who are little more than slaves. Their favorite pastime is ordering women around, and I've never met one as interesting or hardworking as you. Are you aware that *Don* José is my godfather?"

"Your father must be unusually enlightened if he picked a *cholo* as your godfather."

"The godfather at my christening was the time-honored white aristocrat, wealthy enough to raise me in comfort if I was orphaned. After he died, I started calling *Don* José godfather, very much against my father's wishes." She grinned charmingly.

Henning found it easy to picture her as a willful girl appointing her own godparent over a blue-blooded father's objections.

"What can you tell me about a desert called the Wrath of God?" he asked.

"It's south of here," Martine said, "and is Peru's most notorious hellhole. Why?"

"I've been challenged to a horse race there."

Her eyes opened wide.

"Surely you won't accept," she said. "People die in the Wrath of God. Trying to cross it killed all but one of the men who tried. Did José Geldres propose this race?"

"Good guess," Henning replied.

"It wasn't a guess. He's the one who finally conquered the Wrath of God, on his gray stallion. You've no doubt heard how he bought Goliat?"

"Many times."

The story was famous. Her godfather had purchased the big gray from a wily horse trader who routinely raised his prices when buyers tried to pay. After accepting the man's first quote, *Don* José had sliced off the tip of Goliat's ear—reducing the stallion's value and foiling the inevitable attempt to sell him for more.

Since then, the big gray's endurance had become legendary.

******

That night at Valencia, Henning told Belisario about *Don* José's challenge.

The old aristocrat summoned his jolly, round maid, Chabuca, and asked her to serve dinner in his study. Briskly he led the way there.

He and Henning sat in facing chairs as Chabuca removed a chess board from the table between them and laid out place settings.

"What conditions did you agree on?" Belisario asked, rubbing his hands together.

"Negotiating terms would have been pointless," Henning replied. "There are none under which I could possibly win. However, if I return Sultán to you, you can trade him to *Don* José for workers. I suggested that, but he wouldn't hear of it. Perhaps you can convince him."

"You don't think Sultán can beat Goliat?" Belisario sounded offended.

"Not carrying a man my size. I outweigh *Don* José by at least a hundred pounds."

"With determination any obstacle can be overcome."

"Not this one. Are you familiar with the English sport of flat racing?"

"Before my wife died, she and I attended some prestigious races in London."

They paused while Chabuca served *rocoto relleno*, hot, apple-size red peppers stuffed with sautéed beef and hard-boiled egg, then topped with melted white cheese.

After Chabuca left, Henning asked, "Did you see any handicap races in London?"

"Yes. The horses started from staggered positions so the youngest, the females, and those with the worst past performances had a better chance of winning."

"Races are also handicapped by making some entries carry extra weight. In a two-mile race, fifteen additional pounds slows the fastest horses to where lesser animals can beat them. No horse could possibly win while carrying a hundred more pounds for five hundred miles."

"Are you suggesting we propose a handicap to compensate for your weight?"

"I'm suggesting we propose a trade—Sultán for workers."

"You don't know Geldres. Once his mind is made up, he won't budge. But maybe he'll accept a handicap." Belisario finished chewing and swallowed. "Of course you'll condition Sultán and stay here at Valencia while you do it."

"That's a major assumption," Henning said. "Getting him ready will take months."

But if negotiating a trade proved impossible and a handicap could be arranged, this race would be a fascinating challenge. *Don* José wasn't alone in wanting more juice from life.

******

"This race is an opportunity to demonstrate my bloodline's quality," Belisario told Henning at breakfast the next morning.

By the time they set out for Dos Palos, the old aristocrat's enthusiasm was out of control. For miles he rambled on about his breeding program and bemoaned his fellow breeders' failure to acknowledge his horses' excellence.

When his excitement at last subsided, he abruptly announced, "Sugar prices have fallen to where my expenses are higher than my income. My next payment on your loan will be late."

Having anticipated this, Henning had a ready answer. "Prices will go lower before they go back up. But if you agree to one condition, I'll give you all the time you need."

"What condition?"

"I want periodic breakdowns of Valencia's income and expenditures," Henning replied, returning to a subject they'd often discussed and never resolved.

"I go over the income and expenses with you every—"

"From memory, aided by notes on scraps of paper. I need a detailed accounting showing every transaction to the penny."

"I don't have time for such foolishness. I've never kept books."

Henning tried a fresh approach. "You can be sure Emiliano Cabrera does. Otherwise his investors wouldn't loan him money."

"Cabrera has investors?"

"How else could he buy out so many of his neighbors? And as his hacienda grows, his cost per ton goes down. That's why he can undercut your price. To compete, you'll have to reduce Valencia's expenses, which requires knowing exactly how much you spend and for what. You need proper books kept by an expert."

"I suppose you have someone in mind."

"Yes, you don't know her, but—"

"Her," Belisario growled. "A woman? You can't be serious."

"She's coming, now or later."

"No she's not." Belisario's posture stiffened.

"If I don't grant an extension on your payment," Henning said, his voice turning hard, "Valencia will be mine."

"So you've become an investor rather than a friend?"

"I'm trying to be both. Please don't force me to choose."

When Belisario spoke again he was closer to accepting the inevitable. "Tell me about this woman you want me to hire."

"Her name is Encinas Peralta. She runs my water business in Iquique."

"Cortéz has no end of accountants. Why bring someone from so far away?"

"Because I doubt anyone in Cortéz can interpret numbers half as well as she can."

"Who'll run your water business?"

"I'm closing it. A competitor completed a pipeline that delivers water for a fraction of what it costs me to bring it by ship."

"Will this woman come here for part-time work?"

"She has talents besides bookkeeping and will work full time. To start with, I'm pretty sure she can convince your neighbors to have you mill their cane."

"Emiliano Cabrera has processed their cane for years despite my efforts to lure them away. Why would this woman succeed where I didn't?"

"Because she succeeded where I didn't. She doubled my water sales in a month."

"How much will I have to pay her?"

"Ten percent of the profit on the milling business she brings in," Henning said. "For that, she'll also keep your books and help you lower costs."

Belisario winced. "Ten percent adds up fast."

"That's good news because you'll get nine times as much, plus lower expenses."

Near Dos Palos, Belisario—still pretending he had a choice—agreed to try Encinas.

José Geldres received them with glasses of lemonade and three chairs arranged in a triangle on his porch.

"Word is Emiliano Cabrera can't bring Kanakas," Belisario began the obligatory chitchat. "Imagine my disappointment."

"The greedy son of a whore must be apoplectic." *Don* José smirked. "He stood to make a fortune. Why would the good Lord allow such a nice man to suffer so cruelly?"

"I don't know," Belisario replied, "but I'll put something extra in the collection plate next Sunday. Maybe He'll do it again."

Several subjects later Belisario and *Don* José launched an animated discussion of the proposed race. When *Don* José refused to trade workers for Sultán, Belisario looked relieved. Recognition for his breeding program was clearly more exciting than getting more *serranos*.

"You'll have to give us a handicap," Belisario proposed. "After all, you weigh a hundred pounds less than Henning. How about subtracting ten minutes a day from his time?"

"Thirty would be more reasonable," Henning broke in, wishing he and Belisario had discussed that detail earlier.

Wagging his finger *Don* José declared, "The difference in our ages more than compensates for the weight discrepancy."

"Surely you can appreciate the enormous disadvantage my extra hundred pounds will be," Henning pressed.

All three stubbornly clung to their positions. Then Belisario abruptly accepted Geldres's terms and they shook hands, sealing their agreement.

"How long will it take to get Sultán ready?" Belisario asked Henning.

"Six months."

"Let's schedule the race for February," *Don* José proposed.

On the ride back to the Valley Belisario was euphoric. But Henning was deeply disappointed. To start with, February was Peru's hottest month, a terrible time for a desert race. Worse yet, Belisario had failed to negotiate a handicap, throwing away Sultán's one hope of victory along with Valencia's only chance to get desperately needed workers.

******

Despite Henning's disadvantage, he did the only thing his Prussian determination would permit. He decided to beat José Geldres anyhow, then threw body and soul into conditioning Sultán, starting with five-mile workouts every other day.

On one such ride he came upon Martine Prado near Toledo's entrance. She joined him and every second day for a month afterward was waiting at the same time and place.

"This race is the most exciting thing to happen around here in years," she said one afternoon on the bridge across the Chiriaco River. "Everyone is talking about it, even my father. I've never seen him so excited."

"I doubt the race will live up to expectations," Henning said. "Weighing a hundred pounds less gives *Don* José a telling advantage."

"You're looking for sympathy in the wrong place. I'll probably be the only white person in Peru cheering for him." Cocking her head, she changed subjects. "Tell me more about the woman you're bringing to keep Belisario's books."

"There's nothing to report aside from what I already told you."

"I get the impression you're holding something back."

"I may have neglected to mention a detail or two."

"Such as?"

"She used to be the madam at a bordello."

Henning didn't know where he'd found the nerve to say that. He wanted the Valley to accept Encinas and take her seriously. But he knew Martine appreciated honesty and felt positive he could trust her with a secret. And she wasn't a prig. She hadn't been in the least embarrassed when he'd accidentally seen her risqué jade fist amulet.

Besides, it was exciting to go beyond normal bounds with her.

"I can't believe you told me that," she teased, green eyes playful. "You're normally so secretive. I assume what she did for you wasn't related to her former profession?"

"She ran my water business in Iquique," Henning said.

"You couldn't find a man for the job?"

"None as competent and trustworthy."

"It's impressive you hired a woman, but how could you trust someone with her past?"

"Stepping outside sexual boundaries doesn't automatically mean a person is dishonest."

"Men frequently extend that kind of latitude to others of their gender," Martine said, "but never to women. Does Belisario know what she used to do?"

"I didn't see any reason to bring it up."

"How long have you known her?"

"We met when I was eighteen," he said. "I was nineteen the first time I saw you. Your father had just been named ambassador to Argentina. You two were in Lima preparing to leave for Buenos Aires, and in the evenings you were the *Plaza Central's* main attraction."

Martine's mouth formed an unspoken oh. "You were there? Were we introduced?"

"Not until we met aboard *Daphne*. Fate has brought us together several times, almost as if we were meant to be in each other's lives."

Martine went silent—not the first time she'd dropped a curtain between them.

"You're my first real male friend," she'd once told him. "The others were hoping to charm me into giving them what men want most from women."

Fearing he'd shown too much interest, Henning set out to repair the damage.

"I'm afraid we won't be able to ride together anymore," he said. "Sultán needs to get accustomed to working alone."

To properly prepare the little chestnut, he should have made that change already but hadn't wanted to deprive himself of Martine's company.

"I understand." Her expression shifted from defensive to disappointed.

When they said goodbye at Toledo's front gate, Martine was sorry their daily rides were over. She liked the way Henning talked about subjects other than himself, and without the usual male condescension. And despite occasional evidence to the contrary, she sensed that he enjoyed their friendship for what it was. And wasn't angling for more.

As he left, she admired the way his hands held his reins—gently as if they were alive.

CHAPTER FIVE
IF GRANDMOTHERS HAD WINGS

Two days after leaving Cortéz on a southbound freighter, Henning found everything in good order on Altamira Island. Before reboarding his ship under a cloudless sky, he told Alcalino about the upcoming race and said, "I'll be here less than usual for a while."

His young manager listened stoically. If only Eduardo would do the same. But he'd react with disapproval and unwanted advice.

Henning reached Iquique after dark and hired a cab. Passing the theater's brightly lit marquee he saw that La Biscaccianti was performing. Eduardo was inside no doubt, enjoying his favorite singer. In Iquique's conservative British atmosphere coins wouldn't be thrown, of course, as they'd been in San Francisco's boisterous Jenny Lind Theatre.

Henning had the driver stop at Eduardo's house and slid a note under the door. He was eager to deliver his news and be done with the inevitable grumbling, but wouldn't be able to do that until tomorrow.

When Henning went down for breakfast, Eduardo was at the foot of the hotel's grand staircase.

"Your note didn't sound urgent and I was entertaining a lady," he said with his trademark wink.

"There was no hurry," Henning replied.

"That would be a first. You're always in a hurry."

Flabbergasted when Henning told him about the coming race, Eduardo grumped, "For years I've begged you to take time off and enjoy yourself. But this race will replace your usual job with one that's equally taxing."

"I'll enjoy the challenge."

"I don't doubt that. But based on your unusually good mood, I suspect you're hoping your time in the Valley will get you closer to a certain Peruvian ambassador's daughter. Or is it a coincidence that she lives where you'll be training? Heed my words. Marrying dried-up old aristocrats leads to mistresses. And mistresses make puritans like you feel guilty."

Chuckling, Henning asked, "How did we get from a horse race to mistresses?"

As they walked to the restaurant, Eduardo's rapid strides revealed his agitation. The race was none of his business, but he was right about one thing. Henning was hoping his months in the Valley would bring him closer to Martine.

******

Back at Valencia, Henning found his instructions had been ignored. Belisario's trainer had ridden the little chestnut too little and fed him too much.

"It's important for you to do exactly as I ask," Henning told Roque. "With perfect preparation Sultán has little chance to beat Goliat, but without it he has none."

"*Sí*, s*í*, s*í*," Roque agreed with typical *serrano* deference.

"Five men riding horses known for endurance," Henning continued, "once tried to follow José Geldres into the Andes toward what they hoped was his hidden treasure. After two days, one of their horses dropped dead and the others were too exhausted to continue. No one knows how much farther Goliat went, but on the return trip he took sick and collapsed. Even so, he found the strength to get back to Dos Palos, where he almost died. A veterinarian said his survival was nothing less than a miracle. A horse with that much heart won't be easily beaten."

When Henning next visited his businesses, Roque again did things his own way—a recipe for failure and a problem that had to be solved. During his next training ride, Henning formulated a plan.

It was unorthodox and would require Martine's cooperation, which she probably wouldn't give. But she might. She was different from the pampered females in other well-to-do families. She groomed and saddled her own horse, went riding without escorts, and wanted to live life rather than pose on a pedestal.

She'd once told José Geldres, "Wealth is a blessing for men but a curse for women. Rich ladies are shielded from work no matter how much better it might make us feel about ourselves. And even though risks are deliciously exciting, we're not allowed to take them."

******

Working Sultán on a Saturday morning, Henning saw Martine riding ahead of him and sped up. She glanced back, then waited.

"I was on my way to see you," he said, stopping beside her.

"Should I be flattered?" She wiped her brow.

"Depends on how you feel about being asked for a favor. Occasionally I have to look in on my businesses, and I'm hoping you'll ride Sultán and keep him in shape while I'm gone."

"You're not going to insist I ride sidesaddle?"

"I'm not joking."

Her tone softened. "I don't know another man who'd offer an important job to a woman. But *Don* José is my godfather. You should choose someone who's on your side."

"I want you."

"What exactly would I do?"

"Ride Sultán every other day and cover as much ground in as little time as possible."

"Sounds like fun. How's he doing so far?"

"If I were a hundred pounds lighter, he'd have an excellent chance of winning."

"Maybe he'll win in spite of your weight."

"And if my grandmother had wings, she could fly."

Martine's shoulders shook as she threw her head back, emphasizing her graceful neck. When her musical laughter subsided, she said, "That felt good. I've been in a black mood since my father started pushing me to marry Luis Bustamante. Our union would ally Toledo with his hacienda, no small matter in Daddy's mind. This morning the gentleman in question told me he's not interested, without even asking if I was. If I weren't too old to be banished to a convent, Daddy would surely do it now."

Daddy—a little girl's word—seemed out of place from such a sophisticated woman.

Encouraged by her openness, Henning asked, "Did you ever come close to marrying?"

"Woe to any woman who passes through that portal in search of happiness. Even in a convent I'd be better off than any wife I know."

"Despite having been rejected by Luis Bustamante," he said playfully, "You look happy."

"I am and you're responsible. Men are forever telling me what I can't do. You on the other hand seem to think me capable of things beyond even my expectations."

"Does that mean you'll work Sultán for me?"

"If you get my father's permission."

"Do you mind trading horses for a while?" Without waiting for an answer, Henning dismounted.

"Are you wondering if I can handle a stallion?" Martine asked suspiciously.

"No, but your father will have misgivings, and I want to be able to say you rode Sultán without difficulty."

"Why do you have such faith in me?"

"Because you deserve it."

******

After his mother's premature death, Henning had been raised by men and similarly deprived of female company in California's goldfields and on Altamira Island. He admittedly knew little about women but thought he understood Martine Prado's unhappiness. His own spirits had been equally low back when he was under his overbearing grandfather's control.

According to José Geldres, Martine's father had trapped her with a provision that cut her out of his will if she left Toledo before marrying. With no intention of taking a husband, she was doomed to live as *Don Manuel* chose until he died.

When she was a girl, her servants had given her the time and attention *Don* Manuel hadn't. She considered them family and felt protective because they had to deal with problems she'd never have. Motivated by love for them, she'd sacrificed her freedom in order to inherit Toledo and improve their lives.

******

The butler showed Henning to a quiet, velvet-appointed drawing room. Its floor had been polished until the rugs seemed to float in liquid. Standing at a bookcase Martine's father pointed to overstuffed chairs then shuffled toward them, leaning heavily on an elaborate walking stick that had been purely ornamental when Henning first saw it.

"Why have you waited so long to pay me the courtesy of a visit?" *Don* Manuel demanded after they made themselves comfortable. "You frequently ride with my daughter."

"I apologize for my oversight."

"As you should. Martine tells me you're a capitalist."

"That sounded like an accusation." Henning chuckled awkwardly.

"May I know the source of your amusement?"

"I find it odd to think of myself as a capitalist."

"What is a capitalist in your opinion?"

"A man who uses money to make money."

"How does that distinguish him from other businessmen?"

"Capitalists are more organized and disciplined."

"Sounds like they take the joy out of doing business," *Don* Manuel said. "That's a shame. It can be one of life's great pleasures."

"I doubt anyone enjoys it more than I do. Nonetheless, I need a break at times, which is why I'm looking forward to my race with *Don* José Geldres."

Having brought the conversation to the subject he'd come to discuss, Henning was thwarted—intentionally he thought—when his host said, "It's interesting that you call Geldres *Don*. My daughter does the same, even though he clearly isn't one."

For too long Martine's father controlled the conversation while Henning impatiently shifted from one buttock to the other.

Finally *Don* Manuel asked, "What brings you here?"

"I'm conditioning my horse, Sultán, for his match race with Goliat. When I leave on business, Belisario Lorca's trainer takes charge. Regrettably, he knows nothing about cross-country racing and doesn't follow instructions. I believe Martine would do a better job and—"

"She's a talented amateur," *Don* Manuel interrupted, "who still has much to learn and won't let me teach her. You're better off with Roque."

"Sultán needs to be worked at high speed, which makes Roque uncomfortable because that can negatively affect a Paso horse's gait."

"My daughter loves going fast. But women shouldn't ride stallions."

"Yesterday Martine rode Sultán two hours without problems, even though I was riding a mare beside him."

"Even so…" *Don* Manuel shrugged. "May I offer the services of my trainer, Marcial?"

"He'll have the same shortcomings as Roque, for the same reasons."

A smile tugged at *Don* Manuel's mouth. "Am I correct in assuming that you think Martine will follow your instructions?"

"Not blindly perhaps, but she'll understand what I'm trying to accomplish."

"If you can get her to do your bidding, you're a better man than I. I'll let her work your horse provided you stable him here at Toledo while you're gone. I want her to ride with Marcial, so they can trade horses if Sultán misbehaves."

Martine's father had given in too easily—not that Henning minded. But he couldn't help wondering if *Don* Manuel saw him as a potential son-in-law. A blue blooded aristocrat, the old man wouldn't see someone without noble blood as ideal. But perhaps rich commoners were preferable to no husband at all.

Stepping into the hall, *Don* Manuel told the maid, "Show *Señor* Dietzel to the door."

Then he started climbing the stairs, moving his hand up the banister only when both feet and his walking stick were firmly on the same step.

******

Sitting on the low stone wall at Toledo's entrance, holding her horse by the reins, Martine asked, "Did you and my father find common ground?"

"He doesn't give his permission easily, does he?" Henning dismounted, then sat down and pointed at her trees. "How'd you get him to let you plant those on prime farmland?"

"My brother talked him into it. No one else could have, me least of all. But Daddy couldn't say no to Pietro."

"He didn't say no to me, either. You have his permission to exercise Sultán."

Impulsively she squeezed Henning's arm, the first physical affection she'd shown him.

Three weeks later Henning returned from Iquique, bringing Encinas. There had been only one cabin available on *Portales*, and since it had two beds they'd shared it. In Cortéz's predawn darkness Henning hired a vehicle to take them to Valencia.

When he introduced Belisario to his attractive new bookkeeper, the old aristocrat's normal crankiness vanished. After breakfast he showed Encinas to her room personally instead of assigning the task to Chabuca.

When he returned, Belisario poked Henning in the ribs and said, "You must be eager to see how Martine did with Sultán. I'll drive you to Toledo while Encinas settles in."

Later as they dismounted from Belisario's carriage, Martine came outside.

"I'm afraid I can't stay," Belisario told her. "My new bookkeeper's waiting. I'll see the results of your work when Henning brings Sultán home this afternoon."

"He's the best horse I've ever ridden," she said. "I'll miss him."

Praising Belisario's horses normally perked him up. But he was already so cheerful he waved a second goodbye as he drove away.

Following Martine to the stable, Henning saw evidence that she'd taken her task seriously. The sun had darkened her skin and lightened her now-shorter hair. She glowed with good health, but her movements were stiff.

"What happened to your foot?" he asked.

"Sultán stepped on it," she replied, then interrupted his offer of sympathy. "Don't worry. This last month was well worth some discomforts. No one could tell me what to do because I was the only one who knew what you wanted."

She swung Sultán's stall door open. Saddled, he was tied to an iron ring near the manger.

"I'm eager for you to ride him," Martine gushed, "so I had Marcial get him ready. When men praise women, it usually means the poor dears did as well as can be expected from mere females. But after you try him, I want the unvarnished truth."

"You'll get it," Henning replied.

After Sultán warmed up, Henning put the little chestnut in the *sobreandando*, a gait with the speed of a trot. Returning later he was surprised to see Martine waiting where he'd left her.

From several yards away, she eagerly asked, "How did he do?"

"Even though he carried less weight than usual with you on him," Henning said, "you somehow managed to improve his condition."

"He carried your weight every time I rode him. I made up the difference with a saddlebag full of parts from one of my father's broken-down machines."

"The results are impressive. Thank you very much." Henning didn't elaborate. Effusive praise made her uncomfortable.

In the past Martine had always been first to say goodbye. But today she didn't want him to go. They sat talking in the screened porch for hours, drinking *chicha morada* and smiling frequently for such serious people.

"What does Goliat mean?" Henning asked as she refilled his glass for the third time.

"In English it's Goliath."

"As in the Bible? David and Goliath? He doesn't seem big enough to deserve that name. I'm accustomed to Germany's draft horses."

"Well, to quote Belisario," she said, "'If you cooked him, he'd feed a lot of people.'"

"Speaking of which, I'd better go. Belisario asked me to get back in time for dinner."

"Stay a little longer. I'll show you a shortcut that will get you there in plenty of time."

CHAPTER SIX
A NEW PLAN

The long, unbending road from the Cortéz post office to the foothills was fuzzy in late afternoon's light.

"He's late. Does he look worried?" Belisario asked, handing Martine his binoculars.

"Henning's face is harder to read than yours," she teased. "Be patient."

Belisario grunted as Sultán slowed to a walk. He knew Henning always began the cooling process by reducing the little chestnut's speed for the final mile. But the old aristocrat was eager to compare Sultán's performance with Goliat's.

If all went according to plan, Sultán had been in a ground-covering *sobreandando* since leaving Sierra Alta's post office. José Geldres and Goliat had traveled that road the previous year, carrying mail in envelopes commemorating Peru's Independence. Postmasters who recorded his departure and arrival times had been astonished that a horse could go that far so fast.

When Sultán reached Belisario, he stopped on his own—flanks heaving, sweat cascading from his belly—and lowered his head.

"How long?" Belisario asked.

Checking his pocket watch Henning said, "Goliat took over an hour less."

"Sultán will do better after he's had more work."

"Look at him," Henning barked. "Do you honestly think he can cut an hour from the time he just made?"

With darkness approaching, Martine and her father's trainer mounted their horses. Marcial was middle-aged, ungainly, and absolutely devoted to his boss's daughter. She had his complete attention as they rode away.

Belisario watched Henning move Sultán forward so he could dismount without stepping on an *algarrobo* seedling. The nearest trees were far away. This offspring had no doubt sprouted in the droppings of a goat that ate seedpods. If it miraculously survived, its roots would extract the earth's moisture so efficiently that all salt grass within its reach would shrivel and die.

"That seedling is more likely to become a tree," Henning said, "than Sultán is to beat Goliat if I ride him. I realize that winning despite my weight would dramatically demonstrate the superiority of your bloodline. But don't let that dream cost you a chance to get more workers."

"I'll consider a lighter rider if you come up with one who's as good as you."

"I already have."

"Martine?" Belisario rolled his eyes. "Women lack strength and endurance. She couldn't beat José Geldres in a thousand tries."

"And I couldn't beat him in a million."

"You could with God's help, which you sure as hell won't get if you don't go to church once in a while."

"Sure as hell?" Henning repeated. "Shouldn't good Catholics say sure as heaven?"

******

Toledo's screened back porch, crowded with sofas and chairs, had hosted a party the night before. Now it was empty except for Henning and Martine.

"Too bad my brother isn't alive," she said. "Pietro was a splendid rider and not much heavier than I am."

"I'd prefer you even if he were available," Henning replied.

"You'd feel differently if you'd seen him ride. Anyhow, this discussion is pointless. Daddy will never let me ride in a race in the Wrath of God. That would be dangerous, unladylike, and far too much fun."

"I managed to convince Belisario. Maybe I can do the same with your father."

"You'd have the advantage of surprise, that's for sure. Daddy thinks all men look down on women. And I can't remember anyone ever mustering up the courage to approach him with a request that was certain to anger him."

"If he gives his permission, will you ride?"

"I would if I thought I could do a good job."

"I wish you could see yourself through my eyes rather than your father's." Henning paused, then took aim at her competitiveness. "Why don't you try to beat my fastest time on Sultán? If you can't—despite your weight advantage—you're clearly no match for *Don* José."

Green eyes flashing she folded her arms and said, "You're trying to manipulate me and it's working. But I can't do anything without Daddy's permission. And he'll never give it."

"We'll see. I'll ask him this afternoon."

******

The maid showed Henning into Toledo's drawing room where *Don* Manuel was hunched over a stamp collection on his desk. Even after imperiously standing, he wasn't as intimidating as last time. When Henning had asked permission for Martine to work Sultán, he'd felt he was asking a favor. This time he was extending a courtesy. Martine was, after all, an adult entitled to make her own decisions.

His hip plainly better, *Don* Manuel remained standing as Henning explained his visit.

"Men's work should be done by men," *Don* Manuel declared, "and there are many better qualified than my daughter. You for one."

"Martine weighs half what I do. If I coach her, Sultán can benefit from my knowledge without carrying my weight."

"You honestly believe she's up to the job?"

"She has a special affinity with horses. She can almost read their minds."

"Horses have instincts—not minds," *Don* Manuel snapped, showing the temper Henning had heard about. "And strong, capable men have died in the Wrath of God. How can you possibly suggest that I permit you to risk my only remaining child's life?"

"I'll never be far away and will keep track of her with this." Henning slid his spotting scope from its case.

"How will you stay close if your weight slows a horse as much as you claim?"

"I'll have a fresh horse every day."

"It's a pity Martine's brother isn't alive. You should have seen Pietro ride. He was outstanding at everything. When he died, I lost more than my only heir."

"By my count you still have an heir."

"Martine?" *Don* Manuel looked pained. "She'll inherit Toledo, raise everyone's salary, and go broke. A woman couldn't run this place even with the best instincts and training, of which Martine has neither. She refuses to learn the correct ways of doing things."

"She thinks for herself. I'll grant you that."

Don Manuel shook his walking stick. "Thinks for herself? She takes positions to spite me—not because she actually believes in them. It was nice seeing you again."

"May I know your response to my request?"

"I'll give it some thought. *Adiós.*"

After his dismissal, Henning met Martine between the stone walls lining Toledo's entrance. Both on horseback, they stopped side-by-side.

Searching his face she asked, "Do I want to know what happened?"

"He said he'll think about it."

"That's his way of saying no."

"Until he says it in a straightforward way, we should take him at his word."

Martine tilted her head to one side. "You're used to getting your way, aren't you?"

"Within the rules of good behavior," he said. "But you shouldn't have to ask permission to live as you want. Your father will keep you under his thumb until you stand up to him."

"You ignore the fact that I always stand up for myself but never get my way."

"You stand up to everyone but your father. Are you afraid he'll cut you out of his will?"

"That would be a high price to pay for riding in a horse race, don't you think?"

"Not if you value your freedom."

Leaning forward in her saddle Martine brushed a thistle from her horse's mane.

"All right," she said. "I'll condition Sultán until my father forbids it, which he will."

******

Riding out of the deep, narrow passageway under fluffy clouds Henning turned toward Dos Palos. José Geldres was sitting on his porch. Judging by the yellow smear on his plate, he'd just finished Huancayo *papas*, a popular dish featuring potatoes in a spicy cheese sauce.

Fanning himself with his *sombrero*, *Don* José stood as Henning dismounted. After observing the niceties and downing a glass of lemonade, Henning made his proposal.

"Having Martine ride in your place violates our agreement," *Don* José replied. "That would be the equivalent of substituting another horse for Sultán."

"We made no agreement as to riders," Henning pointed out. "That was never discussed."

"Not specifically perhaps, but it was understood that you and I would ride. And I'm looking forward to the honor of competing with you."

"What honor comes from winning because of an insurmountable advantage?"

"What honor comes from defeating a woman?"

"Even with Martine riding," Henning said, "you'll be competing against me. I'll help prepare Sultán, plan her strategy, and assist her during the race."

"What if I insist that you ride?"

"I'd pull out of the race rather than invest more time in a losing cause," Henning replied, then gently added, "Let her ride. She'll relish the challenge as much as you do, and I'll make sure you're hard-pressed to beat her."

"I can't let my goddaughter put herself in danger."

"She doesn't need your permission to take risks and this one is small. *Don* Belisario will set up a camp every night. She'll have a tent, cot, medicine, food, water—everything she needs. And I'll have a fresh horse every day so I can watch over her on the trail."

"I know you'll take good care of her."

"That I will."

Henning sealed their agreement with a handshake before *Don* José had time for second thoughts and then left. The old man's decision had been sudden. When he considered the implications, he'd likely change his mind.

******

Every time Henning's father had visited Grandpa Dietzel's farm, he'd come on the latest in a series of mounts that increased in quality as he rose in rank. During those visits he'd let Henning ride his horses and had taught him lessons learned in Prussia's cavalry.

While saddling Sultán for Martine's first try at beating his fastest time, Henning passed along the most important of his father's advice.

"A cavalryman's life depends on his horse," he began, "and my father passionately believed it's critical to water them correctly before, during, and after exercise. Horses that drink too much get waterlogged, which slows them down. If they don't drink enough they dehydrate, which weakens them. And if not properly cooled before drinking they can colic and die."

Looking as skeptical as Henning had felt when his father gave him that same speech, Martine said, "I always let my horses drink their fill and I've never had a problem."

"When you ride as hard as you will from now on, watering requires precision. I want you to use a bucket until you know how much Sultán requires to be at his best. Then count the swallows needed to take in that amount and make sure he doesn't get more or less when drinking from troughs or rivers."

"You're kidding, right?"

"Absolutely not."

For weeks Martine tried without coming close to beating Henning's best time. Prior to her next try, Henning handed her a hand-drawn map with red lines representing the area's irrigation ditches.

"For me," he said, "Sultán did best with fifteen swallows per hour. Good luck."

That day Martine was only minutes short of Henning's best time. Three days later she bested it. After that she took his advice more seriously, and he stopped prefacing it with "I want" or "I don't want", which clearly rubbed her the wrong way.

"What would you think of riding Sultán with those saddlebags full of machine parts from now on?" he asked one morning. "Without the additional weight during the race, you'll feel light as a feather."

Martine enjoyed lowering her record and lost some enthusiasm when the extra hundred pounds slowed Sultán to where she no longer could.

"It helps my spirits when I make really good time," she told Henning after a month. "Do you mind if I occasionally ride without the machine parts and try to lower my record?"

As she finished without the additional weight that day, Henning glanced at his watch and informed her, "You just had your fastest ride by far."

"I didn't like carrying that extra weight," she said, exhilarated, "but now that I see the results…"

"And I didn't see the value of having you sometimes ride without the extra weight, but now that I see what it did for your spirits…"

CHAPTER SEVEN
THE WRATH OF GOD

Two weeks before the race Martine joined Belisario and Henning at Valencia for dinner. After dessert they made themselves comfortable on the living room sofa.

"When the Creator made the Wrath of God," Belisario said, smiling in appreciation of what he was about to say, "he subcontracted the job but neglected to require surety insurance. You know what that is, right?"

"It guarantees a project will be properly completed," Henning replied.

"Exactly. So once the Wrath of God was finished, there was no one to fix the problems."

"What problems?" Henning teased. "Deserts are supposed to be hot and inhospitable, which makes the Wrath of God a masterpiece."

"This is my story and I'll make the jokes." Belisario's pretended offense faded as he continued. "In the late 1500s, sixteen Spanish *conquistadores* from Cortéz were urgently needed in Lima. To get there they had to cross the Wrath of God. Knowing its reputation, they took plenty of extra water. But during lunch one afternoon, their packhorse ran off with it.

"On foot with nothing to drink, the Spaniards found themselves chasing mirages while their tongues swelled and turned black. One night a none-too-clever private named Sancho was disturbed by the other men's snoring and moved away from camp. Next morning his delirious comrades inadvertently left him behind. After wandering in circles for days, they came upon Sancho's corpse, in his sleeping bag, baked as if in an oven.

"That night the sentry challenged a ghostly figure, who goes there?"

"You don't recognize me?" the apparition asked. "I'm Sancho."

"Y-you're dead. We b-buried you," the sentry stammered.

"Owing to my transgressions, the devil took me after I died. And to tell the truth Hell was a relief compared to here."

"Why d-did you come back?"

"The Wrath of God didn't prepare me for Hell's mild climate. Fortunately, the devil took pity and furloughed me so I could get my blanket."

Martine lowered her chin and looked at Belisario from the tops of her eyes.

"Be skeptical if you like," Belisario said, "but there's a written record of everything I just told you, including the part about Sancho's ghost. The *capitán's* diary was found near fifteen human skeletons. And because not even predators survive in the Wrath of God, all the bones were still arranged exactly as when covered with flesh."

As Belisario finished other stories of men who'd died in Peru's killer desert, the mantle clock chimed, followed by a knock on the door.

"That will be my father's driver," Martine said.

As Henning walked her to the door she volunteered, "This morning Daddy forbade me to ride in the race and I said I'd do it against his will if necessary. As you predicted he later told me I can ride and then established that he's still the boss by imposing conditions. As much as I'm looking forward to this, I would have promised almost anything."

Henning smiled. If Belisario's graphic stories of death in the desert had been intended to encourage Martine's withdrawal from the race, the old aristocrat had underestimated her.

Rejoining Belisario on the sofa Henning asked, "Is there a way I can cross the Wrath of God before the race?"

"I can arrange it," Belisario replied, brightening. "Does this mean you might reconsider and ride in the race?"

"No, I just want to see the terrain."

"During the race, I'll have a dozen extra horses on my schooner, *Fina Estampa*, and will unload a new one for you every night. I can do the same beforehand."

"How will you get them ashore?"

"The same way the *conquistadores* did before Peru had docks. We'll push them overboard. Horses are natural swimmers. Once they're in the water, men in rowboats can get hold of their leadlines and guide them to the beach. After they've served their purpose we'll swim them out and winch them aboard."

"How will I find *Fina Estampa* at the end of the day?"

"She'll be anchored where you can easily see her flag."

Next day, Belisario satisfied his sense of fair play by offering to provide horses for *Don* José so he could accompany Henning.

"Not necessary," *Don* José replied. "Nothing has changed there for centuries."

******

Henning took ten days to become the second man to cross Peru's deadliest desert. Though he'd never done anything as difficult, it didn't feel like much of an accomplishment. *Don* José had made the same journey in the same time on one horse—not ten—and without the supplies and comforts Belisario had supplied at night aboard *Fina Estampa*.

When Henning returned to Valencia the day before the race, Martine was waiting to hear what he'd learned. With much to tell her and only one day to do it, he took her to Belisario's library to avoid interruptions.

He'd barely begun when the cook stopped by.

"I have to prepare thirty meals during the race," the man said. "What would you like?"

"I'll be fine with whatever you prepare," Henning said, then waited impatiently while Martine considered and gave her choices, Resuming where he'd left off, Henning was interrupted by another knock.

Mustering his most discouraging tone he asked, "Who is it?"

"The *talabartero*," a shy voice replied. "I need to have *Señorita* Prado sit in the saddle I'm making. *Don* Belisario wants a perfect fit."

Including polite conversation, the fitting took an hour despite Henning's efforts to move it along. As he and Martine returned to the library, someone came up behind them.

"*Señorita*," Belisario's private cobbler said, "can you kindly slip on your new boots before I do the final stitching? Also, the tailor wants you to try on your riding outfit."

When Henning and Martine finally reseated themselves in the library, Chabuca opened the door and poked her head in.

"Lunch is ready," she said.

"It's lunchtime already?" Henning asked, exasperated. "Can you serve it here please?"

"Right away, *señor*," Chabuca responded.

Returning with glasses of lemonade and a plate of hors d'oeuvres, she said, "Lunch isn't quite ready after all. I brought this to tide you over."

Handing Henning his drink, Chabuca let go too soon. He interrupted the glass's fall with his instep, but it shattered on the tile floor. After mopping up the liquid with linen napkins Chabuca hurried away.

She soon returned with the houseboy who swept up the broken glass while she arranged a three-course lunch on the coffee table.

"Belisario's noble intentions are wasting valuable time," Henning told Martine as they ate. "You'd need weeks to properly break in his gifts, which means you can't use them during the race. But the information I have is critical."

"I have to be gracious in response to his generosity," she replied.

Rather than do what she'd interpret as bossing her around, Henning dropped the subject.

Hours later he finally checked off the last note written while crossing the Wrath of God and began a review. When the saddlemaker requested more of Martine's time, she looked relieved and gave more than he needed.

******

In Valencia's guest room, a squeaky bedspring woke Martine. Unable to fall asleep with the race five hours away, she put on trousers and a shirt then hurried outside, hoping to avoid Henning who'd be up by now and eager to review today's strategy yet again.

In early morning's fuzzy light she crossed the yard and turned left on a dirt path between towering walls of sugarcane. Farther along, she passed a field. It had recently been harvested and replanted with six inch sections of cane stalk, laid horizontally in furrows and covered with soil. Tiny brown birds darted among sprouts that were breaking through the ground.

Beyond the last irrigation ditch was nothing but desert. She sat in the dust, knees hugged to her chest. By midmorning she'd be beyond the horizon. Barring setbacks, she and Sultán would reach Belisario's first camp by late afternoon. There the race monitor would record their arrival times. At six a.m. the following morning, the leader would start again. After waiting the amount of time that had separated their arrivals, the other would follow.

For ten days—God willing—she and her godfather would speed along dry washes, scale hills strewn with razor-sharp rocks, and navigate thorn trees and cactus. More exhausting still, their horses would scramble up sand dunes, sinking shin-deep and losing half their progress sliding backward.

Until now Martine had considered the race a glorious challenge and an opportunity to help Belisario. But she'd been deluding herself. Truth be told, she was about to risk her life in a savage desert without a prayer of winning.

CHAPTER EIGHT
FLAWED TACTICS

At dawn Valencia's stable was enveloped in *garúa*, a mist that interfered little with visibility but was surprisingly moist. Carrying umbrellas, Valencia's neighbors had already begun arriving. When Belisario revealed that Martine—not Henning—would ride Sultán, they thought he was joking.

After that news reached the *serrano* and half-breed workers wearing latex coated ponchos outside the surrounding wall, their normally submissive faces showed disappointment. They had looked forward to holding their heads high when José Geldres—an Indian, like them—defeated a white man. Though victims of prejudice, they now showed their own.

"Winning against a woman is meaningless," one muttered amid a chorus of agreement.

Belisario was disappointed when Henning explained why Martine wasn't using her new saddle and boots. But the arrival of newsmen from as far away as Arequipa cheered him. He practically begged the best-known to tell their readers about his beloved horses and bloodlines.

"I've produced twelve generations in forty years," he told one. "Only my son and wife were more important to me."

The change of riders clearly pleased the reporters. A woman racing Peru's best-known horseman in the infamous Wrath of God was a once-in-a-lifetime story. Ignoring Belisario, they badgered Martine with questions. Henning ran them off and took her into the tack room.

"You've taken on an important responsibility," he said, closing the door. "Valencia's future depends on winning this race, and those jokers are wasting time you should use to get yourself mentally ready."

"Unlike you," she replied frostily, "I don't live by a code that forbids me to enjoy life. And as far as I'm concerned those reporters are a blessing in disguise. Answering their questions calms my nerves."

"I know how you feel but—"

"You can't possibly know how I feel. Men's lives prepare them to compete, but women are simply taught to wait adoringly at the finish line."

"This time the woman will compete and the man will wait."

"Not quietly, as a woman would. You'll constantly order me around, as you are now."

Henning's voice lost its edge. "All right. Go ahead, talk to the reporters if it helps."

She dropped into a chair and stretched out her legs. "No other man would have selected me for this. Thank you. And you're right. I should gather my thoughts."

"In order to win, you have to know it's possible. And it is. You have Sultán in top condition, and we have an excellent plan. But you need to—and deserve to—believe in yourself as much as I do."

She stood. Henning risked a fatherly hug. She neither returned the favor nor pulled away.

The stable boy Belisario sent to help with last-minute preparations had disappeared, leaving Henning to do everything. Martine followed him outside to the hitching rail where he'd left Sultán, saddled and bridled. Henning worked the little chestnut around him on a long line, making the circles larger as people gave way.

When Sultán was warmed up, Martine put her foot in the stirrup and lifted herself into the saddle in a single, graceful motion.

"I still have a lot to do," Henning said. "I'll catch up with you on the trail."

One with her horse, Martine rode away. Left behind, the reporters gathered around Goliat, José Geldres, and a man who'd arrived the previous afternoon. Geldres had hired Bartley Carrick, the most successful trainer at Lima's race track, as his assistant.

"Will you ride with *Señor* Geldres?" a reporter asked.

"Not at my age," Carrick replied, his simple, error-filled Spanish hinting at an Irish brogue. "I'll go to the camps on *Señor* Lorca's ship."

When *Don* José reached the starting line on Goliat, he didn't acknowledge Martine. Clearly he regretted having agreed to let her ride. Back then, everyone had thought the race would be held in quiet obscurity. But thanks to the newspapers, people everywhere were eagerly anticipating it, and the vast majority of Peru's population had Indian blood. Defeating a white man would have made Geldres a national hero.

After spreading the legs of his tripod, a photographer asked Martine and *Don* José to pose side-by-side on their horses.

"Is that one of those newfangled boxes that produce tintype likenesses?" Belisario asked.

"The latest model," the photographer replied. "Hold still and look natural."

He removed the lens cap, silently moved his lips as he counted, then replaced it. Next he asked the riders to dismount and stand next to one another, bracketed between their horses. They were holding their poses when Goliat pinned his ears and lunged at Sultán's neck, mouth wide open. At the last second, Martine's father stepped between them—his walking stick raised to hold Goliat at bay.

"That picture won't be any good," the photographer grumbled. "I'll need another."

"You'll have to take individual shots," *Don* Manuel insisted. "I won't permit my daughter anywhere near that gray devil."

With Martine's attention on Sultán, *Don* Manuel watched her with a strange combination of fatherly pride and disapproval. He was undoubtedly pleased with his daughter's natural beauty and her stateliness—so like his own. But he also seemed embarrassed, probably by her unladylike athleticism and the snug trousers that were manly even though cut to fit her shape.

While the photographer took a shot of Martine on Sultán, *Don* Manuel's trainer, Marcial, sidled closer to *Don* José and Bartley Carrick.

Later his jaws tightened as he walked away, then stopped beside Martine and whispered, "I don't agree with what *Don* José said."

"What did he say?"

"That it was a miracle no one was hurt when you brought Sultán too close to Goliat. And that women shouldn't handle stallions."

"He blames me?" she exclaimed.

"To your marks," the starter called.

Firmly gripping Sultán's reins Martine lined up as close to Goliat as she dared. Again *Don* José ignored her.

Have you hardened your heart because your only chance for glory is to beat me badly and you feel guilty? she wanted to ask.

Belisario began the countdown at five. At zero, Martine relaxed the reins and Sultán surged forward. The Race of the Century, as newspapers were calling it, had begun.

Goliat's burst of speed seemed ill-advised at the beginning of a ten-day marathon. Martine's spirits sank as she quickly fell behind. Henning had instructed her to give *Don* José the lead. But she wasn't giving him anything. He was taking it—and far more than anticipated

Martine cast a panicked look over her shoulder. Henning had left too soon to see that his strategy was already failing. He believed that if the two stallions dueled at top speed for five hundred miles, Sultán couldn't win. Not after a lifetime of languishing in a stall while Goliat carried his master through the rugged Andes.

He'd instructed her to go slow and give Goliat a commanding lead, reasoning that when *Don* José looked back and couldn't see her in the vast desert behind him, his sense of urgency would diminish. And rather than risk injuring Goliat to increase a substantial lead, he'd slow down. But he hadn't once looked back and was increasing his speed.

Henning had hoped a slow pace would leave Sultán with enough in reserve to catch Goliat late in the race. But Goliat's lead would soon be insurmountable.

******

Belisario invited the spectators into his house where thick walls insulated them from the heat. They were sipping cool drinks as Henning tied canvas water bags behind his saddle and followed the hoofprints into the desert. He was perspiring after rushing through his chores, and the temperature—already oppressive—would continue to climb for hours.

On a flat stretch he saw a distant lake. A mirage, it vanished then reappeared farther away. Looking down from Vista Bluff he saw a thermal spring. Beyond its clouds of steam, Martine had Sultán in a slow *paso llano*. They were where Henning expected. But where were *Don* José and Goliat?

He asked his sweat-drenched mount for more speed. Earlier it had accelerated when he simply shook his spurs, making them ring. This time he had to use them.

"You've done a great job sticking to our schedule," he said, coming alongside Martine.

"It's your schedule." Her voice was raspy. "If it were mine, I'd have changed it. *Don* José has been out of sight for two hours."

"Are you drinking plenty of water?"

"I finished it." She pointed to the gourd bouncing with Sultán's movements.

"I'll fill it and then go ahead to see where Goliat is."

"The last of my water was too hot to drink," she said. "I had to pour it out."

"These," he said, uncorking a water bag, "keep water fresh and cool by allowing a little to evaporate through the canvas."

"During training you always watered Sultán first," Martine said after a long gulp. "Don't worry about me if that's what you're doing. I'm fine, but your plan needs adjusting."

Henning shook open and partially filled a canvas bucket. Martine held it and while Sultán drank, Henning refilled her flask.

"I'll be back after I check on *Don* José," he said, back on his horse. "We'll adjust our tactics if he hasn't slowed down."

Because his horse would work only one day, Henning demanded everything it had. The animal was spent when it finally came alongside Goliat.

"I brought water," Henning said.

"I don't need it," *Don* José said curtly.

"If you're worried about the extra weight, don't. I'll bring water to you periodically, as I do for Martine."

"There are springs for the first two days. You can bring me water after that."

Henning hadn't seen any springs today or during his first crossing. The race was a few hours old and *Don* José had already surprised him three times—with his unconventional start, his knowledge of the land, and his ferocious competitiveness.

******

Though they were riding toward one another, Henning didn't see Martine for an hour.

"*Don* José is still pulling away," he said, pouring her horse's drink first this time. "Speed up as soon as this water clears Sultán's stomach."

When she asked the little chestnut to speed up, Martine felt his hind legs drive them forward in a ground-covering *sobreandando*. Carrying those extra hundred pounds of machine parts had done wonders. Henning's exhausted horse quickly fell behind.

"Don't slow down for me," he shouted across the rapidly widening gap.

Following Goliat's hoofprints in dusty rock-strewn soil, Martine paralleled reddish brown hills against which the eternal wind had piled contrasting sand. After several exhilarating hours she veered toward the coast, where the footing became loose and deep.

Soon after spotting the oversize Peruvian flag flying from *Fina Estampa's* mast, she saw a horizon where steely gray ocean met bright blue sky. A mile short of the beach where men were putting up tents and corrals, she slowed Sultán to cool him.

Her sense of urgency now gone, Martine felt the effects of a punishing day. That morning she'd put on a custom-made blouse Belisario had given her. It didn't cover her as thoroughly as the men's shirts she usually wore. Both arms were an angry, glowing red below the three-quarter length sleeves. And her neck stung where sunburned above the low collar. Henning had warned her to do everything exactly the same as she had while training. She should've listened.

If only he had been equally astute when planning today's strategy.

As she crossed that day's finish line, Belisario glared at his watch. The old aristocrat held his temper while Marcial unsaddled and cooled Sultán. But by the time Henning appeared on the distant horizon, his patience was exhausted.

"Goliat is forty-eight minutes ahead," he told Martine. "You'll begin tomorrow's race almost an hour after *Don* José does. What went wrong?"

"Ask Henning," she said, overcome by fatigue. "I did as I was told."

As Henning's spent horse finally plodded across the finish line, Belisario growled, "Why did you have Martine go slow? Correct me if I'm wrong, but I thought our goal was to win."

"I wanted Goliat to have an early lead," Henning explained, "but not forty-eight minutes. *Don* José outsmarted me."

After dismounting he handed his horse over to Marcial, then gave Sultán a rubdown and a few swallows of water.

"Let's go see how much Goliat's performance took out of him," he said, turning the little chestnut loose in a corral.

Across camp they found Goliat in a pen, showing no sign of his exertions.

Returning to Sultán's corral, Belisario took Henning aside. Looking over her shoulder, Martine saw he old aristocrat's angry gestures and was glad she'd kept going.

Later in the largest of the tents his crew had erected on carpet-covered platforms, Belisario proudly told his guests, "This one is for dining and the others are for sleeping. You'll each have one to yourself."

The dining tent's interior was laced with appetizing smells and the table was set with linen, china, crystal, and silverware. *Cholos* dressed in white served a sumptuous meal, then seconds, and finally dessert and coffee.

After Geldres and Carrick had left, Belisario lit a cigar.

"I owe you both apologies," he told Henning and Martine. "I've behaved badly, but I never dreamed Sultán would be so far behind. Tomorrow he'll go faster, right?"

"He's too far behind to catch up that way," Henning replied.

"I don't understand."

"The only way to beat *Don* José now is to make him complacent. Fortunately he's leaning in that direction already."

******

"How long ago did Goliat get here?" Martine asked when she reached the following night's camp.

"He gained another eighteen minutes today," Henning replied.

"That's bad."

"No, it's good."

"It's good that I'm sixty-six minutes behind?"

"Of course not, but *Don* José gained forty-eight minutes yesterday and eighteen today. You averaged the same speed. That means he's content with his lead and has slowed down."

While everyone else relaxed after dinner Henning and Martine went outside where a gentle sea breeze had cooled the superheated desert. By the time they reached Goliat's corral, they had dry foreheads for the first time all day.

"He looks wonderful." Martine sounded discouraged.

"Yes, but his flanks are sunken," Henning pointed out, "and Sultán's are full. That's because Belisario supplements hay with oats while *Don* José uses *algarrobo* seed pods. They're considered nutritious, but I had some tested and they contain mostly sugar. In the days to come Sultán's superior nutrition will give you an advantage."

"Here comes my godfather." Martine sounded tense. "I wonder if he's still ignoring me."

Lost in conversation, *Don* José and Bartley Carrick stopped and turned their backs.

Approaching from behind, Martine heard her godfather say, "I wonder if all Germans have such lofty opinions of themselves. Apparently Dietzel thinks a woman can outride me with nothing more than the benefit of his advice. She'll need a lot more than that."

Turning, *Don* José seemed surprised to see Martine so close. Gruffly, he said, "If you overheard anything you didn't like, announce yourself next time."

"Everyone is entitled to his or her opinion," she replied coldly.

His smug look increased her determination to beat him.

CHAPTER NINE
ALL THE NEWS THAT'S FIT TO PRINT

Goliat's lead gave him an unanticipated advantage. Leaving camp in early morning's coolness, he covered ground Sultán had to cross later, when the day was hotter. Despite this, Sultán held his own for the next four days, twice losing minutes and twice gaining them. On the seventh day Henning told Martine to narrow the gap all she could before the noonday heat.

By then Sultán was closer than at any time since the race's early hours.

What Henning saw when he studied *Don* José through his spotting scope that afternoon was daunting. If the man had shortcomings, they were well hidden. Compact, he was light in the saddle. His perfect balance made him easy to carry on climbs and descents, and he always found the least demanding route. He was by far the most skilled rider Henning had ever seen.

But casually slicing off part of Goliat's ear—combined with *Don* José's failure to observe the fine points of feeding and watering—showed a lack of concern for animals. And that could be his undoing.

Rain in the mountains had been exceptionally heavy that year and two rivers, miles apart, were flowing for the first time in decades. Having forded both during his pre-race ride, Henning knew that. But *Don* José didn't.

Hidden in a gully, Henning watched Goliat suck his fill of water from the first. Underway again, the big gray went too fast after drinking too much. But without paying the price. If *Don* José's good luck continued at the next river, Henning's all-or-nothing gamble would fail, and Martine would lose the race.

From the same gully Henning watched Martine approach the river. Anticipating the water he'd told her to expect, she slowed Sultán to cool him. Then she watched the little chestnut's throat while he drank—counting swallows no doubt—and pulled his head up when he'd had enough. Underway again, she restrained his speed until the danger of colic had passed.

She'd learned well.

Belisario danced a jig as Sultán reached the finish line at Los Altos Beach. "With three days to go, we made up a third of our deficit," he exulted.

"Don't celebrate where *Don* José can see you," Henning cautioned. "There's no point in motivating a man we've worked so hard to lull into complacency."

During her dismount, Martine's knee buckled as her foot touched ground. She landed hard in a puff of dust.

"Give me a second," she said when Henning offered his hand. "My leg's asleep."

Rubbing her calf she looked up gratefully as he coated her cracked lips with cocoa butter.

Cheerful later at dinner, *Don* José clearly didn't feel threatened by a woman who'd collapsed and needed help to get up. His lead was still substantial, forty-four minutes.

Don José, Belisario, and Bartley Carrick were immersed in conversation when Martine excused herself and Henning followed her outside.

"I don't need a chaperone in the middle of an uninhabited desert," she said, then added, "Sorry. That was clumsy. I was trying to say that I need to be alone so I can turn off my brain."

"I know how you feel," he replied. "See you in the morning. Sleep well."

Henning looked exhausted as he walked away, which surprised Martine but shouldn't have. He was crossing the Wrath of God for the second time in three weeks. And was riding back and forth between her and *Don* José, covering more ground than either of them.

She dropped into a chair near her tent and looked up. The moon was nowhere to be seen, and in the absolute darkness she saw countless stars and the blurry splash called the Milky Way.

Waking from a catnap, she saw Marcial standing nearby.

She touched his shoulder as she passed and said, "Thank you, but there's no need to protect me out here."

"You need rest," he replied. "When *Don* José came I asked him not to wake you."

She would have preferred to hear what her godfather had come to say.

******

Barely into the race's eighth day, Henning trained his spotting scope on *Don* José and Goliat. Yesterday Sultán had cut their lead. Today Henning had instructed Martine to conserve the little chestnut's energy for a big push tomorrow. The race's outcome now depended on whether *Don* José sped up. He'd considered that no doubt but so far hadn't done it.

Over his shoulder, Geldres again confirmed Martine was nowhere in sight. He seemed comfortable with that. And why not? Going faster in such harsh terrain would jeopardize the finest horse he'd ever owned, and for what? Sultán was miles behind and had expended a tremendous amount of energy yesterday.

At least, those were *Don* José's thoughts as Henning imagined them.

That afternoon a man on foot closed in on Martine from behind as Sultán slowed after a climb. Too far away to help, Henning raised his scope. His concern lessened when Martine waved to her pursuer. She kept moving after he caught up, forcing him to jog while they talked.

Out of breath after a while, the slender *cholo* knelt to write on a pad of paper as Martine pushed on. Back on his feet, he opened his wooden flask and drank deeply. Earlier Henning had stepped off his horse and had felt the ground's blistering heat through his boot soles. Now he chuckled as the stranger alternately stood on one, then the other of his thin-soled city shoes.

Closer now Henning saw dimples, a v-shaped mouth, and skin the color of mahogany.

"You must be Henning Dietzel," the *cholo* said cheerfully.

"And you are…?"

"Andrés de la Borda at your service." He tipped his hat with easy charm.

"Do I know you?"

"You do if you read the *Lima Correo*."

"You're a reporter?"

"Soon to be the best-known in the republic."

"How'd you get out here in the middle of nowhere?"

"The same way your horse did, except I wasn't thrown overboard when I arrived." De la Borda pointed toward a beached rowboat and a ship anchored in the ocean beyond.

"How did you know to wait for *Señorita* Prado here instead of inland?" Henning asked.

"José Geldres told me it's easier to ride near the ocean here."

"You went through a lot of trouble just to interview a contestant in a private race."

"Private?" De la Borda's forehead furrowed. "Thanks to me—if I do say so myself—this is the most famous race in Peru's history."

"Any chance your self-congratulation is a bit exaggerated?"

"What was the name of the horse Francisco Pizarro rode when he conquered the Incas?"

"I don't know."

"Few people do, but half of all Peruvians know the names of Goliat and Sultán. And the others will before I'm through."

Henning clucked and his horse sped up. Jogging alongside, de la Borda yanked a pad of paper from behind his belt.

"I don't give interviews," Henning said.

"Because I'm a half-breed?"

"Because I had a bad experience with a reporter in Germany."

"José Geldres's helper, Bartley Carrick, is only available to him in camp. Meanwhile you're out here, bringing food, water, and advice to *Señorita* Prado. How do you justify such an unfair advantage?"

Henning' status as a gentleman had been questioned. He couldn't resist explaining. "I'm carrying supplies for both contestants. And if he'd wanted one, Geldres could have picked an assistant capable of riding with him."

Panting and speaking in short bursts, de la Borda changed subjects. "My readers would be interested…in knowing how much… money is riding…on the race's outcome."

"People are always interested in things that are none of their business." Henning said, then left the prying, out-of-breath reporter behind.

But only briefly. De la Borda was waiting at the finish line in Belisario's camp.

CHAPTER TEN
SURPRISE AT THE RIVER

On the race's ninth morning Henning handed Martine the map he'd drawn the first time he crossed the next fifty miles. Then he quizzed her until satisfied she knew what to do.

"If she doesn't do well today, the race is lost," Belisario said as Sultán left the starting line three quarters of an hour after Goliat. "You should ride with her and make sure she keeps her wits about her."

"I hope she does more than that," Henning said. "I told her to try for the lead today."

Studying *Don* José an hour later, Henning focused his scope and whispered, "If you're as bored as you look, I have good news. Today will definitely be memorable."

Later with the temperature at its peak, Goliat was shin-deep in a river, drinking his fill. Nearby *Don* José—on hands and knees—did the same, then splashed his face and arms. Back in the saddle, lost in thought, he turned Goliat toward the opposite bank. Something smashed through the brush on the riverbank behind, then plunged into the water.

Geldres twisted in his saddle. Hooves atomized water into a halo around a fast-moving horse and rider. *Don* José froze as if astonished that Martine was so far from where he'd thought.

Sultán bolted past. Geldres swung his quirt, stinging Goliat. The big gray nearly caught up before running out of steam. Soon Martine was far enough ahead that Henning could see her only from the waist up. When she disappeared, Goliat was resisting ever-more-vigorous encouragement from *Don* José's spurs. The frantic dash after a cool drink had given the big gray a stomach ache. He'd be himself again tomorrow, but today he'd finish second.

Elated, Henning mounted up. It wasn't Martine's nature to risk everything on one throw of the dice, but she'd trusted him and done just that.

And it had worked.

******

Shaded by date palms, Henning waited at the finish line. Nearby, *Finca Las Palmas'* pickers buzzed with discontent. The oncoming rider was light-skinned and riding a chestnut. They'd hoped for a fellow *cholo* on a gray.

Henning's earlier arrival on a bay had also disappointed them. After seeing Martine take the lead he'd pushed his horse of the day hard and reached *Finca Las Palmas* ahead of her. But by the time she finally came in sight, she was long overdue.

"Something's wrong," Belisario said. "Martine always slows Sultán for the final mile. But this time he's been poking along ever since I first spotted her."

Later the little chestnut crossed the finish line in silence so complete Henning could hear his hooves whisper in the sand.

"Congratulations on taking the lead," a stranger told Martine. "I'm Santiago Galante, owner of *Las Palmas.*"

"Thank you for your hospitality," she replied, dismounting.

After miles at a relaxed pace, Sultán wasn't overheated. Nonetheless, Henning began the usual cooling routine.

"Why didn't you finish faster?" Belisario asked Martine, unhappy with her answer before hearing it.

"You should congratulate her," Henning snapped. "She had to catch Goliat precisely at the river. I doubt *Don* José himself could have done it as well."

Belisario lowered his voice. "To be honest I haven't understood his strategy for days. His lead would be insurmountable if he hadn't squandered it."

"Indians don't think ahead," Galante volunteered. "Look how they run their farms. Once they have enough food for a few months, they stop working."

"José Geldres supplies three times more workers than any other labor agent in Peru," Henning said icily. "I doubt he does that without planning."

"I was joking," Galante said.

"I'm sure you didn't intend to offend," Henning replied, "but you were serious."

"I have some confidential news for Henning," Martine said.

"If you require privacy, use the courtyard behind my home." Galante pointed to a Spanish style bungalow, nestled among palm trees, then left as Marcial started Sultán's rubdown.

Belisario, Martine, and Henning formed a tight circle, heads together, tilted downward.

"Well, what is it?" Belisario demanded.

"I'm afraid the race may be over," Martine said.

"You're not that far ahead," Henning joked.

"I'm serious. Sultán fell and now he limps if I push him beyond a walk. I'll show you."

After tying the free end of Sultán's leadline to his halter—creating makeshift reins—Martine suggested, "Let's do this someplace where no one else will see."

In Galante's courtyard, a roof shaded the perimeter and the center was open to the sky. Martine put her foot in Henning's cupped hands and swung onto Sultán's back. Urged forward, the little chestnut responded reluctantly. Asked to speed up, he resisted until she thumped him with both heels. After that, his shoulder dipped every time the hoof beneath bore weight.

"Is there anything we can do?" Martine asked as she came back.

"You can start by getting off."

After she slid to the ground, Henning led Sultán in tight circles, studying his movements. Squatting, he placed his thumb on one side of the little chestnut's cannon bone and his fingers on the other. Sliding them up and down, he checked the tendons, ligaments, and knee.

When he probed Sultán's shoulder, the little chestnut flinched.

"Acts like a sprain." Henning filled his palm with liniment and cupped it to the tender area. After the hair absorbed it, he massaged with such concentration he didn't notice the approaching *cholo* until it was too late.

"Not this guy again," he said under his breath. "I'm surprised he came so close without being acknowledged. *Cholos* don't usually do that."

"I take it you don't care for *Señor* de la Borda?" Martine asked.

"Nor do I trust him. Have you read his articles?"

"Of course. You can't protect me from everything."

"Then you know *Don* José is his hero and you're his villain."

"I like the nice things he writes about *Don* José. But I hate being portrayed as a cheater."

"My photographer wants some images of *Señorita* Prado on Sultán." De la Borda waved to a nearby *cholo* who held a bulky camera.

"We're busy," Henning replied as the man stopped beside de la Borda.

"Now that the *señorita* has the lead," the photographer pressed, "these images will appear on the front pages of newspapers throughout Peru. But the light is fading, and—"

"Some other time."

"Pushing this man works in reverse," de la Borda broke in. "But I haven't yet told him about my friend Armando Jáuregui, who lives nearby and works miracles with lame horses."

"Can someone fetch him?" Belisario asked.

Henning winced. De la Borda had been fishing for confirmation of a suspicion. And now he had it.

"Jáuregui won't leave his farm," the reporter said. "You'll have to go to him."

Missing Henning's signal to hold his tongue Belisario asked, "Where does he live?"

"Less than a mile away. It'll be worth the trip. He's a *brujo* and knows more about lameness than even the best veterinarians."

"What are the chances such an eminence would be so close right when we need him?" Belisario asked, his words dripping sarcasm.

"Take your horse to him. You won't regret it."

"Why help us," Henning asked, "after making *Don* José Geldres a hero and accusing us of having an unfair advantage?"

"*Don*?" de la Borda echoed. "That's not the way gentlemen normally refer to *cholos*."

"You haven't answered my question. Why would you help us?"

"Because the *cholos* and *serranos* who want *Don* José—as you call him— to win are no more numerous than the women who believe *Señorita* Prado is heroically representing their gender against impossible odds in a male dominated world. Without a winner, no one will remember this race. But with one, it will live on in folklore and advance my career."

"At least you're honest," Henning said.

"Yes, and I'm telling the truth about Jáuregui. Take Sultán to him. You won't regret it."

Distant shouts announced that Goliat and *Don* José had been sighted. De la Borda dashed off to interview the famous half-breed who'd lost his lead one day from the final finish line. Burdened by his equipment the photographer fell farther behind with each step.

"What did de la Borda call Jáuregui?" Henning asked Martine.

"A *brujo.*"

"A witch doctor?"

Henning didn't offer his opinion of witchcraft. Martine's jade hand amulet did more than protect her from the evil eye. It guaranteed she'd be offended.

CHAPTER ELEVEN
THE WITCH DOCTOR

"It's been two hours since you massaged Sultán's shoulder," Martine said looking into the little chestnut's stall, "but he doesn't look any more comfortable and still won't eat. Let's take him to Jáuregui. What harm can it do?"

"More importantly," Henning responded, "what good can it do?"

"We'll never know if you stubbornly refuse to give him a chance. Have you forgotten that witch doctors gave us quinine—not to mention the tonic that saved Marco Lorca's life?"

"Rest and nourishment will do Sultán more good than going out in the dark on a footpath where he could easily aggravate his injury."

"But he's not eating or resting. Let's see if *Don* José knows anything about Jáuregui."

"I don't put much stock in competitors' opinions."

"Because we tricked him and you think he'd do as much to us?"

"That was a tactic—not a trick. Taking advantage of an opponent's weaknesses is neither underhanded nor in violation of the rules."

"But is it fair to provoke mistakes? Doing that would never occur to a man with a heart as pure as *Don* José's."

Turning toward voices, Henning saw Bartley Carrick leading Goliat toward them, followed by *Don* José and de la Borda. When the others stopped, Carrick led Goliat in a circle.

"When I was a stable boy," he began, "Lima's finest veterinarians pronounced my employer's best horse permanently lame. I led that horse three hundred miles to Armando Jáuregui's place, which took twenty days. You can stroll over there in less than an hour."

"Did Jáuregui cure the horse?" Henning asked.

"Would I recommend him if he hadn't?"

Looking back at his stomach, Goliat pawed the ground and buckled his knees, preparing to lie down—symptoms of colic. Henning surged forward. Carrick wasn't strong enough to keep the big gray on his feet. Thrashing around on the ground, Goliat could easily twist an intestine and die in agony.

Henning snatched Goliat's leadline, forced the stallion's nose straight up, then locked both elbows.

"*Don* José," he roared, "give de la Borda your whip."

"I'll use it if that's what you want," *Don* José offered.

"I need someone who can hit him harder than you can. His life depends on it."

Don José handed over his riding crop as Goliat sagged further.

"Hit him," Henning bellowed. "Now, on the rump. Don't let him go down."

De la Borda swung. Goliat lunged and locked up again.

"Again. Harder. Don't stop until he moves and keeps moving."

Over and over de la Borda brought the whip down, each impact exploding on Goliat's hindquarter. Finally the big grey minced forward, his strides gradually lengthening.

A half hour later Henning handed the leadline back to Bartley Carrick.

"He'll be none the worse for wear by morning," Carrick said, examining the welts that had risen on Goliat's rump.

"Now it's my turn to do a good deed," de la Borda offered. "I'll take you to Jáuregui."

"Please." Martine touched Henning's arm. "If the race ends like this, we'll never know who would've won. I'll go with you."

"You should get a good night's sleep," Henning said.

"How can I possibly do that? If Sultán is still lame in the morning, we'll forfeit the race."

"All right." Henning raised both palms as if to hold her at bay. "Let's go see the mysterious *Señor* Jáuregui."

******

Pointing at an adobe hovel silhouetted against the starry sky, de la Borda said, "That's his house. Wait here. He doesn't much care for strangers."

A dog stepped out of the brush and raised one paw, then quivered and growled. Martine flinched when a man with a white eye materialized and commanded, "Get off my property."

An ancient musket pointed at them reinforced his demand.

"*Señor* Jáuregui," de la Borda said. "Don't you recognize me?"

"Of course. I'm not blind in both eyes."

"I've come to talk with you."

"Would I live out here if I wanted visitors in the middle of the night? Come back tomorrow."

"That will be too late."

Squinting with his good eye, Jáuregui stared as if amazed to see a woman in pants. Grabbing his musket's barrel, he set the butt on the ground and asked, "Why are you here?"

"We've come on a time-honored mission." De la Borda replied, with the flowery language of his articles. "We need the assistance of a medicine man."

"Get to the heart of the matter."

"We brought a lame horse that needs treatment."

"Follow me." Near his front door Jáuregui pointed at de la Borda and told Henning, "If anyone else had asked, I wouldn't treat your horse at this ungodly hour. But thanks to his article, people bring me lame horses from far and wide and I have money for the first time."

Jáuregui went inside, then reappeared with a lighted lantern hanging from each hand and his arms cradling a beat-up wooden box.

"Take your horse to that tree," he ordered Henning.

Stopping beneath a horizontal branch, Jáuregui hung the lanterns several feet apart on nails and said, "Tie your horse between them."

While Jáuregui examined Sultán, Henning studied the colored bottles and clear jars in the box. Square, round, oval shaped, and hexagonal, most contained liquids and powders. The one Jáuregui opened released the pungent smell of sauerkraut.

"What's he going to do," Henning whispered to Martine, "heal Sultán or eat him?"

She turned, concealing her amusement from Jáuregui.

"Let me see your horse move," the old *brujo* commanded.

Henning led Sultán away, then back

"Again. Faster."

Next Jáuregui poured sauerkraut juice into a can. Its tangy aroma engulfed them as he uncorked other bottles. Henning recognized only one of the competing smells, kerosene.

"Wait on the other side of that cactus." Jáuregui pointed. "If you watch me, I'll stop."

"Sultán won't stand still for a stranger," Martine said.

"He will for this stranger," De la Borda insisted, motioning for her to precede him.

"What do you suppose he's adding now?" Henning asked as they reached their destination. "Eyes of newts? Bat's wool? Unicorn tails?"

Martine's melodious chuckle rewarded him.

"Jáuregui doesn't want people stealing his secrets," de la Borda said.

"I hope they're worth stealing," Henning quipped.

Sultán's shoulder had a glossy shine when Jáuregui called them back. His foul-smelling potion had been applied precisely where Henning concentrated his earlier rubdown.

"Imagine how fast Sultán will go trying to get away from that smell," Henning whispered.

When certain no one was looking, Martine stepped onto a rock, then took his face between her hands and kissed his forehead.

"Thank you," she said. "Tonight was the perfect time to unveil your sense of humor."

Returning to *Las Palmas* Martine led Sultán and Henning followed, liking what he saw. The little chestnut was moving well, his eyes and ears revealing only minimal discomfort.

In his stall Sultán immediately began devouring hay.

"Ready to admit Jáuregui is a miracle worker?" Martine said through a yawn.

"I'll wait until we see what happens tomorrow." Henning checked his pocket watch. "The race's last leg starts in three hours, and you're exhausted. Time for bed."

CHAPTER TWELVE
THE SEA OF DUNES

Eager to reach Palo Verde—where the race would end—Belisario had sailed during the *madrugada*, the hour before dawn. His schooner was no longer visible when Henning and Martine rode between rows of date palms toward the starting line. By then, the only remaining evidence of Sultán's injury was the yellow hair bleached by Jáuregui's concoction.

After the race's first day, Martine had gone back to practical wrist-length shirts and worn riding gloves and a broader-brimmed hat.

"My father criticizes my clothes as unflatteringly masculine," she'd told Henning.

"You're dressed perfectly for the conditions," Henning had replied, stopping short of admitting that he liked the way pants revealed her curves.

Finca Las Palmas' pickers were waiting at the final starting line.

"*Don* José would win easily if he wasn't competing with two people," one complained. Seeing Martine and Henning too late he turned away, embarrassed.

Henning gritted his teeth. De la Borda's recent articles had made much of Martine's so-called unfair advantage.

"I'll ride with you more than usual today," he told her with what he hoped was contagious enthusiasm.

"People think I'd be lost without your help," Martine said lifelessly.

"They're wrong. You've ridden an outstanding race. The one with the unfair advantage is de la Borda. People believe his accusations simply because they're in print. If he was as fair-minded as he tries to appear, he'd praise you."

"If you really mean that, let me ride my own race today." A pause, then, "Please."

With Valencia's future at stake, Henning's instinct was to deny her request. But it was reasonable. She'd be on Sultán's back, listening to his breathing, monitoring his pulse, bowel movements, and urination. And sensing how much strength remained in his tired muscles. She better than anyone, would know what he could do and when.

And she'd have more energy doing what she wanted instead of what he decreed.

"Go ahead," he said. "Do it your way. You've earned that right."

Martine touched his shoulder, her second display of affection in six hours. "What if I lose?" she asked.

"Don't even consider that possibility. Concentrate on how good it will feel to win."

"Do you really think I have a chance?"

"A good one, but don't forget to follow the carriage road all the way around the Sea of Dunes. If you cut across you'll be disqualified." Seeing her expression, he smiled and added, "I've told you that too often. Sorry."

The morning was still cool when Sultán started down the trail, too slow for Henning's taste. He urged his horse forward, intending to stress that she could pamper the little chestnut or win—but not both. Then he stopped. He'd promised she could choose her own strategy.

Bartley Carrick brought Goliat, saddled and showing no sign of yesterday's colic. Carrick had the big gray circle him on a long line then change direction and speed up. Goliat's nostrils dilated, taking in additional oxygen and his veins expanded to circulate blood more efficiently.

Henning had never seen a horse warmed up as skillfully. Goliat was as ready as human hands could make him.

The pickers cheered as *Don* José mounted up. A moment later the whistle blew and Goliat leapt forward. He was twenty-four minutes behind. But due to Sultán's slow start, the distance between them was less than at last night's finish line.

Though fresh, Henning's horse barely kept him close enough to see Goliat catch Sultán. Expecting the big gray to take the lead, he was surprised when the two stallions disappeared over a distant ridge, matching each other stride for stride.

At noon Henning left the carriage road where it began the twenty-mile semicircle around the Sea of Dunes. Going cross-country he'd travel less distance and could perhaps catch Martine and *Don* José. He skirted a pyramid-like dune and saw a seething black cloud coming toward him at ground level.

Stopping with his back toward the wind, he folded his bandanna into a triangle and tied it behind his head. Then he unrolled his sleeves. As the storm's leading edge stung him with sand he pulled his shirt collar high for protection. When he looked down, his horse appeared to be up to its chest in a river of blowing sand.

Underway the instant the storm let up, Henning was making good time when his mount dropped to its knees then scrambled back to its feet. Still aboard, he saw the hole where a forehoof had broken into a rodent's tunnel. Urged forward, the horse limped badly. Leading it, he'd never catch Martine and Geldres.

To bring them water he'd have to find a horse in Palo Verde, then backtrack on the carriage road until he met them. He slogged on foot through loose sand to the top of a dune. Ahead was another expanse of unrelenting wasteland, absolutely lifeless except for a soaring vulture-like bird. The thing was huge.

Later he came over a rise and saw more barren ground, very much like what he'd just crossed except for a greenish slope that hinted at copper ore. Surely he'd see Palo Verde from the next horizon. But when he got there, he found only desert and a riverbed that had probably been dry for centuries.

From the next high ground, he finally spotted Palo Verde at the foot of the hill where he stood. He hurried down the slope and along deserted streets to the *Plaza Central*.

The bunting-draped platform in its far side was packed with well-dressed men. In their midst—wearing his best suit—Belisario was surrounded by reporters.

"Excuse me please," Henning said, lifting himself into the saddle.

Seeing him on horseback, the group blocking his way opened a path. Near the observation platform, he stepped off his limping horse and shook hands with Martine's father. When he relaxed his hand, *Don* Manuel didn't release it.

"You're supposed to be watching my daughter," the old man said. "Why are you here?"

"My horse hurt his leg. I had to take the shortcut through the Sea of Dunes. Can you please ask Belisario to bring me a replacement?"

"Getting a horse from his ship will take too long. I'll borrow one."

Henning had unsaddled his horse by the time *Don* Manuel returned with two *cholos*.

"I'm Mario Ortiz," one introduced himself. "You can use my *patrón's* horse." Ortiz pointed to the arch where Romero Boulevard ended. "That's the fastest way to his stable."

"I wouldn't go that way," *Don* Manuel warned. "That arch is the finish line and the *Guardia Civil* has reserved Romero Boulevard for Goliat and Sultán."

"It'll take forever to go around with all these people in the streets," Ortiz said.

Saddle over one shoulder, Henning hurried under the arch. Ortiz followed with the water bags. Spectators on Romero Boulevard's sidewalks had overflowed into the street, narrowing it to less than half its usual width.

A commotion sped from the edge of town toward the plaza, bringing electrifying news. Riders were coming. Henning's scope brought them closer. They'd been stopped by the *Guardia Civil*. He didn't recognize their horses.

The tip of a baton dug into Henning's chest. The officer holding it grabbed his arm.

"I'm taking water to Martine Prado and José Geldres," Henning explained.

"I don't see any water." The officer shoved Henning against the crowd. "Walk in this street again and you'll go to jail."

On both sides of the street, spectators who'd come early had been pushed into Romero Boulevard by later arrivals.

"Get behind us," a man said. "We were here first."

From the back row, Henning could see over people in front of him but couldn't find Ortiz, who had the water bags. Martine and Geldres had left *Finca Las Palmas* with enough to drink but were expecting him to take care of their horses.

Where was Ortiz?

A second wave of anticipation swept through the crowd, accompanied by cheering. Seemingly out of nowhere two horses charged pell-mell down the middle of the boulevard, people scurrying out of their way. Sultán and Goliat had reached Palo Verde faster than Henning thought possible. And five hundred miles into the race, there was no clear leader.

They were neck and neck, pressed together on a narrow path through packed humanity. Over and over, *Don* José's heavy wooden stirrup hammered Martine's shin, yet her face showed only determination. Near the finish line Sultán forged ahead, by a nose, a neck, then half his body.

Excited onlookers pressed against a vendor's cart, and it rolled into the street. Reaching for every possible inch, one of Sultán's rear hoofs deflected off its side. His hind legs collapsed beneath him. Forelegs braced, he slid until his knees buckled.

Martine was launched over his head and landed face first in the dirt.

CHAPTER THIRTEEN
THE DISUNITED STATES

With Sultán sprawled across the finish line, Goliat thundered past. As the little chestnut scrambled to his feet, Belisario grabbed his reins. Henning clawed through bystanders and knelt beside Martine. She was on her back, not breathing, eyes staring without seeing.

Abruptly she gasped, coughed, and blinked grit from her eyes.

"I'm okay," she said hoarsely. "Just had the wind knocked out of me."

"Where's the nearest doctor?" Henning shouted.

A boy stepped forward. "Shall I bring him, *señor?*"

"As fast as possible." Henning held out a coin.

The boy grabbed it and broke into a run. Henning brushed aside the hair clinging to Martine's sweaty face.

"How's Sultán," she asked.

"He's fine. Don't try to get up. The doctor will be here soon."

"Did we win?"

"That depends," Henning replied, telling her as much as he knew.

"Of course, you won," Martine's father declared. "Sultán clearly reached the finish line before Goliat."

"Daddy."

Kneeling beside her, *Don* Manuel said, "I'm as surprised to be here as you are to see me. I'm glad I came. I've never been more proud—not even of Pietro."

"Are you sure I won?"

"Absolutely positive."

"The mayor," Andrés de la Borda said, "is of the opinion that the winning horse had to cross the finish line with its rider in the saddle. Goliath did. Sultán still hasn't."

"The mayor has no authority over this race," *Don* Manuel insisted.

"Oh but he does," de la Borda declared.

"Do you know something we don't?" Henning broke in.

"*Don* Belisario Lorca made some arrangements he may have neglected to mention."

"He's right." Belisario looked mortified. "I agreed to appoint the mayor as final arbitrator of disputes. At the time I didn't realize he and *Don* José are friends."

"Step aside," *Don* Manuel commanded, clearing a path for the town doctor. "May we kindly have some privacy?"

Spectators backed away as the doctor checked Martine's cuts and bruises.

"She seems okay," he said, "but I should examine her more thoroughly in my office."

"Will someone please offer a lady a drink?" Martine asked.

Reappearing, Mario Ortiz handed her one of Henning's water bags. Normally so formal she ate sandwiches with a knife and fork, she pulled the cork and guzzled from the spout, water trickling down her shirtfront, teeth unnaturally white in her dirt-streaked face.

After Henning helped her up she and *Don* Manuel followed the doctor.

Belisario and Henning found the mayor next to the stairs leading up to his observation stand. He was a *cholo*, round, of medium height, and *trigueño*—a dark golden brown.

"You were closest," he said to two men. "Tell me what you saw. You first."

Both told the same story. As Belisario started toward him, the mayor spun away. Two steps at a time he hurried up to his canopy-shaded platform. With other city officials, Martine's empty chair, and José Geldres behind him, he faced his audience, a speaking trumpet to his lips.

"Witnesses, myself included," he began, "agree that Goliat crossed the finish line while Sultán was still on the ground."

"Sultán," a *cholo* shouted, "would have won but for a clearly intentional act."

"That unfortunate event must be considered accidental unless proven otherwise," the mayor declared. "Do you have such proof?"

"Nothing besides common sense."

"Why would a *cholo* speak up for Martine?" Henning asked.

"Gamblers find it difficult to resist forty to one odds," Belisario replied. "He probably bet on her, and he won't be the only one. Let's stir them up." Shouting he told the mayor, "Sultán had the race won when he was knocked down by a vendor's cart. Whether on purpose or not, he was unfairly prevented from crossing the finish line even though he got there first."

The crowd buzzed with conflicting opinions, then went silent as *Don* Manuel and Martine arrived. *Don* Manuel joined Henning and Belisario while Martine wearily forced herself to climb the observation platform's stairs and sat beside *Don* José.

Opening a book to a dog-eared page, Belisario projected his voice. "The rulebook of the British Horse Racing Society states, 'a horse shall be considered to have completed the race as soon as its nose reaches the finish line. The first to fulfill this requirement is the winner.'"

"That rule governs races in Britain—not here," the mayor declared.

"He's itching to declare Geldres the winner," Henning said from the corner of his mouth.

Resting the open book on his nose, Belisario whispered, "I'm afraid he's made his decision and it's not the one we want. When in doubt he's sour as vinegar, but right now he's smiling so hard he has the driest teeth in town."

A man seated near Martine on the platform stood and said, "Perhaps a tie should be declared. Would that be acceptable, *Señorita* Prado?" When she didn't answer he added, "That way you and *Señor* Geldres will both be winners."

"A tie would make us both losers," *Don* José snapped. "Neither would get any reward for months of hard work."

"I'll make my decision known after a one hour recess," the mayor announced.

In Palo Verde's finest eating establishment, Belisario and *Don* José joined the mayor and other city officials at the head table. Thirty minutes later Martine arrived—hair brushed, wearing a conservative white blouse and ankle-length maroon skirt.

Standing and pointing to the chair beside him, the mayor told her, "I saved this for you."

"That was very kind." She smiled pleasantly. "But I have a previous invitation."

The mayor followed with his eyes as she joined Henning at a table for two.

"You're making the mayor jealous of me," Henning joshed as she sat across from him.

"Why do you suppose *Don* José was opposed to a tie?" she asked.

"Why should he settle for that when he's certain to be declared the winner?"

"It's not like he has no legitimate claim to victory. He was first across the finish line."

"But he wasn't first to get there." Henning stood. "Excuse me. I'll be right back."

Motioning to Henning, Belisario had left the head table. In a corner, they spoke at length.

"He's obsessed with having Sultán declared the winner," Henning explained as he rejoined Martine.

"Does he need workers that badly?"

"Absolutely, but that's not why he's fired up. He wants the distinction of having bred the horse that defeated the invincible Goliat. He begged me to convince you to sit with the mayor."

"Is that because the mayor has an eye for the ladies?" Martine bristled. "Does he want me to charm the old goat?"

"He asked me to give you Sultán as incentive."

"Why would that motivate me?"

"Because you'd have to give him to *Don* José if you're not the winner."

"I've never wanted a horse as much," she said, "but I won't playact to get him."

"On another subject, it's time for me to admit I was wrong and you were right. Jáuregui is indeed a miracle worker." Henning grinned.

"I think you deserve the credit for that particular miracle. Before Jáuregui's rubdown, you gave Sultán one that lasted an hour—not a few minutes like his."

******

In the deserted plaza, Martine and Henning climbed the stairs to the mayor's empty platform. Weary, they sat silently watching two clouds drift across the darkening sky. One had fallen behind by the time Martine saw *Don* José come out of the restaurant, flanked by Belisario and the mayor.

Shoulders slumped, *Don* José stared at the mayor's platform as if trying to decide if his seat there was worth the walk. Finally he sat on a low adobe wall with Belisario and the mayor on either side, talking back and forth across him.

"Belisario is smiling a lot," Martine said. "Is that a good sign?"

"Probably not," Henning teased. "He only resorts to charm in desperate situations."

Martine was saddened by the sight of *Don* José looking exhausted and ancient. She'd always regarded his age as the reason for his wisdom, but his years were also a burden. The last ten days had taken every last drop of his energy.

When a crowd streamed out of the restaurant, the mayor patted her godfather's shoulder, then strode toward the observation platform.

"I don't belong here," Henning told Martine. "See you later."

He and the mayor nodded as they passed each other on the stairs.

"Your honor," Martine greeted the mayor on the platform.

"I trust you have no ill effects from your fall," he said.

"Not yet, but I'm dreading tomorrow."

Looking at the rapidly filling plaza the mayor said, "They're going to be unhappy with me. I've decided to resort to the politician's traditional remedy for difficult choices and postpone my decision."

If he was giving her an opportunity to influence that decision, he was wasting his time.

Later, the mayor told his disappointed audience to return in the morning and escorted Martine to the stairs. While descending, she saw *Don* José, still sitting on the adobe wall.

"Were there strings attached when you gave me Sultán?" she asked Henning as she stepped down to the ground.

"Just that he goes to *Don* José if the mayor decides in his favor."

"Come with me please." She shuffled stiffly across the plaza.

Don José gathered himself as they approached.

"Please don't get up," Martine said, then sat beside him. "Henning just gave me Sultán."

His watery eyes skewering her, *Don* José said, "Sultán won't be his to give until the race has been decided. And maybe not then."

"Right now he's mine," she said firmly, "and I'm giving him to you."

"Before the winner is declared?"

"This instant."

"Why?"

"Because I know how much pleasure he'll give you. And because Andrés de la Borda was right. Henning's help was an unfair advantage."

Don José looked at Henning. "Is it all right with you if she does this?"

"Absolutely."

"Then I should reciprocate."

"By giving me Goliat?" Martine teased impishly.

"By supplying both Valencia and Toledo with unlimited workers for as long as I'm able."

"That's not why I gave you Sultán. You don't have to bring Valencia workers unless the mayor says you lost the race. And even then you don't have to bring Toledo any."

"I prefer to do things voluntarily. It's nicer that way, don't you agree?" *Don* José's smile collapsed his face into a network of lines, deepest at the corners of his mouth and eyes.

"Absolutely." Martine winked.

"Thanks for being kind enough to overlook my rudeness during the race."

Henning couldn't understand Martine's mumbled reply but would have given anything to make her look half as happy.

******

The following afternoon in the crowded *Plaza Central*, the mayor's announcement was simple.

"Under the rules," he said with finality, "José Geldres clearly won. It's my pleasure to sanction his victory."

Martine's initial disappointment subsided when she considered Toledo's workers. From birth, people of their race were treated as inferior. They deserved better. When she told them who'd won, she'd make it clear they could celebrate without hurting her feelings.

As people lined up to congratulate *Don* José, de la Borda approached Martine.

"On second thought," he said, "I believe you won and not in the least unfairly. That's what I wrote in tomorrow's article. The truth is the truth, and it's my job to tell it."

"You're an unusual man," Martine replied.

When the last of *Don* José's admirers finally left, Martine hobbled up and wrapped her arms around him.

"I want an honest answer," she said.

"You don't have to put me on my best behavior," he teased. "I've never lied to you and never will."

"But sometimes you spare my feelings by being less than candid. Did you do your very best or hold something back because I'm your goddaughter?"

Don José's brow furrowed. "During the race, you mean?"

She nodded.

"At the risk of offending, I can honestly say that I tried my very best to avoid the disgrace of losing to a woman. You have every right to take pride in your accomplishment, as does Henning. He came up with a strategy well-calculated to take advantage of my weaknesses."

"What weaknesses?"

"You know how we *cholos* are." *Don* José's eyes twinkled. "We can't stand prosperity and are no good at planning ahead."

"Henning didn't say that. In fact, he stood up for you when someone else did."

"I know. Marcial told me. You like Henning, don't you?"

"I'm not sure how much, but yes." Martine blushed through her dark tan.

******

Next afternoon back at Cortéz, British freighters were tied up at every berthing. *Fina Estampa* had to anchor with an overflow of ships in the harbor. As Belisario's crew rowed him to the wharf, he couldn't think of any possible explanation for the unprecedented number of ships.

Ashore amidst frantic activity, he asked the dockmaster, "What's going on?"

"A civil war over slavery," came the answer, "is imminent in what the British are calling the Disunited States, and growers there produce most of the world's cotton. British merchants anticipate a shortage and are buying all they can get, wherever they can find it."

"How many of these ships are here for sugar?" Belisario asked.

"None. There's no market for sugar. The price is too high."

Belisario's sigh was explosive. If the Brits were buying cotton in Cortéz, they were getting it from Emiliano Cabrera. Like Belisario, the Valley's other growers had planted sugarcane. Once again their ruthless enemy had been first to see the future and had outmaneuvered them.

This was Belisario's worst day since his wife died. First the mayor of Palo Verde had stolen his and Sultán's rightful places in Peru's equine history.

And now this.

CHAPTER FOURTEEN
DOG IN A CLOWN SUIT

The following month, Emiliano Cabrera came to Valencia with ten underlings and a beautifully marked Dalmatian dog. A week earlier he had invited Belisario to his home on Mount Olympus, clearly wanting the old aristocrat on unfamiliar ground for whatever he had in mind. Watching the arrival of Cabrera and his entourage through a window, Belisario's eyes lost their usual twinkle.

"That bastard is unquestionably a genius," he told Henning, "but at times he plays stupid little games. I wouldn't meet at his place, so he sought an alternate advantage by bringing enough advisors to outnumber mine."

"Be careful," Henning cautioned. "Napoleon used similar tactics to great advantage when negotiating surrenders."

"Well, this is a pretty small stage for such high drama. But he can't resist. Watch. When I welcome him, the *pendejo* will stay mounted and oblige me to look up from an inferior position."

Cabrera did as predicted. Invited inside, he brought his dog without asking permission. As he came through the door, his slope-shouldered silhouette looked like a bottle.

Belisario had painstakingly prepared his living room for the only man in the Valley with an equally elegant one. The number of visitors forced Valencia's staff to bring two additional sofas, overcrowding a room filled with furniture and heirlooms handed down for generations.

"He likes to unsettle things with last-minute surprises," Belisario whispered.

"It doesn't hurt to have all those advisors while all you have is your *mayordomo* and me," Henning said. "Why didn't you bring Encinas?"

"Because I don't want Cabrera to know I get advice from a woman."

Cabrera sat between his attorney and accountant.

"I'm here to buy Valencia and am prepared to be generous," he began, his otherwise vibrant face marred by cold, dead, shark-like eyes.

"I'm not interested in selling under any circumstances or at any price," Belisario replied.

"Why not? You were losing money until your bookkeeper wiggled her ass and tempted my milling customers to bring you their business."

"*Señorita* Encinas tempted them with a better price—nothing more," Belisario growled.

Cabrera thumped his pipe against his boot heel, dislodging ashes on the Persian carpet.

"For years, our neighbors have brought me their cane for milling," Cabrera said, dipping his pipe in a pouch of sweet-smelling tobacco. "Next week a judge in Cortéz will order them to resume doing so and to pay a penalty for violating their contracts."

"They didn't sign contracts with you. I know that for a fact."

"The law recognizes implied as well as written contracts," Cabrera's lawyer broke in. "I can absolutely guarantee that Judge Benavides will rule in *Señor* Cabrera's favor."

"As he always does," Belisario grumbled, "even when Cabrera's cases have no merit."

"Without that milling income," Cabrera's accountant interjected, "you'll lose money and go broke in a matter of—"

"You know nothing about my finances," Belisario snapped, losing his grip on his notoriously slippery temper.

"I'll bet a thousand dollars my estimates are accurate within five percent." Cabrera's accountant offered a sheaf of papers. Belisario crossed his arms, refusing to accept them.

"Why fight a war you can't win?" Cabrera asked.

"The objective of business is to make a profit—not fight wars," Henning broke in.

Cabrera chuckled caustically. "Profits increase after wars are won, which means they go hand in hand."

"They don't have to," Henning said.

"They do if one of the parties insists. Look, you've loaned Belisario a considerable sum and he's behind in his payments. If I buy him out you'll get your money the easy way. Otherwise you'll have to foreclose and wait for my friends in the courts to sort things out. In either case, you'll wind up selling to me because I'm the only buyer. But by then I'll be offering less."

"I'll gladly give *Don* Belisario an extension on his payments and lend him more money."

"Well, *Herr* Dietzel, now I'm where you were a few minutes ago," Cabrera said.

"And where is that?"

"Eager to know more about a potential adversary."

"This has gone far enough," Belisario broke in. "The meeting is over."

Outside, Cabrera and his men mounted their horses while the Dalmatian toured the yard lifting its leg and claiming ownership of trees and shrubs.

Looking down at Belisario, Cabrera said, "Last chance to reconsider."

"Valencia has been in my family for two hundred years. When Marco Venicio, comes of age he'll be the fifth generation to work it."

Cabrera rode away.

Watching, Belisario joked, "His manners leave much to be desired but what can you expect from someone whose dog wears a clown suit?"

"They have excellent bodyguards in Chile," Henning said, "and I'll be there next week. I'll bring you one."

"Absolutely not. I don't need a bodyguard."

"Marco does, especially after you told Cabrera he's your reason for not selling."

Belisario's demeanor went from confident to uneasy.

A week later Judge Ramón Benavides ordered Valencia's neighbors to mill their cane at Noya. Without that income Toledo's meager bank account would soon be depleted. Belisario had been outmaneuvered in the opening battle of his war with Emiliano Cabrera.

******

The postal clerk took the letter off his scale and licked a stamp, then positioned it on the envelope and banged it with his fist. Belisario paid and turned on his heel.

Outside, he and Henning crossed the street and Belisario led the way to a bench in a quiet corner of Cortéz's *Plaza Central*. Once they were seated he said, "Despite owing you a great deal already and being behind on my payments, I need another half-million *reales*."

"I'll put up the money in exchange for a five-year partnership and a quarter of your profits," Henning replied.

"There haven't been any profits for months."

"There will be if we join forces."

"If we do that, who'll be the boss?"

"I will," Henning said, "but after our partnership ends, I'll have no authority and no right to any of Valencia's earnings."

"Valencia is mine. Why should you get the final word?"

"Because you won't like the changes that have to be made."

Belisario puffed out his chest. "You think you know more about farming than I do?"

"No. That's one of the reasons I'd rather be your partner than foreclose."

"What changes will you make?" Belisario asked.

"Planting cotton for one."

"I'd prefer half sugar and half cotton. That way, I'll be covered if the market changes."

"The market for sugar won't improve for years. It's gotten so expensive that even the well-to-do use it sparingly and lock it up between meals. But with civil war in the United States, the South can no longer supply Europe's cotton. The price will probably double."

"I can't afford a cotton gin."

"I'll put up the money. The cost will be insignificant compared to the return."

"With my luck, the South will continue to export cotton despite the war."

"Not after the North blockades its ports."

"I'll be bankrupt if I plant cotton and you're wrong."

Three hours later they signed a five-year partnership agreement.

The next day Henning paid off Valencia's debts, arranged to have a gin built, and ordered a boatload of the world's finest cotton seed.

******

Don Manuel Prado's dinner guests were due in an hour. In Toledo's smoking room, Martine closed the door behind a cat and brushed the gray hair from its favorite chair. Then she went upstairs to change clothes. She'd be unwelcome at her father's all-male gathering but had important information for Henning.

After bathing she did something admittedly unusual, styled her hair and put on makeup. Then she selected her only frilly outfit, a floor-length lace dress with a matching bolero style jacket, fold over collar, fitted waistband, and layered overskirt.

By the time she came downstairs her father and his neighbors were behind closed doors enjoying after-dinner cigars.

The smoking room had masculine décor and its occupants wore special jackets and caps, courtesy of their host. Like the curtains, these were velvet and said to absorb smoke.

Henning and Belisario were alone at the non-smokers' table.

"Don't be surprised if you get invited to *Don* Manuel's dinner parties whenever you're in the Valley from now on," Belisario whispered, leaning close. "I think he sees you as a potential son-in-law who could support Martine in the style to which she was born."

"Hope you're wrong," Henning said quietly. "His recommendation would guarantee that she'll never be interested in me."

"She already is, but it's still a long way to the altar."

The room's sanctity was violated by *Don* Manuel's imported Irish Setter. It snuck in as a servant opened the door, then dashed through the room sniffing trouser legs and crotches.

"Dogs use their noses to gather the information we humans get by way of gossip." Belisario cackled. Attracted by his joviality the dog sat at his feet.

Before the door was closed, Henning saw Martine in the hallway. Then one of several servants who'd brought drinks and hors d'oeuvres delivered a note. Written with distinctive flourishes, it read: 'May I please speak with you? M.'

When Henning returned Belisario asked, "What was so important it couldn't wait?"

"Cabrera's wife left him," Henning replied. "Martine believes she contributed greatly to his success and expects Noya to go downhill without her."

"She might be right," Belisario said, standing to announce this development. The other guests too took pleasure in their enemy's misfortune. Encouraged by their rejoicing, the dog dashed about, bracing his forepaws against men's stomachs so they could pet his noble head.

"Maybe Cabrera's wife got tired of his dirty tricks," Belisario told Henning. "Last year he stole Julio Echeverría's customers by selling them sugar for less than cost. After Julio went broke, Cabrera bought a first-class hacienda for a pittance. He plans as carefully as you do. Difference is, you don't hide behind phony smiles…or any smiles for that matter."

Belisario poked Henning's ribs and Henning smiled, just to prove he could.

******

When Emiliano Cabrera had first purchased land in the Valley, its farmers ground sugarcane with devices powered by oxen. Cabrera's new steam driven mill dragged them into the future, but they still considered his use of fertilizer a waste of money—even though their country's guano and nitrate had revolutionized agriculture in much of the world.

By the time Henning revealed his intention to bring nitrate from his mine, their contract had made Belisario's consent unnecessary. He refused it anyhow. Rather than force the issue Henning promised the nitrate would cost nothing if it didn't more than pay for itself.

Three weeks later Henning reached Cortéz with the first shipload.

Belisario met him with wagons. As stevedores filled these with plump gunnysacks, the old aristocrat slashed one open and grabbed a pinch of its contents. He sniffed, tasted, and hurled the granules to the ground declaring, "This salt won't do any good."

"It'll be free if it doesn't," Henning reminded.

"Not by the time it's hauled to Valencia and spread on the fields. Do you realize how long that will take? How many men and wagons will be required?" When their eyes met Belisario added, "Apparently not."

Nearby, a tall broad-shouldered man with green eyes rotated his head from side to side, scanning the area.

"Who's the red-headed brute standing there like a bulldog?" Belisario whispered.

"Our partnership contract requires you and Marco to have bodyguards, remember? This gentleman is yours. The one I lined up for Marco will arrive soon."

"Don't bring another Chilean. I don't much like them."

"O'Higgins is Irish—not Chilean. I'm bringing an Irishman for Marco too. They're excellent bodyguards."

Belisario's face twisted with disapproval. "What the hell kind of name is O'Higgins?"

"It's famous in Chile."

"Is this guy related to whoever made it that way?"

"I don't know, but he was the most highly recommended bodyguard I could find."

"You've come for nothing," Belisario told O'Higgins. "I don't need protection."

"A line in *Don Quixote* explains why that kind of courage is sometimes unwise," O'Higgins replied.

"Which line?"

"'Fear has many eyes and can see things underground.'"

Belisario pounced. "My point exactly. Fear makes us see threats that aren't there."

"That's one possible meaning," O'Higgins conceded. "Here's another: fear sharpens our senses and helps us detect threats we wouldn't otherwise notice."

Galled by O'Higgins' success in using his favorite author's words against him, Belisario was silent as the convoy climbed the coastal mountains. His mood improved as the wagon reached the summit. He had the driver stop above a view of the Chiriaco Valley.

After checking their surroundings for danger, O'Higgins studied the scene below.

"You're fortunate to have enough water to maintain such a paradise," he told Belisario.

"If you think this view is beautiful now," Belisario said, "you should have seen it before sugar and cotton pushed out the other crops."

"It's still captivating. All those fields stretching on and on like a giant chessboard."

"I see it as a patchwork quilt," Belisario corrected, "because the squares vary in size."

"It's been eight years since I first saw this view," Henning chimed in. "Even that recently, the fields were smaller and the green had more hues and tones."

Catching Henning's eye Belisario tapped a finger against his temple, enjoying one of those increasingly rare moments when they agreed.

CHAPTER FIFTEEN
THE CHINCHA ISLANDS WAR

Pleased with the workers' progress, Henning rode across Valencia's just-plowed fields. All around him, *cholos* dropped seed in furrows, and close behind, others covered it and compacted the soil with their bare feet. The resulting cotton crop would be Valencia's most profitable ever.

Cotton had been unknown in Europe when Alexander the Great invaded India. One of his amazed entourage described it as 'trees on which wool grows.' But hand picking the sticky green seeds from cotton bolls was time-consuming and for centuries it was grown in small amounts, usually for personal use.

In the seventeenth century the use of African slaves made large scale production possible in the southern United States. In the early nineteenth century Eli Whitney's invention of the cotton gin made it faster and more profitable. For decades after that, America's southern planters exported once inconceivable quantities, earning enormous profits.

And in 1860—with civil war looming in America—Emiliano Cabrera planted cotton anticipating the shortfall that would come if the angry words hurled back and forth between America's North and South became bullets and cannon balls. He had guessed right, and now Henning was preparing Valencia to also benefit from this new market.

He turned his horse toward the Chiriaco River, where sunlight sparkled on the water's corrugated surface. Last night's rain had left a puddle across the road where a tree shaded three people. Closer now, he recognized a woman and two men.

The man on horseback, Emiliano Cabrera, held a riderless gray. On foot, Encinas and Federico García, the slaver who managed Cabrera's hacienda, faced each other gesturing angrily. He grabbed her collar. She threw herself backward. He held on and backhanded her with all his weight behind the blow.

When she cried out, he spit in her open mouth. She doubled over, gagging. He pushed her face-first into the yellow-brown puddle.

What the hell?

Henning spurred his horse forward. García whirled around. Henning swung out of his saddle. He hadn't used his boxing skills for years. If he still had them they'd be rusty. Shaking with rage, he rolled his hands into fists.

García's huge paws closed, then snapped open. His short arms weren't meant for boxing. But his barrel chest and low, ape-like center of gravity were perfect for no-holds-barred brawling. Henning would be in trouble if those powerful hands got hold of him. Rolling on the ground, García would resort to biting, choking, gouging eyes, and kneeing testicles.

García crabbed sideways with a predator's caution, then saw an opening and lunged. Stepping forward with his left leg, Henning threw a punch at that square jaw. Weight shifting toward García's bullish charge, he rotated his shoulders and hips. When his fist connected he scarcely felt the impact, but García's legs folded. Eyeballs rolling back, he crumpled to the ground.

Cabrera released the second horse's leadline.

"Your turn," Henning growled.

"I don't fight over whores."

"Get down or I'll drag you down."

Cabrera's riding crop stung Henning's face. He grabbed it and pulled. Cabrera held on until cantilevered beyond the point of no return. His sneer gone, he hit the ground. Henning manhandled him to his feet. Slammed against the tree, Cabrera released a burst of spittle-laced air. Henning grabbed his collar, doubled his other fist, and cocked his arm.

Cabrera went limp forcing Henning to hold him upright. Unable to hit someone who offered no resistance, Henning let go. Cabrera landed on his backside, struggling to draw breath.

García had been eager to fight before going down. Now unsteady on his feet, he warily kept his distance.

"Get out of here, both of you," Henning roared.

On wobbly legs, García brought Cabrera's horse.

Back in the saddle, his arrogance restored, Cabrera snarled, "Gentlemen don't settle differences with their fists."

"They do if one of the parties insists," Henning needled, using Cabrera's own words against him.

Gesturing at Encinas, still sprawled in the puddle, Cabrera asked, "Is this whore's unborn bastard yours or a by-product of tactics used to persuade my customers to have Valencia process their cane?" Seeing Henning's puzzled expression, he added, "You didn't know? Why else would she wear baggy clothes? Does Belisario know she wags her tail in men's faces?"

Cabrera and García rode off, slowly as if leaving on their own. Both were dangerous, but in different ways. The impulsive García would be eager to return with help and weapons. But Cabrera would favor a devious approach, one where only he knew what was coming and when.

Encinas staggered from the puddle, one cheek swollen and purple. Henning wiped blood from the corner of her mouth with his thumb.

"That jackass called me a lowlife whore," she sputtered. "*Pendejo.* What right does a slave trader have to look down on me? At least the body I sold belonged to me."

Looking down he saw a white, dripping cotton blouse and skirt clinging to an enlarged abdomen and breasts.

"Yes, I'm pregnant," she said, seeing where his eyes were aimed.

"What happened before I got here?"

"García remembered me from the House of Smiles and Cabrera offered to pay me if I'd spend some nights with him now that his wife is gone. I guess he didn't like my answer."

"I don't understand. You're pregnant. Why would he want to…?"

"Some men find pregnancy arousing. Girls at the House of Smiles charged more when they were in a family way."

Encinas had become more sophisticated after associating with the Valley's elite. Now her sneezes were delicate and her profanity rare. But she still knew things most women didn't.

"Where's your horse?" Henning asked.

"He ran off." Encinas pointed. "That way."

"Take mine and ride to Valencia as fast as possible. I'll follow when I find yours."

"You can't ride a sidesaddle."

"Let me worry about that. I want you far away if Cabrera and García come back." He boosted Encinas onto his horse and she left, stirrups dangling below her feet because she hadn't let him take time to adjust them.

Henning was still looking for Encinas's horse when Martine rode from a stand of cattails, leading it.

"How long have you been watching?" he asked, uncinching Encinas's sidesaddle.

"Long enough to see you handle Emiliano Cabrera as if you didn't know he's a personal friend of the president. Someone was watching from much closer, but I didn't see who."

Henning swung aboard Encinas's horse, sidesaddle under one arm.

"You fought for that woman," Martine said as they started toward Valencia. "Are you in love with her?"

"She's a good friend."

"Only a friend?"

"Why do people say 'only a friend?' Who's more important?"

"You say that as if you let one down." Her earnest expression invited him to confide.

"During the gold rush," he said, "a *Californio*, Domingo Santa María, lost his *rancho* because I wasn't there when he needed me."

"That was a long time ago. You should forgive yourself."

"I'll never be able to do that."

They kept their mounts in a fast *sobreandando* all the way to Valencia. Anxious to reveal Encinas's past before someone beat him to it, Henning went looking for Belisario. Martine found him first and he invited her for lunch, delaying Henning's confession.

Partway through their meal the maid answered a knock on the door and called Belisario.

Returning, the old aristocrat somberly asked Henning, "May I talk with you in private?"

"Bad news?" Henning asked in the kitchen near a pot of steaming coffee.

"Bad enough that you'll be lucky to avoid the sharp edge of my tongue," Belisario snapped. "One of my neighbors just informed me that my bookkeeper was once a prostitute. You should have told me that before you brought her."

"I wish I had."

"I'm glad you didn't." Belisario grinned wickedly. "I wouldn't have let her on my property, and I'd have missed out on a splendid employee and a good friend." Seeing Henning's astonishment, he broke into a rumbling chuckle and added, "I wouldn't take this so well if it had come as a surprise, but Encinas tells me everything. I know she's pregnant. Is that what you're getting ready to tell me?"

"Did she tell you what happened today?"

"Yes. Damn, I wish I could have seen the king of the Chiriaco Valley pulled off his horse by a mere commoner…no offense intended."

"None taken."

Henning had never seen Belisario react calmly to bad news. Yet the old aristocrat was unfazed by Encinas's past or pregnancy. The likely explanation was that he'd fathered her unborn child. If so, Henning was glad two such good and lonely people had found each other.

******

Henning had brought a bodyguard, Bardan Murphy, to protect Belisario's son. Together at the ship's rail, they waited while the mooring lines were secured. Trained by O'Higgins, the dedicated Murphy had reflexively protected Henning throughout the voyage. Seeing Cortéz's crowded dock, he became even more alert.

From the gangplank Henning spotted Belisario across the wharf, shaded under the leafy branches where he always waited to avoid being jostled. Henning and Murphy were halfway through the packed crowd when Belisario started toward them with O'Higgins following.

"As usual, O'Higgins is in perfect position," Murphy pointed out, "far enough away to have a clear view of *Señor* Lorca's surroundings but close enough to protect him if necessary."

While introducing Murphy to Belisario, Henning felt an envelope thrust into his hand.

"Payment for your nitrate," Belisario explained. "When a man's right he's right. That stuff is miraculous. I've never had such a crop. And better yet an English company is going to buy everything I produce for the next two years."

"Have you signed a contract?" Henning asked.

"Not yet."

"Don't sign one that specifies an amount. Prices will go higher as the shortage worsens."

"My buyer won't sign a contract unless it locks in the price," Belisario said. "Everyone is going along with that."

"After two bad years no one else can afford to wait. But we can."

"We'll lose a sure sale."

Henning didn't reply. He didn't enjoy arguing as much as Belisario did.

"Are you still confident the South will lose America's civil war?" Belisario asked.

"Absolutely. The North has a two-to-one manpower advantage, and slaves are a large percentage of the South's population. They can't be armed for fear they'll turn their guns on their masters. And keeping them in line ties up troops. On top of that, the South has little industry. New York alone manufactures more than the entire Confederacy."

As always, parrying one of Belisario's arguments led to the next, "If things are that one-sided, the war won't last long enough to do us much good."

Henning sighed. "Win or lose," he said, "the South won't export cotton for a long time."

"My western fields are ready to plant but I'm out of nitrate so I'll have to—"

"Don't worry. I brought more." Henning jerked his thumb toward the ship he'd just left.

"On whose authorization?"

"You seem pleased with the results so far." Henning held up Belisario's envelope.

"Nonetheless, you should have consulted me. Our partnership agreement relieved you of that obligation, but courtesy demands it."

"You're right. I'll do that from now on."

******

Next time Henning brought nitrate, Belisario met him at the dock. While the bags were transferred from ship to wagons, they ate lunch in an exclusive restaurant's private dining room. Belisario seemed agitated as they finished a plate of his favorite appetizer, *chicharrónes*.

Dipping one of the crisp pork rinds in red onion relish, the old aristocrat said, "Captains bringing news of America's civil war report an uninterrupted string of Southern victories. On your advice I kept my cotton when everyone else sold theirs. Now my warehouses are full and buyers have stopped coming."

"They're not in New Orleans if that's your worry," Henning assured him. "The South's ports are blockaded. And many growers who shipped with blockade runners are now keeping their cotton off the market, hoping that will force England to aid the Confederacy."

"What if the English do take their side?"

"Why would they? They've abolished slavery in their own country. And their navy routinely stops suspicious-looking ships and frees any Africans they find."

"If the cotton buyers aren't in New Orleans, where are they?"

"In Egypt, where they won't find nearly as much as they need. By the time they come back here they'll be offering twice the previous price."

"By then the South will have won the war. Their troops are eighty miles from Lincoln's capital in Washington. The North may have more people and factories, but the South obviously has more fighting spirit."

******

On November 20, 1864, *Intrepido* made a routine delivery to Altamira Island. Its captain, Gustavo Medina, was somber as he hurried down the gangplank and handed Henning a recent *Lima Correo* with a banner that screamed: Spanish Warships Deliver Demand.

Before Henning could read the article, Medina summarized it: "Four months ago, Peruvian workers attacked Spanish immigrant laborers at the Hacienda Talambo, killing one and injuring others. Last week nine Spanish warships called at Callao and Admiral Pinzón demanded an apology and compensation for the victims. Our government considers this an internal matter to be handled by our courts, but Pinzón was adamant. If you ask me, Spain wants an excuse to reconquer us forty years after we won independence from her."

During the next of *Intrepido's* twice-a-week deliveries, Medina reported, "The Spanish increased their demands to include payment of debts they claim we owe under the treaty that ended our War of Independence."

Later he brought news that Spain—which had never recognized Peru's independence—had sent a commissary to negotiate.

"That's a deliberate insult," Medina announced with wounded national pride. "Spain's commissaries deal with her colonies. But we're an independent nation. Queen Isabella should have sent an ambassador."

Next Spanish marines occupied the Chincha Islands and Medina reported, "Spain has long coveted our guano, and more so after she began spending millions to modernize her navy."

A subsequent *Lima Correo* editorial asked: 'With Admiral Pinzón's marines on the Chinchas, will he finance his blockade by selling their guano? And will he seize other islands?'

Every time *Intrepido* tied up after that, Henning rushed to the dock, braced for bad news. But with the Chinchas occupied, his sales doubled and Peru's neighbors—Chile, Bolivia, and Ecuador—took her side.

"All three have stopped selling coal to fire the Spanish ships' boilers," Medina reported. "And Chile is sending us supplies and volunteers. Rumor is, the United States invoked the Monroe Doctrine and called for Spain's withdrawal. But in the midst of their civil war, the Americans can't enforce those demands. All they can do is make it illegal for their citizens to buy Pinzón's guano, an empty gesture since Spain hasn't yet attempted to mine it."

With their supply of guano cut off, Americans were sending a steady stream of ships to Altamira Island and paying the highest price ever.

A month later Medina told Henning, "So far, Pinzón's ships are monitoring U.S. vessels, but not interfering with them. However, he increased the patrols between here and the mainland. I think he's looking for me so he can cut off your supplies and put you out of business."

"If the Spanish confiscate or damage *Intrepido* I'll replace her," Henning promised. "But don't get careless. I can't buy another you."

"You're paying more than enough to justify my risks. And if I were easily frightened, I wouldn't have named my ship *Intrepido*."

******

Next time Medina stepped off the gangplank Henning asked, "Were you able to find out if Cortéz or Iquique is blockaded?"

"There are rumors covering every possibility," Medina replied. "Some say neither is. Some say both are. Others say one is and the other isn't."

"The Spanish have had me trapped on this island for months," Henning muttered, "and during that time I haven't heard a word about my cotton and nitrate businesses. Can you find a blockade runner to take me—"

"The Spanish won't interfere with British vessels picking up nitrate at Iquique or cotton at Cortéz," Medina interrupted. "They haven't forgotten what the English did to their invincible Armada. Chances are your other businesses are fine. And if not, you can't do anything about it."

Medina was right. Henning had a more pressing problem. Spain's navy was trying to cut off the food that sustained his workers. Last week they'd gotten close enough to fire on *Intrepido*.

After the Spanish navy closed down Peru's ports, Medina's brother and fifty men had brought wagonloads of supplies to remote coves and loaded *Intrepido* with rowboats. Medina then eluded the Spanish by sailing on moonless or foggy nights.

"Ships selling contraband coal to the Spanish were banned from Chile's ports," Medina told Henning during his next delivery. "Spain retaliated by bombarding Valparaiso and destroying Chile's merchant fleet. To their credit, the Chileans stood firm and now all South America's Pacific ports are closed to the Spanish. They can't re-provision or give their crews shore leave."

"You've been a true friend," Henning replied. "Without you I'd have been shut down."

"And without you I'd be bankrupt. You're my only remaining customer, and I won't let those Spanish sons of whores put us out of business."

A man of honor, Medina would do his best to keep that promise. But stopping Henning's supplies wasn't the only way the Spanish could ruin him. Their blockade had prevented him from depositing monetary instruments at mainland banks, so he'd been receiving cash. Unable to pay Peru's government its two-thirds share of each sale, he'd accumulated a fortune. If Admiral Pinzón's men looted his safe, he'd be a pauper who owed millions to a bankrupt government.

******

Silvery moonlight knifed through a gap in the cloud bank, illuminating Henning's most trusted workers. For days one crew had dug in hard ground behind Altamira Island's beach, while another built a tower beside the hole.

"This area is off limits to everyone but those actually working here," Henning had told his manager, Alcalino Valdivia, on the project's first day, "and they're sworn to secrecy. Keep everyone else away. The more people who know about this, the more likely the Spanish will find our safe if they come."

When all was ready, Henning's safe was rolled from his office over a series of parallel poles. Each time the rear pole came free, it was picked up and put in front until the ponderous iron box reached the tower and was lowered into the hole. Then the block and tackle's framework was disassembled and became an innocent-looking stack in the lumberyard.

By descending a ladder and unlocking the safe's door, Henning could add to its contents. The hole was surrounded by enough dirt to fill it. After that, leveling a pile of topsoil would erase all evidence that something was buried there.

Back when Felipe Marchena worked half the island, he had built a two-story house on its highest point. After the Spanish fleet entered Peruvian waters, Henning had moved in with two diggers, sharp-eyed ex-hunters chosen to scan the surrounding ocean with spotting scopes from the second floor. He'd been told they could see a small bird fluff at three hundred yards.

Neither had yet failed to sound the alarm bell long before anyone on an approaching ship could possibly have heard. Each time it rang, Henning rushed home to identify its flag. Spain's had three horizontal stripes—red, yellow, and red. If Henning saw those colors, he'd run Peru's flag up the pole on his roof, signalling his diggers to bury the safe.

His simple plan required teamwork, luck, and timing. All evidence of the safe had to be gone before Spanish marines came ashore.

CHAPTER SIXTEEN
TWO VERY DIFFERENT DEATHS

Twelve years earlier *Andrew Chesterton* had been the first ship Henning loaded at Altamira Island. In June, 1865 Captain Lewis Eddings brought her back for the twenty-seventh time. After his vessel was secured to the loading platform, Alcalino drove him to Henning's office. There they found Henning at his desk near a row of pegs holding white smocks.

Following a hearty *abrazo*, Eddings said, "My ship came in from the other side. How'd you know to send your carriage?"

"We keep track of incoming ships these days," Henning replied, handing Eddings a smock. "This will keep your clothes clean while we drive to my house for lunch."

When they were seated at Henning's second floor dining table, he shook a dinner bell. Its melodious ring brought servants up the stairs. One laid out place settings. The other set a pedestal serving bowl beside Henning and reached for the ladle.

"Serve our guest first," Henning said gently.

"How much guano do you have left?" Eddings asked as he sampled the delicately seasoned clam chowder. "When I first came, the mound was eighty feet tall and visible from thirty nautical miles. Now I can't see it from half that far."

"The mound is less than half its original height. Last week diggers exposed the tip of a rock formation, meaning at least part of the island is taller than we thought and I have less guano than I'd hoped."

On catlike feet, a *serrano* silently entered the room. Staying near the wall, he stopped at each window and scanned the ocean with his eyes, then through a scope.

"Please excuse Usco," Henning said. "He's watching for—"

"I see what he's doing," Eddings interrupted, "and I have good news. The Confederacy surrendered in April. With America's civil war over and our military no longer tied down, it's unlikely the Spanish will move against you. We need your guano, and a faction in Washington is eager to punish Spain for meddling in our sphere of influence. If she interferes with you, our navy will attack Pinzón.

"Have you heard if Iquique's and Cortéz's ports are open?" Henning asked.

"The Spanish didn't blockade either one, and for good reason. Britain has warships protecting her sources of cotton and nitrate."

******

Admiral Pinzón's warships finally succeeded in forcing three engagements with his country's former South American colonies. In November 1865, seven months after the end of America's Civil War, the Spanish were humiliated when the Chileans captured one of their ships during the Battle of Papudo. Twelve weeks later they fought an inconclusive engagement against a joint Peruvian-Chilean fleet at the Battle of Abtao.

A month after that, seeking a decisive victory, Pinzón's ships confronted the powerful shore batteries protecting Lima's port at Callao. The daylong engagement ended with both sides claiming victory.

Weeks later Captain Medina brought the best news yet.

"The Spanish evacuated the Chincha Islands," he told Henning gleefully, "and were last seen going toward their colony in the Philippines. If you want to take the money from your safe to a bank, you're welcome to come along when I go to Lima tomorrow."

On the voyage to Callao, Henning saw passenger ships and freighters that had hidden in ports during the two-year-long Spanish blockade. The railway station was jammed with soldiers and sailors headed for Lima to celebrate. Henning hired an army sergeant and three corporals to help put his trunks in a compartment on a train and watch over them.

But first he haggled over their fee—as a tourist would have—to keep them from suspecting the value of what they were guarding.

"Can you gentlemen stay with me a bit longer?" he asked at the depot in Lima.

"Sorry," one replied, "but there's a hero's welcome waiting for us in town."

"Stay with me another hour," Henning said, "and you'll have enough money to take admiring young ladies to dinner for a month."

The sergeant and his men transferred Henning's trunks to a carriage and accompanied him through streets jammed with laughing, hugging, chanting people.

When the driver stopped in front of a British bank the sergeant exclaimed, "My God. You have money in these trunks."

Henning's surprised protectors unloaded his cargo before collecting their reward and rushing off to join the celebration.

The bank manager had security guards clear the lobby and lock the doors. For hours, tellers counted the contents of Henning's trunks while executives stacked bundles of currency and other monetary instruments in the safe. After his deposit had been totaled Henning slid the receipt and a guaranteed check into the pocket behind his lapel.

Then, flanked by bank guards, he fought through packed streets where military men were energetically kissing as many females as would permit it.

In Peru's National Treasury, the astonished cashier accepted Henning's check and took it straight to Minister Luis Guzmán.

"I assume this is the government's share of your guano sales during the war?" Guzmán asked, coming out from behind a magnificently carved door.

"Yes, and this is a list of those sales." Henning handed over a sheaf of papers.

"We figured you'd disappear with our share. Instead you've paid several times what we estimated you owe."

"You've been more than fair with me," Henning said. "How could I be less with you?"

"Your honesty was the reason I resisted Felipe Marchena's efforts to have your guano lease revoked. Turns out you're even more honorable than I thought. Peru's treasury was empty before you brought this check. Now we can hire employees and start functioning again. If it's ever in my power to reward you, I will. And I'll keep that promise."

******

In Iquique, Eduardo handed Henning a bank statement showing a sizable balance and said, "The nitrate business flourished while you were gone."

Four days later in the Chiriaco Valley, Henning found Belisario—happy, healthy, and full of news as they settled into their usual garden chairs.

"Encinas's son, Antonio, is beautiful beyond words," the old aristocrat began, "He was huge and a specialist in Lima had to deliver him. And you greatly underestimated Valencia's profits. My half is more than enough to pay off your loan and end our partnership. But I trust your feelings for Martine Prado will bring you back to Valencia often."

"They will," Henning replied, "if she's still interested after not seeing me for two years."

"*Dios mío*. Has it been two years? It didn't seem that long."

"It seemed a lot longer out on Altamira Island."

Henning's visit to Toledo began well. Martine's father left them alone in the library. After their long separation, Henning had wondered if he'd still feel the same. He had his answer in seconds. She was as enchanting as ever.

For a while.

Eduardo had long theorized that Martine appealed to Henning because she was an aloof, unobtainable challenge. But she'd never been more distant than that afternoon, and Henning found it frustrating—not attractive. For hours he sat as close as he dared, wanting to kiss her while she treated him with the formality people usually reserve for uninvited guests.

Henning invited her to go for a ride and was turned down. He apologized for his long absence, hoping in vain she'd acknowledge it hadn't been his fault. Then he said he'd missed her, inviting a response that never came.

Her father joined them and invited Henning to dinner.

Martine answered before he could accept. "Not tonight, Daddy."

"May I see you tomorrow?" he asked.

"I'll be busy."

During his ride back to Valencia, Henning couldn't make sense of Martine's behavior. He'd never been more alone than when sitting next to her that afternoon. Had his expectations been too high after they'd been apart so long or was it time to find someone else?

******

Every night since returning to Iquique, Henning had slept badly. And for the first time ever he'd lost interest in business. Unable to shake his persistent sadness, he rode to the hamlet of *Placeres*, Pleasures, named after its many delights. Unknown there, he wouldn't feel self-conscious comforting himself in ways long familiar to most men his age.

His first stop was a saloon packed with card tables. After observing for a while, he sat at a blackjack table. Relaxed by a drink, he developed a system for remembering what cards had been played and soon had stacks of chips in front of him.

After another drink Henning decided he still didn't like alcohol's taste or effect. In a bit of a fog, he lost a stack of chips and took those that remained to the cashier's cage.

"Care to buy a lady a drink?" he heard as the cashier pushed his winnings beneath the wrought iron grill.

Turning, he saw an attractive blonde in tight gingham. They sat together at a table.

"Bring the lady whatever she wants," Henning told a passing waitress.

"And for you, sir?"

"Nothing, thank you."

"It's terribly inconsiderate to make a lady drink alone," the blonde pressed.

"I've had too much already," Henning said. "If you're paid by the drink and want to find someone else, I'll understand."

"You're having second thoughts, aren't you?"

"About what?"

"About being unfaithful to your wife."

"She's not my wife…or even my girlfriend. But I am finding it difficult to let go."

"I'm not supposed to tell people my real name," she confided. "It's Lourdes."

Women in her profession were skilled at arousing clients and getting them upstairs quickly. But Lourdes—like Encinas at the House of Smiles years ago—seemed to genuinely enjoy his company. She told him about a romance she'd recently ended. He reciprocated, without saying anything that would identify Martine.

Later in an upstairs room, Lourdes was the perfect antidote for his loneliness. But when they finally woke up the next morning, she was a stranger who no longer found him interesting.

Two hours later in Iquique, Henning tied up his horse and walked into his office.

"Don't look so sad," Eduardo greeted him. "Your unwanted freedom will soon be revealed as a blessing in disguise."

"If so, it's the best disguise I've ever seen," Henning said.

"Don't make finding someone new into a project. Just let it happen, and if it doesn't, enjoy yourself. I'll introduce you to some eligible ladies."

The first had shoulder-length black hair and personality to spare. The fifth had blonde hair, blue-eyes, and singular intelligence. All were attractive, pleasant, interesting, and interested. But none was Henning's type. At thirty-five he still didn't know what his type was. Encinas and Martine couldn't have been more different.

******

On their way back to the wharf after lunch, Henning and Eduardo detoured through a quiet English-style neighborhood with white picket fences and flower gardens.

"Think you'll ever marry?" Henning asked, passing a row of tall sunflowers.

"No," Eduardo replied. "The frying pan is as far as I want to go."

"When you're getting to know a woman, how can you tell if she's your type?"

"By taking her to bed." Eduardo grinned. "That sounds harsh, but it is the best way."

"I hate to admit it, but my real feelings do come out after making love."

"Why don't you call it sex? That's what it is."

"Whatever you call it, I've always believed in finding the right woman first."

"Does every woman you sleep with have to be the love of your life? Can't some simply be enjoyed and—contrary to what priests tell us—made happy?" Looking at a lady bent at the waist over a flower garden, Eduardo quietly added, "Mercy. Look at that. Women are like gourmet food at a buffet. A sample here and there is better than a heaping platter of only one."

"Have you ever been in love?"

"Like you think you are with Martine Prado? No. But that's not love. You'd have neglected her in favor of your work if you'd won her heart. She's ice cold, and that's not what you need." Eduardo frowned. "Or maybe it is. Maybe you're attracted to withholding women. Some men are."

"That's an interesting thought," Henning said, his brow furrowed, "one that never occurred to me."

******

Belisario's invitation to attend the wedding of his son and Alicia Montez surprised Henning, who'd introduced them. He'd met her on the ship that brought him to see Belisario after the Chincha Islands War. When the gangplank was lowered in Cortéz, she'd noticed Marco on the wharf, glowing with vigor and attracting more than his share of female attention.

"Who's the gentleman that waved to you?" she asked Henning.

"Marco Lorca. He's here to pick me up. It's nice to see him looking so well. When he was a boy, he was so frail his nursemaid gave him fortified tonic four times a day."

"That must have been some tonic," Alicia exclaimed, eyebrows arched. "Will you introduce us please?"

Ashore, Henning had enviously watched their conversation lead to mutual attraction.

Invited to their wedding, he traveled to the Valley for the second time in three years. The dusk-to-dawn celebration after the ceremony was flamboyant even by Belisario's standards. A five course dinner was followed by dancing to the music of a chamber orchestra.

Not by accident, Henning found Martine alone near the waxed dance floor, radiant in a pearl-gray gown.

She greeted him with surprising enthusiasm.

"I've missed you," he said, too pleased to hide his happiness.

When her father joined them, she started across the room with a quick, "Nice to see you."

Don Manuel followed, shaking what Belisario called his scolding finger.

Henning stifled a sigh.

Typical of Belisario's extravagance that night, he had a boy doing nothing but cleaning ashtrays. After lighting a cigar the old aristocrat leaned the still-burning match inside one. He beamed with approval when the boy collected it before the flame went out.

Turning to Henning he said, "Seeing you again is a treat. Yesterday we talked for hours though we've seen each other only once in three years. I find it tiring to have a five-minute conversation with most people."

"Apparently some of my friendships here didn't survive my absence during the Chincha Islands War," Henning replied, watching Martine and her father quarrel in a distant corner.

"If you're feeling sorry for yourself, there's something you should know. For years, Martine's father has pushed her to show interest in you—even in front of me. I can only imagine how bad it must be when they're alone."

Called to pose for a photograph with Marco and Alicia beside a sparkling white, six-tier wedding cake, Belisario excused himself. He was still posing with different family groups when Henning strolled to the sitting room. There he saw Martine sitting alone, her folding fan creating a breeze that bounced her curls. As he turned to leave she pointed to the chair beside her.

"I owe you an apology," she greeted as he sat down. "You've been a better friend than I have. When you were gone so long during the Chincha Islands War, my father became obsessed with the notion that I had lost my last chance to marry. I didn't show how glad I was to see you earlier because I don't want him to start again. He did anyhow, as I'm sure you saw."

"Thank you for telling me."

"I have an ulterior motive. You're persistent, but I'm sure you'll eventually give up on me. Thing is, you're close to your goal if you can be satisfied with what I can give—even though it's less than you want." As if flirting, she took her lower lip between her teeth. "Write me when you feel like it, and you'll get answers. Whether they're satisfactory or not will be up to you. Why are you smiling?"

"Because I'm happy," Henning replied.

In truth, he was amused. He and Martine were exactly where he and Encinas had been when their relationship ended. One wanted more than the other could give.

But this time, the usual male and female roles were reversed.

******

After a difficult first day back in Iquique, Henning started a letter to Martine. He was interrupted when the night supervisor brought word that his loading dock's conveyor system had broken down, delaying a shipment for E. I. du Pont de Nemours. He woke the mechanics at their homes and stood over them until dawn to make sure du Pont's nitrate went out on schedule.

He'd resolved to write Martine every night, but the emergency had prevented that. With Encinas, he'd allowed urgent matters to take precedence over important ones. He didn't want to repeat that mistake with Martine. Sluggish with exhaustion he wrote her a lengthy letter and delivered it to the post office in time for the mail boat.

After that he wrote every night. And to explain why he didn't hear back, he imagined scenarios that justified Martine's silence and allowed him to believe he was important to her. Finally he received what he hoped was her first of many letters.

Disappointingly brief, it said: 'I've been meaning to answer your letters, but Daddy is dreadfully ill and I can't find the time or energy. Please understand. I'll write when I can. M'

Henning sighed. His personal life never went down the road he wanted. But that was often his fault. Trying to make Martine feel loved, he'd made her feel pressured. She'd asked him to be satisfied with what she could give, and instead he'd inadvertently demanded too much.

******

The following month a ship brought a letter from Belisario.

'Please come as quickly as soon as you can,' was all it said.

Something was wrong. Determined not to fail Belisario as he had *Don Domingo Santa María*, Henning dropped everything and skipped lunch. Carrying a hastily packed bag, he reached the dock in time to board the mail boat for its return voyage.

Late the next morning, a maid he'd never seen before led him to Valencia's stale-smelling library. O'Higgins nodded to him from a dark corner. The shades were down. Across the room Belisario slumped in a chair, lap covered, watching Henning stride toward him. The old aristocrat rose for a feeble *abrazo*, then grabbed the arms of his chair and lowered himself, eyes wide with effort out of proportion to the task.

"Why the new maid?" Henning asked. "Where's Chabuca?"

"I sent her to work for *Don* Manuel Prado," Belisario replied feebly. "She idolizes Martine and will be happier there now that Marco Venicio no longer needs her."

"How is Marco?"

"He grew faster and stronger while I got older and slower, but never once tried to elbow me aside. He was a good son. I should have put him in charge of Valencia years ago, before it was too late."

Henning's heart sank as he draped Belisario's blanket across the withered legs from which it had fallen.

Belisario looked up gratefully. "Marco was all I had after his mother died. He was so sickly I feared I'd lose him too. But after his health improved I assumed he'd run Valencia long after I was gone. I never dreamed I'd outlive him."

Throat constricting Henning asked, "What happened?"

"I'm supposed to think he was killed when his carriage overturned, but the accident was eerily similar to the one that killed Martine Prado's brother."

"His bodyguard must have seen what happened."

"Murphy too was killed, along with Marco's wife, Alicia. I find it suspicious that three people died in a one-vehicle wreck on flat ground, don't you?"

"Very. I'll bring someone to help O'Higgins protect you."

"Why? Cabrera has no reason to harm me. I've signed Valencia over to you." Belisario held up a hand to silence Henning's protest. "There's no alternative. I'll never be able to pay what I owe. You saved me twice. Doing it again will only lead to a fourth time."

"Let's form another partnership."

"I'm not interested in being your partner. I don't have the strength or money to go on. Hell, I sold my schooner and didn't even clear enough to plant my fields."

"How much do you need?"

"Don't pity me," Belisario bellowed. "Let me do what I want. This is my fault. Encinas took time off to help her son, Antonio. While she was gone I made mistakes and now I'm paying the piper." A cat made figure eights around Belisario's ankles. Getting no response it left, tail twitching. "Valencia is like that infernal cat. It'll make unwanted demands as long as it's mine. Six months ago I borrowed money from someone else rather than have you impose conditions. Emiliano Cabrera bought that debt and I'm behind on the payments. You'll have to pay him off. Truth is, having you take over is a relief. I'll be glad to be rid of everything but my horses."

"Take them with you. They're rightfully yours."

"Not according to the law. Besides, I can't afford to keep them."

"Valencia's stables are on prime farmland," Henning said, formulating his proposal as he spoke. "When I take over I'll tear them down and build new facilities on land too poor for crops. I'll need someone to oversee it."

"You want me to work for you?"

"You won't be working for anyone. You'll have complete control of the horses and everything related to them."

"How soon do you need an answer?"

"Why don't you accept now? We'll select a spot for the stable this afternoon and start building your new house."

"Are you sure you want that?"

"Positive. No one else understands your bloodlines well enough to breed the quality of horses I'll get from you."

Belisario leaned back. "I'd be a fool to say no."

After lunch, they sat talking in the garden until it was time for Belisario's nap.

"I think I'll visit Martine Prado while you're asleep," Henning said.

"Last I heard you'd had enough of her."

"Since then I decided her friendship will be sufficient."

"She and her father have been in Lima for weeks."

"Do you know why?" Her last letter hadn't mentioned a trip.

"All I know is *Don* Manuel's behavior was becoming peculiar."

******

Henning had made an appointment to pay off Belisario's loan at Emiliano Cabrera's office in Cortéz. To his surprise, Cabrera wasn't there and he was directed to Juan Luis Moreno's small, spartan cubicle. Bald and not-soaffectionately known as The Vulture, Moreno had for years helped Cabrera feast on the carcasses of haciendas ruthlessly driven out of business.

After issuing a receipt, Moreno said, "*Don* Cabrera still wants Valencia and will pay more than previously offered."

"Your boss doesn't give up easily," Henning replied.

"He doesn't give up, period."

"I'm not interested in selling, but how much is he willing to pay?"

Cabrera's uncharacteristically generous offer didn't surprise Henning. The man had probably murdered three people to get Valencia, but now he had to be more artful. The authorities would be suspicious of another accident.

Outside, Henning climbed into his carriage and started for his next appointment. Curious about tactics Cabrera had used to get other properties that weren't for sale, he'd arranged to visit Patricio Rendon. Wealthy before Cabrera ran him out of the Valley, the patrician but *nouveau* poor Rendon lived in a dingy one-room apartment. Its amenities were a chair, a folding cot, and a Bunsen burner for cooking. Judging by Rendon's prominent ribs, he seldom used the burner.

Rendon offered Henning the chair, then sat on the cot and described the events that preceded his downfall.

"Cabrera's assaults always begin with seemingly harmless harassment," he said by way of summary. "At first you'll think it's a stupid game, but it will actually be a distraction to get you to watch one hand and lose track of the other. Don't drop your guard—even briefly—or you'll wind up like me."

Before leaving town, Henning arranged for a grocer to bring Rendon weekly deliveries.

That afternoon from horseback, Henning took his first careful look at Cabrera's Hacienda Noya. The cane was taller than Valencia's. Methods and machinery were the latest from the United States. Roads and irrigation ditches were perfectly maintained. Henning saw nothing he would have done differently except for the French flag near Noya's entry gate. It flew higher and was larger than the Peruvian flag beside it.

After dinner Belisario and Henning sat reading in Valencia's library. Both lowered their books after Henning said, "I can't tell you how impressed I was with Noya. The one exception was the insulting way Cabrera flies the

French and Peruvian flags. If I flew the Prussian flag at Valencia—which I will never do—it would be smaller than the Peruvian and on a shorter pole."

"The story I heard," Belisario volunteered, "was that Emiliano Cabrera's grandfather, seven times removed, changed his name from François Caban to Francisco Cabrera so he'd fit in after settling in Peru. Mortified by his ancestor's concession, Cabrera goes out of his way to remind everyone of his…" Belisario waved his hand in circles, then came up with, "frenchness."

"I had a talk with Patricio Rendon this afternoon. Apparently when Cabrera wants to take over a hacienda he starts by harassing the owner in seemingly insignificant ways."

"I'd call it probing. The bastard wants to see how his intended victims react. He started that way with me too."

"Did it do him any good?"

"Absolutely. By the time he was through, he knew how to make me so angry I couldn't think straight. Remember the day he brought his lawyer, accountant, and Dalmatian dog and then goaded me until I said I wouldn't sell because I wanted to leave Valencia to Marco Venicio? I couldn't have given him more useful information but was too angry to realize it. Now it's your turn. The day you foiled his takeover of Valencia, he named Noya's fields after battles—such as Jéna and Auerstädt—where Napoleon's French troops demolished the Prussian army's towering reputation."

"If he wants to rile me, that won't do it. I'm more Peruvian than Prussian these days."

******

Henning tied his horse to the hitching rail at Hotel Las Flores. Late for his lunch with Belisario, he crossed the lobby to the dining room. With no carpets, curtains, or tapestries to absorb sound, the masonry-walled, high-ceilinged room echoed with voices, footsteps, and the music of a string quartet.

Following the waiter to where Belisario sat, Henning heard the national anthem of Prussia's age-old enemy, France. Passing a table where men stood at attention, he saw Emiliano Cabrera smirking in their midst. After Henning sat at Belisario's table the orchestra returned to its usual music.

"Why did they play *La Marseillaise?*" Henning asked.

"As a petty torment, courtesy of Emiliano Cabrera," Belisario replied. "The bastard saw you coming, jumped up, and passed out coins to the musicians."

"Well, we won't let him spoil your birthday," Henning said gently. "Hope you're hungry. I had the chef prepare your favorite meal."

Henning waved to the waiter who brought shrimp salads and a cut glass cruet of dark red dressing. Belisario poured some on his fork and tested it.

"You know me well," he said, drenching his salad.

Belisario's mood improved with each course. First winter squash soup followed by mint sorbet to cleanse the palate. Next a plate with potato balls, baby peas, and lobster tail. Then more mint sorbet and finally chocolate cake rounds.

After lunch, Henning folded his napkin and stood. The string quartet broke into *La Marseillaise* as he and Belisario crossed the room.

"Better get used to that," Belisario said when they were outside. "I have a hunch you're going to hear it often."

******

The day the horse farm was ready, Belisario left the house where he'd been born and at Henning's insistence took all the furniture he could squeeze into his new residence. After Encinas moved in, Henning sent workmen to add bedrooms for her and Antonio. True to form, the Valley's residents disapproved of unmarried people living together. But many surprisingly gave Belisario credit for helping raise the blond, blue-eyed boy who was clearly his.

"It's already taken care of," Henning replied when Belisario asked how much the additional rooms would cost.

After confirming that Encinas wanted to manage Valencia despite what had happened to Marco, Henning assigned O'Higgins to watch over her. Three days later the *Guardia Civil* allowed O'Higgins to inspect the impounded wreckage of Marco Venicio's carriage.

"The brakes work perfectly, which makes the accident all the more difficult to explain," O'Higgins reported to Henning. "You'll need a bodyguard while I'm watching over *Señorita* Encinas. If you want, I'll send for Bardan

Murphy's brother, Patrick. He was once my protégé and would love to work for someone other than his skinflint boss."

"Write a letter asking him to come at once and offer the salary he deserves," Henning instructed. "I'll mail it this afternoon with a check for travel expenses. I want both of you to watch over Encinas by day and to sleep at different times so she's also protected at night."

******

On a schooner's deck watching Peru's monotonous coast slide past, Henning began his return voyage to Altamira Island. Martine and her father were still in Lima and he considered stopping to see her. But she wouldn't like that—not with *Don* Manuel pressuring her to show interest in him.

He spent hours under a pleasant sun, dozing and bringing Martine up to date in a letter. She'd be sorry to read about Marco Venicio's death but delighted that Henning had foiled Cabrera's attempt to add Valencia to his empire. She'd also be glad Henning had put Belisario in charge of the horse farm, giving him reason to live.

The schooner's deep hull made crossing Altamira's shallow bay impossible, so Henning was taken to the dock in a launch. Waving goodbye to the men who'd rowed him ashore, he was drenched by a brief cloudburst that ended as Alcalino Valdivia rode up on his bicycle, then leaned it against a warehouse and dashed through the curtain of drops still falling from the eaves.

"You've done a superb job here," Henning said as they entered his office, "but it's time to shut down."

Altamira's guano had been lowered to where Henning's *serrano* diggers were mining veins that twisted among rock formations—slow and sometimes unprofitable work.

The following afternoon Henning found the dining hall ready for a farewell party. As he'd come to expect from Alcalino, everything was as requested. And there was a surprise from Henning's stoic *serranos*. On the wall behind the head table a crude, hand-lettered sign in *Quechua* read: 'Good Memories Make Leaving Painful.'

He dreaded the coming party's small talk and forced laugher. It would take time he should devote to Valencia's numerous problems. He felt certain he could revive his new hacienda. But that would be difficult. His previous ventures had all taken unforeseen twists and turns, some so serious they might have deterred him if he'd anticipated them. More than once he'd been tempted to quit. But he'd persisted and eventually landed on his feet. And he would again…no matter how many aces Emiliano Cabrera had up his sleeve.

******

From *Intrepido's* bridge, Captain Medina cautiously directed his schooner's maneuvers. Her flat bottom was designed for shallow water, but with the tide low he had to be extra careful crossing the shallow bay toward Altamira Island's dock.

Once *Intrepido* was tied up, porters—surrounded by armed guards— rolled a trunk on wheels down the gangplank. Medina caught up with it on the dock just as Henning left the dining hall through a door framed by bougainvillea. He looked as concerned as Medina had felt picking up a trunk filled with enough cash to pay each of a thousand workers a year's salary. Bringing that much money had been risky. But no one would cash checks for *serranos*.

"Hope you're not sending your workers to the mainland in that," Medina said, pointing at sleek clipper anchored offshore. "Such a splendid vessel is above such humble work."

"Her crew just brought her from a Boston shipyard," Henning said.

"Who does she belong to?"

"She's your reward for outstanding courage and loyalty during the Spanish blockade."

"I-I don't…know how," Medina stammered, "to thank you."

"There's no need. You earned her."

"I'll miss you."

"Not necessarily. My neighbors and I need a supplier for our nitrate mines. With two ships, you could do the job nicely."

"Where do I sign?"

"Your word is good enough."

Medina turned toward the clipper. "She's sleek as a hornet. I think I'll name her that."

For two days *Hornet* and *Intrepido* ferried workers to the mainland. As each man boarded, Henning gave him a wallet containing his accumulated pay plus a bonus.

When he and Alcalino were the only ones left on the dock, Henning handed him a check, explaining, "The amount matches your outstanding work. Captain Medina will take you to Iquique and Eduardo will show you how to run my dock. Then he'll take over my nitrate mine so I can concentrate my attention on Valencia."

According to a short note Henning had received from Martine, she'd be home soon after he returned to the Valley.

'Sorry I haven't been in touch,' she'd written, 'but I've been frantically busy taking care of my father. I fear you and I won't see each other much after I return to Toledo."

******

Henning moved into Belisario's old house and poured heart and soul into Valencia. When Martine and *Don* Manuel got home from Lima, he was working sixteen hours a day, sleeping little, and eating on the run. Even so, he sent his driver with a note inviting Martine to dinner. In the unlikely event she accepted, he expected her to insist on coming in her carriage so *Don* Manuel wouldn't see them together.

To his surprise she accepted his offer to pick her up. Arriving late because of last-minute problems at the mill, Henning parked and dashed up the stairs. Sad-eyed and somber, she was waiting on the porch swing.

During the drive to the main road, Henning slowed his carriage as it passed through black and yellow butterflies swarming in a ray of sunshine.

"You don't see such beauty in Lima," Martine said. "It's good to be home, and even better to get out of the house."

Henning suspected her father was seriously ill, but if she wanted him to know she'd tell him. He let her control the conversation throughout dinner. Not having seen each other for so long, they had much to talk about. And Henning's one attempt to learn about her current situation was gently deflected by questions about his.

"Should I have dessert served in the sitting room?" he asked after the main course.

"Regrettably, I have to go," she replied.

"May I offer you a glass of wine?"

"No, thank you. I've been gone too long. Really."

Swallowing his disappointment, Henning drove her home and escorted her to the door.

"Can you come for dinner every Tuesday?" he asked when she didn't invite him in.

"Not for a while," she replied. "I shouldn't have come tonight, but I'm glad I did. Thank you for a wonderful evening."

The following Tuesday Henning brought dinner in blanket-wrapped pots warmed with hot rocks. The maid's gloomy scowl disappeared as she opened the door.

"*Señor* Henning," Chabuca said, savoring the food's aroma. "The *señorita* will be glad to see you. She needs to forget her cares for a while."

Martine was at the dinner table. Chabuca replaced her half-eaten sandwich with Henning's offering served on china plates with silverware and starched napkins.

For weeks after that, Henning brought dinner every Tuesday. Though he didn't once see *Don* Manuel, he suspected the worst because Toledo's fields hadn't been replanted.

Martine's birthday fell on a Tuesday that year. Henning brought one of her favorite meals, two dishes rarely served together because they shared the same basic ingredient. *Papas a la Huancaína* consisted of boiled yellow potatoes served on lettuce, topped with spicy yellow dressing, and garnished with black olives, white corn, and slices of hard-boiled egg. *Causa*, the second dish, was layers of mashed potato separated by crab salad, cheese, and avocado, then topped with a spicy sauce. Served cold, both were ideal for the hot weather.

Since Henning's last visit, Martine had decorated the dining room with shelves, positioned at different heights in no recognizable pattern. Varnished hardwood, they varied in size. Their knickknacks and flower vases added texture and color to dull, white walls. Henning flattered himself by imagining she'd put them up for him.

Her father shuffled in, a list in one hand, a pencil in the other. His black and tan hound followed, bringing the pungent smell of wet fur.

"Damn dog was in the irrigation ditch again," *Don* Manuel said, staring as if wondering who Henning was.

The dog recognized Henning immediately and slung its tail from side to side.

Despite stifling heat the once elegant *Don* Manuel wore a shapeless wool bathrobe over a suit. His slippers were caked with mud. Due to his weight loss, his skin hung in folds.

"Always use cottage cheese when making *causa*," he said looking at his daughter's plate. "It doesn't clog the bowels." He turned imperiously and left, his dog close behind.

Martine shouted for Chabuca and went after him.

When she returned, she somberly said, "It will be best if you don't come back for a while. It's demeaning for a proud man to be seen in my father's condition."

As if he hadn't heard, Henning asked, "What do you do in your spare time these days?"

"During Daddy's naps, I read. That's the extent of my recreation."

"Let's take a ride tomorrow."

"I can't leave Daddy alone."

"Surely Chabuca can look after him for an hour."

"It takes two people to help him up the stairs," she said, "or take him to the bathroom. Or get him back on his feet when he falls."

"I'll bring my maid to help Chabuca while we're gone. If you'd rather do something besides ride, we—"

"I appreciate your concern, but I don't want your maid or anyone else to see my father right now. I prefer to have people remember him as he was."

"Please let me know if I can be of assistance. I'll gladly bring Valencia's workers to help plant your next crop."

"Daddy doesn't want to farm this year. And please don't ask if Toledo can survive without income because I don't know."

******

Henning too had problems, inherited from Belisario. The United States was again exporting cotton. After America's civil war ended, southern plantation owners had devised a system for exploiting their freed slaves as sharecroppers. The resulting abundance had driven cotton prices down with Valencia's warehouses full of it and another crop ready to harvest.

Henning had sold that cotton at a substantial loss and planted sugarcane. But with his usual foresight, Emiliano Cabrera had long since switched to sugar and then streamlined Noya's operations so he could sell for less. Unable to compete, many of the Valley's growers were going broke. And Henning's plan to become competitive would take time to bear fruit.

To avoid meeting with an unfortunate accident in the meantime he began carrying a rifle. It was in the scabbard on his saddle the next time he reached Cortéz's central roundabout, where five streets radiated from a statue of Emiliano Cabrera's grandfather.

Looking up at the bronze reproduction of a man he wished had been childless, Henning heard the all-too-familiar strains of *La Marseillaise*. By now he'd heard France's national anthem played on everything from pan flute to guitar. This time it was dominated by an accordion.

"I'll pay you to stop," Henning offered the gypsy musicians.

"That would get us on *Don* Cabrera's wrong side, a very bad place to be," the violinist replied without missing a note.

A group of nuns sauntered by, mouths drawn into tight little bows. Like everyone else in town they knew what was going on. And not knowing the whole story, they found it amusing.

On the outskirts of Cortéz, a *cholo* crept up behind Henning and began *La Marseillaise* with a blast on his trumpet. Henning's startled horse leapt, slammed to the ground stiff legged, and whirled. Henning landed hip first.

Ignoring a stab of pain he vaulted to his feet, angrily ripped the trumpet from the wide-eyed *cholo's* hands, and bashed it against one of the whitewashed boulders separating traffic from the statue. When exhausted, Henning returned the instrument with enough coins to buy another. By then, the horn appeared to have been dropped from a cliff and to have hit every protrusion on the way down.

Still fuming, Henning rode downtown with a new question for Cabrera's long ago victim, Patricio Rendon.

"I sold to Cabrera after his harmless pranks led to one that almost killed me," Rendon answered. "I advise you to do the same."

******

The day her father was buried, Henning saw Martine for the first time in months. He was standing with the bereaved beside a freshly dug hole in Toledo's family plot when she appeared on foot—expressionless behind a veil—following *Don* Manuel's casket and pallbearers.

"Thank you for respecting my father's privacy," she told him after her father had been laid to rest between her mother and brother. "I was too sad to have been good company. I didn't realize I loved him so much. Or maybe what I think is sadness is really fear that his dementia is lurking somewhere in my future."

Henning offered his arm, then covered her black-gloved hand with his as they followed the other mourners to the house.

When Marco Venicio Lorca passed away, his death had cut short a promising life. *Don* Manuel's had ended one that was burdensome. Friends and family were glad his suffering was over. But to Henning's astonishment as well as her own, Martine missed him.

******

Emiliano Cabrera stepped from his carriage in front of his Cortéz headquarters. Entering his office, he looked up to see if the hinged window above the front door was leaning at the correct forty-five degree angle.

"*Señorita* Alvarado," he scolded. "You've forgotten to open the transom."

His secretary jumped up and grabbed the pole used to manipulate the latch.

"I'll take care of that immediately," she said. "Beautiful day, isn't it?"

"You'll be amazed how much more you can accomplish if you avoid comments on the weather," Cabrera replied. The woman was more trouble than she was worth. Only yesterday her mother had begged him to raise her salary.

"She can't support herself on what you pay," the old lady had pleaded. "Today I caught her scraping plaster off her closet wall and using it for face powder."

He'd squelched her pathetic bid for sympathy with, "If plaster isn't a satisfactory substitute, find her a better paying job."

Mateo Morales, Cortéz's most feared attorney, sat near the desk in Cabrera's private office. He trimmed two cigars and handed one over.

When both were lit, Morales said, "I've drawn up the Demand for Payment and the Eviction Notice."

"Have them served this afternoon." Cabrera released a puff of blue smoke.

"On the day of *Don* Manuel's funeral? Is that a good idea? Why the hurry?"

"Remember the Eviction Notice you served on Belisario Lorca after his son's death? That looked like a sure thing too. But *Herr* Dietzel came to the rescue. He's sweet on Martine Prado. I don't want to give him time to raise money and pay me off."

"Don't worry, he's spread thin. Furthermore, he and *Señorita* Prado are no longer close. If they saw each other at *Don* Manuel's funeral this morning, it was the first time in months."

"How do you know?"

"The best way to learn people's secrets is to talk with their servants." Hands clasped behind his head, Morales looked pleased with himself.

Cabrera studied his ceiling fan and the belts connecting it to a small windmill on the roof. Losing Valencia after killing Marco Lorca had been a severe setback. He'd heard that Belisario Lorca had described it as, "A surprise arranged with my help as well as God's."

But Cabrera wasn't worried about divine intervention. After seeing other landowners pray in vain for assistance against him, he believed in a distant God who played little role in human affairs.

"Two ambitious, incorruptible prosecutors have reopened the investigation into Marco Lorca's accident," he told Morales. "They questioned me yesterday. If Dietzel tries to help *Señorita* Prado, we'll have to stop him without calling attention to ourselves."

CHAPTER SEVENTEEN
A BITTERSWEET PROPOSAL

Martine had slept fitfully the week before her father's burial. When the guests left, she lay down in her funeral gown and drifted off. Wakened by knocking on the front door, she checked the mirror to see why her cheek ached. The initials monogrammed on her pillowcase had left a mark. Rubbing it, she heard another knock.

Chabuca would have answered by then if she was indoors. Smoothing her hair and straightening her skirts, Martine hurried downstairs.

"Who's there?" she asked through the closed door.

"It's me," a familiar voice said. She opened the door and saw a man who wasn't the *me* she'd expected.

Frowning he said, "You're looking at me like I have a hump and a limp."

"That's because you recently served legal papers on my father."

"And today I'm serving you." He handed her an envelope sealed with a dollop of red wax. "Take those to your attorney. He must respond in writing within—"

Putting a finger to her lips, Martine stopped him mid-sentence.

"Go away," she said, closing the door.

Through a window she watched him drive off, then sat in a chair on the back porch reading the documents. When finished, she went down the steps to the yard and approached the swing her father's servants had hung from a branch when she was little. It had been too high for her then, and she'd had to be lifted up to sit in it. But she was taller now and the seat was the perfect height.

Unfortunately her father's debts had also grown, and Martine's worst nightmare was coming true. Instead of making Toledo into a utopia for her workers, she was going to lose it—and them—to Emiliano Cabrera. Or was this an attempt to exploit her ignorance?

She felt a spark of hope. Her father had never mentioned a loan or overdue payments. At his office desk, she found the key in its pigeonhole and unlocked his filing cabinet. Walking her fingers across folders she found one labeled 'Mortgage.' As she read the documents inside, the spark went out. *Don* Manuel had used Toledo as security for a loan.

"Much of which you wasted on ridiculous luxuries like monogrammed sheets," she muttered, rubbing her sore cheek.

With three payments past due, the mortgage had been sold to Emiliano Cabrera. The only way to prevent foreclosure was to pay him off.

Though Toledo's losses had eroded her father's fortune, Martine expected a substantial inheritance. She took the folder marked 'Financial Records' to her father's desk. Her chin propped up with a fist she soon found that her father's payments to creditors had stopped months ago because there was no more money. He hadn't told her about the loan. If he'd had a plan for repaying it, he hadn't mentioned that either.

A year ago Fernando and Elena Murillo, had lost their farm to Cabrera. Martine had seen the first sign of trouble in their bathroom where imported packages labeled Gayette's Medicated Paper for the Water-Closet had been replaced by newspaper squares impaled on a spindle. The day Cabrera's henchmen evicted the Murillos, he'd brought a Dalmatian dog as if to a picnic.

Light swirled across a wall. Seeing Chabuca in the doorway with a lantern, Martine asked, "Were you in the garden?"

"Yes. What would you like for dinner?"

"I'm not hungry, thank you. See you in the morning."

"Are you okay…after the funeral and everything?"

"Can we talk tomorrow please?"

Chabuca's steady gait echoed down the hallway. Martine picked up a lantern and went to her room. In her dressing table mirror she saw a pale complexion and bloodshot eyes. After putting on her nightgown she slid between the blanket and top sheet.

Angry and frustrated, she managed to get between the sheets on her next try.

Tomorrow she'd take the Eviction Notice to her father's younger brother, an attorney. Alfredo and *Don* Manuel had been estranged for years, but her uncle was fond of her. Surely he could do something. By the time she fell asleep Martine's pillow was damp with tears.

She lurched awake in the midst of a nightmare. She'd been aboard a ship, its steering wheel spinning wildly as rough seas pushed it on an erratic course under a moonless sky. Alone and soaked with ocean spray, she'd dashed here and there looking for someone to help her.

Still perspiring, unable to sleep, she stared at the familiar swirls in her room's plaster ceiling as the meaning of her dream became clear. Uncle Alfredo couldn't help, nor could any other lawyer. Emiliano Cabrera had far more influence in Cortéz's courts, thanks to Judge Ramón Benavides.

To save Toledo she'd have to bend her knee, perhaps even beg.

That would be excruciating. But Toledo was more important than her pride.

******

The walls of Valencia's library were lined with bookcases containing every book Henning owned. He'd even kept the weather-beaten volumes read that brutal winter he'd spent alone in California's Gold Country while other prospectors sheltered in San Francisco.

Reading his latest purchase, Henning sat in sunlight streaming down from the dormer. When the maid announced a visitor, he returned *The Art of War* to the gap it had left on a shelf. The owner of Cortéz's bookstore had said Emiliano Cabrera considered it the best book he'd ever read. Eager to understand his enemy, Henning was studying it for the third time.

His impatience to resume reading evaporated when the maid said his visitor was Martine Prado. She entered the library looking eager to make a good impression, in a stylish high-necked, long-sleeved, green dress with a form-fitting bodice.

She'd favored dresses with narrow silhouettes long before they'd come in style with their emphasis on the bust, waist, and hips. But in keeping with her no-nonsense personality, she'd resisted the addition of corsets and padding to improve her figure.

Henning rolled his sleeves down and buttoned them.

Without preliminaries or artifice Martine offered something Henning wanted more than anything else in the world. But her marriage proposal was more bitter than sweet.

"I don't know if your interest in me still goes beyond friendship," she explained when he didn't respond. "But even if it doesn't, there are excellent reasons for us to wed. We're far past the usual age for marriage and without prospects. Our haciendas share a common boundary and will operate more efficiently if combined."

"You don't think you're being overly sentimental?" he teased.

Intent on her purpose, she missed his irony. "Not in the least. Marriage is my only alternative to having Toledo fall into Emiliano Cabrera's hands, and you need more land in order to compete with him."

"Are those good enough reasons to marry someone you don't love?" he asked, fishing for a sign of affection.

"It's done all the time," was her disappointing reply. "Marriage is a common way of joining people for mutual advantage."

"Among the highborn perhaps, but we commoners sometimes marry for love."

"And wind up barely tolerating one another. You and I have been friends for years. We know one another's faults, yet we get along. What better foundation for a marriage?"

"If we marry we'll be together for the rest of our lives. That's a long time for people to put up with each other's faults when they're not in love."

"We won't spend all that much time together. After years of saying you want a personal life, you still work every waking second. You claim your efforts to have a fuller life have been foiled by circumstances beyond your control. But you'll clearly never find a woman as interesting as your work."

How could she believe that? He'd adored her for eighteen years and had pursued her long after other admirers switched their affections to younger women. With very little encouragement he'd find all the time she could possibly want.

When Henning replied, his tone was professional.

"What's Toledo's financial condition?" he asked.

"People assume my father settled substantial monies on me before his death. However, his fortune is gone and Toledo's debt is enormous. Worse yet, Emiliano Cabrera purchased our mortgage." Martine handed him the

Demand for Payment. "If he takes over Toledo, his advantage over Valencia will be insurmountable."

A union with Martine would have advantages, the greatest of which was that she might come to love him once they were working toward a common goal. And combining Valencia with Toledo would create the third largest estate in the Valley, making Henning a force even Emiliano Cabrera would have to reckon with. But paying off Cabrera would cost a once unimaginable sum, and Henning's finances were precarious.

"If we were to marry I'd heed your counsel," he said, "but I'd make the final decisions."

"I'm offering you the Valley's best land. Surely I'd be entitled to a voice in running it."

"You'd have a substantial voice, but a business can't have two bosses."

"So you'd be able to overrule me anytime you please?"

"Only when neither of us can convince the other and we can't reach a compromise."

"A man gains certain physical rights by marriage." Looking uncomfortable, Martine shifted her weight. "If we marry I want your word you won't take liberties, even though they're not considered liberties with a wife."

"I wouldn't dream of insisting, but I might try friendly persuasion."

Trying to find something to do with her hands, Martine said, "I was pregnant once. My father found a French doctor who saved my reputation for a reasonable price, but the experience soured me on intimacy. In those days I was starved for praise and didn't realize my fiancé was manipulating me." She looked down. "He'd call me Sleeping Beauty and promise to wake me with the delights of love. You could count the number of times it happened on the fingers of one hand. The day I told him I was pregnant, he left me to face the repercussions alone." She squared her shoulders. "No man ever touched me before or since."

"I'm not a virgin either," Henning said, trying to put her at ease. "And there's something else you should know. In California, Mexicans robbed and murdered five of the best men I've ever known." Leaving out the gory details, Henning told her how he'd recovered the stolen gold and killed three of the bandits. "I've never told that story to anyone but you, Eduardo, and Alcalino," he concluded. "Being a pacifist, Alcalino was horrified."

"I'm no pacifist," Martine said. "I'm glad you have a backbone. You'll need it. Emiliano Cabrera will come after you with a vengeance if you stop him from acquiring Toledo, especially after you previously kept him from taking over Valencia."

"It will take every penny I can borrow to pay him off. We'd have to live frugally."

"That's fine with me. But I would like to have a priest perform our ceremony even though you're not a believer. You'll have to pledge to raise our children—if any—in the Church. I'm thirty-seven. It isn't recommended for women my age to have babies, but it happens."

"If we marry and have children, I won't object to their attending church. But once they're old enough to think for themselves, I won't force them."

"Did you go to church as a boy?"

"Yes, my family was Lutheran, but I found the mythology difficult to accept. After my father was killed in one of Prussia's wars, my grandfather stopped taking me. He said my father's death made it obvious that his interest in God wasn't reciprocated." Henning rubbed his eyes. "If you want your children raised Catholic, why aren't you troubled that I'm not one?"

"How you live all week is what matters to me. Not what you do on Sundays."

And it doesn't hurt that I'm the only bachelor in the Valley who can raise the money to pay off Emiliano Cabrera. Henning pushed the unwelcome thought aside.

"One last thing," Martine said. "I want Toledo's workers paid better."

"I'll pay their back wages and offer them a way to earn more than they do now," Henning replied, "but they'll have to work harder."

"I won't have them driven like mules."

"I favor motivation that comes from within." He described his incentive plan.

That afternoon Martine gathered her workers and told them, "Henning Dietzel and I may wed. If we do, Toledo will be combined with Valencia."

"Valencia's workers are very happy with *Don* Henning's incentive plan," an overseer said enthusiastically. "If you marry, can you please ask him to pay us the same way?"

******

Henning was in the saddle, ready to leave, when Belisario rode in.

"Can we go over the latest invoices for the horse farm?" the old aristocrat asked.

"Can it wait?" Henning asked. "I'm on my way to visit José Geldres."

"I keep forgetting to tell you…*El Loco*, the old hermit who lives in a cave near Dos Palos has begun stopping people, claiming he's the law and demanding to see what they have in their pockets and saddlebags. He's harmless but persistent and can waste a great deal of time. If you have a sheath knife, wearing it will keep him at a distance."

"I'm no knife fighter."

"And I wouldn't want you to terrorize a harmless old man. The point is, *El Loco* won't come near you if you're carrying a blade."

Henning took the invoices to his office and returned with a sheath and Bowie knife hanging from his belt.

"You did well to take my advice," Belisario said. "*El Loco* won't delay you now."

"I'm going to invite José Geldres to my wedding" Henning explained, "which will likely lead to a long conversation, and I don't want to be on the trail after dark."

"Are you sure you know Martine well enough to marry her?"

"I fell in love with her eighteen years ago and probably know her as well as you knew your wife when you married."

"My wife was uncomplicated, like Encinas. You'd be better off if you'd stayed with her."

"I would have if we'd been in love."

As Henning unsaddled at Dos Palos, José Geldres brought the usual lemonade and chairs out onto his covered front porch.

"Martine and I are engaged," Henning began once they were seated.

"Your interest in my goddaughter has long been apparent. When did you become promised to her?"

"I gave her a ring this morning."

"As recently as that? Why share such a momentous day with me?"

"You understand Martine's heart and I need to know what she wants in a husband."

"Not even she knows that. Unlike most women, she doesn't long for someone like her father. He was everything she doesn't want."

"I'm not like him." Henning crossed his legs and folded his hands.

"As far as she's concerned, all men are like him. At first she'll suspect you of wanting to run her life—as he did—and will keep you at arm's length. And because she could never please him, she won't make much effort to please you. I'll never understand how *Don* Manuel loved Pietro and not her. They were twins, so much alike that their mother called them one person divided in two. The day Pietro broke a leg in Cortéz, Martine—at Toledo—felt pain in the same spot. After Pietro's death she missed him so terribly that she'd put on his clothes, tuck her hair up inside his *sombrero*, and stand in front of a mirror. They looked very much alike and that was her way of bringing him back to life. She once told me, 'If Pietro and I say exactly the same thing, Daddy treats me like a silly girl but takes Pietro seriously.' She resented the way men have status and women don't. She sympathized with *cholos* and *serranos* because we—like women—aren't allowed to live as we wish. Come inside. I want to show you something."

As they stood, a lizard scampered off, its tail leaving a drag mark in the dust between its footprints.

Henning followed *Don* José across the living room and into a bedroom. On top of the dresser angled across one corner was a framed daguerreotype photograph of Martine as a girl.

"She looks sad," Henning said.

"Yes. Even back then she was too serious. That photo was taken at her fifth birthday party. Her father had scolded her for reprimanding a friend who'd been rude to a maid. He demanded to know why she couldn't get along with other little girls and she told him, 'Because it's wrong to be mean to people.' But *Don* Manuel didn't think *cholos* are people."

Don José pried up a loose floorboard with his pocketknife, then reached into the cavity and withdrew a silver box. When he opened the lid something inside glowed.

"Thirty years ago I set this aside for Martine's wedding day," he said, dropping a heavy gold bracelet on Henning's palm. "It's the most exquisite artifact I've ever seen."

"We can't accept this," Henning said. "It's far too valuable and—"

"That's not up to you. You'll have endless strife if you try to make Martine's decisions for her."

Don José's eyes lingered enviously on the Bowie knife. Jim Bowie had been Henning's childhood hero, and his mother had saved for months to buy it. She'd believed in doing nice things for people and would approve of giving it to someone who'd treasure it. Henning unbuckled his belt, then slid the knife and sheath free, and handed them over.

"A dagger of this design," *Don* José said, "will be useful in many ways."

"Such as stopping *El Loco* from demanding to see what you're carrying?"

"Too late. He died. But that doesn't detract from your gift's value."

"It's hardly the equal of yours."

"The price of gifts is meaningless. What matters is the pleasure they bring, and I'll enjoy this knife at least as much as Martine does her bracelet."

Still concerned about the disparity, Henning said, "I have a colt, Emisario, who's Sultán's full brother and promises to be as good. I want you to have him after I finish his training."

"Thank you. Goliat is old and before long even Sultán will find it difficult to take me to my bank." *Don* José pointed toward Las Casitas Canyon. "You probably think it's strange I refer to it as my bank. Everyone knows I don't trust them, but mine is more reliable than most."

CHAPTER EIGHTEEN
EVEN BEES PAY THEIR WAY

The Valley's church was too small to accommodate everyone who'd been invited, so the marriage ceremony was held at Valencia. As music from a borrowed organ increased in volume, people on benches in the yard fell silent. Then, under a late afternoon sun, *Don* José escorted his goddaughter down an aisle between vases of Peruvian *amancae* lilies, toward the side porch.

The long train of Martine's ivory gown swept the ground in front of Encinas, who followed in the same cadenced walk. Encinas wasn't a typical maid of honor and Emiliano Cabrera had made sure everyone knew why.

"None of us is perfect," Martine had defended her choice to a friend bold enough to question it, "but I admire her decency—yes, decency—as well as the honesty and hard work that brought her success in a man's world."

The Valley's convent had provided the altar where Henning waited with his best men, Eduardo and Belisario, in black dinner suits with long tails. After *Don* José climbed the steps and delivered the bride, the Valley's priest began the ceremony.

"O God in heaven, bless these friends of ours who are about to give their vows...."

Afterward the bishop himself—tall miter on his head, golden staff in one hand—sprinkled the bride and groom with holy water.

Martine had invited over a hundred of Toledo's and Valencia's administrators and overseers. One took a swig of *pisco*, raised his bottle, and shouted, "Long live the most beautiful bride ever."

The woman beside him—clearly his wife—pretended to slap his face while onlookers giggled. To call attention away from this distraction, *Don* José initiated the applause as the newlyweds came down the stairs toward the reception line. Martine's Uncle Alfredo was first to congratulate them, followed by friends, neighbors, and finally a long line of workers.

As his employees came through, Henning took each man's hand in both of his and thanked him for coming. As far as *Don* José could tell, he addressed every man by name. But Martine's look of approval faded whenever he lovingly touched her arm, neck, or shoulder.

Don José wished he'd mentioned Martine's disapproval of public affection. But when she pulled away from his touch, Henning's spirits weren't visibly dampened. He was probably expecting her to be more receptive when they were alone.

Don José didn't think she'd warm up that soon.

******

Out of respect for the newlyweds' first night together, the guests went home soon after dinner, leaving Henning and Martine alone in the living room.

"Why do you call our combined hacienda Valencia?" were her first words in private.

"I'll call it Toledo if you like," Henning replied.

"That would be nice." She looked around. "Living here will feel strange. I was in my father's house all my life, except when he was Peru's ambassador to Argentina." She yawned. "It's been a long day and I'm exhausted. I think I'll go to bed."

As if by appointment, Chabuca appeared and led the way to the bedroom where the staff had put Martine's furniture and clothing. Later Henning saw a sliver of light beneath its closed door on the way to his room. His bride was awake—probably reading—two hours after leaving him alone on their wedding night.

The next morning Martine was still in her room when Henning left for the fields. He came back for lunch and ate alone. During supper she didn't encourage his efforts at conversation and went from the table to her room.

"What are you reading these days?" Henning asked at dinner the following evening.

"A book about Europe's labor unions," Martine replied. "What do you think of workers banding together to improve wages and working conditions?"

"I wish them every success."

"That's a surprise. May I ask why?"

"If the unions fail, labor unrest will bring revolution, maybe even communism. In my opinion capitalism will be well served if unions succeed in eliminating worker abuse."

For an hour Martine animatedly described the progress made by England's unions. The next night Henning reopened the subject and again the conversation flowed. But when he described the wagon he'd designed for hauling cane to the mill, Martine squelched a yawn.

During his first trip to Iquique after the wedding, Henning left Encinas in charge. Martine protested, but he overruled her. Encinas was more adept at business and Toledo was still hard-pressed by Emiliano Cabrera's Hacienda Noya.

******

Three months into their marriage Henning had seen but one of the attributes *Don* José had promised. Martine was a hard worker, unlike other highborn ladies who boasted they'd done something after they'd had servants do it.

During Henning's next trip to Iquique, Martine—on her own—took charge of the *mayordomos de campo* who supervised fieldworkers. At lunch the day he returned, Henning complimented her on a job well done and encouraged her to continue. He didn't think he deserved lavish gratitude. But she didn't even seem pleased.

Before their marriage he'd had his hacienda running like a fine Swiss watch. Now after borrowing money to pay her debt to Emiliano Cabrera, he was working all day and half the night to make the payments. And so far she'd showed no appreciation.

On his way to bed that night Henning was galled by the light under her door. As always she was reading during his only free time.

He knocked and heard, "Can it wait until tomorrow?"

"No." He opened the door, half hoping she'd be naked.

Pulling the covers to her neck, she sat up.

"I'm killing myself," he said, "to save your hacienda and—"

"What I see," she fired back, "is a man doing whatever he wants with my property."

"Toledo would be Cabrera's property if I hadn't borrowed a fortune and paid him off."

"That was the best investment you'll ever make and you know it." The headboard's mirror reflected her shapely, bare back.

"It's impossible to please you," Henning snapped.

"Not at all. I simply want a voice in running Toledo. I deserve to make decisions—not just suggestions."

"You can't make good decisions without experience and training."

"You gave Encinas a chance. Why do you trust her more than you do me?"

"I don't. She had an eighteen-year history of running businesses. If you want, I'll have her teach you what you need to know, starting with accounting."

"I have less than no interest in that."

"Then you'll never be able to run Toledo."

Chabuca appeared in the hallway to Henning's right, clearly concerned by the angry voices. As he faced her, she covered her mouth and fled.

"I'm sick of your sacred numbers," Martine spat out the words. "As well as your absurd claim that they predict the future."

"Numbers—not your prayers and witch's amulets—saved Toledo from Cabrera."

"Why can't you give me at least *some* authority?"

"Because a business can't have two bosses."

"Toledo does—you and Encinas."

"No. I'm the boss and Encinas does what I ask. But if you were in her place we'd quarrel day and night."

"Would you like to point out more of my faults?"

"I don't know where to start. You're so deeply rooted in old-fashioned ways that—"

"Those roots mean I won't blow over in the wind coming out of your mouth. You're not the only one disappointed with our marriage. Life will be better for both of us if I move back to my father's house."

"I'll take you right now if you want."

"Tomorrow morning will be soon enough."

By the time Henning reached his room Martine had slammed her door twice, and he regretted his impulsive offer to take her back to her old house. But how else could he have responded without seeming to beg?

The next morning Martine packed her clothes in trunks and her tall, thin manservant, Pedro Malaga, put them on a wagon.

"I'll send Pedro and Chabuca with you," Henning said. They'd take excellent care of her.

With no indication of how much he hated to see her go, Henning let Martine struggle aboard the wagon before assisting Chabuca.

Once seated he unnecessarily cracked his whip above the horses' backs.

Halfway to the house where Martine grew up, they passed the beekeeper's cottage. Openings through its covering of yellow-blossomed vines showed a door and two windows, the only visible evidence of the structure within. Fuzzy-bodied bees buzzed from hives and swarmed among nearby fruit and nut trees.

"I'm told you're selling our honey," Martine said. "It used to be enough for the bees to pollinate the orchards. But since you took over, even they have to pay their way."

Alone on the drive home Henning experienced the sense of loss he'd endured when his mother died. If anything, today was even more painful. He and the love of his life had drifted apart without ever getting close.

The next day he sent O'Higgins to protect Martine and her servants.

A week later José Geldres came visiting and Henning had lunch served in the garden.

"I'm not surprised Martine is staying elsewhere," *Don* José said upon hearing the news. "I feared she'd find it difficult to lose the freedom she expected after her father died. Forgive my personal question, but are you giving her an allowance?"

"I gave her the honey business," Henning replied. "It makes a good profit and will teach her about commerce."

"Having her own income makes her independent. Is that a good idea?"

"How else can I show her it's safe to love me?"

******

By 1869 Peru's guano industry was fading, her silver sales were stagnant, and the world was extracting quinine from the bark of cinchona trees planted with smuggled Peruvian seed in Asia. Tens of thousands of *serranos*, *cholos*, coolies, Negroes, and Kanakas were suddenly unemployed, converting Peru's centuries-old worker shortage to a glut. José Geldres's trips to find workers for Toledo had become a thing of the past.

"I found Goliat dead in his corral last Sunday," *Don* José said after reaching Toledo on a horse Henning couldn't remember having seen before, "and I buried Sultán two weeks later. It was as if they couldn't stand being idle. Riding this nag is a long step down."

"Take Emisario home with you," Henning said. "I've finished his training."

"Is he safe for an old man?"

"With his spirit he'll never be foolproof. But then again you're no fool."

Lonely now that he no longer visited friends in the Andes, *Don* José was making monthly visits to the Valley. He typically spent two days with Martine, one with Henning, and another with Belisario, Encinas, and young Antonio.

During their Easter get-together on his sunny patio, Henning tilted his chair back and said, "I wish you'd come more often and stay longer."

"And I'd give anything to see you and Martine get back together," *Don* José replied.

Juan Alba, the cook Henning hired after sending Chabuca to look after Martine, brought two bowls of *suspiro limeño*, rich creamy caramel topped with delicate meringue. To prolong his enjoyment Henning took small bites.

"I miss my son," *Don* José said between mouthfuls.

"I didn't know you had one."

"Years ago his mother took him and disappeared. I spend time with Encinas's boy, hoping he'll fill the vacancy. But we're opposites. My first thought when I wake up is, 'Good morning, God.' His is, 'Good God, morning.' He seems perpetually melancholy, perhaps because he's a bastard. Or maybe he's just that way."

"I doubt I'll ever have a son," Henning mused, "considering Martine's age."

"It's even less likely with her living elsewhere and you working such long hours. Neither of you has any sense of balance. A good life has to contain the necessary ingredients in the right amounts. The recipe doesn't allow for leaving some things out and replacing them with an excess of the others, which is what you and Martine do. She spends most of her time alone, and you put too much of yours into making everything perfect."

"Can you suggest anything she might like to do together?"

"You've been married four months. I know you're strapped for cash, but a honeymoon could be the best investment you'll ever make."

CHAPTER NINETEEN
THE BLONDE NATIVE GIRL

The following morning Henning sent an overseer with a note inviting Martine to dinner and offering to pick her up.

Her reply read: 'Thank you. I'll be ready at six.'

Elated, Henning told Juan Alba, "My wife is coming for dinner. Will you please prepare your very best *lomo saltado*?"

"I take it that's her favorite dish?" The normally somber Alba surprised Henning with a lopsided grin. "Tonight's will be fit for a queen provided I get the right ingredients."

"I can provide perfectly aged meat, and I'll have whatever else you need brought fresh from the garden."

"I'd rather select it myself if you don't mind."

"Better yet. And this afternoon I'll buy Martine's favorite wine in Cortéz."

"In Cortéz," Alba exclaimed, eyebrows raised. "That will take the rest of the day. I've never seen you leave your work that long."

"Which tells you how important tonight is."

In Cortéz Henning bought several bottles of dry white wine imported from Chile's finest Jesuit winery. Next he rented a shiny black landau carriage with white leather seats and a top that could be raised and lowered.

"Follow me," he told the driver, "and please don't wear your uniform. I want it clean and perfectly pressed tonight."

At Toledo the driver polished the carriage, then bathed and put on his uniform. By that time, Juan Alba had beef tenderloin strips, minced garlic, hot and sweet peppers, red onions, potato cubes, and sliced plum tomatoes in separate bowls—ready to be flash fried with vinegar and soy sauce, then served with steamed rice.

In his gray alpaca suit—twenty years old and none the worse for wear—Henning called for Martine with the carriage's top down. They made small talk during the drive. When Henning opened the front door, they were greeted by the aroma of frying meat, garlic, and onions.

"That smells like an outstanding *lomo saltado,*" Martine declared with an overdue smile.

Dinner began in silence punctuated by the ring of silverware on translucent bone china.

"I've never tasted better," Martine said as Alba brought second servings on clean plates.

"It's time we went on a honeymoon," Henning began when they were alone again. "Is there someplace you've always wanted to go? Paris? London? Hamburg?"

Martine touched her napkin to her mouth. "I don't enjoy cities much, but I'd love to see the Brazilian Amazon. My brother, Pietro, said it's wondrous."

"How soon can you be ready?"

"When does the next ship leave?"

"I'll find out tomorrow." Henning dipped his table knife in a bowl of salt then tapped the blade to sprinkle it on his food.

They talked until after midnight. Rather than invite her to spend the night and risk being turned down, Henning escorted Martine to where she was living. Later back at Henning's, the driver slept in a guest room.

When Henning brought Martine's ticket the following afternoon, she was sitting on the lid of her trunk while O'Higgins struggled to close the latches.

She looked up after studying her itinerary, then pretended to wipe sweat from her brow and said, "Whew."

She didn't elaborate in front of O'Higgins, but Henning understood. She was relieved they had separate staterooms. Henning had hoped she'd protest the expense and suggest they share one.

"Can you find room in your trunk for these?" He handed her a gift-wrapped package.

Inside she found three ankle-length sun dresses. All left the neck and upper chest bare, had snug bodices and short sleeves, and were made of lightweight Peruvian Pima cotton.

"Thank you," she said. "They're perfect for where we're going."

Clearly aware his presence made them uncomfortable, O'Higgins left the room.

"I've been petty and unreasonable," Martine said, shutting the door behind him. "You took on an enormous debt to save Toledo and are working unbelievably long hours. I should be helping. If you're still willing to have Encinas teach me accounting, she can start when we get back from Brazil."

******

Henning had chosen this particular ocean liner because it sailed within view of southern Chile's sensational shoreline. Chiloé, Corcovado, and Guamblin Island seemed even more spectacular after Peru's sterile, monotonous deserts.

"It's as beautiful as you promised," Martine told him after two days of islands, beaches, fjords, peninsulas, waterfalls, and forests where rainfall was measured in feet.

Their first night in the Strait of Magellan, they watched the fiery eruption of a Tierra del Fuego volcano then hurried below as fierce winds and powerful currents buffeted their ship.

By the time the pitching and rolling had lasted long enough to make even Henning queasy, the sound of Martine vomiting came through the wall between their rooms. Disappointed her first storm at sea hadn't had a different effect, he took her a pitcher of water and a glass from the galley.

Beyond sight of shore, the voyage north along South America's Atlantic coast was dull until the afternoon their vessel was suddenly surrounded by yellow-brown water. Hours later there was still no sign of the ocean's normal blue-gray.

"What causes this color?" Martine asked a sailor who'd been staring at her the way most men once had.

"Silt from Brazil's Amazon River, ma'am," he said, coming closer and tipping his hat. "The Portuguese were looking for its source when they discovered the river's mouth."

"How far are we from there?"

"Over three hundred miles, ma'am."

"It's hard to believe a river could discolor that much ocean."

"The Amazon isn't just any river."

Next afternoon the sailor rejoined Martine and Henning at the rail.

She greeted him by name and said, "The water's color is deeper here. We must be near the Amazon."

"We're on it, ma'am."

"You sure?" Shading her eyes, Martine looked left then right. "Where are the banks?"

"The Amazon's mouth is two hundred miles wide. You won't see land until we make port at Macapá."

After their ship docked the next day Henning and Martine transferred to an English freighter from Dover. *Armstrong* was scheduled to follow the winding Amazon for twenty-three hundred miles to Iquitos, Peru, where stevedores would unload construction material to sustain that area's rubber boom. Then it would return to England with rosewood, sarsaparilla, wax, exotic animals, and tropical fish.

Armstrong left port as Henning and Martine settled into their cabins. When they met on deck, Macapá was a distant speck. In every other direction, they saw only water.

"Will we always be so far from shore?" Henning asked when the captain happened by.

"Not always, but for days at a time."

"Hardly a feast for the eyes."

"This isn't a tourist cruise. We stay in the middle of the river so we don't have to worry about hitting small craft. You won't see either coast most days."

"By coast, do you mean riverbank?" Henning asked.

"Yes. The natives call them *costas*, not entirely inaccurate when you consider that much of the Amazon is over fifty miles wide."

Henning's face twisted with disappointment. Having entered a world like no other, he and Martine were missing it. The ticket agent in Cortéz hadn't mentioned that *Armstrong's* only objective was making good time.

On the third day *Armstrong* delivered cargo to a village. Martine and Henning went ashore with the captain.

Pointing to a small steam-powered riverboat with *Amazonas* painted on its stern, he told Henning, "If you want to see something besides the middle of the river you should transfer to that ship or one like it. Mind you, I can't refund your ticket."

Armstrong's captain introduced them to Hector Renaldo. His white moustache—waxed and turned up at both ends—matched the perpetual smile beneath it. He was fluent in Spanish, rare in Portuguese-speaking Brazil.

"I've spent thirty years on this river," Renaldo told Martine. "You won't regret changing ships. *Amazonas* is always near shore where you'll see some of the world's most unusual flora and fauna. I don't normally carry passengers because my ship has only one private room, mine. But it's yours if you want it."

Tiny, the room had no windows and a bed barely big enough for Martine.

After due consideration, she said, "There's room for a hammock. This will be fine."

Henning hid his surprise and went shopping with Renaldo while Martine settled in.

"How long have you two been married?" Renaldo asked as Henning paid for the longest hammock they'd found.

"We're on our honeymoon," Henning replied.

"In that case you're still protective of your privacy." Renaldo's wink rivaled Eduardo's most mischievous.

Back aboard *Amazonas*, Renaldo took Henning to the wheelhouse. Pointing to a cot near the steering wheel, he said, "While you and your bride are aboard, I'll sleep here, and my deckhands, as always, will sleep in that shelter near the bow. As you can see, we're too far from your room to eavesdrop on what happens there."

That afternoon Henning and Martine sat at the rail, laughing and talking as *Amazonas* chugged upriver. They saw swarms of brilliant blue and yellow butterflies, flocks of herons, and huge water lilies. And finally a school of much-feared piranha fish. Capable of stripping the flesh from a human skeleton in seconds, they looked disappointingly placid.

The next day Henning and Martine alternated between boredom and enchantment. At times they saw only yellow-brown water and a green, unchanging wall of vegetation. But often enough the river's next bend revealed orchids, otters, alligators, or giant turtles.

When *Amazonas* stopped, a seemingly deserted settlement sprang to life. Martine was approached by a boy with high cheekbones and black bangs cut straight across above his eyes. He offered to sell her a live boa constrictor or a smaller snake with alternating black and orange stripes. Henning bought both. Before reboarding, Martine opened their bamboo cages and watched them slither into the jungle.

"That was more satisfying than anything else I could have done with them," she told Henning. "Don't be cross with me, please."

"Sorry if I look disappointed," he said. "I'm not. I was thinking that setting them free was in keeping with your own need for freedom."

"If my father had bought those snakes, he'd have scolded me for lack of gratitude."

For days Renaldo pointed out plant and animal life unknown in the outside world. He also took Henning and Martine ashore to see a trailhead where explorers had hacked their way into thick jungle searching for a lost city. And when they passed a large cross in a village where missionaries spread their religion and imposed their culture, he muttered profanities.

Even more than Renaldo, Martine called Henning's attention to extraordinary sights. Incredibly observant, she saw every detail in flowers and birds that were blurs of color to him. And though he was eager to see a jaguar, she was the one who did.

"Over there," she whispered, "just beyond the big tree."

Henning was still looking when she told him the big cat had disappeared.

Near Santarém, Renaldo abruptly shut down the engine and spun the wheel, forcing *Amazonas* into a tight turn that sent creaks and groans through her hull. Looking where he was pointing, Henning caught a glimpse of a young blonde girl. Then there were only bushes and ferns where she'd been.

"Did you see her?" Renaldo asked.

"Yes," Henning replied. "You're not going to leave her, are you?"

"Don't worry. She lives here. You can be sure her mother is nearby."

"Who is she?" Martine asked.

"I couldn't tell. All three look alike from a distance."

"There are other blonde children?" Martine was incredulous.

"I'll tell you the story at dinner."

Renaldo spun the wheel, returning his ship to its former course.

CHAPTER TWENTY
CONFEDERATES AND EGRETS

Waiting for dinner in a thatched restaurant ashore, Renaldo lit a cigar and began his promised tale.

"Just four short years ago in 1865, thousands of southerners who couldn't live with the outcome of America's civil war fled what they saw as unbearable oppression. They eluded the victorious Union armies and took their silverware, linen, and slaves elsewhere. Many came to Brazil where land is cheap and slavery legal. Not to mention that we'd sympathized with the Confederacy during the war. Some two hundred *confederados* settled near Santarém."

"They probably thought its remote location would isolate them from a world that had turned against slavery," Henning offered during a pause.

"They said as much," Renaldo continued, "before setting out to reestablish the gracious lifestyle they'd known in Dixie and pass their slaves along to their posterity. But life in the Amazon is difficult, and they soon went elsewhere. The blonde girl you saw this afternoon is one of their half-breed daughters, born of native women."

"Are you serious?" Martine asked.

"Absolutely." Renaldo shrugged. "The existence of such children is ironic considering that *confederados* passionately believed in their racial superiority and had brought their women."

"Men!" Grinning, Martine added, "Present company excluded of course."

In Santarém's market the following afternoon, Martine and Henning found themselves surrounded by people of every conceivable racial mixture.

"I don't understand," Martine said as they left, "how those southern aristocrats could bring themselves to have relations with women they considered inferior mongrels."

"Maybe Renaldo was simply entertaining us tourists with a tall tale. Do you believe hundreds of *confederados* actually brought their slaves out here in the middle of nowhere?"

"After seeing the pottery in that market I'm sure at least a few did." Seeing Henning's frown, she asked, "You didn't notice the bowls, plates, and cups with Confederate flags painted on them?"

******

That afternoon, *Amazonas* passed a beach covered with huts. Naked boys sprinted toward the river, broke into pairs, and launched narrow canoes. One in the stern and the other in the bow, they paddled out and stopped at right angles to *Amazonas*. When its wake reached them they bobbed up and down on their waterborne seesaws, giggling and waving goodbye.

"Those boys live in a place like nowhere else," Martine said, "yet they're like children everywhere."

"Do you want children?" Henning asked.

"Very much, but at my age it's too late."

Later *Amazonas* left the main river's panoramas and entered a tributary's smaller, more intimate world. Torrential rain drove Henning and Martine under the corrugated metal roof with Renaldo and his deckhands. When the sun reappeared, the honeymooners found a semblance of privacy behind crates stacked on the ship's stern.

The yellow sun dress Henning had given her left Martine's upper chest and back bare. He hurried to their cabin, then returned and handed her a bottle of peppermint oil to repel the mosquitoes that came out when the sun went down.

"Will you please put some on my back?" she asked.

He spread the tangy smelling oil on the exposed skin she couldn't reach. Martine didn't object when he applied another coat.

Reflecting from the river, the setting sun's rays bathed the ship in soft light as she backed into him and snuggled closer. Resisting the urge to wrap his arms around her, Henning froze. Anything he said or did could ruin the moment.

The following evening they were again shielded behind the cargo on *Amazonas'* stern.

"Those would look wonderful in my garden. What are they?" Martine pointed to large trees, their trunks held above the water line by aerial roots resembling spider legs.

"I'm pretty sure they're mangrove trees."

When a swarm of mosquitoes enveloped *Amazonas*, Henning and Martine repeated the previous night's routine. This time he rubbed the oil in more thoroughly and she snuggled against him sooner. A breeze tucked the thin sun dress between her legs. Looking down, Henning saw the outline of her stomach and thighs. And their enticing junction.

"You're different when relaxed," she said, doing nothing to spoil his view. "Lately our conversations remind me of the ones we had back when we went riding together."

"Me too."

"In one sense, we're not truly man and wife yet." Her breathing was shallow, faster. "Regrettably, I don't know what to do. My fiancé was very rough and in a terrible rush. All I remember is that it hurt and left me pregnant."

Henning hugged her tighter.

Darkness came fast on a narrow river between tall trees. A sudden downpour drove them under the corrugated metal roof they'd shared with Renaldo and his men during previous rains. But tonight Renaldo was in the wheelhouse and his men were in their shelter.

Lightning periodically illuminated the huge raindrops, and the metal roof made them audible. Anonymous in the inky blackness, Martine expanded on what she'd said previously.

"After the abortion, Daddy did everything he could to make sure I didn't further risk my reputation. He sent chaperones wherever I went and drummed the fear of syphilis and damnation into me. From that day on I did as he wanted, but for my reasons—not his. I was certain my fiancé had lost interest because I was no good at lovemaking."

In a bright flash of lightning, Martine's face resembled cold hard marble, but her eyes sparkled with excitement. When the rain stopped she led the way to their claustrophobic cabin. Inside, Henning untied one end of his hammock, creating space for them beside her bed.

He lit and dimmed the lantern. Then, hands on Martine's shoulders, he turned her away from him. She tensed as he unbuttoned her dress. Sensing he was moving too fast, he sat beside her on the tiny bed and gathered her in his arms. When she relaxed, he eased her back until she was flat, then knelt on the floor and ran his fingers through her hair.

The worst of her tension faded though he still saw her vulnerability. She didn't fear physical pain, as her courage in the Wrath of God had shown. But she had fastidiously kept her emotions—and him—at arm's length since their marriage. Now that buffer was gone and she was available.

"Roll over," he said. "I'll rub your back."

When she was face down, he opened her dress and uncorked a bottle releasing the faint aroma of coconut oil. Once applied, it left a sheen that highlighted the lithe muscles bracketing her spine. He massaged her neck and shoulders. Then—thumbs near her backbone, fingers wrapped around the curve of her ribs—he worked his way down her backbone.

When he reached the small of her back, Martine stiffened. Bypassing her buttocks and thighs, Henning surrounded a calf with both hands, gently probing its firmness.

Later as he worked his way higher, she tensed again.

Reversing directions, he said, "You have an exquisite body."

"If only that were true." She rolled over, hands covering her breasts. "Thank you for the compliment, but I'm skinny."

"How can you not know how gorgeous your body is? I prefer it to the so-called full-figured women that painters glorify. Will you be more comfortable if we stop here for tonight?"

"No, I don't want that," she said.

Martine dimmed the lantern further, then slid her dress down and kicked it off. In the tropical heat she wasn't wearing the layers of undergarments he'd expected—just pale blue pantalets and a matching camisole.

Henning reached for her jade amulet's chain.

She clutched it, explaining, "It only protects me if I'm wearing it."

Henning took off everything but his drawers. They were knee-length and no more revealing than a swimming suit, but she shut her eyes. Now naked, he crowded onto the cot beside her. Wrapping her in his arms he rolled over, putting her on top. When they kissed, Martine's lips were hard and tightly clamped. The next time they were slightly open. The time after that they were loose and soft.

Spreading her legs she slid downward. Her eyes flashed as their most intimate parts touched. Henning felt heat and dampness. Reaching around her, he unlaced the garment covering her chest. She pressed against him, concealing her breasts but not the scent of lilac cologne between them.

"I'm ready," she breathed, interlacing her fingers with his.

After a sudden indrawn breath Martine's face assumed its usual dignity. Henning would have preferred to see and hear her pleasure. Striving to be gentle, he didn't get as lost as he liked. But what the moment lacked in power and abandon was made up for by its sweetness.

******

Brazil's travel posters featured macaws and toucans. But the majestic egrets appealed more to Martine. Up to four feet tall with a four-foot wingspan, they were most beautiful in flight, but also fascinating while standing on one long leg in the river's shallows or stalking their prey with measured strides that produced no ripples.

They entered schools of fish stealthily—not alerting them until the first was impaled. Then they danced like jugglers on stilts, flipping their victims in the air before swallowing them headfirst.

At sunset a week after first making love, Martine and Henning saw a large flock of the snow-white birds. They flew over *Amazonas*, legs trailing, necks collected into s-shapes. Then changing direction in perfect unison, they headed for a tree and spread out before gliding in to land from all sides.

"They've paired up," Martine said, pressing her hip against Henning.

"Must be mating season." He slid one arm around her.

Next morning at *Amazonas'* rail, Martine told Henning, "I've seen trees—mangroves for example—that I'd love to have in my garden. I'd take seedlings home if I thought they'd survive."

"I doubt tropical trees would do well in the desert," Henning said, "but egrets would."

"I couldn't bear to confine them in cages and feed them in bowls."

"We could put in a lake stocked with frogs and turn them loose in your garden."

"Seriously? Where would we put a lake?"

"Between the willows and the irrigation ditch. Losing a little farmland is a small price for an aphrodisiac with such a powerful effect on you."

"I assume you're referring to what happened after we saw that flock last night. What did you do differently? I didn't notice anything new, but…" Her afterglow reappeared.

"Last night was special because you finally let yourself go."

"I've always thought certain delights are reserved for men." Martine looked up at him. "Apparently they're also available to women lucky enough to find the right man."

Captain Renaldo coughed, announcing his arrival.

"Can egrets be caught without hurting them?" Martine asked.

"Those long legs are easily injured," Renaldo replied. "Aside from that, egrets are hardy, though I wouldn't recommend hiring inexperienced people to capture them. They have a long reach and bills as sharp as daggers. I once saw one slam its beak through a hardwood oar."

"Can you find someone to catch a few for us?" Henning asked.

"I don't know. I've seen them shot but never captured alive."

Martine winced. "How awful. Why shoot such beautiful, harmless creatures?"

"During mating season," Renaldo replied, "they grow those plumes used on ladies' hats and are slaughtered by the hundreds. Ounce for ounce their plumes sell for more than gold. I imagine the locals could take them alive, and it shouldn't be difficult at night. Like most birds they can't see in the dark. How many do you want?"

Eyebrows raised, Henning turned to Martine. "A dozen females and two males?"

Martine nodded, adding, "They'll also need frogs to eat during the voyage to Peru."

"I'll see what I can arrange." Renaldo crossed his fingers behind his back where only Henning could see. A romantic, he must have overheard their conversation about aphrodisiacs.

"I hope," Martine said after Renaldo strode away, "this won't get frightfully expensive."

"It'll be worth whatever it costs. Your face is glowing like it did last night."

She leaned close and whispered, "If you saw more than my face, I'll never let you leave the lantern on again."

******

At a restaurant in Macapá, back at the river's mouth, Martine and Henning were partway through breakfast.

Lifting the cover from a wicker basket between them, she said, "I'm told these rolls are so tasty because they're baked over wood that produces fragrant smoke. Our honeymoon has been full of delightful new experiences. Wish it wasn't ending."

"It doesn't have to," Henning replied. "Where would you like to go next?"

"Can you take more time off?"

"Enough to do anything you want."

"I've always been curious about the place where you got your start."

"Germany?"

"No, San Francisco."

"Despite what you said about not liking cities?"

"I've always imagined San Francisco as special."

"It was when I was there. I'd love to see what it looks like now."

"But if we go, what will we do with the egrets?"

"Ship them to Toledo," Henning said. "Encinas can make sure they're well taken care of until we get home."

"Without us to look after them, they'll never survive the voyage."

"They will if we provide incentive."

Later under Macapá's broiling sun, Henning bought Martine a parasol in an open air market. It was across her shoulder—blue silk dome rotating one way then the other—as they left a cab and entered a freight company that specialized in transporting wildlife. The spinning stopped when Martine heard the cost of shipping her egrets.

Her breath warm in Henning's ear, she whispered, "Negotiate a price that doesn't make me feel so extravagant."

"Sorry but your wish can't be my command this time," he said quietly, then told the agent, "I want the first mate to oversee the egrets' care and will give him a sizable bonus for every one that reaches Cortéz alive."

"I'll tell him," the agent said.

"May I please speak with him?" Martine asked.

"He's not here," the agent replied, clearly opposed to female meddling.

"In that case, we'll come back later and take him to lunch," Henning said firmly.

As they waited for their food that afternoon, Martine described the care and feeding of egrets and the first mate took notes.

"They'll get the best treatment possible," he promised, getting up to visit the washroom.

"Do you trust him?" Martine asked in his absence.

"Absolutely," Henning replied. "He wants that bonus."

When the mate returned, Henning started to give him an unsealed envelope addressed to Encinas Peralta. Changing his mind, he handed it to Martine and said, "I drew this map last night so Encinas will know where to put the lake and what size to make it. Do you want any changes?"

She studied it and replied, "Looks perfect. Thanks for asking."

"No need to thank me. It's your hacienda, too." Henning passed the envelope to the mate and said, "Give this to whoever picks up the egrets in Cortéz."

CHAPTER TWENTY-ONE
THE MIRACLE TREE

When California-bound fortune seekers crossed Panama during the gold rush, they had to hike, ride mules, and paddle canoes for a week. Henning and Martine made the trip in five hours on a railway built to help that route compete with Nicaragua's Vanderbilt Road. The journey's hardships were gone—replaced by padded seats and a drink cart full of tinkling glasses, pushed by a steward wearing white gloves and a pillbox hat.

Soon after leaving the Atlantic Ocean behind, Henning leaned against one of their car's windows and fell asleep. Martine moved across the aisle to join a priest. They were still talking when the train slowed and Henning woke to a view of Panama City and the Pacific Ocean.

"That priest was at the San Francisco mission for years," she told Henning as they left the depot. "Hearing his stories made me all the more eager to see California."

At the dock where ships once picked up men hoping to strike it rich, they boarded a passenger liner of a radical new design. Not many years after having proven superior to clipper ships, paddlewheel steamers were already being replaced by deep-hulled vessels with underwater propellers.

"What got you interested in San Francisco?" Henning asked as he and Martine unpacked in their cabin.

"A book about Junipero Serra, the priest who founded California's missions," she replied. "Fascinating man. I would love to have met him."

Leaning on the deck's rail as their ship left the harbor, they watched porpoises jump back and forth across the bow's wake. When the playful mammals swam away, Martine yawned and said, "Time for my nap."

Wide awake after sleeping on the train, Henning didn't want to lose her company and began telling tales of the gold rush. She chuckled at his versions of characters' accents.

"Sean O'Reilly was an Irishman," he began another story, "capable of using the English language's most objectionable word as a noun, verb, adjective, and adverb—sometimes all in one sentence. He didn't even realize he was doing it. His daughter's friend, Hope, came to dinner one night and while they ate O'Reilly said, 'This is the best effing beef I've had in months.'

"'I'm not allowed to listen to that kind of language,' Hope said and scurried out the door.

"'Putrid mouth,' O'Reilly's daughter chastised him.

"He stared at her and in his thick brogue complained, 'What the eff did I say?'"

Encouraged by Martine's laughter, Henning continued. "Another time, O'Reilly sidled up to a pair of hefty ladies of the night in a saloon. Hearing their accents, he asked, 'Are you lassies from Scotland?'

"One glared and snapped, 'Wales you bloody idiot, Wales.'

"'Allow me to rephrase that,' he said, then calmly took his revenge. 'Are you whales from Scotland?'"

******

Once an outpost, months from the East Coast, San Francisco had become a metropolis served by a transcontinental railroad that brought people from New York in ten days. Most *Californios* had lost their land to squatters. Indians had all but disappeared—victims of starvation, bounty hunters, and white men's diseases against which they had no immunity. Caucasian women and children were plentiful. Gold was mined by *hydraulicking* with high-pressure water hoses that pulverized entire hillsides, creating rivers of mud that sometimes buried crops in the valleys below.

"You would have loved the old San Francisco," Henning said the afternoon they arrived.

"I love it now," Martine replied.

And he loved the way she thrived in the city's pleasant temperatures and reveled in its vitality. Peru's heyday was long gone, but California's was in full bloom. Lima's historic landmarks were centuries old. San Francisco's were so young she could remember what she'd been doing when they were built.

That night Henning took her to the California Theater to hear Agnes Schmidt, considered the finest *prima donna assoluta* alive. During intermission they stepped outside for fresh air and instead found men smoking.

Wrinkling her nose, Martine suggested, "Let's go across the street."

On the opposite sidewalk, a row of A-shaped signboards advertised other theaters.

Glancing at them Martine asked, "Why isn't there one for the Jenny Lind Theatre? I want to go there so I can see the mahogany you imported."

"Unfortunately it went up in smoke," he replied. "Tom Maguire rebuilt the Jenny Lind three times. Tired of losing it in fires, he finally built a sandstone palace beautified with oak bought from someone else. Too big for a theater, it's now City Hall."

"When we get back to Toledo…" she paused, then plunged ahead, "why don't you move in with me?"

Martine had been saving this invitation since their last day on the Amazon River, waiting for just the right moment—which this wasn't. Blurting it out impulsively, she'd caught Henning off guard.

Too bad. If she'd waited for the right time, she could have enhanced a romantic moment—not that they needed enrichment.

******

By day Henning showed Martine the sights. In the evenings they ate in exclusive restaurants and watched famous performers in luxurious theaters.

"Could we go to a ballroom before we leave?" she asked one night as they stood looking down on the city from the Palace Hotel's penthouse.

The night they first met at a party aboard *Daphne,* a guano freighter anchored off Peru's Chincha Islands, Henning had seen how much she enjoyed dancing.

"You can't imagine how uncomfortable I'd feel," he pleaded. "I can't dance."

"I can teach you enough to get by." Martine moved her feet in time with music drifting up the stairwell from the hotel ballroom.

"I hate disappointing you, but I can't make a public spectacle of myself. Could we dance here in our room?"

"Why do you care how you look to people you'll never see again? Have you ever danced?"

"Never in public." Henning quickly changed the subject. "I heard about a fascinating investment opportunity today. I'm going to look into it tomorrow. Care to come along?"

Silently shaking her head Martine watched the moon rise between a church's twin steeples.

"I'm glad we came here," Henning said.

Martine denied him the "me too" he'd sought.

******

California had been settled by risk takers. After the gold ran out, they speculated on land, oranges, Belgian hares, Mexican limes, and silkworms. The latest so-called astonishing opportunity was eucalyptus.

Henning had first heard of the miracle tree when gold rush prospectors brought seeds from Australia and sold them to farmers who needed windbreaks. Now their lofty silhouettes were everywhere and Californians were obsessed with their economic potential.

Stopping Henning and Martine outside their hotel, a huckster in an expensive brown suit launched his pitch.

"Eucalyptus will produce more wealth than gold did," he began. "In Australia it's used to make wagons, ships, and agricultural implements. The oil and resin are perfect for medicines, soap, and scented products. It grows fast and re-sprouts after being cut down, making it ideal for firewood, paper, and cardboard. The Central Pacific and Sacramento Valley railroads plan to use eucalyptus ties. They're also planting eucalyptus to beautify land adjoining their tracks in anticipation of selling it. Shares in tree farms are going fast, but I still have a few."

"I heard that a previous attempt to use eucalyptus ties failed because they crack easily and won't hold spikes," Henning said.

"That little difficulty will be solved by using a different species."

Henning preferred to hear that from a disinterested expert, and that would be better done when Martine wasn't standing next to him, leaning toward the hotel's entrance.

"Little does he know you'd never invest in someone else's tree farm," Martine said as they crossed the lobby. "But you might start your own, right?"

At the registration desk the clerk pointed out two men with their hat brims pinned up on one side and told Henning, "If you're still looking for information about eucalyptus, you should talk to them. They're Australian lumbermen."

After tipping the clerk Henning took a step toward the lumbermen and stopped.

"Go ahead," Martine said, sighing. "Take them to dinner. I'll eat in our room."

******

Well into their meal on the outside terrace, Henning asked the Australians, "Is there a variety of eucalyptus suitable for railroad ties?"

"Why ask us?" the bearded one replied. "This town is full of experts, never mind that none have ever worked with eucalyptus."

"Yanks hear how we use it in Australia," the other added, "and assume they can do the same, but eucalyptus matures slowly. Ours comes from centuries-old virgin forests. No one alive today will see decent lumber from the trees here."

Henning had the information he wanted but was enjoying the lumbermen's enthusiasm and colorful accents, which were more engaging than the stuffy British monotone. He stayed with them until after midnight. Martine was asleep when he reached their room.

The next morning's golden sunlight reflected from east-facing windows as they began their trip home.

"Can you kindly stop at this nursery?" Martine asked the driver partway to the docks.

Returning with a clerk carrying a box of eucalyptus seedlings, she explained, "Souvenirs for my garden at home."

"They'll be a nice addition to your forest," Henning said.

"And dancing would have been the perfect ending to our honeymoon," she chided.

CHAPTER TWENTY-TWO
MATHEMATICAL FORMULA FOR LOVE

"You're dying to know many egrets survived the voyage from Brazil," Henning told Martine as the cab carrying them stopped at Belisario's old house. "You should continue on to your father's house. I'll join you after I finish here."

"I'll send Pedro to help," Martine said as Henning stepped down to the driveway. "He'll be ecstatic to know you're moving in. His not-so-subtle efforts to get me back together with you reminded me of a child trying to reunite estranged parents."

After packing his clothes and personal effects, Henning put the trunks on the porch with his dresser and custom-made, extra-long bed. He was locking the house when Pedro arrived and began loading a wagon.

"See you later," Henning told Pedro as he rode away.

By the time he caught up with Martine, she was in the forest she called her garden, explaining where she wanted a *cholo* to plant her eucalyptus.

Riding in from one of the fields, Encinas called out, "Welcome home." When closer, she pointed to sprawling nests in nearby trees and told Martine, "It's mating season. A worker's son climbed up this morning and found more than enough eggs to replace the two egrets that died on the way from Brazil."

"It's dangerous for children to go near the nests," Martine said. "Mother egrets use their beaks like daggers."

"I made that abundantly clear. Would you like to see your lake?"

Encinas led the way on foot, stepping aside at the last moment to reveal a deep blue expanse of water with a mirror-like surface. After a wind gust, the reflections re-appeared.

"It's even more beautiful than I imagined," Martine enthused. "I love the cattails."

"I had them transplanted from the river to provide the frogs with nesting places."

"Did we send enough frogs?" Henning asked.

"See for yourself." Encinas pointed to swarms of tadpoles wriggling near shore.

"I'd like to start supervising the overseers tomorrow," Martine said. "After being cooped up on a ship for weeks I'm bored silly."

Henning hid his disappointment. Characterizing their voyage home as dull was Martine's third apparent retaliation. After he'd compounded his failure to take her dancing by being absent their final night in San Francisco, she'd lost interest in lovemaking. Then she'd asked him to sleep in another room after joining her in the house where she'd lived during their separation.

Maybe he was overreacting. He'd already seen indications that her lack of interest in intimacy was only temporary. Sleeping alone, however, was another matter.

In a way though, it made sense for them to sleep separately. Their differences were never more apparent than at bedtime. Moments after going full speed, he could fall asleep. But she lay awake, sometimes for hours, if he turned off the lantern before she'd read long enough. He slept deeply, seldom waking before morning. She slept lightly, woke frequently, and often couldn't go back to sleep.

But having her lying next to him was Henning's idea of heaven. And had been even during the voyage home when they'd been alone in the same bed.

******

Henning and Martine were still in separate rooms when the *amancaes* bloomed. He'd read about these wild spider-lilies in Charles Darwin's *Voyage of the Beagle* and had seen them on the hills behind Lima. Nonetheless, he was amazed by the intensely green foliage and greenish-yellow blooms blanketing one of Toledo's hillsides.

Martine's custom was to admire what she called "my *amancaes*" from a distance during the first days of their short lifespan, then pick bouquets for her dinner table and nightstand. On the way to her bedroom the night before she was to reenact her annual ritual, Henning handed her a folded sheet of parchment where he'd written:

'One *amancae* = one loving thought of you.'

"Not that I think it's possible to reduce love to mathematics," he clarified, continuing to his room.

Standing nearby, Martine's faithful maid Chabuca giggled like a nervous schoolgirl.

Martine knew why the instant she opened her door. Vases of *amancaes* covered the floor except for a path to her bed and from there to the bathroom. Masses of stemless blossoms hid her bedspread and the tops of her dresser and nightstand. More floated in the sink and bathtub.

She exhaled a sigh. Henning's grand gesture was well-intended, but aside from her two bouquets, she preferred *amancaes* in their natural setting. He'd clearly had these cut while she was in Cortéz that afternoon. And since they'd been carefully and evenly harvested she hadn't noticed their absence. But in years to come, there'd be fewer *amancaes* because the hundreds in her room hadn't yet borne the seeds that would have produced future flowers.

And now she was supposed to show gratitude, difficult because Henning's well-intentioned surprise hadn't pleased her. Frustrated, she swept the flowers from her bed with both hands, made a backrest of pillows, kicked off her shoes, and made herself comfortable with a book. But her thoughts were elsewhere and by the time she reached the bottom of the first page, she couldn't remember what she'd read at the top.

Filling her room with *amancaes* was typical of Henning's tendency to go too far. He'd worried about the impression he'd make on strangers rather than take her dancing. Then looked into an investment on their honeymoon. And now this lavish effort to get her back in his bed. She imagined him making advances, which she fended off by throwing *amancaes* in his face. The image brought an amused snort.

The thing was, Henning's tendency to overdo also had a positive side. Who else would've gone to the trouble and expense of bringing egrets to Toledo and providing a lake instead of cages?

A vase of *amancaes* in one hand, she knocked on the door of his room.

"Who is it?"

"Your wife."

"No need to knock. You're always welcome," Henning teased.

He was in bed, propped up on an elbow, a book on the mattress in front of him.

"You were right." She raised the vase as if for a toast. "There is a mathematical formula for love."

"It would have taken a thousand times more *amancaes* to show how much I love you," Henning said. "But I knew you wouldn't want me to harvest that many. And since the flowers I cut hadn't yet gone to seed, I bought enough to replace the ones they would have produced."

"You thought of everything. And you know me better than I thought. May I join you?"

"Please do."

Early next morning, rich golden sunshine greeted Martine as she opened the curtains.

"What a glorious day," she announced.

"And waking up together with you," Henning said, "makes this one extra special. Did you sleep well?"

"Well enough. May I have Pedro move my clothes and dressing table in here today? He'll be more than delighted to see us in the same room again."

"Why don't you have him bring your bed too? You'll sleep better without me thrashing around next to you."

Eyes wide with mock surprise, she said, "That's a promising compromise. Would you consider another?"

"Of course."

"I've arranged for Encinas to begin my accounting lessons, which should help me see Toledo through your eyes. In return, will you please discuss future decisions with me before finalizing them?"

"Absolutely. And when we don't agree I'll do everything possible to meet you halfway."

******

In September, 1875, Henning reached his loading dock in Iquique on a dilapidated side-wheel steamer. Disturbed by the ship's noisy arrival, lustrous black sea lions sunning themselves on the adjoining beach galloped across the sand on their flippers and slithered into the water.

At the bottom of the gangplank, a surprised Eduardo greeted Henning in his usual pungent style. "If you sent a letter saying you were coming, you got here before it did."

"I came on short notice," Henning explained. "The government is preparing to nationalize nitrate exactly as it did guano. And for the same reason…money."

"I heard that rumor too."

"It's not a rumor. Congress just passed the Nitrate Nationalization Act. The mines are to be confiscated as soon as the army arrives to do the dirty work. The government will compensate the owners with bonds."

"And by the time they mature, the treasury will be empty," Eduardo said angrily. "You'll lose three million dollars even if they don't take your wharf and loading facility."

CHAPTER TWENTY-THREE
THE BAD SIDE OF WAR

Weeks later, one of the Peruvian navy's ironclads tied up at Iquique's municipal wharf and the national army band silently marched ashore, instruments in hand. Facing the ship they launched a stirring rendition of the national anthem. As the last notes faded, soldiers along the ship's rail shouted, "Long live Peru," and Minister Raul Rubio strutted down the gangplank.

An honor guard, holding Peru's flag high, escorted Rubio's carriage to the town's best hotel while marines and military matériel streamed ashore. Formerly Peru's Minister of Guano, Rubio was now Minister of Nitrate. After his speech from the hotel balcony, he sat for newspaper interviews in the lobby.

The following morning he set out for the nitrate mines on horseback, leading columns of cavalry, infantry, and artillery.

******

Iquique's Horseshoe Bar had a wall thermometer near the lavatories. Customers usually gathered there to discuss the weather, but today everyone's attention was on the man who had breezed in with a satchel and stood on a chair to announce, "I'm Fidel Alonso, a reporter for Chile's *El Corvo* newspaper. I came here directly from the ship that brought me because it leaves for Valparaiso in two hours and I have to dispatch my first article with it. If any of you are dispossessed Chilean mine owners, I want to pass your stories along to people back home."

Halfway out the door, Henning spun around and followed Alonso to a table, then said, "I'm Prussian—not Chilean. I own Salamanca, a nitrate mine that's about to be confiscated, and I'd like to know what to expect. May I eavesdrop on your interviews?"

"As long as you're quiet. I only want to hear from Chileans." Alonso took blank paper from his satchel and opened an ink bottle, releasing a tangy metallic smell.

"My name is Óscar Dimas," a man introduced himself. "Like most of the Atacama's nitrate miners, I'm Chilean. The goddamn Peruvians seized my mine yesterday. I'll be glad to help you tell the world about those thieving sons of whores."

"What happened when the soldiers reached your mine?" Alonso asked, pen poised as Dimas sat down between him and Henning.

"An artillery unit surrounded my property and loaded its cannons. Then armed soldiers escorted Raul Rubio to my office and he gave me a half-hour to pack my personal belongings. Thirty minutes later a sergeant brought one of my horses as if it was a favor and threw me off the mine I built from nothing. He wouldn't even let me put one of my own saddles on my horse. All I have left after sixteen years of hard work is that horse, the clothes I'm wearing, and the contents of a satchel. I lost my machinery, wagons, house, furniture…Raul Rubio is the most heartless prick God ever created. He even hired my administrators and workmen."

By the time Dimas finished, angry men were standing five deep around the table.

"This morning *El Corvo* ran a caricature of Minister Rubio," Alonso told his audience.

His flat cheeks wrinkled with amusement he handed a newspaper to Dimas, who snickered and passed it on. When it got to Henning, he saw a drawing of a man with unruly eyebrows and prominent ears—a club in one hand, a pistol in the other. The caption read:

'Stealing the Fruit of Better Men's Labor.'

Sneering Dimas said, "It should say the fruit of better men's labor and investment."

"Why didn't you clear out rather than risk getting shot or jailed?" Alonso asked. "You didn't have a prayer of stopping an army."

"When you're about to lose everything," Dimas replied, "you can't help hoping for a miracle. Who knows? Maybe the expropriation will be repealed or won't affect everyone. Perhaps God will take pity on you or…"

He threw his hands up in disgust.

******

As a gray dawn turned blue, Henning vaulted the low rock fence and unlocked the door to Salamanca's headquarters. Inside, he took his spotting scope to a window. At this hour he normally watched baby foxes playing near the entrance to their underground den. But this morning his attention was on a cavalry column, flashing in and out of sight as it came toward him across rolling country.

Wind had piled sand against the rock wall surrounding the office. Unable to open the gate Eduardo repeatedly kicked the gritty pile holding it shut. Roaring drunk at breakfast, he was grim and purposeful as the pounding hooves grew louder. He yanked the gate open and faced the accountants behind him, spreading his arms to keep them from scurrying past him.

"Don't let those *pendejos* see your fear," he bellowed.

The cavalrymen stopped in a windswept cloud of dust. Swords scraped the insides of metal scabbards, then glistened with reflected sunlight. Still fresh after the brief trip from last night's camp, the lead horse pranced and pawed the air.

Henning's eyes scanned his flushed accountants as they rushed through the door to the windows, mesmerized by the spectacle outside.

"This will only affect me," he announced. "They'll probably offer to keep you in your jobs, and I won't hold it against anyone who stays."

"Damned if I'll work for thieves," Eduardo growled.

The thump of hard-soled boots penetrated the door. Flung open it crashed against the wall. Soldiers with drawn pistols burst in followed by Raul Rubio.

"Your title please," Rubio demanded.

Having considered Rubio a friend when the man was Minister of Guano, Henning looked him in the eye and asked, "How can you possibly justify—"

"I don't have to justify anything." Rubio held out his hand. "Your title."

Henning handed over a certificate from the safe. Rubio struck a match, then lit two corners and dropped the flaming document on the floor.

"By congressional decree, that title is invalid." Rubio took a paper from his document case. "This is its replacement and that's the current owner." He tapped his finger against Henning's name at the top of the page.

Henning frowned. "I don't understand."

"The Treasury Minister, Luis Guzmán, hasn't forgotten that you voluntarily paid four million dollars in guano taxes after the Chincha Islands War. This is your reward. You now own Peru's only private nitrate mine. Congratulations."

******

Four years later, the War of the Pacific snuck up on its participants. After their mines in Peru were confiscated, Chile's nitrate barons had received permission to work Bolivia's deposits. Later during a dispute over taxes, Bolivia's government seized Chilean-owned Antofagasta Nitrate & Railway Company. The day its assets were to be auctioned off, Chile's army invaded.

Peru was sucked into the conflict by a mutual defense treaty with Bolivia.

After reading that Chilean warships had blockaded Iquique, Henning sailed from Toledo to Arica, then continued on horseback to avoid Chile's marauding navy. En route, he heard that five blockaders had departed leaving two aging wooden vessels to starve the city.

From the top of the cliffs behind Iquique, Henning used his spotting scope to locate the Chilean warships, far offshore beyond range of Peru's coastal batteries. He hurried down the road and across town. With no freighters coming or going, his loading dock was deserted except for Eduardo's parked carriage.

He swung the office door open.

"You made a long trip for nothing," Eduardo said from behind his desk. "Luis Guzmán can't help us this time. Only Peru's navy can do that, and I doubt the admirals have the balls."

"Where are your sympathies?" Henning asked.

"Is that why you came? You don't trust me? Well, I don't side with Chile or Peru. My loyalty, as always, is to you."

"I didn't doubt that for a second. I was just thinking that being Chilean puts you in a difficult position."

As the sun appeared to slide into the ocean, Eduardo left Henning at his usual hotel. The lobby was deserted except for the desk clerk. Also serving as janitor, he was sweeping.

"Welcome back, *Señor* Dietzel," he greeted. "You'll have our best room as soon as I clean it. Would you like to eat dinner while you wait?"

In the dining room, the cook—doubling as a waiter—told Henning, "Thanks to the blockade, I can't offer a choice. You'll have to take what you get."

"That'll be fine," Henning said.

The customer at the next table was served a questionable stew.

"Precious little meat in here," he complained.

"Blame the blockade—not me," the cook snapped.

Henning's potatoes and steak were served by the manager, who often embarrassed Henning with special treatment. He'd evidently decided that only someone important could have kept his nitrate mine when everyone else lost theirs.

Henning cut the steak in two and passed half, on a saucer, to the man at the next table.

******

In his office on the wharf, waiting for Eduardo's return, Henning heard a commotion and hurried outside. Stampeding from town, a mob spread out as it charged toward the beach. The men in front rampaged onto Henning's dock, pushing and shoving to get the best views.

Both wooden-hulled blockaders, *Virgen de Covadonga* and *Esmeralda*, had come closer. Two huge ironclads, belching rolling black clouds, bore down on them.

"The Chileans will turn tail," a man shouted. "They're overmatched."

"No," an army sergeant bellowed gleefully. "The damn fools are going to fight."

The crowd roared with anticipation.

"What's going on?" Henning asked.

"The ironclads are ours," the sergeant said, "*Huáscar* and *Independencia*. They'll make short work of those Chilean antiques."

Hit by cannon fire *Covadonga* headed for the open sea pursued by *Independencia*. *Huáscar* stayed behind to deal with *Esmeralda*. Through his spotting scope Henning saw one of *Esmeralda's* cannon balls bounce off the Peruvian vessel's armor.

The Chilean crew positioned their corvette in front of Iquique and zigzagged, making her a difficult target and forcing *Huáscar's* gunners to risk hitting their countrymen on shore. One of the ironclad's cannonballs tore into a wave near Henning's wharf.

With *Esmeralda* now in range, Iquique's shore battery opened fire and scored a hit, bringing black smoke from *Esmeralda's* stack.

"She won't be so nimble after losing a boiler," the sergeant rejoiced.

Having fired numerous times and scored only a minor hit, *Huáscar* resorted to ramming. With the vessels still in contact, a handful of Chileans stormed aboard the ironclad. The rattle of small-arms fire was followed by silence.

At close range *Huáscar* raked the Chilean vessel with grapeshot and backed off. Her captain must have thought the sailor climbing *Esmeralda's* mast would raise a white flag. Instead he nailed up a tattered Chilean red, white, and blue.

Then a faint "Long live Chile" came across the water.

Another volley left *Esmeralda* in flames. Rammed again, she sank.

Sickened by the joyful cheering, Henning watched *Huáscar* rescue the survivors before steaming off to join *Independencia's* pursuit of *Covadonga*.

"Wish I could be there when they catch her," the sergeant bellowed.

Still celebrating, spectators along the beach headed for town. Henning stayed behind, glad Huáscar had won but sorry for the Chileans who'd died. Esmeralda had fought with Peru against Spain during the Chincha Islands War—which explained why Huáscar had so diligently rescued the survivors.

All night, Iquique's residents celebrated with fireworks and alcohol. The next day their joy turned to horror when word came that *Covadonga* had lured *Independencia* onto a reef. Then shot her to pieces while she was hopelessly stuck.

Esmeralda had been avenged with cruel irony. During the Chincha Islands War she'd captured *Covadonga* from the Spanish. And now *Covadonga* had destroyed Peru's finest warship, quite possibly changing the war's course and definitely erasing Henning's sympathy for Peru's former ally.

By September, 1880 the Chileans had captured Iquique and swept the Peruvian navy from the sea. Next, General Patricio Lynch sailed his troops around Peru's heavily defended south and landed in her vulnerable north. His announced purpose was to stop overland shipments of foreign arms and cut off tax revenues from sugar growers, who were almost single handedly financing Peru's war effort.

But quoting unnamed spies, Peru's newspapers accused him of planning to fill Chile's war chest with money extorted from landowners in wealthy areas such as the Chiriaco Valley.

******

In a hurry to deliver his news, José Geldres pushed Emisario hard. Near Toledo he slowed the little chestnut and lit one of his custom-made, hand twisted black cigars. He smoked half, then snuffed it out and was chewing the rest when he saw Henning riding toward him.

"This morning," Geldres said as they stopped side by side, "I spoke with refugees in Cortéz. They say General Lynch is working his way toward the Valley, collecting *cupos*." Seeing Henning's puzzlement, he added, "A *cupo* is money paid to stop the destruction of something."

"We called it protection money in San Francisco." Henning stiffened with outrage. "It was collected by the lowest of the low. When I helped Chileans there stand up to a gang that demanded it, I never imagined their government might one day extort it from me."

"If you don't pay, Lynch's men will burn your hacienda."

"Any chance Peru will send troops to protect us?"

"Every available man is defending Lima. We'll have to use our wits. Lynch's troops will also steal horses that tickle their fancy. Fortunately my farm is remote. It's probably not on their maps and definitely not worth their time. I can hide a few of your best animals there."

"I'll have *Don* Belisario send you the ones he wants to save."

"The Chileans will definitely like the one you're riding." *Don* José dismounted, then trudged up to Henning and touched his horse's ear. "If you cut that ligament, this ear will hang pointed at the ground. Military officers are too vain to ride lop-eared horses. But don't disfigure more than one or the Chileans will know you did it on purpose." Geldres spat out a gob of well-chewed tobacco. "Our horses have more to fear from us than from Lynch's men. If this war lasts much longer, we'll have to eat them."

CHAPTER TWENTY-FOUR
CITIZEN OF A NEUTRAL COUNTRY

The arrival of Chile's army was announced by columns of smoke boiling skyward north of Toledo.

"Someone's *cupo* must have been more than he could pay," Henning told Martine.

"Hope that doesn't happen to us," she said.

Henning hated seeing her face furrowed with concern. He'd decided to let Lynch's men burn some of her beloved hacienda. Each time he'd started to tell her, the words had stuck in his throat. He was making the right move but had broken his promise to hear her out before finalizing major decisions.

Next day, the sound of hard-soled boots on Toledo's cobblestone driveway brought Martine to an open window where gauze-like curtains billowed in and out as if the house was breathing in anticipation. Soldiers filed into the yard. A colonel on horseback—sword in hand, blade resting on his shoulder—rode to the porch and ordered his bugler to blow a summons.

Martine watched Henning step outside to face rows of armed men and a round-shouldered colonel with skin the color of a dried carrot and a tight collar that pinched his neck into a stack of wrinkles.

"Greetings from Commander Lynch," the colonel said. "My name is Agustín Talavera. And you are?"

"Henning Dietzel. I own this hacienda."

"Have *Señor* O'Higgins come outside with his hands up."

Already at the door O'Higgins opened it and presented himself, hands raised. After frisking him, a sergeant confiscated his pistol and took him back inside at gunpoint. The fact that Talavera knew about O'Higgins meant he had a local informer.

Confirming Henning's suspicion, the colonel said, "I understand you were in California during the gold rush. Commander Lynch was also there. Perhaps you met him?"

"Wish I'd had the pleasure."

"I'm sure you do. His friendship would be useful right now." Talavera consulted a notebook. "Toledo has been assessed a hundred thousand dollar *cupo.*"

"I'm a citizen of a neutral country and have documents to prove it. You've no right to ask me for anything."

"I'm not asking. I'm demanding."

"Chile started this war because its people were mistreated in Bolivia. My government likewise will react to abuse of its citizens."

"You're wasting time *señor,*" Talavera blustered. "We destroyed a railroad because its English owner refused to pay his *cupo*. If we're not afraid of the British, we definitely won't pee down our legs at the mention of Prussians. Pay or we'll burn your hacienda."

"I can replace everything here for a fraction of what you're asking."

"Don't be ridiculous. Your mill alone is worth that much."

"Not any more. It's worn out. I'll have to build another even if you don't burn it."

Martine stepped away from the window, then reappeared in the doorway and stepped onto the porch, a storm brewing on her face.

"*Señora* Dietzel I presume," Talavera said. "Evidently she wants to discuss something before my men light their torches. You have five minutes."

A sergeant herded them to the living room and stood in the entryway.

"You broke your promise," Martine whispered through clenched teeth.

"You're right. I should've explained what I'm doing."

"Explained?" she fumed. "You said you'd ask my opinion before finalizing decisions. This is a terrible time for my world to go up in smoke. I missed my last two monthlies. I'm pregnant."

Because she was past child-bearing age, Henning hadn't expected children.

"Why didn't you tell me?" he asked, hiding his joy from the sergeant.

"It would have been cruel to raise your hopes for nothing. I wanted to be sure."

"Three more minutes," the sergeant broke in.

"The mill is nearly worn out," Henning whispered. "I'll have to replace it even if the Chileans don't destroy it."

"What if the fire spreads to the house or my garden?"

"I'll make sure it doesn't."

"Can't you just pay the *cupo*?"

"I intend to, but rather than spend money we'll need to put Toledo back on its feet after the war, I'm trying to negotiate a lower amount. When we go outside, act as if this conversation disappointed you."

She didn't have to act. Her anger remained white-hot as the sergeant took them outside, where Henning resumed negotiation with Colonel Talavera.

"If you make an example of me by burning the mill and stop there," he began, "I'll give you thirty thousand dollars."

"Triple that and I might consider it."

"Thirty thousand is everything I have. However, it's gold bars—not paper."

Talavera's interest sharpened.

"My men," he said, "will search the house and garden after you take your gold from its hiding place. If thirty thousand is truly all you have, I'll burn the mill only."

"Do I have your word as a gentleman?"

"Yes, but if you have more money than you admit, I'll take it all and burn your hacienda to the ground."

"Then we have an agreement." Henning left his hand outstretched until Talavera reluctantly shook it, without meeting his eyes.

******

Perspiring in Toledo's dining room, Talavera removed his tunic and draped it over a chair back. While Chabuca—accompanied by a major—went for Toledo's measuring string, Henning and O'Higgins muscled hutches away from a wall. Startled by a sudden metallic clatter, Talavera spun to face it. His jacket had fallen, hitting the floor buttons first.

He was on edge, making Henning's plan dangerous.

Using twine knotted at regular intervals, Henning measured from the corner and from the floor, and marked a now-exposed spot on the wall. When he picked up a meat cleaver, Talavera moved his hand near his holster. It stayed there as Henning hacked plaster off the wall and began chipping away at mortar between the adobe bricks.

"Bring him some proper tools," Talavera ordered Chabuca. Again she left the room under escort. Glaring at Henning, Talavera snarled, "You're wasting time. Keep working."

Henning's progress improved after Chabuca brought a hammer and chisel.

"Come on. Hurry up," Talavera snarled, still not satisfied.

But Henning stuck with his plan. According to Lima's newspapers Chile's most important backer, Britain, had criticized General Lynch's collection of *cupos*. Lynch had no doubt warned Talavera that harming civilians would cost Chile vital English armaments, which should give Henning some latitude.

"Faster," Talavera snapped.

Offering his tools, Henning said, "You're welcome to do this if you prefer." Talavera shook his head.

A chair chattered noisily as Henning slid it across the tile floor, then stood on its seat. Once he'd broken the bricks into pieces and extracted them, he felt inside the cavity and flung his hammer to the floor, shattering a tile.

"*Sangre de Cristo*," he cursed. "I must have measured wrong."

"You've been pissing around too long." Talavera jerked his revolver from its holster.

"Allow me to handle this, sir." A major spoke with deference, but then stepped in front of Henning as if to shield him.

"What's the use of having a pistol if I can't shoot some cretin who's wasting my time?" Talavera bellowed. "Answer carefully, Major Moore. Are we here to make friends?"

Standing at rigid attention, Moore barked, "No, sir."

"Does our mission include practicing gracious manners?"

"No, sir."

"Are we here to mollycoddle people?"

"No, sir."

"Do we have orders to collect *cupos*?"

"Yes, sir."

"So you do understand our mission after all." Glaring at Henning, Talavera growled, "Get it right this time."

"I won't work with you pointing a gun at me." Henning's bluff would fall flat if Talavera smelled fear.

"With you dead I can still find the money," Talavera threatened. "I'll just have my men tear down that whole wall."

"That will take a month of Sundays. It's three feet thick."

"Maybe I'll start by shooting you in both kneecaps."

Martine close behind, Talavera's aide rushed in and saluted. "The cavalry selected the best horses in the stable, sir. Would you like to see if any are up to your standards?"

Talavera holstered his weapon and went outside.

"What went wrong?" Martine asked Henning, exploring her front teeth with her tongue as she always did when distressed.

"Everything's going according to plan," Henning assured before a soldier escorted her out.

O'Higgins stood, then dropped back into his chair when the man guarding him cocked his pistol. In English he asked Henning, "Do you think this fat son of a whore would shoot me?"

The soldier's expression didn't change.

"I don't think he speaks English." O'Higgins said. "An Irish proverb says, 'If you're the only one who knows you're afraid, you're brave.' But you're being unnecessarily brave."

Returning, Talavera looked daggers at Henning. "Your only horse worth a damn has a lop ears. Quite a coincidence I'd say." He lifted the pistol from his holster and cocked it. "Find the money now. No more games."

Henning hammered a square of plaster and scraped the debris away, exposing lighter colored bricks. Removing them revealed a hollow from which he lifted a strongbox. He set it on a table and opened it.

"How much are they worth?" Talavera demanded, staring at the gold bars inside.

Major Moore examined the weight and purity markings. Calculating in his head he replied, "A hair over thirty thousand dollars."

"Have the men search the house," Talavera commanded. "Empty every drawer. Turn over furniture. Break open patched walls. Make certain there's no more money anywhere." Then he told the sergeant, "Organize the men outside and search the grounds."

******

The thought of dirty, sweaty strangers pawing through her personal belongings disgusted Martine. She followed four soldiers up the creaky staircase and into the master bedroom. Hoping to shame them, she stood inside the door. Facing her, a sergeant with shaggy eyebrows leaned forward until his palms touched the wall, trapping her between his hairy arms.

Nauseated by his rancid breath Martine ignored the lecherous gaze probing her body.

"You shouldn't be alone in a room with four men and a bed," the sergeant drawled, lowering his hands. As Martine backed into the hall, he lifted her blue pantalets from the laundry hamper and sniffed them.

She hurried downstairs, neck veins blue and swollen.

In the dining room her terrifying vulnerability was emphasized when she noticed Henning and O'Higgins, tied back-to-back in chairs.

Through a window she saw men outside filling a wagon with gold, silver, paintings, statues, clocks, and jewelry boxes.

"Surrounded by all this luxury," Talavera said, "your father must have been quite the social lion." Buttoning his tunic he ordered Major Moore to select steers for the men's dinner.

"You promised to leave everything but the mill alone," Henning protested with cold fury. "We shook on it."

"I said we wouldn't burn anything but the mill, which we won't. We'll stop barbecuing when your beef is medium rare."

A platoon carried lit torches past the window.

"The fire may jump into the cane," Henning said. "I'll warn the workers' village."

"Send your maid," Talavera snapped.

"I'll saddle her horse." As Henning led Chabuca to the barn he said, "After you warn the workers' village, notify everyone at Belisario's place."

He didn't refer to it as the horse farm because the sergeant had come with them and some of the horses still there were as outstanding as those he'd sent to Dos Palos.

As the Chileans left, embers from Toledo's burning mill floated into a cane field, igniting flames that raced toward Martine's prized trees. Henning, O'Higgins, and every available man dashed into the cane, swinging machetes, their arms flickering in the smoky moonlight.

Roaring like a freight train, a towering reddish-orange wave bore down on their fire break. When the others ran, Henning stayed behind until the heat was unbearable and his throat felt as though he'd inhaled slivers of glass. Reaching the felled cane, the flames burned themselves out.

Henning's relief was premature. From another direction a second fireball forced him and his exhausted crew back into the cane. Compelled to retreat before the job was complete, Henning waited anxiously. He'd done his best to keep his ill-considered promise to protect Martine's garden, but could only watch the fire jump the unfinished break and roll into her trees.

He organized a bucket brigade to bring water from the lake and then flung water into the fire. When its advance slowed, he grabbed a shovel and threw dirt to smother flames and bury hot spots. But by then the fire had consumed dozens of trees, including Martine's orchard.

Barely able to put one foot in front of the other, Henning found her doctoring burns.

"Anyone seriously hurt?" he asked.

"Not here," she replied. "And one of the overseers said the irrigation canal stopped the fire short of the workers' village and horse farm."

"Sorry we couldn't save all your trees."

"You tried harder than you should have. You might have been killed." Fighting an urge to burst into tears, she cleansed his arms and smeared ointment on the burns.

"*Señora*," a worker shouted, rushing toward her. "We can't find the egrets."

"*Dios mío* I hope they weren't burned alive," she said. "Where did you last see them? I'll help you look."

"We'll find them tomorrow." Gently Henning took her by the elbow and guided her toward the house.

Their bedroom was a disaster. Clothes and drawers were strewn everywhere. Stuffing bulged from slits in the mattresses. Martine swatted pillows to fluff them up while Henning put the least damaged mattress on one of the beds.

They lay on it in their underclothes, too warm for sheets or blankets… eager to talk but respectful of the other's need for sleep.

"Are you asleep?" Martine finally whispered.

"Wide awake."

"When did you hide those gold bars in the wall?"

"The weekend you were at Uncle Alfredo's in Cortéz."

"Secretive as always." Martine flashed that mysterious smile that hid more than it showed. "You put on quite an act before paying our *cupo*. You could've found that strongbox and sent Colonel Talavera on his way in ten minutes. Why didn't you?"

"If he'd gotten his money quickly, he would've tried for more."

"He tried for more anyhow."

"Not as hard as he would have without the long, discouraging wait."

"I wonder if our son will inherit your deviousness."

"Even before he's born you call the baby our son. Why?"

"Because he's a boy."

"How can you be so sure?"

"I just am." She rolled onto her side and backed up until her buttocks were nestled between his stomach and thighs. Henning wrapped his arms around her and forgot the fire, the egrets, and Toledo's uncertain future. Despite his broken promise, he and Martine had finally become one. And soon they'd be three.

"Could you have paid the first amount the colonel demanded?" Martine asked.

"If I had we'd lose Toledo. We may anyhow. The Chileans took Iquique last month. If they shut down the mines, our savings will run out before I finish paying off the loan I took out to pay off Cabrera."

"How can we find out what's happening in Iquique?"

"By going there."

"Promise me you won't do that until the war's over." Still facing away, Martine lifted his hand from her stomach and kissed it.

They remained snuggled together the next morning when wakened by knocking.

"The *mayordomos* confirmed that no one was seriously hurt," O'Higgins reported through the door.

As his footsteps slowly faded, thumps came from the backyard. Metal rings clattered across the wooden rod as Henning threw the curtains open and looked down from the second floor window. Chabuca was at the clothesline outside, beating dust from the entry hall carpet, soiled by countless soldiers' boots.

"Amazing," he told Martine. "She's already working, as if this is just another day."

"Not another day like yesterday I hope." Martine slid the lower window sash up, stuck her head outside, and shouted, "Have you seen the egrets?"

"No ma'am," Chabuca replied.

A butterfly flew through the open window, landed beside its shadow on the bed, and folded its wings. Henning dressed, then took O'Higgins out to a flowerbed and dug up a canvas-wrapped bundle. Opening it, he handed his bodyguard a pistol and said, "To replace the one the Chileans took. Thanks for the encouragement when Talavera threatened to shoot me."

"An Irish proverb tells us that 'two-thirds of help is to give courage.'"

"How do you remember all those sayings?"

"We Irish are born to remember them as surely as the French are born to cook."

Henning wrapped his new lever-action Spencer repeating rifle inside the canvas and reburied it.

As he and O'Higgins sat down to breakfast Martine asked, "Any sign of my egrets?"

"No," O'Higgins replied, "but the crows are back. That's a good sign."

Martine rolled her eyes. "Crows survive anything. Belisario calls them weeds with wings."

Chabuca served scrambled eggs, cheese, rolls, and coffee before they went outside. The fire had devastated the orchard, leaving blackened tree skeletons. Yesterday the smoke-stained fragments on the ground were mirrors hanging from branches heavy with fruit and nuts. Their flashing had repelled birds. Today birds were staying away from the bare trees on their own.

Martine hurried toward the grove where her egrets usually slept.

"José Geldres's warning wasn't as far-fetched as it seemed," Henning told O'Higgins as they followed. "If this war goes on much longer, we'll be eating horses."

The lake was covered with ash and speckled with bloated, dead frogs. Flames had stripped every leaf from nearby trees, but the branches now held something better.

Martine's egrets.

CHAPTER TWENTY-FIVE
NOT IN MY NAME

The thin, haggard owner of a tiny farm on the Rímac River outside Lima had shown himself to be the kind of man Jesus Christ called salt of the earth. He clearly fed his wife and children more that he ate. And though struggling to keep himself and his family alive, he sympathized with Henning's plight and offered what help he could.

"Since the enemy took Lima, it isn't safe there," the farmer said. "You never know when the Chileans will start burning, raping, looting—even fighting among themselves over spoils. You can stay in the barn until things quiet down. I wish I could offer you meals and a room in my house, but…"

Henning had come in response to Eduardo Vásquez's letter, sent before the capture of Lima. Delivered to Toledo by a smuggler, it instructed him to meet Fernando Gálvez, a courier who would wait in Lima until March first. Worried that Gálvez might depart early, Henning left his horse with the farmer and strolled into Lima as casually as he could manage.

The streets were deserted and people were staying away from windows. Avoiding major avenues, Henning saw no Chilean patrols on his way to a boardinghouse too small to have been commandeered by the occupiers. Fernando Gálvez was in his room. He looked young and innocent but was all business as he demanded the password from Eduardo's letter.

"Coyote holes," Henning said.

"*Señor* Vásquez's report is here." Gálvez tapped his temple. "That way it won't fall into the wrong hands."

The news couldn't have been better. After taking Iquique, Chile hadn't nationalized the mines. Better yet, Henning's was prospering despite the conquerors' taxes.

"Don't let the Chileans know you have a nitrate mine in addition to your hacienda," Gálvez warned. "If you do they'll collect another *cupo.*"

Henning smiled. No one who knew him would waste time advising secrecy.

"Anything else you want to know?" Gálvez asked. "I'm getting out of here before the soldiers start patrolling again. Right now they're busy filling ships with plunder. Everything of value—from machinery in factories to zoo animals—will soon be en route to Chile."

"Tell Eduardo I want his safety to take priority over profits," Henning said.

Hurrying back across town he saw men going house to house trying to buy food. Two had succeeded, barely. One had a papaya, the other a half loaf of dry bread. The Chileans had plundered every market in town.

"Give the National Library a wide berth," a man warned, staring at distant smoke. "I hear the soldiers are burning its books."

"As money hungry as they are," Henning said, "I find that hard to believe. Some of those are priceless."

Was it true? Why would anyone burn irreplaceable books, many of them centuries old?

Henning's love of literature got the best of him.

******

Crates on wagons parked in front of the library were full of leather-bound volumes. In a nearby street, soldiers were tossing armloads of lesser books into towering bonfires.

"This library had copies of every book ever published in Peru," Henning told a sergeant with a single thick eyebrow across his forehead. "Many are one of a kind. Why burn them?"

"Those worth saving will be well cared for in Chile. The rest are taking up space we need for a barracks." The sergeant left, sword swinging in rhythm with his walk.

Later he returned pushing a cart full of books

"I'll pay you to give me those so I can take them to the mayor," Henning said.

Wrapping a hand around the hilt of his sword the sergeant snarled, "Go away or I'll arrest you for attempted bribery."

No one was there when Henning picked up his horse at the farm. He left a thank-you note on the kitchen table along with gold coins to buy food for the starving family that had resisted slaughtering his horse for its meat.

Peru's army had disintegrated, leaving Chile's troops unopposed. On horseback, Henning would have to push hard to reach the Chiriaco Valley before Chile's navy delivered men to plunder that area as they had Lima.

******

Fifteen days into the journey, Henning's horse gave out. While leading the exhausted animal the last hundred miles, he wore holes through the soles of his riding boots. Limping badly, he reached the Chiriaco River near Toledo and found it low enough to cross on foot, allowing him to avoid the detour to the bridge.

Footsore and exhausted he reached his house after midnight and found it dark. The staff was huddled near the staircase. When he asked where Martine was, Chabuca's tears overflowed.

"She's been in bed for two weeks," O'Higgins answered. "Dr. Ávila says she may not get better until the baby is born."

Despite his raw blisters, Henning took the stairs three at a time.

O'Higgins caught up at the landing and whispered, "You should wait until she wakes up. She needs her sleep."

"What happened?" Henning asked.

"Complications with her pregnancy weakened her. When José Geldres gets back with the necessary roots and herbs, Chabuca will prepare some of the tonic that helped Belisario's son."

With the fluid strides of a big cat, O'Higgins brought a chair, blanket, and pillow.

"Why don't you get some sleep?" he suggested. "You're worn out, and Martine will probably sleep for hours."

Later—wakened by his wife's faint call for Chabuca—Henning opened her door. He didn't recognize the pale, hollow-eyed creature who gazed up at him from her bed.

******

With the fighting over, Chile's naval blockade cut off Peru's sugar exports. No-longer-needed workers had gone home, leaving once-bustling haciendas nearly deserted and forcing the Valley's elite to grow their own daily bread. Gardens around their palatial homes now produced vegetables and potatoes instead of flowers and ornamental shrubs.

Though officially at war, Chile and Peru hadn't fought a battle for months. Chile's negotiators had proposed a treaty that would transfer the Atacama Desert and its nitrate to their country. When Peru refused to sign, Chile—her treasury drained—had been forced into an occupation she couldn't afford. Her commanders were feeding their troops any way they could.

Their once smooth patrician hands now rough and calloused, the Valley's landowners stored their first crops in food sheds that fall. With crisp military efficiency, soldiers from Cortéz boarded these up and threatened to shoot anyone who broke in. Then they stripped the orchards and seized all cattle and poultry.

Next their commander announced that he would grant renewed access to the food sheds after his men confiscated half their contents.

******

Henning rode cross country to avoid enemy patrols. The Chileans didn't know about Dos Palos, José Geldres's isolated farm. If he unwittingly led them there, they'd steal *Don* José's livestock, Belisario's horses, and anything else that took their fancy.

Leaving the narrow passageway into Dos Palos's natural amphitheater Henning saw *Don* José crossing a cornfield toward his house. A hoe across one shoulder, he was singing with toneless enthusiasm that echoed from the encircling cliffs.

When Henning reached the porch, *Don* José was scrubbing his hands with a brush and lye soap. Pointing at a pitcher with his chin he said, "You're just in time to help."

Henning poured as Geldres rinsed away the brownish suds. Then they sat in facing chairs and *Don* José lit one of his twisted black cigars.

"What brings you on such a hot day?" he asked, enveloped in his stogie's bluish haze.

"Chabuca's tonic—made with the herbs you brought—has done wonders for Martine," Henning replied, "but her further recovery depends on how well I feed her, and the Chileans are taking half my harvest. Can you find it in your heart to let Encinas, Belisario, and Antonio live here so I'll have fewer mouths to feed?"

"Why don't you have them grow their own food at the horse farm?"

"Because the Chileans will take half."

"I can feed them if they help with the farming. Can they get here without being seen?"

"If they come today. Being good Catholics, the Chileans don't patrol on Sundays."

******

Hastily Belisario closed the door behind them to keep the heat out. The curtains were drawn for the same purpose. In the dim room after hours in bright sunshine, Henning's eyes adjusted slowly. Finally Encinas and her son, Antonio, came in focus, standing near the sofa.

Antonio was tall, thin, and looked bored—as usual.

"We can raise our own food right here," Belisario declared after Henning explained why he'd come.

"If you do, the Chileans will take half," Henning said.

"Who'll care for my horses if I leave?"

"Even if you stay they'll have to fend for themselves. The troops took the last of our hay when they confiscated the cattle."

"If I'm not here when the Chileans run out of beef and start eating horsemeat..." Belisario's voice cracked, delaying his next words, "my bloodline will be gone forever."

Touching the old aristocrat's arm, Encinas told him, "If the Chileans decide to take your horses, you won't be able stop them even if you are here."

"You'll still have the stallions I'm keeping for you," *Don* José pointed out, "and I have room for three more. We'll plant corn and wheat for us and feed them the stalks. That will put eight of your horses beyond the Chileans' reach."

After a long pause Belisario said, "This time I'll take mares."

******

Three days later, soldiers parked a wagon in front of Toledo's food shed. With crowbars they pried off the boards nailed across the door. Hearing the screech of nails yanked from dry wood, Martine rang the bell on her nightstand.

Chabuca rushed in. The only servant still at Toledo, she had stayed behind to care for Martine when the rest of the staff left.

"What's happening?" Martine asked.

"Soldiers are taking their share of our food," Chabuca replied.

"Their share? That's laughable. Help me dress. I want those barbarians to know they're stealing from a pregnant woman."

"Please go back to bed, *señora*. I can't go against Dr. Ávila's orders."

"He's not your boss. I am," Martine declared, shuffling unsteadily toward her armoire.

"*Señor*," Chabuca shrieked.

Dressed by the time Henning rushed in, Martine raised her hand to silence him and snapped, "I'll fight you with every ounce of my strength if you try to restrain me."

Henning draped her arm around his neck and shouted for O'Higgins. The big Irishman met them at the landing and steadied Martine from the other side as she hobbled down the stairs, shakily touching every step with both feet.

Henning carried her outside, one arm under her thighs, the other behind her back. O'Higgins followed with a chair. Pale, eyes recessed in dark hollows, Martine sat glaring at the soldiers. They continued loading, embarrassed but undeterred.

After they left, Henning carried Martine to her room and sat her on the bed. Lifting her legs he turned her so she could lie flat.

"Comfortable?" he asked.

"Yes," she said weakly. "Please leave while Chabuca undresses me."

When he returned, she was asleep.

"She shouldn't be so exhausted," Chabuca whispered quietly. "All she did was sit in a chair."

******

Henning and O'Higgins returned to the shed. Vegetables, wheat, rice, and potatoes were scattered where the soldiers had emptied baskets on the floor. While selecting what they wanted they'd trampled much of the rest.

"Didn't leave much, did they?" O'Higgins muttered.

"And most is in bad shape."

"Martine carries the burden of a difficult pregnancy. The best will have to go to her…and Chabuca, of course."

"If they're hungry enough to eat this garbage."

"They'll eat worse and be glad to get it if Peru doesn't sign a treaty soon," O'Higgins said. "Fortunately we still have horsemeat and honey."

"No, we don't. The Chileans took our beehives yesterday. And when they run out of beef, they'll confiscate the horses."

"Can we hide some?"

"Where?" Henning paused, then perked up. "I could dig a cellar, then butcher some, smoke the meat, and store it there."

After working his garden that evening, Henning slept three hours and snuck outside. In the barn he took up a section of plank floor and started shoveling dirt into buckets and spreading it in fields where no one would notice. At dawn he put the planks back and hurried to his garden so the morning patrol would see him where he belonged.

Stopping by the barn that night, O'Higgins said, "I feel guilty eating Toledo's food without doing anything to replenish it. Let me help."

"I prefer to have you protect Martine," Henning replied. "The soldiers raped a woman last week and Emiliano Cabrera remains a threat."

Henning dug until well after midnight. Finally—too tired to continue or walk to the house—he lay down in a stall.

Wakened by footsteps at dawn, he asked O'Higgins, "Why aren't you looking after Martine?"

"Chabuca will ring the dinner bell if anyone comes near the house," the big bodyguard assured him. "I saw men down here and figured I'd run them off before they saw what you're doing. But they were gone when I got here."

"Were they Chilean?"

"I doubt it. Soldiers would have confronted me. May I make a suggestion?

I'm not overly fond of animals. Why don't you watch over Martine and let me do the butchering?"

"Have you ever done that?"

"You can teach me."

"It's not easy and neither is being a bodyguard. We'd better stick with what we know."

Looking around, O'Higgins asked, "How old is this barn?"

"A hundred years according to Belisario."

Cracks between the adobe bricks were crisscrossed by cobwebs. As they did every morning, spiders were abandoning those and retreating inside the walls.

Henning crossed his fingers. "Here's hoping the spiderwebs hold this place together until I can have it rebuilt."

"Why are the old webs thicker than the new ones?" O'Higgins asked.

After touching some of each, Henning said, "The new ones are sticky. The others are coated with dust raised by my digging."

"So the Chileans are making you work harder to feed your family, and you're making the spiders work harder to feed theirs." O'Higgins shivered.

"Take my jacket," Henning pointed to a coat hanging on a nail. "All that digging overheated me."

"You'll cool off soon."

"Please wear it."

O'Higgins slid the jacket on. Typical of the best bodyguards, he always put others first. Henning had never met a better man or one who'd caused him as much worry. Throughout the war, he'd feared some hotheaded patriot would murder O'Higgins because he was from Chile.

Fortunately Toledo's neighbors admired the big bodyguard for standing up to soldiers who got too close to Martine. They considered him a friend and were spreading the word. But that kind of news traveled slowly among people forbidden to leave their property.

******

To prevent patrols from seeing smoke or smelling burning juniper, Henning sealed the smokehouse cracks with mud. Then, by moonlight, he strolled into the field where Toledo's horses were eating weeds. All but one were racks of bones. The plump exception—one of Belisario's favorites—had been well fed before the Chileans stole Toledo's hay.

The unsuspecting bay was rubbing against a tree to rid itself of itchy, dead hair. A pet, it calmly allowed Henning to buckle a halter on its chiseled head, then followed him on a loose leadline. In the barn, it groaned with pleasure and pushed back against Henning's currycomb.

The floor was littered with clumps of dead hair by the time Henning brushed its coat, telling himself he didn't want the meat contaminated. In truth, he was reluctant to kill such a trusting animal. And after skinning and quartering it, he was bloody from fingertips to elbows, as if to remind him of his sin.

While he worked the garden the next day, Chabuca sliced the stringy flesh into strips and draped them over a fence under the hot sun. That afternoon she put the dried meat on the smokehouse curing rack.

Exhausted after twenty-four hours without sleep, Henning got out of bed several times that night to stoke the fire with fresh juniper. The following morning Chabuca sealed the meat in clay pots and he hid them in Toledo's new cellar.

Hours before Henning was to butcher a second horse, the Chileans drove Toledo's herd to Cortéz. No doubt their patrol had seen how thin the animals were, and their officers had decided to slaughter them before their remaining meat was gone.

Sooner than planned, Henning vented the smokehouse—slowly so the Chileans wouldn't see or smell evidence of what he'd done.

******

Killing one of Belisario's prize horses had been necessary but felt like a sin the day Henning saw the old aristocrat pampering his remaining horses at Dos Palos.

"These are the last of your bloodline," he told his old friend. "The Chileans slaughtered every one of Toledo's other horses for meat."

Losing their horses deprived the valley's residents of more than meat. With no draft animals to pull plows, they had to cultivate their gardens with shovels, which meant working less land. The next harvest would be inadequate even before the Chileans took half.

Expecting little response, Henning called a meeting at Toledo. Without horses, his neighbors had to walk, and he was pleasantly surprised by how many came. At meetings on other haciendas he'd been shouted down for suggesting cooperation with the Chileans. Perhaps people had finally realized his plan was the only alternative to starving.

More likely, they hoped he'd serve something to eat.

Once his guests were seated in chairs on the lawn, Henning stood before them.

"I'm nearly out of seed," he began. "I'm sure most of you are in that same predicament. The solution is to grow food for the Chileans in exchange for seed and soldiers to help plant enough for both their needs and ours."

"Why should we feed those worthless pieces of shit?" a man shouted.

Women ignored the vulgarity. Men cheered it.

The meeting's focus changed when a man held a bottle of *pisco* high.

"Made in my new copper still," he announced. "You'll easily notice the improvement."

Passed from hand to hand until drained of its remarkably clear contents, the bottle was replaced by others. Wives couldn't keep their husbands from drinking too much. When Henning was confronted by two angry, scarlet-faced neighbors, O'Higgins stepped between them.

"You're from Chile," Mateo Malaga blustered. "You probably sympathize with them."

Henning moved in front of O'Higgins.

"Who's protecting whom?" Malaga's pockmarked cheeks inflated and a laugh came out in snorts as he glared at Henning, then said, "If you go to the Chileans in my name, I'll..." Letting Henning imagine the consequences, he chanted, "Not in my name! Not in my name!"

His companion joined in. Rather than let his tormenters assume they'd scared him, Henning resisted the temptation to walk away.

"Not in my name! Not in my name!"

Heads turned as the refrain brought Martine outside. The chanting trailed off.

Last time seen in public, she'd had a flat stomach. Now it stuck out like a shelf. A boy stared and giggled. Martine pressed both hands against the small of her back to help support her suspended abdomen.

As Isabella Arrieta started up the steps, Henning dashed past her and helped Martine into a well-cushioned chair

"Please forgive her for not standing," he said.

"Don't be silly," *Señora* Arrieta replied, a smile on the gentle face she'd powdered extra heavily to protect it from the sun. "I remember what a chore it can be to get up out of a chair in that condition."

Face flushed, her husband appeared at her side muttering. He seized her arm and steered her to the steps.

"What was that all about?" Martine asked.

"It's a bad time to be seen with us collaborators."

Martine gave a little jump.

"What's wrong?" Henning asked.

"Our son kicked me." She verified no one could see and guided his hand to her stomach.

"I don't feel anything."

"You will. He's extremely active today."

"Sounds like you're still convinced our baby's a boy."

"He is. Can't you get that through your thick skull?"

"It hurts when you call my skull thick."

"In your case the words are inseparable." Martine's forehead furrowed. "I wish people hadn't seen me looking like this."

"You've never been more beautiful."

"If only that were true."

Something jabbed Henning's palm from inside Martine. He looked up in wonder. Lips pursed she whispered a kiss.

As the guests left, Mrs. Arrieta waved goodbye until her husband stopped her.

"Look how thin everyone is," Martine said. "I must be the only one here who eats three meals a day."

"That's because you're eating for two."

"No. It's because a thick-skulled man takes wonderful care of me."

CHAPTER TWENTY-SIX
BAD TO WORSE

Henning's long hike across the mountains had become a brutal ordeal. Reaching Cortéz on his last legs, he passed a window. His reflection showed chalky skin stretched across protruding cheekbones under limp, silvering hair. He looked like a beggar and would be fortunate if the commander agreed to see him.

Inside Chilean headquarters, his normally powerful voice rasped as he explained his visit at the front desk.

"I'll see if Major Moore is available," the sergeant said. Boots crisply striking the floor he crossed the room, knocked on a door, opened it, spoke, listened, and waved Henning over.

Partway there Henning passed out.

As he regained consciousness, the major bending over him asked, "You okay?"

"Too much sun," Henning replied through a blurry fog.

"Don't get up. I sent for a medic."

"I'm fine." After standing to prove it, Henning leaned against the wall, dizzy.

"You can rest in my office." The major's clipped moustache was familiar. So were his low-cut boots with long tongues that folded down to cover the laces.

They sat on opposite sides of a desk that held a collection of Charles Darwin's books between elephant-shaped bookends.

"You were with the soldiers who collected my *cupo*," Henning said. "You stepped in front of the officer in charge when he threatened to shoot me."

"I remember. You're Henning Dietzel. I'm Jaime Moore."

"Moore isn't a Chilean name," Henning observed.

"I'm English by race but like many of my countrymen, I settled in Chile. What can I do for you?"

"I have plenty of land and water," Henning began, "but no workers, seed, or animals to pull plows. Provide those, and I'll grow enough food for your men. In return I want seed for myself and my neighbors, along with a promise not to touch our crops."

"Your timing is uncanny. I've been ordered to have my men grow food. But doing that in front of hungry people might lead to bloodshed. If you loan me land so remote no one will know my men are there, I won't confiscate any of your neighbors' food or yours."

"Do I have your word you won't take as much as a grain of rice?"

"For someone dealing from weakness, you drive a hard bargain. But it's a fair one. I'll dispatch a seed requisition to Chile. We'll have to take what we get, but what would you prefer?"

"My wife's doctor recommended asparagus, beets, broccoli, cabbage, and spinach."

"What would you like to eat right now? You look half starved."

"Half? More like three quarters. I'll take anything you can spare."

A medic was examining Henning when the sergeant returned with a freshly baked meat pie. Henning rushed oversize bites to his mouth as the medic examined him and issued the predictable diagnosis: "All you need is three good meals a day."

"Come with me, Sergeant Corbo," Moore ordered. "You're going to Chile."

Moore and Corbo slowed to Henning's speed on their way to the dock where *Almirante Cochrane*, an armored frigate, was building up steam.

"Don't let this wind up under a stack of papers somewhere." Moore handed Corbo the seed requisition. "And make sure everything I ordered is aboard *Cochrane* when you return."

As the frigate shoved off, Moore told Henning, "I can offer you dinner, a cot for the night, and breakfast. In the morning I'll have two of my men drive you home."

"If I'm seen with them, my neighbors will suspect me of collaborating."

"In that case my men will only take you as far as the summit, which will at least save you a long, hard climb."

******

Even on the mountain's downhill side, the hike taxed Henning's remaining strength. By the time he reached the Valley's flat roads, every step was an ordeal. His strides had shortened, becoming irregular, and he didn't dare stop for fear he wouldn't be able to start again.

Having overslept, he'd missed the morning coolness. By now he should have been in his house but was still beneath a sun that seemed brighter every time he looked up. Blinding light bleached the color from his surroundings. Overpowering heat bathed him in sweat. And he'd emptied both canteens without satisfying his raging thirst.

Mile after mile, he saw no movement, heard no birds, felt no wind, and smelled only scorched air. The first sign of life was O'Higgins, jogging across Toledo's parched lawn.

Hands cupped around his mouth, the big bodyguard bellowed, "Martine's having pains again. I'm on my way to fetch Dr. Ávila."

Gathering his remaining strength, Henning shouted, "I'll bring Dr. Carmona, too."

Henning trusted Carmona and admired the man's competence and plainspoken explanations. Ávila minced words and always seemed unsure of his diagnosis.

Wearily Henning forced himself up the porch stairs and the inside staircase, then down the hall. Outside Martine's door he stepped around a pile of bloody sheets and blankets.

Face shiny with perspiration, Martine was on her back under fresh bedding.

"I shouldn't have gotten out of bed the day the Chileans stole our food," she mumbled.

After that he heard only, "…bloody thighs…unbearable pain…terrible mistake…"

"Don't worry." Henning squeezed her hand. "You and the baby will be fine. O'Higgins went for Dr. Ávila, and I'll bring Carmona."

Chabuca followed Henning into the hallway.

"You're exhausted and Dr. Carmona is in Cortéz," she said, closing the door. "Why don't you send O'Higgins?"

"He won't be back for hours, and I want Carmona here as soon as possible."

"At least eat and rest a while."

"I'll eat while I'm walking and rest after I get back."

He sat on the kitchen counter, his back against a cabinet, guzzling water as Chabuca refilled his canteens and put more than his normal ration of food in a cloth bag.

As the sun went down, he kissed her forehead and set out in the fresh night air, feeling the first effects of what he hoped was a second wind.

******

Henning returned in a carriage pulled by the skinny horse Major Moore had allowed Carmona to keep because of his profession. The doctor pulled the animal to a stumbling halt at the porch. Rushing to the front door, Henning landed on every third step. Yanking it open he glanced back. Carmona was close behind, medical bag in hand.

At the foot of the staircase, O'Higgins told them, "Ávila sedated Martine, but after he left she started having contractions."

"It's been too long since I felt normal," Martine mumbled when Carmona asked about her symptoms.

She winced as her abdomen tightened. And again when Carmona touched his stethoscope to her stomach.

Leaning close to Henning, Carmona whispered, "The baby's dead. I hope she's not too weak to push it out."

Henning's unborn child—already a beloved son in his mind—was gone. And the most important person in his world was in danger. He wished he believed in a benevolent God who answered prayers.

Carmona plucked a bottle from his bag and set it on the nightstand. The label read: 'Laudanum. Contains Whiskey and Opium. Overdoses can be Fatal.'

The contractions stopped. Carmona ripped off his stethoscope, then pushed Henning into the hall and panted, "I'll have to cut the baby out of her. Bring every towel in the house and have Chabuca boil all the water she can."

Later Henning charged back into the room and dropped armloads of towels on a chair. Carmona handed him a handful of medical apparatus and a bottle of carbolic acid.

"Clean those thoroughly with the acid and boil them ten minutes," he commanded. "Then drain the water without touching the instruments and bring them to me in the pan."

By the time Henning returned, Carmona had arranged cotton balls, iodine, gauze, thread, and adhesive plaster on a dresser.

"What now?" Henning asked.

"For you, nothing. Chabuca has assisted me before and knows what to do."

"Surely I can—"

"What are the names of those?" Carmona pointed at the kettle Henning had brought.

"A knife and—"

"Chabuca?" Carmona interrupted.

"Scalpel, forceps, artery hook, and surgical needles," she replied.

"You'll only be in the way," Carmona told Henning. "Wait downstairs. Patiently. This will take a while."

On a bench at the foot of the stairs, Henning and O'Higgins grimaced every time Martine shrieked. Covered in perspiration when her screams stopped, Henning bolted up the stairs.

Carmona met him in the hall. Blood splattered and fatigued, he said, "I gave her as much laudanum as I dared, but she suffered horribly."

"May I see her?" Henning asked.

"Very briefly. She needs rest."

Chabuca came from Martine's room carrying bloody sheets and towels. While squeezing past her, Henning saw Martine, chalky white.

Most of her faint words were unintelligible. He understood only, "God took our son…sorry…tried so hard…my fault."

"All I want is for you to get well." Henning knelt beside her bed, too terrified to cry.

Martine's eyes closed as he ran his fingers through her hair. When her breathing had been deep and regular for a while, he tiptoed into the hall and shut the door.

"Martine will die if you don't build her up," Carmona said. "Feed her the best you can, even if everyone else has to go hungry. She won't have much appetite and may be despondent, even suicidal. Something chemical affects the female mood after pregnancies end prematurely. Martine blames herself, which will make her symptoms worse. Whatever you do, don't tell her she'll never again be pregnant."

For the first time Henning wished Carmona believed in softening bad news. Or dispensed it in smaller doses.

✳✳✳✳✳✳

Wakened by the hum of subdued voices, Henning looked down from his second-story bedroom window and saw Major Moore's convoy. Quickly he dressed and stomped his feet down to the bottoms of his boots, then hurried outside, passing O'Higgins who was watching the soldiers from a window.

"I wasn't expecting you so early," Henning told Moore.

"We came at night to avoid being seen. These men were farmers before the war. They'll prepare the ground while we wait for seed. All they need is water and a few secluded *hectáreas*."

A swallowtail butterfly settled on one of their draft horses.

"You'll find plows and harnesses in there." Henning pointed to a shed. "When will the seed get here?"

"Soon. Are you sure no one will see my men?"

"Our neighbors are miles away and have no horses. They don't come around."

"My men won't light campfires or do anything else to give away their presence. We don't want people raiding our crops, and you don't need your neighbors thinking you're a collaborator."

A week later the seed arrived and an ample share went to Henning and his neighbors. Nine weeks after that, they and the Chileans harvested beans followed by tomatoes and corn, then carrots, potatoes, and wheat. In the dead of night, military wagons secretly transported the soldiers' crop to Cortéz.

True to Moore's word, his men didn't confiscate any of what Henning and his neighbors had grown. But after troops in nearby Soria heard that their countrymen in Cortéz were on full rations, a general in Lima ordered Major Moore to take half the food he'd let Henning and his neighbors keep.

Moore did everything possible to avoid carrying out the distasteful order. But the best he could do was steal less than the general intended.

To feed both the Cortéz and Soria garrisons, Moore's men planted twice the *hectáreas* next time. By then someone had seen military wagons leaving Toledo at night with freshly harvested food, and spread the news.

The Chileans responded by surrounding their upcoming crop with sentries and warning signs:

Fusilamos a los Intrusos
We Shoot Trespassers

******

Working his garden in early morning fog, Henning didn't see Jaime Arrieta until the old man was within a few yards. His neighbor's normally bouncy walk had gone flat. Stopping at the split rail fence he leaned on it with both forearms, short of breath.

"Good morning," Arrieta said, lips barely moving. Shiny, tight, gray skin hugged his skull and arms. Like everyone else in the Valley, he was slowly starving to death.

"Come inside. I'll have Chabuca fix you something to eat," Henning invited, then helped his neighbor to the library and sat with him on the sofa.

"It was cowardly of me to stop my wife from talking with Martine at the meeting where you suggested growing food with the Chileans," Arrieta said, eyes downcast. "*Disculpa.*"

"But Jaime," Henning's voice was gentle, "how can I forgive you if I haven't blamed you? People's moods were ugly that day. You did well to keep your distance."

"There's something else," Arrieta said. "If we attack the Chileans, we should be led by you—not Emiliano Cabrera. You've always helped your neighbors. He never has. Not to mention that Martine told my wife you were educated at a military school."

"What attack? What's going on?"

"Cabrera's administrator, Federico García, has organized every able-bodied man in the area—except you—into a militia. He says you're a Chilean sympathizer and are growing food for them."

"The Chileans are farming one of my fields, but not because I'm a sympathizer. In exchange, they provide us with seed and promised to stop confiscating our food."

"García brought one of the warning signs posted around their crops. It said trespassers will be shot. Apparently we're supposed to docilely die of starvation while they steal our food. Over fifty men have taken their rifles out of hiding. García's training them for guerilla war. As friendly as you are with that Chilean major, maybe I shouldn't have told you."

"I hope you're not one of García's guerillas?"

"Not at my age. If you'd been asked, would you have joined?"

"No. Attacking trained soldiers is suicide. Besides, Major Moore's men just planted twice as many acres as before. When they harvest that crop, they'll replace what they confiscated from us."

"You believe that after their broken promise?"

"Why not? Moore already gave us more seed."

"He gave us that so we'll raise more food for his men to steal."

"He's a decent man doing his best to avoid bloodshed."

Arrieta left with a bag of potatoes and vegetables. Henning would have also given him meat but didn't want anyone to know he had it. The Valley's landowners might never fire their dilapidated rifles in anger, but while training they were working their gardens less. Their next crops would be too small for their families' needs.

Who knew what they'd do if they found out about the meat under Toledo's barn?

******

The Chileans clearly suspected something was amiss. They'd increased their patrols, making it possible for each to go over less ground, more thoroughly. Every morning one rode through Toledo confirming everyone was where they belonged. After it passed on a Sunday in 1882, Henning set out for Dos Palos.

On foot, he'd be hard-pressed to get back by morning, and if he didn't the Chileans would arrest him. But Chabuca needed roots and herbs for Martine's tonic. And José Geldres brought a fresh supply from the Andes on the first day of every third month.

After the grueling hike had made his thighs ache as if they'd been clubbed, Henning found *Don* José sitting on his porch, sharpening a machete. The old man tested the blade with his thumb and nodded with approval. Backlit by the sun his translucent red ears contrasted with otherwise pale skin.

"I'm here to pick up the makings for Martine's tonic," Henning said, "and to see if you can spare any food."

Don José filled his lungs and emptied them. "We may lose our current crop and can't spare any. My spring went dry. We're digging a well but it's slow going."

In the distance, Encinas climbed out of a shoulder-deep hole and Antonio took her place.

"Is the boy showing any quality yet?" Henning growled. "He's the youngest person here, but moves like an old man."

"There are times when he works hard enough to make me suspect he's your son."

"Which he's not, thank goodness."

"He's not as lazy as you think. In fact, he's an excellent worker once he gets going."

"How long does it take him to get going?"

Already Antonio was leaning on his shovel, mopping his brow.

"When two men work together," Henning said, tying his bandanna around his brow, "the slower speeds up if he's worth a damn. Let's see what Antonio does."

A shovel in one hand, Henning marched over and dropped in beside the startled boy. He began sending dirt arching over the rim of the hole, without speaking. This was a test—not the start of a relationship.

Antonio sped up. Soon Henning couldn't tell who was accomplishing more. Lungs working like bellows, both shed their shirts. When the kerchiefs on their foreheads could absorb no more, they scraped sweat from their eye sockets with their fingers and kept digging.

The hole was a foot deeper than Henning was tall when he finally slowed, giving in to pain and fatigue. Antonio didn't follow suit. And speeding up to match the boy's pace would take energy Henning couldn't spare. He had to get home before the morning patrol.

"Well done," he said, patting Antonio's back. "Put that much determination and energy into everything you do and you'll go far."

The boy's smile was out of proportion to a simple compliment.

Belisario and *Don* José lowered a ladder. After climbing out, Henning was surprised by Encinas's unusual warmth as they touched cheeks, their usual greeting.

Following Henning to his horse, *Don* José needled, "Who'd you just see in Antonio?"

"He can't possibly be mine," Henning said. "But if he were, he'd work like that always."

"Are you exactly like your father?"

"Once you get a notion in your head, you don't let go, do you?"

"You should ride one of Belisario's horses back to Toledo. You're exhausted."

"No. My heart would break if the Chileans got their hands on another of his horses."

From the road, Henning looked back and saw blurs of dirt flying from the hole. Antonio was behaving like a son trying to impress his father, which seemed to substantiate *Don* José's absurd suspicion.

But if Henning had planted that seed, he'd know it.

He got back to Toledo just ahead of the morning patrol. He'd risked imprisonment to bring food. Instead, he'd have to share what little he had at Toledo.

A week later Henning made an overnight hike to Dos Palos and delivered what he claimed was rabbit. Having often eaten horsemeat, *Don* José must have recognized the stringy meat. But he held his tongue, in deference to Belisario no doubt.

"It did Antonio good to win your contest with him," he told Henning. "He took extra turns digging until we hit water. And when we planted, he was a whirlwind."

******

By the time the horsemeat ran out, the pots under Toledo's barn contained smoked frogs Henning had caught in traps and egrets he'd shot until he could no longer get close enough.

"Rabbit and crow," he'd told Martine, who didn't question his explanation.

Off and on, Henning considered taking everyone who depended on him to Ecuador. Problem was, Martine wasn't strong enough to travel hundreds of overland miles and Chile's navy was sinking blockade runners.

Every night, exhausted by work and worry, Henning fell asleep so quickly it felt like passing out. In the mornings he regained consciousness more than woke up. He was burned out, used up. In the mirror he saw a man ageing before his time. His despair increased every morning and evening when—on Dr. Carmona's instructions—he forced himself to read to Martine.

So far, there'd been no sign she heard him.

CHAPTER TWENTY-SEVEN
THE RANSOM NEGOTIATOR

Early one morning eight months later, Henning found a friend asleep on his front porch.

"Good morning, *señor*," Alcalino Valdivia greeted. His Indian side was more visible, his European side less so. And his black hair was graying at the temples.

"It's good to see you," Henning said. "How long have you been here?"

"Ten hours *mas o menos*."

"All night?"

"The house was dark. I didn't want to bother anyone."

"Welcoming you is no bother. Come in. Chabuca's cooking breakfast. It's almost ready."

Until recently, another mouth to feed would have been the worst possible news, but things had changed. Henning's garden was producing generously. Numerous trees in Toledo's orchard had recovered from the fire and their branches were heavy with fruit and nuts. The Chileans were feeding themselves. And José Geldres's new well was producing enough water to make Dos Palos self-sufficient again.

Equally important, Cabrera's guerrillas—weary of playing soldier— had gone back to working their gardens. And their sudden congeniality showed that they knew Henning was the reason Major Moore provided them with seed and no longer allowed his men to confiscate any of their crops.

As they waited at the dining room table, Henning relieved Alcalino of the obligation to make small talk. "What brings you here? Is something wrong in Iquique?"

"No," Alcalino replied. "Eduardo heard about the food shortage and sent me to help you. How's your new baby?"

"He died before he was born." As Alcalino's mouth formed a silent o, Henning steered the conversation elsewhere. "I get the feeling something bad also happened to you?"

"On my way here I tried to visit *Don* Diego de la Torre in Lima. I had worked up the courage to ask if he's my father but never got the chance. The Chileans have arrested him and are demanding a thousand U.S. dollars for his release."

"Money-grubbing bastards." Henning slammed his fist into his palm. "What did they accuse him of doing?"

"He proudly admits spending the last of his fortune to finance guerrillas in the *sierra*. And because they warned him not to get on the Chileans' wrong side, relatives won't pay his ransom. If you'll loan me the money to do that, you can reimburse yourself with deductions from my salary."

"That won't be necessary. I owe him much more than a thousand dollars."

During Henning's first year on Altamira Island, *Don* Diego had foiled Felipe Marchena's efforts to destroy him and his reputation.

As always when someone important to Henning was threatened, his thoughts turned to Domingo Santa María, the *Californio* he'd failed during the gold rush, the friend he'd been too busy to help.

******

Every morning and evening Henning brought fresh *muña*, a mint-like Peruvian herb, to scent Martine's bedroom, then read aloud while she lay motionless, eyes closed. Physically she'd healed, but she'd lost interest in life and was always asleep—or pretending to be—when he entered her room.

"I think I'll ask Uncle Alfredo to negotiate *Don* Diego's release," Henning told Chabuca when she brought Martine's breakfast on a tray the morning after Alcalino's arrival.

"It would be better for you to go to Lima yourself," was her unexpected response.

"Dr. Carmona said it's essential I read to Martine twice every day, even if she doesn't seem to hear."

"She hears, *señor*, but it isn't helping. Dr. Carmona's prescription isn't harsh enough."

"What makes a gentle lady say that?"

"O'Higgins can explain better than I."

O'Higgins was leaning against the wall outside Martine's bedroom. He listened to Henning's question, then moved farther from the door and answered, "Everyone has a private devil as well as a guardian angel. You're helping Martine's devil get the better of her. She's too sure of you. Go to Lima yourself. Chances are she'll get better if she thinks her withdrawal is driving you away."

"I'm no good at playing hard to get."

"That's because you haven't seen how well it works. Martine has the sadness that afflicts people who no longer want anything. Make her want you."

"And what will the Chileans do if I personally pay *Don* Diego's ransom after swearing it took every cent I had for Toledo's *cupo*?"

"I served in Chile's military. The unit that jailed *Don* Diego is far removed from the one that collected *cupos*."

The following day Henning applied for a travel permit at Chilean headquarters. Denied, he asked for Major Moore's help. Moore took him to an office where the base commander sat behind a desk near a map-covered wall. Flanked by assistants, he held a document and was mulling over whatever he'd just read.

When he saw Henning, he asked, "Isn't this the farmer who helps us grow food?"

"*Sí, comandante*," Moore replied. "He's been denied a permit for travel to Lima and wishes to appeal."

"If I remember correctly," the *comandante* said as if Henning wasn't there, "this man made an agreement with us and kept his word. But General Mendoza didn't let us keep ours."

"*Sí, comandante*."

"Issue a travel permit and arrange passage for him on our next ship to Lima."

"We can't put a foreigner on one of our warships," a junior officer protested.

"Why not?" The *comandante's* tone was such the officer couldn't think of a reason.

Back in Moore's office the major and Henning sat on a sofa.

"I heard about your wife's stillbirth and depression," Moore said. "You didn't deserve that burden on top of so many others."

"Neither did she."

"When we collected your *cupo* I envied you such a spirited woman. And I admired your gentleness with her. I'll light candles for you both in church next Sunday." Moore picked up a letter opener by its blade. Tapping the handle against his other palm, he asked, "Are you aware of how deeply Emiliano Cabrera hates you?"

"He and I are competitors. It's only normal for us to be adversaries."

"He despises you in a way I find monstrous—not natural. Did you know he was training guerrillas until recently?"

Henning looked surprised to discourage Moore from asking for names.

"Cabrera did that," Moore continued, "because I asked him to, hoping to keep someone else from actually starting an insurrection. I wanted the Valley's men busy until I could calm them down by sharing our next crop. Cabrera drank too much one night and told me you'd meet with a training accident if you joined his little army. I'd hire more bodyguards if I were you."

******

After collecting *cupos* and stealing thousands of national treasures, the Chileans had resorted to holding wealthy Peruvians for ransom in a notorious Callao prison. Popularly known as Hell on Earth, it had a reputation for vermin, torture, and untimely deaths. This encouraged its inmates' friends and relatives to part with outrageous sums without hesitation.

Henning met with the ransom negotiator, Colonel Rodolfo Bartolomé, at Chilean Military Headquarters in Lima. Handsome and a smooth talker, Bartolomé was notorious for seducing impressionable young Peruvian ladies. His eyes widened as he saw Henning, well dressed and of good bearing.

They sat together on an imperial settee while a junior officer served tea. Bartolomé's office had formerly belonged to a Peruvian general. Paintings in hand-carved frames on the walls now showed Chilean rather than Peruvian dignitaries. Henning recognized only one, General Patricio Lynch who now ruled Peru and had been nicknamed its 'last viceroy.'

Unaware that Henning knew he'd offered *Don* Diego to Alcalino for a thousand dollars, Bartolomé said, "*Señor* de la Torre was financing men who attacked and murdered Chilean soldiers. I can't release him for less than ten thousand dollars."

"De la Torre is an old man without friends or money," Henning replied coldly. "A month ago you offered him to his illegitimate son for a thousand dollars."

"I can't entertain such a ridiculous offer."

"Then you'll get nothing." Henning stormed out.

Two days later he sauntered into Chilean Headquarters and asked for a second meeting. He thought Bartolomé would make him come back later, to give the impression he was in no hurry to make a deal. But the colonel immediately had Henning brought to his office.

Without rising from the chair behind his ornate colonial desk, Bartolomé said, "*Señor* de la Torre has been transferred to the infirmary downstairs."

"An attempt to worry his family no doubt," Henning said gruffly, then sat on the opposite side of Bartolomé's desk. "As I said before, the only person who gives a damn about him is his son, who works for me. I'll loan him a thousand dollars—not a penny more."

Bartolomé dropped his price to five thousand. Henning crossed the room with long strides and reached for the doorknob.

"Prices are determined by demand," he said over his shoulder. "If *Don* Diego had any value to anyone besides his son, he'd have been ransomed long ago."

"Would you like to see him?"

"Trying to soften my heart is a waste of time." Henning opened the door. "He's an old man I scarcely know. I'll pay a thousand dollars and take him with me right now. But first you'll have to prove he's alive."

"With pleasure. Come with me."

"Why? I'm not interested in listening to him beg." Henning strode to the window and looked down at the exercise yard. "Have him brought outside. I can see him from here."

CHAPTER TWENTY-EIGHT
COMING APART AT THE SEAMS

Diego de la Torre was stern, formerly wealthy and powerful, and as decent as any man anywhere. Looking older than when Henning last saw him, he shuffled out of Chilean Headquarters, the lower half of his face obscured behind a beard, his body engulfed in a baggy, worn-out brown suit that had once fit perfectly.

Henning drove closer and dismounted from his carriage. Before he got to the other side, *Don* Diego had struggled aboard.

"I hope you jewed those bastards down," he said, edges rough as ever.

"I'd be Peru's richest man," Henning replied, "if all my negotiations were as successful."

"Good." *Don* Diego cackled. "Who'd you deal with?"

"A colonel by the name of Bartolomé."

"That son of a whore fancies himself quite the bargainer, but he has gut wind where his brain should be. I'm sure he was no match for you."

Back in the driver's seat, Henning picked up the reins and clucked at the horses.

As they rounded a corner he said, "I'm taking you to Toledo. Bartolomé said you financed guerrillas who ambushed Chilean army units in the *sierra*. If they killed friends or relatives of soldiers stationed in Lima, you won't be safe here."

"I'm not strong enough to go by land and we can't go by sea. The goddamn Chileans want Peru to suffer so we'll sign their stinking treaty. Their navy won't let anyone or anything into or out of our ports."

"We're going on a Chilean warship." Henning savored *Don* Diego's perplexed reaction.

"Don't go any further out of your way to help me," *Don* Diego finally said. "I can't repay you."

"You paid in advance back when Felipe Marchena was trying to take my guano business and send me to jail for counterfeiting."

"I've done favors for a lot of people. But you're the only one who came after the Chileans locked me up."

"Thanks to Alcalino. When he found out you were in prison, he asked me to loan him money for your ransom. But I preferred to bail you out myself."

"I backed guerrillas that killed people. Pacifists don't condone that sort of thing. Lino won't be happy to see me."

"You're wrong. You can't imagine how worried he was. Let's get you some grooming supplies and new clothes."

At a general store Henning helped the old man to the sidewalk and hired an attendant to watch the carriage while they were inside.

As a clerk took *Don* Diego's selections from shelves, Henning asked, "Do you know why Alcalino became a pacifist?"

"His mother's boyfriend often beat her. Watching her suffer bruises, black eyes, and broken ribs that didn't heal properly, Alcalino became a pacifist. Knocking hell out of her boyfriend would have done more good. The bastard eventually beat her to death, and Alcalino found the body."

After locking his purchases in the carriage's trunk, Henning asked the attendant to be extra vigilant and took *Don* Diego to a bath house, then a restaurant.

"Wish I'd gotten to know Lino better," *Don* Diego said after the waiter took their order.

"There's still time."

"Not according to those goddamn Chilean army doctors." *Don* Diego slashed a finger across his throat. "I have a disease called cancer. Hope you don't regret paying good money for a man who's near death."

"I'd do it again." Henning hid his sadness. "You'll live a long time yet. There's an outstanding doctor named Carmona near my hacienda. He'll keep you going."

"What's Lino doing these days?"

"He runs my sugar mill and is adding a room to his house so you can live there. But he's worried it won't be up to your standards."

"After Hell on Earth, Lino's house will be paradise. Even better because I'll be with…"

"Your son," Henning finished the thought. "Why is it difficult to call him that?"

"That would be admitting I slept with an Indian maid while my wife was still alive."

"Your maid must have been special. And smart, like her son and granddaughters."

"Alcalino had children this late in life?"

"His wife is a fair bit younger. You'll like her. She's good to him and the girls."

"Having missed so much of Alcalino's life makes me sad." *Don* Diego's expression matched his words.

"I admire the way you supported your country against its enemy while your peers sat on their hands."

"Thanks for trying to pick up my spirits." *Don* Diego cleared his throat. "My *peers*, as you call them, were too dignified to do anything but pray and hide their money. I should have hidden some of mine so I wouldn't be a burden to…" he grinned, "my son."

"You won't be a burden. He's looking forward to learning from you."

"I don't have anything more to teach him."

"Not about business perhaps, but you can make him wiser."

******

On October 20, 1883, the Treaty of Ancon officially ended the War of the Pacific and transferred the Atacama Desert and its nitrate to Chile. Eager to shed the burden of maintaining troops on foreign soil, the Chileans speedily withdrew their army. A few days after the last soldier left Cortéz, Henning sailed to Iquique.

Behind his desk at the wharf, Eduardo stared as if he couldn't believe his eyes. "You've changed," he said.

"It's been three years since we last saw each other," Henning replied, "long enough for Encinas to ask her question a hundred times."

"What question?"

"She couldn't believe I trusted you so completely with a million dollar business. I told her I had no doubt about your competence or honesty. Have you eaten?"

"Yes, but I wouldn't mind eating again."

As the waiter served pancakes and hot chocolate, Eduardo asked, "How are Martine and the baby?"

"She had a stillbirth." Henning didn't look up. "And has been bedridden ever since. Physically she's healed, but she's lived in a private, silent world for over a year. I miss her."

Back at the office Henning went through filing cabinets. The first was half full of deposit receipts. The next was stuffed with invoices and tax bills, all stamped paid. According to bank statements in the third, over two million dollars had passed through Eduardo's hands since Henning was last there.

Minister Raul Rubio had been astonished when Henning voluntarily paid Peru's guano taxes after the Chincha Islands War. Now Henning understood how it felt to admire scrupulous honesty.

"You never even drew your salary early," he told Eduardo.

"I was working so hard I didn't have time to spend it," Eduardo joked, then turned serious. "Chile reaffirmed her pledge to leave the mines in private hands. You'll be a multimillionaire if you concentrate your energy here."

"I'll look after things while you take a vacation, but then I'm going to put Toledo back on its feet and try to do the same with Martine."

"Toledo has been nothing but trouble. If I were you I'd give up on it. But not on Martine. You'll never love another woman as much as you do her."

******

A month later Henning got off a ship and picked up his carriage at Uncle Alfredo's house in Cortéz. Driving home, he passed his mill's charred iron skeleton. José Geldres had brought Toledo's *serrano* workers back from the Andes, and they were widening the approach road.

"You got here in the nick of time," the foreman greeted. "*Señorita* Encinas couldn't answer my questions, and without those answers we won't finish in time to get our bonus."

O'Higgins' last letter had said Martine was out of bed, taking a renewed interest in life.

In a rush to get home Henning said, "I'll be back this afternoon."

"Is that a promise?" the foreman asked.

"You have my word."

Henning drove to the house, wondering what he'd find. When he'd come home after ransoming Alcalino's father, Martine hadn't reacted to his return. But his latest absence had lasted much longer.

Hurrying up the porch stairs, Henning was startled by a hummingbird with an orange chest and iridescent green head. It hovered blurry and buzzing in front of him, then darted away. He decided it had been a good omen when Martine opened the door. In the daylight instead of a darkened bedroom, her skin seemed paler and her gray hairs more numerous. But her eyes—so long melancholy—now shone brightly.

Henning's joy was so sublime that smiling would've cheapened it.

"You were in Iquique too long," she greeted, backing up to let him in.

He reached out to hug her. With O'Higgins looking on, she pulled back.

"I came as soon as I heard you were out of bed," Henning said. "You look wonderful."

"Seeing Toledo come back to life has been an even better tonic than Chabuca's. I'm going to start supervising the overseers as soon as I get myself in shape."

Those words made the best afternoon of Henning's life less than it might have been. Martine's miraculous recovery, like her marriage proposal, had been inspired by love of Toledo—not of him.

"I have something for you." He ducked into the library and came out with a gift-wrapped package. "This isn't your present. That's in the carriage shed."

"Must be big."

"Not nearly as big as they will be."

"They? How intriguing."

Henning gestured for her to go first. They crossed the lawn, walking in and out of the shadows of Italian cypress trees, striping the grass like rungs on a giant ladder. Henning's boots thumped on the shed's plank floor. He stopped between a carriage and a line of saplings in planter boxes. Ordinary-looking, they were half his height.

"I first heard about rainbow eucalyptus in San Francisco during our honeymoon," he said. "They turned out to be rare. I bought these from a man who raises them on a pulpwood plantation in the Philippines. When they get bigger and start shedding strips of bark, they'll look like this."

He lay the package on a work bench. Hair falling forward on both sides of her face, Martine unwrapped a painting of trees marked with vivid slashes of blue, purple, orange, maroon, yellow, and pink.

"The artist must have exaggerated the colors," she exclaimed.

"I'm told the actual trees are even more spectacular."

"They'll be the highlight of my garden if they look half this good." Next time she spoke, her voice was subdued. "For over a year while I was ill, you gave me everything you had—even though I couldn't give anything back. Thank you."

"Thank *you*." Henning wanted to tell her he would have given up on any other woman...that she was and always would be the love of his life. But that would probably be more than she wanted to hear. Ending a long pause he added, "Are Encinas, Belisario, and Antonio back at the horse farm?"

"Yes, and *Don* José brought our workers back from the *sierra*."

"I know. I passed a crew widening the road to the mill so it'll accommodate the boilers and girders when they come from England."

Martine's eyes opened wide. "You're going to build our new mill?"

"The biggest and most modern in South America."

Henning spent the rest of the afternoon bringing Martine up to date on his plans. After he finished, she went to bed. By then it was too late to go back and answer his foreman's questions. He hadn't forgotten his promise or taken it lightly. But he'd been unable to tear himself away with Martine back from wherever she'd been.

He'd pay his workers' bonuses even if they didn't finish the job on schedule.

******

Emiliano Cabrera slid open the curtain and stared from his carriage's passenger compartment. The size of the stark steel skeleton was surprising, but shouldn't have been. The crew from England's Babcock, Wilcox & Company had been working on it since January.

Attracted by the newly erected smokestack—visible for miles—other neighbors too had come to Toledo. They'd left their carriages and gathered together, faces showing disapproval of the unsightly, soon-to-be noisy intrusion into their tranquil, picturesque valley.

Cabrera pulled the curtain across his window, signaling his driver to take him home. He'd seen enough. Toledo's new mill was huge. The payments would be the same. And he knew something Henning Dietzel didn't. Peru was coming apart at the seams.

Armed peasants had taken over haciendas. Black slaves had overpowered their masters and were loose in society without money or food. Rogue militias were collecting tribute from anyone with anything of value. Chinese were being murdered at random, whether or not they'd been among those who fought alongside the Chileans to avenge their mistreatment in Peru.

Only Cabrera, Dietzel, and a handful of the Valley's other landowners had planted that year. Penniless after the war with Chile, the rest had avoided debtor's prison by selling their land or abandoning it and disappearing. In either case, their former properties had become part of Cabrera's empire. The only person buying, he'd been able to name his price, which he'd done without interference from a conscience.

The Chilean withdrawal had left Peru with no government, no economy, and no law enforcement. After seven presidents in five years, an unavoidable civil war would soon pit Miguel Iglesias's troops against those loyal to Andrés Avelino Cáceres.

Cabrera came as close to smiling as he ever did without an audience. He'd get a new mill—and the rest of Toledo—when Dietzel inevitably defaulted on his payments to Babcock, Wilcox & Company.

CHAPTER TWENTY-NINE
THE VULTURE

Answering a knock on the door, Henning and Martine saw Juan Luis Moreno, who received a commission on every acre he added to Emiliano Cabrera's Hacienda Noya. His ruthless negotiating skills had inspired a nickname, The Vulture.

"I know it's late." Thrusting both hands in his pockets, The Vulture managed to look embarrassed. "Perhaps I should come back tomorrow?"

He was notorious for arriving unannounced at day's end, then returning the following morning as an invited guest.

"Coming here was a waste of time," Martine snapped, her tone intentionally brittle. "We'll never sell to your boss—not under any circumstances."

The Vulture said a polite *adiós* and rode away.

When they re-seated themselves to finish their interrupted dinner, Martine lowered herself, without letting gravity take charge, typical of her resistance to outside control. Then her irritation surfaced in the form of rhetorical questions. "How stupid can he be? Why would we sell after building a new mill and harvesting our first crop in five years?"

"Maybe he knows something we don't," Henning replied.

"Such as?"

"Perhaps his boss has a plan to put us out of business, and he wants to arrange a deal before it's too late to get a commission."

"How could Cabrera possibly drive us out of business?"

"When I ask myself that question, I always get the same answer. By stopping us from exporting our sugar, which won't be difficult with Peru in chaos."

Appetite suddenly gone, Martine pushed her plate away and asked, "What if you're right and he succeeds?"

"We'll lose Toledo, if my nitrate profits can't pay for our new mill."

"Can we borrow money if we need it?"

"Not with civil war on the horizon."

"I wish The Vulture hadn't come tonight," she said. "I was relaxed and ready for a good sleep. Now I'll lay awake all night wondering what Cabrera has in mind for us."

Henning let out a burst of air as Martine left the table. She always went to their bedroom first. By the time he arrived, her eyes would be closed whether she was asleep or not. They hadn't made love since before their son's stillbirth.

With his usual forthrightness Dr. Carmona had cautioned Henning to expect that, explaining, "She's worried you'll be repelled by what you see. During her operation I concentrated on saving her life and didn't fret about the scar."

Henning went to their room early and caught her sitting up, reading. He expected her to be unhappy he was there so soon. Looking up from her book, her eyes said otherwise. Rather than risk another rejection, Henning took his nightshirt behind the dressing screen as usual.

"Hurry." Martine's voice was husky, "unless you want this mood to go away."

He slid between the sheets. She struggled to remove her nightgown with one hand while the other held the bedding over her. When he took off his nightshirt, Henning made sure he didn't pull the comforter away from the area of her disfigurement.

Taking her face between his hands he softly kissed her. She rolled over and backed into him until they were snuggled together on their sides. She seemed in a hurry. Henning sensed she wanted to make love in that position so he wouldn't see her scar.

"Not like this," she said, stopping him. "It reminds me of the way turtles mate without seeing each other's faces. Can you just hold me a while please?"

Later she crawled on top. He liked having her there, free to move as she wanted. As she skilfully hid her stomach, he glimpsed white stretch marks from when her engorged breasts had been ready for the son who never arrived.

She kissed him gently then passionately, grinding her body against him. Watching the storm in her eyes, Henning slid inside her. He wanted to see her arousal and to show her his. She understood and kept her eyes open as she kissed him again. Then she froze, shoulders suspended above him, nipples swollen, face twisted as if by silent agony. Her orgasm—always private in the past—was obvious…and unbelievably exciting.

Martine watched Henning's face when his turn came, then went limp and lay plastered to him as if she had no skeleton. Later—as though coming out of a trance—she flopped onto her back breathing slowly and deeply.

"Seeing your excitement was incredibly arousing," she finally said. "Why?"

"Perhaps it's true," Henning replied, "that the eyes are the windows of the soul."

He was almost asleep when she broke the silence. "If need be, would you pay for Toledo's mill by selling your nitrate holdings?"

Henning's eyes snapped open, that delicious sense of wellbeing gone. Why had she chosen tonight to renew their physical relationship? Did she want him to pick Toledo over his nitrate business if one had to be sacrificed?

******

Without declaring themselves in favor of either aspiring president, the *Frente Popular's* soldiers had marched into Cortéz, seized the docks, and imposed an export tax. Their leader, Rafael Burga, soon proved himself masterful at maximizing the amount collected when growers dispatched sugar to foreign buyers.

Slender, wily, and a skilled extortionist, Burga knew when to leave questions unanswered, when to bestow uninvited confidences, and when to act on his threats. A dark-skinned *cholo*, he also resented the way Cortéz's white elite had treated him and was now in a position to demand their respect along with sizable chunks of their profits.

Standing at the window in his commandeered office, Burga shaded his eyes with one hand, watching a pelican glide low over the ocean. Intent on the water, it alternately flapped its wings and coasted, then splashed into a swell and reappeared with an expanded throat pouch.

Burga's peacock blue uniform was the equal of those worn by guards at the president's palace and had vertical red stripes down the legs. A row of sparkling brass buttons held the jacket shut. And his shiny helmet had a rakish plume. His men wore street clothes and visored military caps.

The new export tax fed and armed his troops, but bribes went in his pocket. Though getting rich on them, he had no enthusiasm for the one Emiliano Cabrera had just offered.

"Why would I deny your competitors the use of Cortéz's port?" he asked. "The levies I collect from them support my army."

"Perhaps I was unclear," Cabrera said. "I want you to stop only one of my competitors, Henning Dietzel, from shipping sugar."

"How much is it worth to you?"

"A thousand British pounds if you kill him while you're at it."

"Two thousand, and I may or may not kill him." Burga's tone said he wasn't open to discussion.

"Half now and the balance in three months," Cabrera countered, "provided Dietzel is dead…or at least hasn't found a way around you."

"There is no way around me," Burga declared, "as you'll learn if you don't make your next payment on time."

CHAPTER THIRTY
PETITE FIRING SQUAD

Legs wide apart, hands clasped behind his back, General Burga blocked the entry to Cortéz's wharf. Closer now, the oncoming wagons rumbled on cobblestones bracketed between rows of breeze-tossed willow trees. All week, Burga had been expecting them and their cargo, sugarloaves wrapped in Toledo's distinctive blue paper.

The graying blond man leading the caravan must be Henning Dietzel. Mounted on a golden palomino and flanked by bodyguards, he looked calm and confident. Like the other landowners, he'd be determined to bully his way out of paying Burga's export tax. And he'd attempt to do so with the arrogance whites typically reserved for half-breed *cholos*.

Señor Dietzel was in for a surprise.

"Stop," Burga held up his hand. The wagons' dust kept coming and engulfed him.

"I assume you're Henning Dietzel and this sugar is from the Hacienda Toledo?" Burga said, brushing his uniform with both hands.

"Yes."

"We've been expecting you."

Thirty *Frente Popular* ruffians in dirty clothes sprang from behind a nearby wall, rifles at the ready. Outgunned, Henning's bodyguards raised their hands while Burga's men collected their firearms.

"If any of you come to town again you'll be shot," Burga announced. "Allow me to demonstrate. You and you...against that wall."

Burga stabbed a finger at Henning, then the lead driver. By the time their backs were against the bullet-pitted adobe wall, the driver was blinking fast between involuntary gulps.

Boots crunched in gravel as a two-man firing squad formed in front of them.

Burga cupped his hands around his mouth. "Ready." Rifles were snugged to shoulders.

Dietzel's body tensed. The driver made the sign of the cross and kissed his thumb as a dark spot slowly spread down one leg of his trousers.

"Let him go," Dietzel said, sidestepping in front of his driver. "If he did anything wrong, it's only because he was following my orders."

"Standing in front of him won't do any good," Burga roared. "The bullets will go right through you. Aim."

Burga paused. The driver, a fellow *cholo*, didn't deserve to die. He'd been ordered to the wall with Dietzel so no one would suspect his boss had been singled out for murder, which would cast suspicion on Emiliano Cabrera. Only one of the would-be executioners held a loaded rifle. The other had been instructed to pretend his weapon misfired.

Burga frowned. About to die, Dietzel had done something completely unexpected. He'd offered his life to save a *cholo's*. For that, he deserved to live, and why not? Burga had promised to stop Toledo from exporting sugar. Shooting Dietzel had been optional.

"I won't kill anyone today," Burga announced. "But if any of you return to Cortéz, you'll be shot on sight." He turned to a man attaching a camera to a tripod and added, "You alone will have the honor of shooting these gentlemen today. Get good likenesses and post them in the guardhouse at the entrance to town."

Burga's men drove Toledo's wagons onto the dock while the photographer took a close-up of Henning and group pictures of the drivers and bodyguards. Nearby, a cook lit a fire under a grill, filling the air with the sound and smell of frying bacon.

"I was watching when you thought you were going to be shot," Burga told Henning. "You've got balls but won't have them long if I see you again. By the time you walk home I will have sold your sugar, wagons, and horses. Consider the proceeds a one-time ransom."

The general ordered mounted men to herd Henning and his drivers across town and leave them on the road to the Chiriaco Valley.

"Don't let them stop, eat, or drink," he ordered sternly. "And if anyone causes problems, shoot him."

******

For the third time since General Burga stopped him from exporting sugar, Henning rode away from Toledo. Martine's goodbye kiss fresh on his lips, he was already lonely. And worried. She'd been despondent since he'd sent the workers home but so far hadn't come close to the deep depression that followed their son's stillbirth.

And she wouldn't as long as his nitrate sales continued paying for the new mill, keeping Toledo out of foreclosure. Beyond the stable Henning rode past empty worker housing, then warehouses filled with year-old sugar, and finally idle farmland with weeds higher than his horse's belly. These sights made it easier to leave.

Wearing white clothes to reflect heat and a broad-brimmed *sombrero* to shade his face, Henning began his long journey with a two-day ride. In La Rioja, a tiny fishing village unworthy of General Burga's attention, he left his horse with the same farmer as always. Then a fisherman rowed him out to an anchored schooner, *Duquesa*.

When *Duquesa* stopped in Callao an old acquaintance came aboard. Andrés de la Borda was as thin and angular as when he and Henning had met in the Wrath of God Desert. Chasing stories for the *Lima Correo* had kept him fit.

"*Señor* Dietzel," the reporter greeted. "I can't believe my good luck. I was in Cortéz last week and heard some intriguing rumors about you."

After his articles about the match race between Sultán and Goliat, de la Borda had become Peru's most widely read reporter. People who valued privacy avoided him. Henning intended to do the same. Emiliano Cabrera was eager to know how Toledo was paying for its mill. Henning didn't want him to get that information from a de la Borda article.

"Where are you headed?" Henning asked.

"Iquique," de la Borda replied, "to find out what happened after Chile took over."

"You won't like what you see. Things are better than when Peru was in charge."

De la Borda winced. "That's bad news, but the truth is the truth and it's my job to tell it. Can you point me in the direction of any good stories?"

"If you promise not to use my name." Henning instantly regretted his remark. People who shunned publicity were usually hiding something, and reporters believed anything worth hiding was worth finding.

"You have my word," de la Borda said. "My interest in you is personal— not professional."

Finding that difficult to believe, Henning asked, "How goes our civil war?"

"Cáceres's attack on Lima forced Iglesias to abdicate. As soon as Cáceres consolidates his power he'll run General Burga out of Cortéz and open the port to everyone, you included. And Emiliano Cabrera won't be able to do anything about it."

"There isn't much you don't know, is there?"

"There'll be less after I return from Iquique."

Next morning their ship passed Iquique's lighthouse and swung toward the docks.

Ashore Henning said, "*Adiós.*"

He took the long way around and made sure he wasn't followed. But de la Borda was waiting at the railway station with a self-satisfied smile.

"I'd planned on staying in Iquique," he explained, "but I've decided to start my research in La Palma. Is that where you're headed?"

"No, I'm going farther."

Henning didn't want to travel with such an observant companion, but the alternative was to wait a week for the next train. He maneuvered de la Borda into the line, ahead of him.

"Mind if I travel with you?" de la Borda asked over his shoulder at the ticket window.

"You'd be wasting your time where I'm going."

De la Borda bought passage to La Palma. When Henning purchased his ticket, he spoke too quietly for the reporter to hear.

Their train climbed a series of switchbacks to the plateau behind town. Picking up speed it started across a wasteland of chalk, gypsum, and salt. After an hour of this monotonous landscape, de la Borda opened the window. Hit by a burst of air, he closed it halfway.

"It's as hot outside as it is in here," he complained. "But it smells better. I hate this place already. If I had a wife as beautiful as yours, I wouldn't leave her to come here. But you have to pay for your new mill and she can't come with you, can she? Under Peruvian law, haciendas are up for grabs unless the owner or a member of his immediate family is in residence. With you both gone, Emiliano Cabrera could legally take Toledo."

"You said your interest in me is personal. How about your interest in Cabrera?"

"My interest in him is decidedly professional. I find you both intriguing, but for different reasons. When I was last in Cortéz, I interviewed everyone I could about him but only spoke to your wife about you. She wouldn't tell me if General Burga is preventing Toledo from exporting sugar. But Toledo's unplanted fields answered that question.

"I couldn't help wondering why everyone there lives together in one house. It's unheard of for whites and *cholos* to share the same roof. Then I saw all those bodyguards and realized that protecting people is easier in a small area. But protecting them from whom? My theory is that during our civil war, Emiliano Cabrera can do whatever he wants. And with no government or *Guardia Civil*, only an army of bodyguards can keep him at bay."

A square, roofless structure of stacked rocks flashed by. De la Borda swiveled his head for a second look.

"Why slits instead of windows?" he asked.

"That's a bunker built during the War of the Pacific."

De la Borda shut the window to keep incoming air from fanning his notebook's pages and scribbled a notation.

"Those umbrella-shaped trees are *tamarugos*," Henning volunteered. "Their taproots go as deep as fifty feet and find water where nothing else can grow."

On the window's inner surface, their images held a constant position while the arid landscape raced past. De la Borda was studying Henning's reflection—not the passing scenery. Henning made sure his expression revealed nothing.

The train slowed on the outskirts of La Palma, then passed buildings with corrugated metal walls and roofs. Their faded signs offered goods and services. De la Borda turned his notebook's page.

"Any good stories here?" he asked.

"The La Palma and Santa Laura Saltpeter Works are both worth your time. There's also a unique swimming pool made of iron plates from the hull of a salvaged ship."

"I wouldn't mind a nice, cool swim." De la Borda patted his brow with a handkerchief.

The train stopped beneath the station's high metal roof. De la Borda stood and pulled his luggage from the overhead rack.

"*Adiós* in case I don't see you again," he said, waving from the end of the car before descending the metal steps.

Hours later on a sidetrack, the brakeman uncoupled a line of empty gondola cars while Henning stepped off the train and started toward a waiting wagon. He sped up after seeing de la Borda in the train's other passenger car.

"Let's get out of here," he ordered the driver.

Looking back through shimmering heat haze, Henning saw only the cars left behind when the train continued on. But later his spotting scope revealed a lone rider. He told his driver to stop, then pulled his rifle from its scabbard. After he levered a shell into the chamber, he let the hammer down to half cock.

When de la Borda caught up, his eyes were slits beneath a hat brim that shielded them from direct sunlight, but not from rays reflecting up from the sand.

"I need more information for my articles," he said, "and won't likely find another source as good as you. I already promised not to use your name, and I won't."

"It's hard to take you at your word when you persist in following me."

"I already know you own a nitrate mine out here and a wharf in Iquique. No secret is safe *from* me but yours are safe *with* me. If I intended to write about them, I'd have done it by now."

"Why didn't you?" Henning returned the rifle to its scabbard.

"I can write an article now or a book when you own the whole Chiriaco Valley. I'd much rather author your biography. And when the time comes, I can't interview you if we're on bad terms, can I?" He shifted uncomfortably in his saddle.

"Why don't you tie your horse behind the wagon and ride with me?" Henning suggested.

"With pleasure. This horse I rented is a boneshaker."

An hour later they stopped beside a manmade crater swarming with men and mules.

"You own Toledo and all this too?" de la Borda exclaimed. "How rich are you anyhow?"

"I'm a pauper compared to Colonel John North who bought God knows how many mines after it became obvious Chile would win the War of the Pacific. He paid a fraction of their value because everyone thought Chile would nationalize nitrate."

A familiar voice added, "Some say North had taken out insurance by bribing the officials who decided against nationalizing the mines."

"Eduardo Vásquez," Henning said, "meet Andrés de la Borda, a *Lima Correo* reporter."

"Why is your view of Colonel North so cynical?" de la Borda asked Eduardo.

"It's realistic—not cynical," Eduardo replied. "Money and corruption go hand in hand, except for those rare occasions when idealists like Henning get rich."

"Colonel North also controls the Atacama's railways, a bank, and a company that sells food and water to the mines," Henning said, trying to change the conversation's subject.

"Henning supplied this area's water," Eduardo offered, "until North started piping it in."

Catching Henning with a forefinger to his lips, de la Borda said, "Don't worry. I won't mention you or your businesses, past or present."

The driver showed de la Borda to Salamanca's guest quarters, leaving Henning and Eduardo in private.

"We've accumulated enough for a down payment on another mine," Eduardo said. "There's a good one on offer. Can I show it to you?"

"I don't want to take on more debt until Toledo is profitable again."

"You once told me Toledo keeps you from having all your eggs in one basket. If you keep it much longer you'll wind up with no eggs and no basket."

"If I had to get rid of one or the other I'd sell Salamanca."

"Which would bring us to a parting of the ways. I'm not cut out to be a farmer."

They'd had this discussion before, but neither had stated his priorities so clearly.

******

"I try not to worry about things I can't control," Henning said, settling into his chair in Salamanca's office.

"It's usually unproductive," de la Borda responded from across the desk, "but have you seen these?" He handed Henning a metal token stamped with Emiliano Cabrera's profile.

"Sure. Cabrera pays his workers with them."

"If he gets his way, they'll soon be accepted throughout the Chiriaco Valley and Cortéz."

"Why would he want that? He pays with tokens so his workers can't spend them anywhere but Noya's company store."

"What he loses there will be replaced a thousand times over if he can pay his bills with money he doesn't have to earn."

"You don't honestly think people will accept his tokens as money?"

"Many already do, partly because years without a national mint have created a shortage of coins and currency. But also because merchants can't refuse thousands of new customers. Cabrera closed his company store and Noya's workers now do their shopping in Cortéz. His tokens have become money by definition."

"The new government in Lima won't let him get away with that."

"By the time Cáceres's government branches into the provinces, Cabrera will have the best friends money can buy. He'll be able to purchase anything he wants—including land—with money he manufactures. Even his enemies will have to go down on one knee in front of him."

"And people call capitalism immoral. At least it's based on earning money—not creating it by sleight of hand."

"For the unscrupulous, capitalism involves accumulating wealth by any means possible."

That night Henning wrote Martine, asking her to save upcoming issues of the *Lima Correo*. Before accepting de la Borda as a trusted friend he wanted to be sure the man's coming articles didn't reveal anything they shouldn't.

CHAPTER THIRTY-ONE
DOUBLE DOUBLE-CROSS

Henning and Martine finished breakfast as the sun rose above distant brown peaks. Today Henning wouldn't go through La Rioja on his way to Iquique. General Burga's men had scattered two days before President Cáceres's federal troops reached Cortéz. With its port again open to him, Henning had rehired Toledo's workers, and they were planting his next crop.

Pointing to the *Lima Correo* newspapers on a nearby table, Martine told Chabuca, "You can burn those. *Señor* Henning has read them."

True to de la Borda's word, his articles had made no reference to Henning. And his exposé decrying the acceptance of Emiliano Cabrera's private money had created a furor. But Henning still had a fight on his hands when he refused to take Cabrera's tokens as change.

"I'll miss you more than ever this time," Martine said.

Instead of saying goodbye at the front door, she walked Henning to the stable. When he was ready to put his foot in the stirrup she hugged him a very long time.

Finally letting go she said, "When people part company the one left behind suffers most."

Her words stayed with him. He wrote her every night for a week and sent his accumulated letters by ship when next in Iquique.

'Uncle Alfredo delivered an envelope with six wonderful letters today,' she replied. 'To prolong the pleasure of reading them, I'm limiting myself to one a day.'

A week later Henning read: 'You won't get a letter every day, but I always have several going and add to them as the spirit moves me.'

Picturing Martine at her wall mounted desk, he replied, 'Being a typical, orderly Prussian, I write my letters at the same time every night and finish one before starting another—not very artistic I'm afraid.'

Early on, Martine limited herself to news. The fields were finally replanted. The leaves on her favorite tree were mysteriously turning brown. A mother egret had defended her chicks from a desert fox. Alcalino's daughters were ill.

Gradually her letters grew thicker and the contents more personal.

'I'll be inconsolable if I ever have to leave the Valley, all the more so if Emiliano Cabrera winds up with Toledo,' she wrote when he couldn't come home for Christmas.

Henning's answer, full of reassurance, was apparently what she needed because her response revealed a carefully guarded secret: 'Long before we lost our son, Dr. Carmona said something was wrong and recommended ending my pregnancy. Knowing how much you wanted a boy, I kept his advice to myself. If I had taken it, I could have gotten pregnant again.'

'After we lost our baby,' he replied, underlining *we* and *our*, 'I hid my feelings so my grief wouldn't increase yours. I wince when I remember what you endured trying to give me a son. My gratitude would be no greater if you had succeeded. Please don't blame yourself.'

Martine's favorite of all his letters, that one went a long way toward unlocking the few remaining doors between them.

******

Holding the drapes open, Henning watched wagonloads of men pass by in predawn's gray light. A seemingly endless nightmare was over. Toledo's fields were being harvested after years of standing idle. And to make matters even better, sugar prices had skyrocketed and he'd had thousands of tons in his warehouses when Burga stopped him from exporting.

That afternoon an unusual vehicle stopped at Toledo's front porch. The first dogcart Henning had seen, it was an open two-wheel conveyance pulled by a single horse, with back-to-back seats. The passenger had prosperous looking bulges of fat above his collar and around his middle.

Jumping down, he said, "I'm Archibald Mackintosh. Is it true you have sugar to sell?"

"Absolutely," Henning replied. "Send your cab back to Cortéz. When you're ready to leave, my driver will take you."

Jolly and talkative, Mackintosh followed Henning up and down aisles between rows of sugarloaves in Toledo's immaculate warehouses. Cone-shaped and wrapped in blue paper the thirty pound, three-foot-tall loaves were stacked on their sides.

"The sugarloaf is arguably the world's most familiar shape," Mackintosh said cheerily. "Thousands of hills, peaks, and other cone-shaped protrusions have been named in its honor. The most striking I've seen is Sugarloaf Mountain, outside Rio de Janeiro. Have you seen it?"

"Only in paintings."

Getting down to business, Mackintosh said, "I'm sure you know England protects its refining industry by charging punitive taxes on sugarloaves whereas raw sugar gets in free."

"There are other places you can sell."

"I can't pay what you're asking—not for sugar that's been in warehouses for years."

"Sugar doesn't deteriorate if kept dry. Every loaf here is good as new."

"What discount will you offer if I take it all?"

"There's a worldwide shortage." Henning chuckled mirthlessly. "What premium will you pay if I let you buy it all?"

Mackintosh removed his glasses and exhaled on a lens. Polishing it with his handkerchief, he said, "You can't blame me for trying."

After lunch—having seen Mackintosh pay for his cab ride with Noya's tokens—Henning drew up a sales contract specifying payment in U.S. dollars.

******

Soon after Mackintosh left, The Vulture, Juan Luis Moreno, arrived with an armed escort. Alerted by the sentry watching the main road, O'Higgins had taken his sharpshooter's rifle to the top of the bell tower overlooking the yard. The precaution was unnecessary. Moreno's visit was brief and the only hostility was Martine's as she ordered him off the property.

"Why does that imbecile keep coming back?" she asked Henning, loose sleeves fluttering as she waved her arms. "We've made it clear we won't sell."

"You'll have to admit," Henning teased, "that it's considerate of him to warn us every time his boss has a new plan to drive us out of business."

"This time let's counterattack rather than merely defend ourselves," she blustered, running her fingers through her silver-streaked hair. "Pietro's motto was, 'Have your enemy for breakfast lest you become his dinner.'"

"Cabrera's never been more powerful. If we fight him now we'll lose. But if we wait until he's down we might be able to keep him from getting back up."

"First we have to we knock him down."

"Not necessarily. Ambitious men eventually overreach themselves. I did when I built Toledo's new mill too soon. Somewhere along the line, Cabrera will make a similar mistake."

"If he does, it will be probably too late to do us any good."

"It's never too late."

"It is if you're dead."

"If Cabrera decides to go that far he'll send Federico García," Henning said. "And O'Higgins will be ready because he has men watching García day and night."

******

Alcalino helped *Don* Diego down the back porch steps and into Toledo's park, forty acres of grass, shade trees, manmade lakes, and exotic plants. As the old man struggled to get one foot in front of the other, people vacated the nearest bench. After strapping a legless chair to it, Alcalino placed pillows across the seat and backrest.

Sitting there, *Don* Diego watched one of his granddaughters hide in a clump of silver-plumed pampas grass while the other counted to fifty. Laughing and happy they played until their mother called them. Then Alcalino started a conversation, speaking slowly and listening patiently, difficult with so many questions that he feared he didn't have long to ask.

When *Don* Diego was too weary to project his voice, Alcalino helped him to his feet and they returned to the house.

"Dr. Carmona says I'm getting better," *Don* Diego wheezed later, seated on the living room couch, "but it doesn't feel that way."

"You are," Alcalino said, patting his father's bony shoulder. "I can see it. When you're stronger we'll go to the workers' *fútbol* games and take the girls for hikes along the river."

"Keep him looking forward to better times," Carmona had recommended. "Hope is the best medicine of all."

As Alcalino's relationship with *Don* Diego improved, the old man's impending death became both more and less painful. More, because he dreaded losing the father who'd only begun revealing his private thoughts. Less, because they were having conversations fathers and sons usually postponed until too late.

Alcalino's daughters adored their *abuelo*. But Estella, their mother, found him intimidating and resented the extra work and strain on the household budget. After Henning increased Alcalino's salary her complaints continued, then mysteriously stopped. Alcalino found out why the day he came home early and saw *Don* Diego helping with her housework.

"It's embarrassing to have such an important man hanging my laundry and sweeping my floors," he heard his wife say.

"I'm glad I'm finally strong enough to do it," *Don* Diego replied. "Don't worry. No one—Alcalino least of all—will ever know."

Alcalino backed out the door and returned at his normal time, feeling more love than ever for the father who'd ignored him before inexplicably going to the opposite extreme.

Later Estella came to enjoy *Don* Diego's gruff, profane humor. And to appreciate the way he accepted her and his granddaughters despite their Indian blood. Jealous of his Wednesday visits to Cortéz—dressed in a suit Henning had bought him—she told Alcalino she suspected the old man had found female companionship.

"I wish," Alcalino replied. "But he's visiting an old friend he no longer likes."

******

Don Diego hadn't seen Ramón Benavides since their close friendship at Lima's premier university. But the judge's initial formality and caution faded as they met every Wednesday afternoon in his living room, their camaraderie fueled by the expensive wine *Don* Diego brought.

Benavides's droopy eyelids made him seem unworthy of trust, and his high forehead made him look intelligent. He was both. Unfortunately his intelligence was all that remained of the promising young man *Don* Diego had befriended a half century earlier.

But that didn't stop the weekly visits. *Don* Diego wasn't there for old time's sake. He was there to repay Henning. And one afternoon a chance presented itself as he nursed three inches of wine while Benavides finished off the rest of the bottle.

"Emiliano Cabrera," the judge said with the slow, deliberate speech of a man trying to hide his inebriation, "is preparing litigation to slash Toledo's share of water from the river."

Back at Toledo *Don* Diego told Henning, "I can stop Cabrera for you. Being overly honest you won't like how I do it. But in my opinion bribes are an acceptable way of protecting yourself from men who use them to gain unfair advantage. Put up the money and I'll do the rest. I can't get you a receipt, of course. You'll have to trust me."

"I'd be a fool not to. How much do you need?"

"I don't know yet, but it'll be plenty. Benavides is many things—but not inexpensive."

******

At Uncle Alfredo's suggestion, Henning hired Epaminondas Mastorakos, a Greek immigrant, to defend against Cabrera's lawsuit. Henning didn't reveal that the verdict had already been arranged because he wanted Mastorakos to do his best to win.

Handsome with long, curly hair, Mastorakos sometimes lost his train of thought when he saw pretty girls.

"Don't worry," Martine said after Henning mentioned this disconcerting habit. "Women are unwelcome in Peru's courts."

During the trial Henning listened carefully as the opposing attorney presented Cabrera's case. The preposterous claims were more than he could stomach. Though he usually let experts do their jobs without interference, he found himself repeatedly leaning close to Mastorakos and suggesting ways to expose Cabrera's lies.

On the trial's second day Judge Benavides interrupted Mastorakos's rebuttal and said, "You're wasting the court's time. *Señor* Dietzel is obviously using more than his fair share of water. I rule in favor of *Señor* Cabrera." He thumped his gavel, finalizing the verdict.

"My God," Mastorakos sputtered as he and Henning left the courtroom. "That wasn't a trial. It was a one-act play, and the ending was written in advance. You won't receive a bill for my services—not after being victimized like this."

Alone and outraged, Henning drove back to Toledo wondering what had gone wrong. He'd been double-crossed. But by whom? All he knew for sure was that reducing Toledo's water allotment meant thousands of acres of cane would wither in fields he could never plant again.

Mastorakos's unassailable case hadn't even been heard. Benavides must have received two bribes, with Cabrera's being larger. But why had *Don* Diego been acting so strangely?

At Toledo Henning drove straight to Alcalino's house. Estella was sweeping the porch in a cloud of dust.

"Haven't seen him since last night," she replied.

Henning checked back in an hour. Again in two.

The third time *Don* Diego was on the porch, alone. He spoke first. "Sorry to put you through that, but you're a shitty actor, and a convincing performance full of outrage was needed. Benavides doesn't want Cabrera to know he was betrayed."

"Seems to me that we were the ones betrayed," Henning said.

"Looks that way, doesn't it? But don't worry. Benavides had good reason for not hearing your attorney's rebuttal. He was providing grounds for an appeal to the Superior Court in Lima. Cabrera's suit won't stand a chance in front of an impartial judge."

Henning appealed and Benavides's verdict was overturned.

A month later *Don* Diego was hospitalized after having lived two years beyond Dr. Carmona's most optimistic prediction. In his final hours the old man sent for Henning and Alcalino. He thanked Henning for his friendship and told Alcalino, "I'm ashamed to admit that I helped your mother raise you because it was my duty. Back then I didn't know you were a gift from God."

CHAPTER THIRTY-TWO
ALL HIS WORLDLY GOODS

Following a midnight rainstorm, the newly washed air smelled of orange blossoms. Unable to sleep, Henning sat in pitch darkness on his front porch. He struck a match, turned it upside down until the flame spread up the stick, then lit a kerosene lantern. It produced more light than its whale oil predecessor, enough to see Martine's black cat arch its back as he reached down to pet it.

"What are you doing up so early?" Henning asked when Alcalino brought Toledo's fastest horse, saddled and ready to go.

"I wish I could do more to help on such an important day," Alcalino said.

"Do you know what's happening?"

"Only that it's a secret."

"Not from you." But then Henning played his cards close to the vest. "Emiliano Cabrera found my Achilles' heel. If I don't stop him today we'll lose Toledo."

"God will help you, *señor.*"

"God helps those who help themselves."

"He also helps those who help others, and that's you."

"That remains to be seen," Henning said.

A civil war on top of the one with Chile had left Peru in shambles. For months it seemed that only Cabrera and Henning would survive. The gentlemanly barons who owned the Valley's other haciendas were near bankruptcy. For generations they'd traveled the world and sent their children to schools in Europe. Now most were selling their land to Cabrera for tokens, and the holdouts would soon be forced to do the same.

And yesterday Cabrera had finally discovered Toledo's hidden vulnerability.

******

Henning had almost reached the Alvarez farm when the rising sun set the edges of scattered clouds aglow. Shading his eyes he scanned the trees along the Chiriaco River. The Vulture, escorted by Federico García, had visited Mario Alvarez yesterday. And as always, one of O'Higgins' men had García under surveillance.

When O'Higgins passed along that man's report late last night, Henning had instantly known what was afoot. Too small to interest Cabrera under normal circumstances, the Alvarez property was between Toledo and the river. Toledo had the perpetual right to bring water across it. If Cabrera bought it, he could petition Judge Benavides to redefine the word perpetual.

And without *Don* Diego's intervention, Benavides would comply, leaving half of Toledo without water.

A column of smoke widened as it rose from Mario Alvarez's chimney. Halfway from the milking shed to his house, Alvarez stooped to adjust his boot. Straightening up, he saw Henning.

"The Vulture was here yesterday," he said. "That crazy *pendejo* Cabrera wants to buy my farm with Noya's tokens. But I want to retire in Europe where his private money is no good."

"I'll pay U.S. dollars," Henning offered.

"I figured as much. Care to join me for breakfast?"

Twelve hours later at dinner, Henning told Martine what he'd done.

"What if Cabrera offers more?" she asked.

"He can't. I brought Uncle Alfredo from Cortéz and closed the deal this afternoon. Cabrera could have bought the Alvarez farm yesterday if he hadn't insisted on paying with tokens. For once his greed cost him."

Martine poured two glasses of wine, then handed one to Henning and raised the other.

"A toast," she proposed, "to the first of what I hope will be many land purchases."

"There'll be at least one more. Cabrera's trying to get his hands on Luis

Bustamante's hacienda. Tomorrow I'm going to buy it out from under him. Let me show you why."

Henning went to his office and returned with sheets of paper covered by calculations.

"Buying the Bustamante hacienda is smart," Martine said. "I don't need numbers to tell me that."

"I know you think mathematics are cold, but I like them for one of the same reasons I love you. They never lie to make me feel good."

"My accounting lessons with Encinas," she said good-naturedly, "taught me that making mathematics tell the truth is easier for you than for me."

The addition of Bustamante's acreage made Toledo the Valley's second largest hacienda. But the down payment drained Henning's bank account to a dangerously vulnerable level.

******

Awake for what seemed like hours, Martine rolled onto her side and glanced at the clock beside the framed photograph of her dog, Oso. Now dead, he'd been excited when it was taken and his tail was a blur.

"How'd you sleep?" Henning asked from his nearby bed.

"I can't stop thinking," she replied. "Since you paid dollars for the Bustamante hacienda, the remaining landowners are demanding the same. But Cabrera is insisting on paying with tokens. Obviously he knows we can't afford more property."

"He's wrong. I told the sellers to hold on a few weeks longer so I can concentrate my resources here and buy their land with dollars."

"You're going to sell your nitrate holdings?"

"Would you if they were yours? Don't forget what Encinas taught you."

"I think she'd say that in the sugar business you'll have only one serious competitor. But with nitrate you're up against giant, well-financed companies and barons like John North, who ran you out of the water business."

"You're right, but my decision was based on a personal consideration. I could never ask you to leave Toledo. Now come over here and convince me I'm right."

"Why don't I go over there and thank you instead?"

She'd never been more beautiful than during that short walk from her bed to his.

******

At sunset three days later Henning stepped off the gangplank at his wharf in Iquique, where Captain Medina's supply ships, *Hornet* and *Intrepido*, were being unloaded.

"I'm going to offer Salamanca to John Cowden," Henning told Medina as they stood under huge kerosene lanterns that made it possible for his stevedores to work at night.

"Damn," Medina said. "Cowden supplies his own mines. If he buys Salamanca I'll be out of customers."

"Why don't you go into the passenger business? There's a propeller-driven steamship, *La Gallega*, for sale. You can sell *Intrepido* and *Hornet* to get a down payment, and I'll help with your other start-up costs. Interested?"

Peru's largest, most important cities were along her coast. Traveling between them, people went by ship—not overland. Prices were high and waiting lists long.

"That's an easy decision," Medina said. "Passenger ships earn twice what freighters do."

In Iquique Henning's hard-fought negotiations with the president of an English mining concern yielded an unheard-of price for his wharf, loading facility, and warehouses. Two days later John Cowden agreed to buy back the nitrate mine he'd sold Henning decades ago. The price was several times what Henning had paid—but below market value due to special conditions.

Next Henning took what was probably his last train ride to Salamanca. By the time he revealed what he'd done, he was sitting near Eduardo's living room window and they were watching a spectacular orange and pink sunset.

"Damn," Eduardo exclaimed. "I'll hate leaving here."

"I know. That's why the purchase contract gives you five percent of Salamanca and a contract to continue as manager."

"You could've gotten a better price without those conditions."

"True. But you love it here, don't you?"

"If your goal was to leave me speechless you've succeeded."

Eduardo knelt in front of the fireplace and lit the newspaper under logs and kindling he'd arranged earlier. The flames cast shadows in his face's lines and colored his brown eyes amber.

Finally able to speak, he cleared his throat and said, "It's amazing how chilly the desert gets this time of year."

The two *amigos* were soon drinking wine in front of a crackling blaze. They talked about getting back together during the big San Francisco fire, stopping the Hounds from extorting protection money in Little Chile, Henning's risky cinchona shipment to New York, and rebuilding after Iquique's tidal wave.

Now and then Eduardo placed another log in the flames and refilled their glasses. At dawn both men moved closer to the glowing embers and wrapped themselves in blankets. They ate Eduardo's favorite breakfast, *bistec a caballo*, fried eggs atop Argentine flank steaks.

After Henning saddled his horse, they exchanged what he feared was their final *abrazo*.

Eduardo's youthful posture had been ramrod straight, but now his back was curved and his head and shoulders bent forward.

"The way things worked out," he told Henning, "you seem taller than ever. I was hoping you'd wind up stooped over so I could finally look you in the eye."

"Maybe you'll get another chance. As alike as we are, we'll probably find each other in the next life."

"You don't believe in a next life any more than I do."

"No, but after all we've been through together, our friendship can't just end."

"Why not?" Eduardo shrugged. "Everything ends somewhere."

"Not the universe. It goes on forever."

"That's impossible."

"No. Think about it. If it ends, what's there? A brick wall? And if so, what's on the other side?"

******

The closer Henning got, the more he looked forward to giving Martine the good news. He picked up his carriage at Uncle Alfredo's and made excellent time on Cortéz's almost deserted streets, then across the bridge and along the coastal highway. Finally, the steep mountain grades slowed him.

He sped up again on the downhill side, then—luggage in hand—burst into Toledo's living room. On the couch Martine marked her place in a Bible with its attached ribbon and stood to greet him. Already across the room, he scooped her off the floor.

"I got great prices," he said. "If Emiliano Cabrera wants more land he'll have to outbid me to get it and he'll have to pay with dollars."

Setting Martine down, Henning didn't see her recently acquired worry lines. In fact, she'd never looked so happy.

******

On Mount Olympus Emiliano Cabrera stepped into his new Phaeton carriage. "Get me to Cortéz fast," he told the driver.

As his coach raced toward town yielding right-of-way to no one, Cabrera recalled that morning's conversation with Luis Sarmiento.

"President Cáceres outlawed all but government-issued money," Sarmiento, the vice-minister of Peru's treasury, had begun. "I have orders to remove your tokens from circulation. This reminds me of the time I charged your neighbor, Henning Dietzel, with counterfeiting because he paid his workers with scrip. Don't worry. I won't come after you if you convince me you were unselfishly preventing economic collapse during a national emergency."

"I don't suppose you accept tokens?" Cabrera said, taking out his wallet. As Sarmiento politely chuckled, Cabrera folded a wad of hundred dollar bills and handed it over, then asked, "What happened at Dietzel's counterfeiting trial?"

"We didn't get that far. He turned out to have nine lives."

"Only nine?" Cabrera had replied. "That means he's down to his last one."

Consulting his watch as he stepped from his carriage at Noya's office, Cabrera told his driver, "Barely over an hour. Well done."

At his desk he pored over maps. Largely because of him, the Valley's hundreds of farms had been consolidated into giant haciendas, the biggest of which were Noya and Toledo. Of the other thirteen, seven were for sale, and six others soon would be. This time he wouldn't be able to pay rock bottom prices because he'd have to outbid Henning Dietzel.

At least he was well prepared. While paying his bills with tokens, he'd stockpiled a fortune in crisp, new U.S. dollars.

******

In 1892 José Geldres's arthritis forced him to sell Dos Palos. To preserve his independence, he declined Martine's invitation to live at Toledo and instead rented a room in Cortéz. Two months later he walked into Dr. Carmona's office, complaining of chest pain.

Later that day, *Don* José summoned Martine's Uncle Alfredo from a hospital bed.

Down the hall a baby halfheartedly cried as Alfredo, tall and solemn, strode into *Don* José's room.

"Years ago we spoke at your brother's funeral," Geldres began.

"I remember," Alfredo said. "You recommended I get to know my niece, who's also your goddaughter. Does she know about your condition?"

"She doesn't even know I'm in the hospital."

"I'll tell her."

Sitting beside the bed, Alfredo asked questions and made notes for his new client's Last Will and Testament. *Don* José signed it the following afternoon. Hours later he died at an age his obituary described as 'advanced' because no one knew when he'd been born.

*****

Alfredo Prado hadn't knocked on Toledo's door for years. Seeing her normally reserved uncle's distress, Martine disrupted his plan to deliver the news gently.

"Something terrible happened, didn't it? What? Tell me now, please."

"*Don* José had a fatal heart attack," Alfredo said, coming inside.

"*Dios mio.* You just tore my heart out. Was he in pain?"

"He was doing his best to stay alive. That usually means a person's suffering isn't burdensome."

"Wish I could've said goodbye." Fighting to control her emotions, Martine led the way to the library where Henning was on tiptoes reaching for a book.

She cleared her throat and said, "*Don* José passed away."

"What happened?" Henning took her in his arms.

"Heart attack." Martine pulled back, embarrassed by his affectionate display. Uncle Alfredo—like her father—was from an era when men and women never touched around others.

She felt her self-control ebbing and barely reached the bathroom before releasing a flood of tears that made her reflection in the mirror seem to dissolve.

When she returned to the library Henning picked up a bell and rang in vain for a servant.

"I'll get us a pot of tea," he offered, heading for the kitchen.

Handing a document from his leather case to Martine, Uncle Alfredo said, "*Don* José's Last Will and Testament. He left you his worldly goods."

Martine had never heard a relative—except Pietro—refer to Geldres as *Don*. He would've liked that.

When Henning returned, Uncle Alfredo handed him a rolled-up parchment. "This map shows the location of the Inca tomb where *Don* José found his artifacts and stored his valuables. He asked me to give it to you with this note."

"'If you're as decent as I think,'" Henning read aloud, "'you'll solve this map's mysteries.' Strange thing to say. Mysteries are solved by being smart—not decent."

After lunch Alfredo left Henning and Martine to reminisce about the man who'd been their dearest mutual friend. When neither had more to say Henning unrolled the map on the coffee table, his fingers along the edges to hold it flat.

With Martine looking over his shoulder, he said, "Guess I'm not as decent as *Don* José thought. "There's no scale, nothing to show which way is north. And what are those wavy lines and zigzags. Ravines? Hills? Trails?"

Stubbornly he rotated the map one way and another, trying to unlock its secrets. Finally he released its edges and the parchment rolled up.

"Bedtime," he said.

When Henning came to breakfast the next morning Martine was already at the table, a newspaper beside her empty porridge bowl.

"Uncle Alfredo sent *Don* José's obituary," she said. "I wish someone had written such nice things when he was alive to enjoy them. Have you had any inspirations regarding his map?"

"Sorry, but I doubt we'll ever know what he left you."

******

Dividing the proceeds from his nitrate properties into down payments, Henning purchased six of the Valley's remaining haciendas, to Cabrera's seven. Between them they now owned the entire Valley. But this accomplishment soon increased their problems.

Cabrera's worsened when Tuco Zamora, a *cholo*, organized Noya's workers and set out to improve wages and working conditions. His demands ignored, Zamora called a strike.

Forced to increase salaries Cabrera later rescinded the pay hike, blaming low sugar prices and setting off several rounds of tit-for-tat. Again Noya's mill workers walked out. Cabrera's friends in the government sent soldiers who forced them back to work. The strikers set fire to Noya's mill, destroying it. Cabrera sent his cane to be processed in the small refineries acquired when he'd bought out competitors. Then those were sabotaged.

Toledo was spared this strife because its workers earned more than the strikers has demanded. But when Henning's best customer switched to less expensive beet sugar, his income no longer covered expenses, and he couldn't make up the shortfall because he'd sold his other sources of income.

CHAPTER THIRTY-THREE

A DEAL WITH THE DEVIL

La Gallega, Peru's fastest passenger liner, was the first propeller-driven ship Captain Medina had handled. He enjoyed nothing more than taking her wheel, as he had shortly before Henning and Martine joined him on the bridge.

"The view up here is beautiful," Martine said.

Medina spun the wheel, alternately catching and releasing its spokes. *La Gallega's* bow swung toward Callao.

"Dry land has rivers and oceans have currents," he said. "Both are helpful when they flow in the right direction, but we've been bucking an unusually strong Humboldt Current all day. You should get there in time for the show, but if I were you I'd change into my evening clothes now."

In their cabin Henning put on a white tie, and black dinner suit. Top hat in hand, he went on deck and watched Callao grow from a narrow sliver to a wide panorama. When Martine joined him, she wore a form-fitting blue evening dress and silver shoes.

From the docks they took a *calesa* to the railway station, a train to Lima, and a cab to the *Teatro Municipal.* The curtains were still closed as the usher hurried them down a hallway behind the top tier of luxury boxes on the back wall.

A man came through a door and stared at Martine as she passed. Even at fifty she was striking, and the dimly lit corridor made her young again. The usher stopped in front of the center box. When Martine pivoted toward the door, Henning saw the profile of her high, still-firm breasts.

"The president sits here when he attends," the usher said. A bell tinkled as he pushed the door open.

With every seat empty, Henning and Martine chose two in front.

"There's a sold out sign on the ticket counter," she said. "Why is this box empty?"

"I didn't want to share you on our anniversary," he replied, "so I bought all the seats. You have the second-best view in the theater."

"There's a better one?"

"Yes." He stared at her. "Mine is much better."

That evening's show was a comedy. After Martine had said she'd like to see it, Henning had surprised her with tickets.

The lights dimmed and Martine pressed a silk-covered leg against Henning's. The first act featured a buffoon constantly on the verge of losing his baggy trousers. Henning didn't find him funny but Martine couldn't stop laughing. During the last act she took advantage of the privacy and leaned her head on his shoulder.

When Henning was a sailor, shipmates had ridiculed him for choosing Encinas Peralta every time they went to the House of Smiles bordello.

"A stranger," one had said, speaking for all of them, "is more exciting."

Henning hadn't agreed then and still didn't. To him, bonds formed over time made sexual relationships better. The longer he'd known Martine, the more appealing she'd become. Maybe that was only because he'd never felt absolutely certain she loved him. But the way he felt tonight was ample reward for that sometimes painful uncertainty.

After the final curtain they strolled to their hotel beneath gaslights that cast flickering circles on the sidewalk. Partway there, Henning put his arm around Martine and pulled her close without breaking stride.

In their room she asked him to look away, a request she always made when undressing in his presence. He'd seen her naked only once since the stillbirth, and that had been an accident. But he'd seen enough to know the scar on her once-smooth stomach resembled a crumpled shirt. Which explained why she didn't want him to see it. Over the years he'd been unable to convince her that he saw the scar as a symbol of her valiant effort to give him a son.

When Henning heard her pull the maroon comforter up to her neck, he sat on the bed. The more he picked at his knotted shoelace, the tighter it got. Watching, she giggled.

"This isn't funny," he declared with a mock scowl.

Soon he was laughing as hard as she was. Finally at ease together, they'd never been happier. And somewhere along the line Martine had become more important than Henning's work. Even with Toledo's precarious finances, this lavish anniversary trip hadn't struck him as frivolous. Saving their hacienda would require hundreds of times what he'd spent.

But on his deathbed, he'd remember tonight.

******

Finished with his errands, Henning went sightseeing along Cortéz's oceanside *Malecón* boardwalk. In no hurry for once, he hunkered down to watch youngsters skip coin-shaped pebbles across a pool left by the retreating tide. Shadows of passing pedestrians flickered across the sand. One stopped and he raised his eyes to see Emiliano Cabrera looking down.

Henning's knees protested as he stood too quickly after squatting too long.

After a lifetime of satisfying many appetites without restraint, Cabrera's largest circumference was his waist. And those cold eyes still revealed his ever-present detachment from all concerns but his own—no matter how much he smiled.

"Knowing your wife will oppose my proposal," he began with decidedly un-Peruvian directness, "I decided to present it when she's not with you."

"I'm listening," Henning said, instantly wary.

"Let's go someplace private. My office perhaps?"

"I've always believed enemies should negotiate on neutral ground."

"We're not enemies. We're potential friends with a rare opportunity to help each other. However, if you insist on neutral ground, I—"

"Your office will be fine."

Henning knew what Cabrera wanted. He wanted it too but had thought Cabrera was too proud. Evidently the man's problems were worse than he'd realized.

With rapid strides Cabrera led the way to a carriage. Henning beside him, he drove in silence, then veered onto a red, brick-surfaced driveway. A waiting *cholo* held the horses while Cabrera and Henning dismounted under a hanging sign that read: Sales Office–Hacienda Noya–Emiliano Cabrera, Proprietor.

Inside, Cabrera hurried past a secretary and unlocked his private office. A sable and white collie lay in the far corner, muzzle nestled in its flank hair. Seeing Cabrera it backed up until pressed against the wall, concentrating on Cabrera and reminding Henning to do likewise.

They sat on opposite sides of the desk. Cabrera folded a newspaper, hiding the rectangular hole from which an article had been clipped.

"I want you to mill my cane," he said, confirming Henning's suspicion. "For a fee, of course. With sugar prices as low as they are, I'm sure you can use the income."

Knowing he'd get better terms if he needed persuading, Henning showed minimal interest. They discussed possible arrangements, finding nothing mutually acceptable.

Frustrated—or playacting—Cabrera angrily leapt to his feet and insisted, "This deal is to your advantage as much as mine. Why should you get the better of it?"

The collie whined. Dropping back into his chair, Cabrera smoothed back the hair that had fallen across his forehead and calmed himself. What choice did he have? His cane needed processing and Henning had the Valley's last functioning mill.

Cabrera made his first concrete proposal.

"Exactly how would that work?" Henning asked.

Slowly Cabrera covered the same ground again, in greater detail. Having understood the first time, Henning pretended to listen while preparing a counterproposal.

"I have some conditions," he said when Cabrera finished. "First, I want you to sell two hundred tons of Toledo's sugar every month."

"If you can't sell it, what makes you think I can?"

"You wouldn't have tried to buy every available hacienda if you didn't have more customers than sugar."

"If I market yours, you'll have to pay a commission."

"No."

Staring past Henning until then, Cabrera looked directly at him. "Then you'll have to mill my cane for a special price." He suggested a per-ton rate.

Henning tripled it.

"That's outrageous!" Cabrera slammed his fist on the desk.

"Not if you consider that I have the only operating mill within hundreds of miles. You'll still make a profit."

"Less than half what I was making before."

"But more than you'll make if we don't reach an agreement." Henning paused, then added, "I also want our contract to specify that disputes will be settled in Lima's courts."

"What's wrong with the one in Cortéz?"

"I prefer Lima's," Henning said, sidestepping an argument that would lead nowhere.

"Are you questioning Judge Benavides's integrity?"

"I'll resist the urge to ask what integrity that might be."

Upset by their raised voices the collie cowered, tail between its legs. The unfortunate animal had more to fear from Cabrera than Henning did. If anything happened to him, Martine would go broke rather than mill Noya's cane. And Cabrera knew that.

CHAPTER THIRTY-FOUR
THE POWER OF PROPAGANDA

Preparing to operate Toledo's refinery around the clock, Henning hired Cabrera's striking mill workers. That afternoon immersed in the smell of molasses, Henning took his new workers to where long time employees could show them how to operate the mill's separators, boilers, steam engines, and water storage tanks.

"I want you to personally teach the workers who'll handle the dry sugar," he told Alcalino. "Sugar dust explosions can be lethal, and I want these men safe and sound with their families every night."

"What does Martine think about processing Noya's cane?" Encinas asked, joining them.

"She doesn't know yet," Henning replied, "but she'll appreciate the irony, don't you think? Cabrera rescinded his workers' raises and they went on strike. Now the same workers will process the same cane and it'll cost Cabrera more than the pay increase he cancelled."

"Those nuances won't occur to her," Encinas said. "All she'll see is her husband helping her worst enemy."

"You don't think she'll enjoy seeing her worst enemy save Toledo after doing everything he could to put it out of business?"

"Subtleties like that won't occur to someone as angry as she'll be."

Encinas was right. Henning should tell Martine about the contract and explain why he'd signed it. But he'd have to work day and night to get ready for Noya's cane. Trying to briefly tell Martine what he'd done would be followed by hours and more hours of angry debate.

Already exhausted and short-tempered, he decided to put off that confrontation as long as possible. Even though that would make it worse.

******

Martine was surprised when Toledo's refinery didn't shut down at the usual time. And bewildered when wagons brought freshly cut cane from the main road rather than Toledo's fields. All week she'd known something was afoot. Chabuca had been taking Henning's meals to the mill and he'd been sleeping four hours instead of the usual eight.

By dawn Henning still hadn't come to bed, and Martine had reached an unthinkable conclusion. Hiking to the mill, she heard squeaking wheels and plopping hooves as wagons rolled to and from the crushers. Less than half were Toledo's. Then she recognized one of Emiliano Cabrera's drivers, confirming her worst fear. Her husband was helping the man responsible for her brother's murder.

Seeing Encinas on horseback and desperately tired, she blurted out, "I won't stand for what you and my husband are doing. It's wrong."

"For you right and wrong are easy to distinguish, like black and white," Encinas said. "But life sometimes forces us to accept a mixture of the two."

"Life doesn't mix right with wrong. People do. And they shouldn't. It's easy to tell the difference."

"Maybe for you," Encinas said, wearily continuing on her way.

Furious, Martine headed for Henning's office.

******

Henning's office door burst open and the chief mechanic rushed in.

"A boiler failed," he said breathlessly. "Repairs will take two days at least."

"What else can possibly go wrong?"

Henning's rhetorical question was answered when Martine charged in— chin first—screaming, "Why are you helping that worthless *cabrón*?"

"Strange word for a lady," Henning said.

"There are more where it came from." She bore down on him, green eyes smoldering.

The chief mechanic left faster than he'd come in.

"I'm milling Cabrera's sugar," Henning said with forced calm, "because saving Toledo is more important than hurting Noya."

"You promised you'd fight that *pendejo* if you could catch him when he's down," Martine fumed. "Well he's down, and if you don't mill his cane he'll stay there. We can finally push him into the fires of hell where he belongs."

"If we do, we'll fall in right behind him. Toledo can't meet its obligations without the money he's paying us."

"You didn't tell me you were considering this. I deserved a chance to talk you out of it."

"You couldn't have. The only alternative is losing Toledo. Look, I got the best of the deal. Cabrera is paying three times the normal milling fee and marketing our sugar without a commission. I doubt he'll be able to afford a new mill when our contract expires. If Toledo's situation is better then, I'll stop processing his sugar and let him go broke."

"If," Martine repeated disdainfully. "Why pass up a sure thing for something that may never happen." She stormed out, unshed tears of fury and betrayal in her eyes.

At dinner Martine was aloof but calm, giving Henning hope she understood his decision even though she disagreed. That possibility faded when he came from the mill at midnight and found her bed and clothes gone. He was working day and night to save Toledo. And she was indulging in petty punishment.

He stormed down the hall and threw open the door to her new room.

Propped up against her headboard reading, she spoke first without looking up. "I'll never accept or understand your treachery."

"Treachery?" Henning growled. "Hell, I just saved your hacienda for the second time."

To release his pent-up rage, Henning scooped up a handful of rose petals floating in a cut glass bowl on her dressing table. Hurled, they splattered against her comforter.

Glaring, she said, "Surely you don't expect that to make me accept what you've done."

******

For years Henning had given Toledo's mill workers bonuses based on how much their shifts produced. After the first day of the new twenty-four hour schedule, he paid the night crew's bonuses as the day crew arrived. Again that evening, he paid the departing workers in front of their replacements.

Seeing the day shift receive more money for the same number of hours, the night crew sped up, setting Toledo's all-time twelve-hour production record. It was broken while they slept and fell regularly for weeks. When neither shift could move faster, both began devising techniques that further increased output.

By then Cabrera's former mill workers were earning twice what he'd refused them, and refining sugar for half what it had cost him. When Martine heard them praising Henning, her anger faded.

But not enough to bring her back to his bedroom.

******

An hour into his explanation, Henning closed Toledo's current ledger and turned to Martine, sitting beside him at his desk.

"My accounting lessons with Encinas," she said, "taught me enough to understand that you're right. Toledo can't survive without milling Cabrera's cane."

"If things get to where we don't need him to sell our cane," Henning offered, "I won't renew his milling contract."

"From what I just saw, that will take a miracle."

"A miracle that may be within reach after I digest this." Henning held up a book with *The Power of Propaganda* in gold letters on its blue cover.

"That must be fascinating. It's held your attention for weeks."

"It begins with a committee the Catholic Church set up to win converts. Then it describes propaganda's evolution into a commercial tool."

"Sounds like plain old advertising to me."

"Propaganda promotes broad goals rather than specific products. For example, a firm in New York uses it to attract European farmers to California."

"So attracting farmers is like converting people to Catholicism?"

"I wouldn't say that." Henning removed his new spectacles. "But attracting farmers is definitely similar to selling sugar."

"Tell me more."

"When France's Emperor Napoleon controlled Europe he banned imports from Britain, denying income to merchants whose taxes supported his archenemy, England. For decades the English continued importing cane sugar while continental Europe grew sugar beets. But now British farmers are raising beets for refineries that once bought from us. With the right propaganda we can get those customers back."

"And stop milling Cabrera's cane," Martine finished his thought. "If you can manage that you're a genius."

"If I had half a brain I would have told you about my deal with Cabrera and we'd still be in the same bedroom."

"You keep promising to discuss things with me," she teased. "When will you do it?"

"Now. I should have started the day we married."

"My impatience is partly to blame," she said. "By now I should know your methods eventually reach my goals. If it's okay with you, I'll have Pedro move my things back to your room." She heaved a sigh, then added. "*Dios mío.* The way I keep moving in and out will make him suspect I'm crazy. Oh, well. Better to have him suspect that than to try to explain and remove all doubt."

******

Henning met Liverpool's sugar importers in a room with a cane field painted across one wall, a reminder of when these men had marketed their product so effectively that England had no market for beet sugar.

"As you know," he told them at a conference table, "sugar beets—unlike cane—can be grown in England's climate, making them cheaper. However, cane has advantages you can exploit with a relatively modest investment in propaganda."

After Henning outlined his plan, a director asked, "How much will it cost?"

"I brought this bid from Barrington & Vickers in New York."

The directors passed Henning's envelope from hand to hand until it reached the head of the table. The man there reviewed its contents, then looked up and asked, "Mr. Dietzel, may I please have a private discussion with the board?"

Later, the managing director joined him in the waiting room and said, "We'll finance your plan. And if it increases sales to previous levels we'll buy Toledo's sugar for ten years."

******

Henning left Liverpool on White Star Line's *SS Majestic*, which had briefly held the Blue Riband for fastest crossing of the Atlantic. She made excellent time to New York where a storm broke as he exited immigration. An unusually profane driver in a covered cab took him to Barrington & Vickers amidst hailstones bouncing on streets and sidewalks like rubber balls.

"I'm sure we can make your trip worthwhile," Winston Barrington welcomed him. "How exactly would you stop sugar beets from taking over England's market?"

"I wrote down a few ideas." Henning handed over the proposal he'd presented to Liverpool's sugar importers. "But you're an expert. Do what you think best."

"You just passed a test. We don't accept clients who tell us how to do our job."

"And I don't hire people to do things I can do myself. The Brits are stubborn. Changing their minds will require someone who knows more about influencing public opinion than I do."

Something in Henning's proposal caught Barrington's eye. He kept reading.

Finally finished he said, "You can offer advice anytime you like."

As Henning had proposed, Barrington began his campaign by exploiting the widely held opinion that cane sugar tasted better.

'The difference,' thousands of posters told consumers in London, Manchester, Bristol, Birmingham, and Liverpool, 'can be appreciated in beverages, baked goods, sweets, jams, and wherever sugar is used.'

After that, banners proclaimed cane sugar 'cleaner and more healthful,' emphasizing that, 'Beets grow underground while cane matures in fresh air and sunshine.' Similar propaganda was scheduled to appear even if cane sugar sales returned to previous levels.

Months after returning from New York, a smiling Henning handed Martine the long awaited envelope he'd picked up at the new post office in Cortéz. Postmarked Liverpool, it was neatly slit open. Inside she found a contract guaranteeing England's sugar importers would buy Toledo's sugar for the next ten years.

"And Cabrera cancelled the contract to build his new mill," Henning said, "which means he couldn't get financing. When our current agreement expires we can stop milling his cane. He's finished. Done. *Kaputt.*"

CHAPTER THIRTY-FIVE
MEORIAL TO A MARTYR

Emerging from Toledo's best field, Henning looked back at the dark, rich soil that had again yielded eighteen-foot cane. The latest crop had been set afire yesterday, burning away the dry leaves and feathery flowers. Today, workers had felled and stacked the bamboo-like stalks. Tomorrow, wagons would take them to the mill.

Hearing wailing from inside the nearby workers' village, Henning turned his horse between rows of houses with common sidewalls. Children should have been playing while their fathers relaxed after work. Instead everyone was gathered near Ana Jaramillo's door, where women trying to console her had instead succumbed to their own grief.

"What happened, Ricardo?" Henning asked a man wearing a black armband.

"This morning," Ricardo replied, "Cabrera's field hands stopped harvesting Noya's cane and staged a demonstration. The army sent troops."

"And?" Henning swung down from his horse.

"Federico García's thugs shot Tuco Zamora and others including Ana Jaramillo's son, Guillermo."

"The soldiers let them do that?"

"They joined in. Unbelievable, no? The Chileans were here for years without bloodshed, but our own troops started killing us an hour after arriving." Ricardo extended his hand. "Let me hold your horse while you deliver your condolences."

"Thank you."

Guillermo Jaramillo had been Belisario's head overseer and then Henning's. Inspired by Tuco Zamora's speeches, he'd quit to help organize Noya's strike. Now washed and in clean clothes, he'd begun changing color but otherwise seemed asleep in the open coffin near his widowed mother's door.

Henning stopped behind a group waiting to offer their sympathy. They stepped aside so he could go first. He insisted on waiting in line.

When his turn came Henning told Ana, "A woman who loses her husband is a widow. A child who loses a parent is an orphan. But losing a child is so unthinkable that no language has a word for it."

"Dear God," a familiar voice male behind them said. "It's true. They murdered him."

Turning, Henning saw Belisario and Martine, their horses ground-tied behind them.

The crowd opened a path. As Martine hugged Ana, the old woman's shoulders shuddered. Both were sobbing by the time they stepped apart.

Henning engulfed one of Ana's dry, wrinkled hands in both of his and said, "I'll see to it that Guillermo has a fitting monument, something that will remind us of how wonderful he was."

Eyes lowered, the old woman managed, "*Gracias, señor.*"

Belisario was waiting next to his horse when Martine and Henning reached theirs.

With the fingers used to scrape pus from a festering sore, a boy—about four—grabbed Henning's hand. He looked up and started to speak, then lost his nerve and backed away.

As Henning wiped the yellowish matter on his pant leg, Belisario snapped, "You should have disinfected all the way to the elbow after the handshake that obligated you to mill Emiliano Cabrera's cane. Why didn't you let his workers shut him down?"

"Because that would have hurt Toledo as well as Noya," Martine said protectively, using the argument she'd rejected when Henning first offered it.

Glowering, Belisario mounted up.

"No need to wait," Martine said. "I'll ride home with Henning."

"Talk some sense into him," the old aristocrat snapped. "Now that Cabrera's field workers have gone on strike, his friends in the government will send convicts to harvest his cane. If Henning processes what they cut, all this suffering will have been for nothing."

He rode away, forgetting to tip Ricardo for tending his horse.

A dog scratched itself with a hind leg, repeatedly thumping its hock on the ground.

Henning took the metal box with the red cross from his saddle and sat on his haunches next to the boy who'd grabbed his hand. Unwilling to let Henning clean and bandage his wound, the boy gave in after Martine knelt beside him.

"Let's open a school for the workers' children," she suggested as the youngster ran off. "We can put it in a warehouse. These are hard times, but it won't cost much."

"Educating these kids will just prepare them for opportunities they'll never have."

"That doesn't sound like the Henning I know and love. How would you feel if someone decided what was beyond your reach and then denied you the tools to get there? *Serranos* have as much right as we do to be valued and educated."

"An education will just make these kids dissatisfied with their place in the world. No one will hire them for better jobs."

"Bettering their lives will take time. Let's help them take the first step."

A flock of birds flashed by, low and fast.

"Okay," Henning said. "Open your school."

He still didn't believe an education would lead to better jobs. But being able to mother the workers' children would compensate Martine for not having her own. And a school would be a fitting memorial to Guillermo Jaramillo.

"Is Belisario right about the convicts?" Martine asked later, as they rode away.

"Yes and that means I have to continue milling Cabrera's cane until our contract expires. Otherwise, he won't need bribes and crooked judges to win a settlement that could bankrupt us."

"I understand. I don't like it, but a contract is a contract." Martine smiled mischievously. "Besides, if I start a fight I'll have to move out of your room again."

"Our room," Henning said with a meaningful look.

******

Ana Jaramillo was guest of honor the day Toledo's *Escuela Guillermo Jaramillo* opened. Before the ceremony she sat on a raised platform with Henning, Martine, and newly hired teacher, Wilfredo Delgado. Then, eyes glowing with pride, she stepped to the podium and praised her son in words that concluded with, "Guillermo died trying to make the world better for us *cholos*. This school will help that happen. But only if parents who saw no need for education recognize that their children will suffer if they don't take advantage of this opportunity."

Her eloquence reminded Henning of how well most *cholos* spoke. It was impressive considering that their only schooling was listening to Peru's highly educated *Dons*.

"Thank you, *Don* Henning," Ana said before sitting down.

Her praise made him uncomfortable. He'd never abused his workers and had always paid them well. But he'd never before helped them without expecting something in return.

Señor Delgado replaced Ana at the podium. Elderly with white whiskers, pumpkin-colored around his mouth, he began, "Education enriches lives and fosters success. And now your children can attend school, a blessing few *cholos* have ever had."

As Delgado droned on, Alcalino's dog—the only one at Toledo with meat on its ribs—trotted in to sniff a trash can. Alcalino took him outside and tied him to a fence, then rejoined Estella and their daughters in the front row beside the refinery's night manager, Dante Acosta, and his wife.

Sexy and promiscuous, *Señora* Acosta wore a dress that emphasized her plump breasts and flat abdomen. Henning sighed with sympathy. He felt sorry for Dante, whose pathetic efforts to stop his wife's straying had included trying to hide his bald spot with colored shoe wax. He didn't deserve his fate but had invited it by choosing beauty over goodness.

And on the subject of injustice, why did Dante's wife have children to neglect while Martine—who'd have been a splendid mother—had none?

Lowering himself into his chair, Delgado announced, "Time to enroll your children."

Alcalino's daughters were first in line. Glancing at the boys behind them, Delgado asked Martine, "What's your policy on girls?"

"Ana," Martine said, "would you like to answer?"

Normally deferential, Ana answered boldly, "*Escuela Guillermo Jaramillo* will take all the girls it can get."

After enrollment, refreshments were served. Standing beside Henning in a corner, Alcalino said, "I hope it wasn't a mistake to enroll my daughters. They'll be the only girls in the school, and the boys will make them miserable. But I'll pick them up, dust them off, and sent them back again the next morning."

"Do you ever wish you'd had boys?" Henning asked.

"Never. My girls stay awake if I don't get home until after they go to bed. The older one has a special little voice she uses to let me know they're waiting for a goodnight kiss. I can't imagine boys doing that."

Henning flashed one of his rare smiles, pleased that a *cholo* son deprived of love had become a *cholo* father who gave it freely.

CHAPTER THIRTY-SIX
THORNS WITHOUT ROSES

Henning and Martine were in the front hall when someone struck the first blow with the brass knocker. Their visitor looked startled when Henning opened the door while still being summoned. His trimmed moustache and severe expression made him look dignified enough to have multiple surnames.

"Franklin Forbes-Finnegan," he introduced himself with a melodious accent. "I represent British Mercantile Bank here in Peru. Forgive me for dropping in unannounced, but I have a proposition. I trust your religious beliefs don't preclude talking business on the Sabbath."

"Not at all," Henning replied. "Come in."

He had a servant restore the shine to Forbes-Finnegan's dusty shoes and then motioned for Martine to lead the way.

"Would anyone like tea, coffee, or something cold?" Martine asked once they were seated in the library.

"Tea would be perfect, as a metrafect," Forbes-Finnegan replied, pronouncing matter-of-fact as a single word.

They discussed the improving market for sugar until Chabuca brought tea and cakes. Then Forbes-Finnegan said, "British Mercantile has loaned money to Emiliano Cabrera for decades, though not since the strike, of course. We consider ourselves enlightened and wouldn't have done business with him if we'd known how harsh he was with employees. I'm in the Valley because *Señor* Cabrera was behind on his payments. Have you heard yet that two of his workers hacked him and his manager to death with machetes this morning? None of Noya's workers will tell the *Guardia Civil* who did it. All they'll say is that Cabrera's abuses finally unleashed the wrath of God."

Henning and Martine stared at each other, dumbstruck.

"I doubt God had anything to do with it," Martine said, recovering from her surprise. "But Cabrera finally got what he deserved."

"It appears British Mercantile will foreclose on Noya." Forbes-Finnegan removed his spectacles and rubbed the indentations on his nose. "Are you interested in purchasing it?"

"Let's discuss that over lunch," Henning suggested.

Chabuca showed Forbes-Finnegan to the washroom, then set an extra place at the table as Henning and Martine seated themselves.

Leaning close Martine said, "I was looking forward to seeing you defeat Cabrera in a glorious, climactic battle."

"In a book called *The Art of War*, an ancient Chinese general named Sun Tzu said the best victory is the battle you win without having to fight it."

"I'm glad you know things like that. If you'd listened to me and gone to war with Cabrera, we'd be bankrupt." These days her hair—more gray than brunette—added dignity to her fierce beauty.

After Forbes-Finnegan returned, Chabuca served pork roast, mashed potatoes, and asparagus.

"Noya was granted to Emiliano Cabrera's great grandfather, seven times removed, by King Philip the Fifth of Spain," the Englishman began as they ate. "Only a small portion lies in the Chiriaco Valley. To the west it borders the Pacific Ocean. To the east it stretches across the Andes into the jungle. It's the size of a small country, over one and a half million acres."

"The only part I want," Henning said, "is what's in the Chiriaco Valley."

"You'll have to buy all or none, and British Mercantile won't carry the loan. If you can't find a lender to pay us off, we'll operate Noya in competition with you."

"How much are you asking?"

"Fifty-five million dollars."

Yet again Henning's knowledge of history had a practical application. U.S. President Thomas Jefferson's Louisiana Purchase, from France, had doubled the size of the United States for fifteen million dollars. Later the

U.S. had bought Alaska, nearly six hundred thousand square miles, from Russia for just over seven million.

"For less than half that amount," Henning said, "the United States made the Louisiana Purchase and bought Alaska. Together those are many hundreds of times larger than Noya."

"Yes," Forbes-Finnegan agreed, "but the Louisiana Purchase and Alaska are useless wilderness. The portion of Noya in the Chiriaco Valley is fully developed farmland in an area where crops can be cultivated year-round. Its profits, combined with Toledo's, can easily service a fifty-five million dollar debt."

"You won't find another buyer," Henning countered. "Building a new mill will cost a million dollars and take a year—during which you'll have no income. Afterward you'll have to operate with disgruntled workers as well as limited knowledge of the sugar business."

"Would you be agreeable to fifty-three million?"

"Fifty is as high as I'll go, and I want a list of Cabrera's customers along with access to his financial records."

After further haggling confirmed Henning's determination to defer unless he got his price, Forbes-Finnegan accepted.

For weeks Henning shopped for a loan. But Peru's banks were investing in mining, and Britain's were put off by Peru's labor unrest. Lenders in the U.S. were keeping their money at home, and France's refused to do business in South America.

Germany's Deutsche Landesbank offered a loan but demanded the security include both Noya and Toledo. In return, Henning asked for a lower interest rate. Landesbank agreed on the condition that one of its accountants live at Toledo, keep its books, and have a veto over nonessential expenditures until the loan balance was reduced by half.

"You've always said a business can't have two bosses," Martine reminded Henning after reading this proposal.

"It should be easy enough," he said, "for men of goodwill to resolve disagreements over something as inconsequential as nonessential expenditures."

"Will Landesbank guarantee to send an accountant with goodwill?"

******

The loan documents were finalized on Uncle Alfredo's office desk, near a statuette of an orator with one hand raised high for emphasis. Word got out quickly. Wherever Henning went for the rest of the day, he was congratulated.

In Cortéz's *Plaza Central* he was surrounded by admirers who shook his hand and lavished him with praise. Their adulation echoed a scene in Lima's *Plaza Central* where Peru's high and mighty of forty-two years earlier had paid homage to Martine's father, the new Ambassador to Argentina. That night—in threadbare clothes, a saddlebag of cash over one shoulder—Henning had hired Alcalino Valdivia and been captivated by Martine Prado. All these years later he wanted to share his triumph with them and others like them—not with people who hoped to gain by flattering him.

"Have you seen this?" A man handed Henning the latest *Lima Correo*, headlined: Peruvian Plantation Becomes Largest on Earth. The accompanying article began, 'Having acquired Hacienda Noya, Henning Dietzel will now provide a third of Peru's sugar exports, making him perhaps this country's most eminent citizen.'

Politely Henning freed himself and left the plaza, looking forward to the evening's dinner party at Uncle Alfredo's house. Martine had invited his closest friends including three he hadn't seen for years, Eduardo Vásquez, Jorge Villegas, and Andrés de la Borda. Decades ago Villegas and Henning had made a small fortune clearing away the dump and wall that surrounded Lima and restricted its growth. And after his articles describing Iquique and the Atacama Desert under Chilean rule, de la Borda had become editor of the *Lima Correo*.

******

Following dinner Eduardo stood, tapping a table knife against a fluted crystal goblet. When the ringing had attracted everyone's attention, he proposed a toast, "To Peru's greatest businessman."

Their glasses drained, everyone filed from the brightly lit dining hall into the warm orange glow of the sitting room fireplace. As they sat on couches arranged in a square, their group conversation broke into smaller ones.

"No more discussing work," Henning interrupted. "I want to know about your personal lives. You first, Eduardo."

"I have a new lady friend," Eduardo began. "We've been seeing each other for a year, but don't get the idea there's a wedding in the offing. I'm not ready to give up my freedom."

"Same old Eduardo," Henning teased.

"With one small change," Eduardo responded. "While you wrote the story of your life, I often tried to take the pen from your hand. I'm glad you didn't let me. I wouldn't have done half the job you did."

"Next." Henning pointed to Encinas.

"My son," she said, "graduated with honors from Cortéz Academy."

"Wonderful," Henning responded. "Give him my congratulations. Who else has good news?"

"My uncle donated a statue of my father to Lima's *Alameda de los Descalzos*," Alcalino offered shyly. "Its plaque commemorates his loyalty to Peru during the war with Chile."

Henning applauded and everyone joined in.

"*Escuela Guillermo Jaramillo* has received a National Education Award," Martine said, taking her turn. "As we celebrate my husband tonight, I can't resist praising his generosity, which was so apparent when he financed Toledo's school with money he couldn't spare."

"Thank you, my love," Henning said. "I wouldn't be more pleased if you'd composed a sonnet in my honor."

She shocked him with a public kiss on his cheek.

Gustavo Medina was next. "Like everyone here, I have ample reason to be grateful to Henning. The best years of my life came after I stopped delivering freight and started carrying passengers, something I could never have done without his help."

"No one here," Jorge Villegas followed, "except Henning, knows I was a dyed-in-the-wool communist before he converted me to capitalism. Thanks to him I was able to retire while I could still enjoy my children and grandchildren rather than be a burden to them."

"I'm working on Henning's biography," Andrés de la Borda said, "and hope to finish it with his discovery of *Don* José Geldres's famous treasure, a tale I'll tell in a way that guarantees private collectors and museums eagerly compete to buy what he finds."

"I'll tell you scoundrels about my personal life," Uncle Alfredo said, "after Henning tells us what happened to his bodyguards."

"I sent them back to Chile," Henning said, "except for O'Higgins."

"Hope that wasn't a mistake," Alfredo said. "Speaking of which, I have something to show you."

He led Henning to his office desk where they hunched over an open ledger.

"These estimates are based on detailed conversations with José Geldres," Alfredo explained, then slid his finger down the page, stopping at each number in a column. "That's how much he received for Dos Palos. That's what he cleared as a labor agent. That's from the sale of Inca artifacts and jewelry. That's the estimated value of the remaining artifacts, and that's what I calculate collectors will pay for his gold coins—dating back to the 1700s— of which there are thousands." Moving his finger to the total Alfredo said, "All told, *Don* José's treasure adds up to a sum that would put a substantial dent in Toledo's mortgage."

"That's a subject for another day," Henning said. "I want to spend tonight enjoying you and the people in the next room."

******

In January, 1895 Horst Beller, a chalky white, balding accountant sent by Deutsche Landesbank, arrived while Henning was in the fields. As soon as Beller's trunk was at the foot of his bed, he demanded to see the head accountant.

Walking with Encinas to her office, he ignored her attempts at conversation.

Inside, he plopped down in her chair and rolled up his sleeves. After securing them with bands he replaced his necktie with a bowtie, explaining, "This one doesn't get in my way."

Having brashly commandeered Encinas's chair, Beller demanded Toledo's ledgers. By the time Encinas brought them, he had donned a pince-nez with round, flat lenses that hid both eyes behind reflections and were held on his nose by a spring-loaded clip.

Twice in ten minutes, Beller's baby-faced assistant, Jürgen Müller, tried to anticipate what his boss wanted next. Both times he guessed wrong and was taken to task.

"*Señorita* Peralta," Beller said, slamming January's ledger shut. "Keep Thursday afternoon open. I'll have questions once I finish reviewing these."

For lunch and again at dinnertime, Beller had his meal and Müller's brought to their desks. They were still working when Henning arrived. Initially impressed by Beller's diligence, Henning was soon offended by the man's arrogance. Nonetheless, he opted to postpone a confrontation until certain it was inevitable.

"That *pendejo* intends to take over all my duties—not just accounting," Encinas sputtered as Henning walked her to her room after dark.

"I'm hoping to rein him in without a war," Henning replied. "Let's see if we can come up with a strategy at lunch in Cortéz tomorrow afternoon."

******

Asked to select a restaurant, Encinas had chosen the Los Portales Hotel's courtyard.

"I regret the way Beller treated you yesterday," Henning began after the waiter seated them beneath flags hanging from poles attached to the building. "He won't bully you again."

"Don't confront him over that," Encinas interrupted. "It's time for me to retire. My son leaves for Heidelberg University soon. Until then I'd like to spend my time with him."

"Take as long as you want. When you're ready to come back, your job will be waiting."

"No. I've wanted to retire for a long time. You should do the same, but I doubt you've yet realized there's more to life than work. After Beller leaves, you can make Alcalino your chief accountant. For a year now, he's managed the mill's day shift on your time and been my apprentice on his. He's more than ready."

Henning hadn't looked closely at Encinas for years. She was heavier around the middle, a common part of aging in a country where rice and potatoes were routinely served on the same plate. And she looked weary.

"Heidelberg University is expensive," he said. "I'll give you a pension and pay Antonio's tuition. What else can I do?"

"Teach Antonio German," she replied. "He's taking lessons in Cortéz but doesn't go as often as he should. And can you please make your offer directly to him? He won't accept if it comes through me."

"I'll bring him here for dinner. The drive will give us a chance to get acquainted."

******

Alone in his bedroom, Antonio sniffed the armpit of his shirt, then took it off and put on another. Next he combed his hair at the small mirror on his wall. Finally, responding to a last-minute concern, he twisted a tuft of cotton around the head of a wooden match and cleaned his ears.

"*Señor* Dietzel is here." Encinas's muffled voice came through the door.

He entered the living room in slacks and a dress shirt, wearing his best shoes instead of the interchangeable ones that fit either foot.

"Please comb your hair better," Encinas said. "You're going to a first class restaurant."

"He looks fine," Henning said.

On the way down the driveway, Henning swerved his carriage to miss a puddle. A newspaper had sunk to its bottom. Magnified by the water, the headline read: 'Toledo Breaks Production Record.'

Henning's sideways glance caught Antonio rolling his eyes.

Later at Los Portales Hotel, the waiter handed over their menu as if presenting rare books to prospective buyers, then noticed a hole in the tablecloth and had it replaced.

"It's amazing the way people bow and scrape for you," Antonio observed when they were alone.

"A disadvantage of wealth." Henning forced a smile.

"Wish I deserved that kind of treatment." Antonio pushed his silverware aside, creating room for his elbows and clearly making a point, though Henning couldn't imagine what it was.

As dessert was served Henning said, "Heidelberg University is an excellent school with a strict admissions policy. You must be an outstanding student." A smile nearly broke through Antonio's sullen expression, but it faded as Henning added, "I understand you're studying German. I can help if you'd like."

"You don't owe me any favors," Antonio replied angrily.

"It would be for your mother," Henning replied, fed up with the smoldering hostility.

Antonio dipped a French *macaron* in his milk. Mushy, it dripped all the way to his mouth. From a nearby table a dowager stared with disapproval.

"No one is good enough for the rich," Antonio scoffed, loud enough for her to hear.

Henning tried again. "Let's speak German for the rest of the evening. It'll be good practice."

"No. You'd be doing it for my mother—not for me."

During the drive home, Henning's attempts to converse in German brought curt responses, and he gave up with a sense of relief. Finding time to give lessons would be difficult while he was still crossing swords with Horst Beller.

He watched Antonio climb down from the carriage at Encinas's house, where bright moonlight highlighted blond stubble along his ears' edges. He must shave them, a strange vanity for someone who'd spent the evening emphasizing that he didn't care what people thought.

Together they walked toward the dark house.

"You would have liked my father," Henning said quietly as Antonio put a key in the lock. "He was a simple man, far less complicated than I. And he would have enjoyed telling you stories of the battles he fought while in the Prussian cavalry. He was twice decorated for bravery."

"Maybe you'll tell me more about him someday. And about the time you took your gold back from ten Mexican bandits."

"There were only six," Henning corrected. "How did you know about that?"

"My mother told me, but only briefly. Maybe someday I can hear the details."

Antonio went inside and closed the door.

Henning couldn't have been more confused. Surly and combative all evening, Antonio obviously wanted to see him again. Why?

******

Having been asked to keep an eye on Horst Beller, Alcalino watched as the proud German seated himself at a portable table outside the refinery's entrance and summoned the first man in line. With great deliberation, Beller then moistened his thumb and two fingers in a saucer of water and rubbed a banknote—confirming that his blue-veined hand held only one.

"Zähle dein Geld," he growled, handing the bill and three coins to Pablo Rios.

His assistant, Jürgen Müller, translated. Rios counted his salary and signed a receipt. Beller gave him a printed notice as the next man stepped forward.

Unable to read, Rios showed it to Alcalino who shook his head in disbelief.

"*Herr* Beller passed these out when he paid the mill workers today," Alcalino told Henning later, handing over the paper.

Henning read it and turned purple.

"Come along," he said. "I want a witness."

Outside Beller's office Henning stopped to compose himself. He looked up at the Latin motto *Tace, ora et labora* chiseled in marble above the mill's double doors. Martine's father had hung it above the previous mill's entrance to remind workers of his expectations: silence, prayer, and work.

Henning had transferred this motto to his new mill. But having come to see it as harsh, he'd recently decided to replace it with the gentler: 'Good Workers Deserve Good Employers.'

"An unnecessary expenditure," Beller had declared, vetoing that idea. "Besides, *Don* Manuel's advice is better."

And now Beller was meddling a more serious way. Henning twisted the doorknob and burst into the room, Beller looked up, eyes watery and bloodshot.

"If canceling the workers' bonuses indicates the extent to which you intend to control Toledo," Henning bellowed, "you and I are going to butt heads right here and now."

"I didn't come from Germany to do as you tell me," Beller said, infuriatingly calm. "I'm here to prevent you from wasting money, and my assistant's calculations show that your bonus plan is without economic justification."

"If your assistant were any more full of shit he'd have brown eyes," Henning fired back. "Those bonuses are based on output, which guarantees the benefits will outweigh the costs."

"You should've consulted the numbers more carefully."

Beller leaned a ladder against the shelves where financial records were stored. From the fifth rung, he pulled a folder from its place, then returned to his desk and put on eyeshades.

"This is Jürgen Müller's evaluation." In a professorial tone, Beller explained page one. On page two his voice lost its edge. "I need to review this more carefully," he said, then changed subjects. "By the way, we need to discuss the school your wife operates for the workers' children. It's—"

"It's none of your concern."

"Everything on your books is my concern. I have authority to veto non-essential expenses, and educating Indians is a colossal waste of money. The torch of knowledge can't be passed to simpletons."

"My contract with Landesbank grants me an allowance. I'll finance the school from that."

Beller tried to relax the tension with a smile. The curve of his mouth—perfect for showing disapproval—wasn't up to the job. He opened another ledger.

"This," he declared, "itemizes the school's expenses back to your loan's effective date. I'll subtract equal portions of the total—plus interest—from your next six allowances."

Alcalino accompanied Henning again on Wednesday when Beller, having reexamined Jürgen Müller's calculations, authorized reinstatement of the bonus plan.

"It took you forty-eight hours," Henning fumed, "to realize something obvious. The only thing your meddling accomplished was to upset my workers."

"I have to be thorough because you don't think things through. For example, you have ten thousand workers living in free housing. If you charge them four dollars a month it will bring in a half-million dollars a year."

Beller wasn't receptive to humanitarian arguments, so Henning tried a practical one.

"At the moment," he said, "Toledo is Peru's only hacienda that doesn't have a union, and I don't want one. They're the first step toward revolution, which could end with both of us hanging from trees."

"Are you trying to scare me?"

"I'm telling you I won't charge for housing."

"You no longer have the final word here," Beller declared.

"And your authority is limited to vetoing non-essential expenditures. Read the agreement your bank and I signed."

"Maybe you should take another look. Evidently you don't realize how much power you granted me."

******

Based on his contractual right to increase Toledo's accounting staff, Beller had added two new accountants and a row of filing cabinets.

"Speaking of unnecessary expenses," Henning told Martine at dinner after the new cabinets arrived, "Beller has expanded his accounting department to where it's too big for Encinas's office. I have to remodel a small warehouse for it."

"You don't seem as upset as I would expect," Martine said.

"That's because this gives me an opportunity to make a point."

After Beller and his staff moved in, Henning brought construction workers who outlined rectangles on the walls and began sledgehammering the bricks inside them.

"Openings for windows," he told Beller. "This was a warehouse, which is why its windows are so high. All you and your people can see are treetops and sky."

"We have enough light," Beller argued, "and your new windows will tempt my assistants' eyes from their work. Don't you ever plan ahead?"

"That's what I'm doing. You spend every second of daylight at your desk and walk back and forth to your room after dark. Everything you know about Toledo comes from invoices. To truly understand an operation this complicated, you need to see it firsthand."

Wiping his forehead, Beller dislodged his pince-nez. As it dangled from its neck ribbon he growled, "Looking at Indians, mules, and dusty roads won't help me increase your profits."

"Please. Let me show you around while the new windows are installed."

Following his two-day tour, Beller hung empty sugar sacks over the new windows.

When Henning told Martine, she described Toledo's head accountant perfectly, "All roses have thorns, but not all thorns have roses."

"Are you ever tempted to remind me you advised against bringing him?" Henning asked.

"No. You wouldn't have gotten a loan if you hadn't."

CHAPTER THIRTY-SEVEN
HENNING'S PERSONAL GLACIER

The Chiriaco River raced down steep Andean slopes, then crept across a flat desert before reaching the Valley. From behind his office desk, Horst Beller had ordered Henning to plant those barren riverbanks.

"We don't have enough water," Henning snapped. "And your authority is limited to non-essential expenditures."

"Water costs money," Beller countered, "and wasting it qualifies as non-essential."

"Congratulations. You've made the ridiculous sound plausible."

"I stand firm based on *Herr* Müller's measurement of the river's width, depth, and flow."

Henning's letter of complaint to Deutsche Landesbank began: "I regret to inform that *Herr* Beller is again overstepping his authority."

The directors' reply threatened to have Landesbank's attorneys enforce Beller's order.

Motivated by the potential cost of confronting Europe's most feared legal staff, Henning invited Beller to dinner. Basking in his apparent victory, Beller was unusually gracious.

"Before we squander money on lawyers," Henning said as Chabuca served fragrant, steaming coffee, "let me show you the land you want to plant."

"Just describe what you want me to see," Beller commanded.

"Only if you'll promise to believe me."

Next morning at daybreak, they set out on horseback with two *cholos* leading pack mules. Beller silently followed Henning toward the Andes all morning and much of the afternoon. But he came alongside as they left the green, sweet-smelling cane fields and entered a barren, colorless wasteland that smelled of baked earth.

"I've just realized the mules are carrying camping supplies," he began, "and since we can't possibly get back to Toledo before dark, I assume we're sleeping out?"

"Don't worry," Henning said. I brought everything you'll need, including a new badger hair toothbrush. I even had Martine inform *Herr* Müller that you won't be back until tomorrow. This time, you can't accuse me of not planning ahead."

"I felt conciliatory after Deutsche Landesbank took my side against you. That's the only reason I allowed myself to be bullied into this useless trip."

Later, the *cholos* set up camp on a bluff. After dinner, Beller trudged away from the fire—wincing with every step—and sat on a rock beside Henning.

"That's the water you called insufficient," Beller groused, glaring at the river boiling from the gorge below.

"And this is the soil you want to plant." Henning picked up a handful and let it trickle between his fingers. "But, maps don't show how poor it is. You have to see it firsthand."

"This area may not produce as well as the Valley," Beller said, "but it'll produce."

"That's best discussed after you see the Valley's west side tomorrow."

"You'll have to tell me what's so interesting there. I won't ride a step beyond Toledo."

"You won't have to. I had a raft built on the riverbank below." Henning pointed. "You'll probably call that a nonessential expenditure, but it's cheap compared to a dispute in court."

Next morning with the raft in the water, Henning waved for Beller to come aboard.

"I can't swim," Beller said.

"This river is smooth as silk and faster than a horse," Henning reassured him. "Come with me and you'll be home for lunch."

"Kindly refrain from praising your careful planning," Beller groused, coming aboard.

With Henning at the tiller the *cholos* pushed the raft into the current, and then started their long ride home.

For three hours and thirty miles, irrigation canals siphoned off the river's water. It was a fraction as wide and barely deep enough for the rudder when Henning steered toward a *cholo* and three horses on a beach.

"The water's shallow from here on," he told Beller after they slammed ashore, "so I arranged alternate transportation."

Henning held his tongue as they rode downstream to where the last water trickled into a muddy depression.

"You weren't exaggerating," Beller said, breaking the silence. "This river doesn't reach the ocean."

"It hasn't gotten that far since the sixties. Most years, we barely have enough water to irrigate the Valley."

"You've made your point masterfully." Beller's expression said his unexpectedly gracious words tasted bitter.

******

Martine and Henning rolled over in their beds, wakened by the early morning ring of the blacksmith's hammer and anvil.

"We own over a million acres we've never seen," Henning said. "If some can be put to profitable use, we can increase our payments and reduce our balance at Landesbank faster..."

"And get rid of *Herr* Beller sooner," she finished his thought. "Which suits me fine. We'll never save enough from our allowance to build more classrooms, and your trip down the Chiriaco River didn't soften our keeper of the purse as much as you'd hoped. He denied my request for funds without even considering it."

The following afternoon Henning rode into the Andes with a packhorse, a surveyor's map, and supplies. Three weeks later he saw a magnificent snowcapped peak straddling the continental divide. He rode toward it for hours, never seeming to get closer. Passing it the next afternoon, he realized it was a glacier. His glacier.

So far Henning hadn't seen a single acre with economic potential. He was sixty-four and the strenuous trip had taken the wind from his sails. His hips and knees ached. He gasped for air when swinging his machete above the timberline, cutting dry grass to fuel his fire and feed his horses. His head on a pillow of rolled-up trousers, he overslept most mornings.

A week later—blocked by dense jungle—he turned back toward Toledo. Still hoping to find what he sought, he went by another route. By the time he got home he'd have ridden two months without once setting foot on land that wasn't his. Reading the surveyor's report had been one thing. Seeing his recently acquired canyons, jungles, and waterfalls was another.

Re-crossing the continental divide, Henning entered a desolate land of rock and dust. Blocked by the top of a horseshoe-shaped cliff, he inched up to its edge. A chill reminded him of his dislike for looking down from great height. He confronted his fear by sitting with both legs over the edge as he studied the terrain and charted a course to the plain below.

Once there, his horses were shin deep in grass. Windblown green waves rolled across its surface as if rushing toward a distant shore. Evidently moist ocean air flowed inland and formed clouds. Then trapped by cliffs and their own weight, these surrendered their rain before rising to continue their journey.

This was the opportunity Henning had sought. Peru's arid coast—home to most of her population—had little grazing land, making beef scarce and expensive. Back at Toledo he proposed to establish a cattle station on this natural pasture.

For the first time Beller approved a nonessential expenditure. The outlay was minuscule. Pens and structures were built with sun-dried adobe bricks, made with clay-rich soil from a riverbed. The native grass was perfect for thatched roofs. Fences were unnecessary because the area was bordered by cliffs on three sides and a forbidding desert on the other. The only significant expenditure was for cattle. Henning imported four bulls and two hundred pregnant cows from Ecuador.

And horses having been in short supply since the War of the Pacific, he'd also bought a hundred mountain-bred Indian mares. Malnourished and stunted, they'd produce quality offspring if bred to good sires, and he knew where to find the best.

Problem was, their owner wouldn't easily make them available.

When Belisario opened the door, his hair was flat on one side.

"Sorry I woke you," Henning said. "I'll come back tomorrow."

"I was sleeping because I was bored—not tired," Belisario grumbled. "Come in. I'm in desperate need of a stimulating conversation."

Henning admired the sunset while Belisario lit a lantern. As its light turned the living room window into a mirror, he joined the old aristocrat on the couch.

"I used this to ward off Lima's nighttime chill while you explored your new property," Belisario said, covering his legs with a plaid lap blanket. "Thank you for sending me. I had a wonderful time, but it's good to be home. You never hear silence in a city." Amused by Henning's expression, he added. "Yes, I can hear silence."

Knowing Belisario's high spirits could end abruptly, Henning made his request.

"I hate saying no after you treated me to a vacation in Lima," Belisario replied. "But those stallions are the last of my bloodline. I don't want them wasted on mares that have no pedigree."

"Down here your sires breed six mares a year. But at the livestock station they'll produce hundreds of offspring. Your bloodline will spread throughout Peru and those sales will leave Beller no choice but to continue funding the horse farm."

"But those representatives of my bloodline will come from Indian mares, and even the best stallions need outstanding mothers to produce quality offspring."

"These mares are excellent," Henning coaxed. "Let me take you to see them."

"At my age I can't ride that far. Let me think about it."

Belisario still hadn't made up his mind when Henning returned the next day. Or the next. A week later Henning brought ten of his new mares to the horse farm. To his delight, Belisario considered their conformation—forged by generations in the rugged Andes—outstanding and gave in.

The livestock operation generated a profit its second year and six times as much the third. By then it needed little attention, but with Beller vetoing every new project he proposed, Henning had nothing better to do.

"You'll never be happy resting on your laurels," Martine told him from her bed one night, a full moon visible through the curtains. "But until Beller goes back to Germany, you should read more or find a hobby. With the right attitude the wait can be as enjoyable as what you're waiting for."

"I don't enjoy waiting and never will," Henning grumped. "Now that I've managed to triple Toledo's mortgage payments, I want to quadruple them."

******

Stepping down from Henning's carriage at the docks in Cortéz, Shaun O'Higgins snagged his sleeve.

"Damn," he said, examining the tear.

The silk shirt was one of several—all Irish green—Henning had given him as going-away presents. After thirty-three years of service, O'Higgins had retired and was returning to Chile.

Before his long-time bodyguard boarded *La Gallega*, Henning handed over an envelope, cautioning, "Open it in private. The contents are tempting and you don't have an O'Higgins to protect you."

"I trust this means I served you satisfactorily."

"You did more to keep me alive than any doctor."

"In George Bernard Shaw's play, *Candida*, there's a good line: "Man can climb to the highest summits, but he cannot dwell there long.' I hope you'll be an exception to that rule."

Their *abrazo* was long and the backslapping vigorous.

"I'll miss your way with words," Henning said as they let go.

"If wars were fought with words, we Irish would be rulin' the world," O'Higgins replied, exaggerating his brogue

******

After seven years at Toledo, Horst Beller sent for his wife. Six weeks later he picked her up in Cortéz with Henning's carriage. When they reached Toledo, Henning and Martine were waiting, him with work gloves behind his belt, and her fluttering a spread-open fan.

"Would you like to join us for tea, *Frau* Beller?" Henning asked after the introductions.

"Not now," Beller answered for his thin, sandy-haired wife. "I've been absent from work long enough for one day."

"I'm a bit tired after my trip." *Frau* Beller's pleasant glow faded. She spoke only English and German so everyone switched to English, the only language spoken by all but not the native tongue of any.

"Perhaps we can play Bridge this evening," Beller surprisingly suggested.

"Six o'clock?" Henning jumped on the opportunity. "Martine and I don't play cards. You'll have to be patient with us." He had a proposal best presented in a congenial atmosphere and knew from experience that Beller enjoyed instructing him.

"We'll be here at six sharp," Beller emphasized, then followed his *frau* and the servants carrying her trunks.

Alone with Martine, Henning said, "He obviously doesn't want his wife talking with us when he's not around."

She grinned. "Apparently he's as strict with her as with us."

That evening Beller came directly from work at precisely six.

Minutes later Henning welcomed Beller's wife at the door, "Please come in *Frau* Beller."

"Kindly call me Karin." She was less pretentious than her husband, who even after years at Toledo insisted on being called *Herr* Beller.

"You're late," Beller scolded as his wife and Henning joined him and Martine.

They ate dinner around a table in Toledo's library, near a window with clear diamond shaped panes. The beveled-edge glass separated the setting sun's rays into splashes of color.

"I love what this window does to sunlight," Karin said.

"The bevels act as prisms creating color diffraction," Beller explained, shuffling the cards he'd brought. "Shall we begin?"

"A friend suggested we start with Whist," Henning said, "because it's similar to Bridge but less complicated."

"That would be like paying checkers in order to learn chess," Beller scoffed. "Whist is a pastime for the simpleminded." He quickly explained Bridge's objectives and bidding process, then announced, "We'll compete as husband and wife teams."

"Shouldn't we put an experienced player on each team?" Karin asked.

"No. Tonight will be more instructive if our hosts see how experienced players work together." With uncanny accuracy Beller sailed cards into tidy piles in front of each player.

Karin played skillfully but unlike her husband was patient when asked to explain rules more than once. Nor did she share the pleasure he derived from trouncing Henning and Martine.

With each loss, Martine's determination increased. Henning didn't mind improving Beller's mood by losing, but did what he could to help her win a victory. Beller ruthlessly denied that pleasure. His meaningful looks ordered his wife to do likewise.

After two hours during which he and Karin hadn't lost a hand, Beller crowed, "Bridge, more than any other mental exercise, requires memory, skill at mathematics, and application of the laws of probability—not to mention the ability to plan ahead."

"I'm going to ask Landesbank to increase my loan," Henning said, nonchalantly broaching the subject he'd had in mind from the beginning. "We need a railway to bring cane from our fields to the mill and another to take our sugar to Cortéz."

"I'll have *Herr* Müller do a study," Beller offered.

"Don't worry, you'll get your railroad," *Frau* Beller told Henning graciously. "My husband is in no hurry to return to Germany. Increasing Toledo's loan will prolong his stay as well as earn his bank a tidy profit."

Her husband glowered, but she hadn't revealed anything Henning didn't know. And he was certain that after recuperating their cost the railways would save enough money to send his stiff-necked accountant home ahead of schedule.

Beller announced the lopsided final score, then said, "Time to call it a night." Standing at a full-length mirror, he tilted his hat until satisfied and proclaimed, "I don't need a study to know those railroads are a good idea. I'll recommend that Landesbank increase your loan."

******

Asking Henry Meiggs to build a railroad across Toledo's flat, uncomplicated landscape was the equivalent of asking Rembrandt to spread red paint on a barn. But Meiggs—who'd fallen on hard times—was glad to get the job. Building the Peruvian Central Railroad, he had laid track that clung to steep Andean slopes like ivy and carried trains from sea level to sixteen thousand feet in sixty miles, thanks to an average of one bridge and tunnel per mile. A lesser man could have built Toledo's railroad—but not as fast, as well, or as cheaply.

After the trains started rolling, Henning proposed more improvements, but Beller was no longer worried about having to leave before retirement.

"No more loans," he snapped.

"I don't need a loan," Henning clarified. "I'll make these improvements with our profits."

"No you won't. Toledo needs to increase its cash reserves as a hedge against hard times."

"If Beller was in charge of rabbit reproduction," Henning complained to Martine at dinner, "they'd be extinct."

His letter of complaint to Landesbank brought a reply that began, "If you fail to comply with the terms of your contract, you will lose a very costly legal battle."

When finished reading, Henning told Martine, "Threats lose impact when repeated too often."

CHAPTER THIRTY-EIGHT
JUDGE BENAVIDES

All afternoon from opposite sides of his office desk, Uncle Alfredo and Henning pored over Toledo's loan contract. By the time Henning got home the sun was down. Martine had eaten but joined him at the dining table.

"Your uncle is confident I can get the court to order *Herr* Beller to stop exceeding his authority," Henning said reaching for a linen napkin Chabuca had folded into a pyramid.

"Doesn't Judge Benavides hear cases involving contracts?" Martine asked.

"No. He retired. Your uncle believes his replacement is on the up-and-up, and I verified that he lives within the means of an honest public official."

"Benavides will get himself assigned to the case if there's a bribe available."

"There won't be. I don't bribe judges and neither do German banks."

"Bribery is part of doing business in Peru for everyone but you. That's why Benavides's house has an ocean view and enough rooms to require four servants."

"Considering the source of his money," Henning said. "You'd think he'd be more discreet."

"Why? No judge in Cortéz has ever been or ever will be convicted of misconduct."

******

Starting up the marble staircase outside the courthouse, Henning saw Uncle Alfredo coming down, a black attorney's robe swirling around his ankles. He gestured for Henning to follow, then stopped beside a window, his reflection looking like an agitated identical twin.

"There's been a change of judges," Alfredo declared. "Your case is postponed for two days, and Benavides will hear it. He wouldn't come out of retirement without incentive. Deutsche Landesbank must have bribed him. You need to offer more than they did."

"I can't march into a judge's office and offer money just because you think Landesbank might have done it. And even if you're right, I'm too late."

"Benavides is always open to a bigger bribe."

"Even if reputable German banks did bribe judges, Landesbank wouldn't bother with no money at stake."

"You can authorize me to proceed and give me the money," Alfredo said firmly, "or lose your case." He strode away, his shadow following like an anxious-to-please Negro porter.

Deep in thought, Henning strolled around the block, and then returned to his carriage, parked beneath a shade tree. Alfredo was in the passenger compartment with Martine. Henning's newly hired driver, a concession to advancing age, was polishing the vehicle's brass.

Henning reached the carriage as Alfredo left.

"Did you see that girl ahead of you?" Martine greeted when he opened the door. "She was dying for you to notice her buttocks. The way she rolled them was nothing short of artistic."

"The only buttocks that interest me are yours," he said.

"Uncle Alfredo just left. He's concerned about the change of judges and is positive Landesbank bribed Benavides. There's still time to top their offer."

"I can't offer Benavides a bribe on the infinitesimal chance that Germany's most respected bank might have done it."

"Why not? This wouldn't be the first time you bribed him."

"Back then I knew Cabrera had offered a bribe. But it's inconceivable Landesbank would stoop to that. So this time I'd be doing it to gain unfair advantage. And a man's honor is lost forever if he tosses it aside when it's inconvenient."

******

Murals depicting Pizarro's conquest of the Incas adorned the chamber's walls. According to a plaque beside the door, these had been painted while a shipload of mahogany was carved into the room's wainscoting, railings, doors, elaborate furniture, and massive judge's throne.

For two days a small audience had listened as Alfredo and Landesbank's attorney battled in the legal profession's unintelligible language. As Judge Benavides looked down from his raised platform the spectators went silent. The room buzzed with disappointment after he announced his verdict would follow a week of reflection.

"Let's hope," Henning whispered to Alfredo at the plaintiff's table, "this means his decision will be impartial."

"More likely," Alfredo said quietly, "the old goat wants to carefully structure his verdict in a way that doesn't leave grounds for appeal."

Seven days later the courtroom was packed. Everyone stood as Benavides came in wearing a white wig and black robe with wing-like sleeves, white ruffled cuffs, and a scarlet sash. He adjusted his collar of gold medallions and climbed the podium steps, then seated himself and banged his gavel.

Skewering Henning with his eyes, he boomed, "This contract calls for interpretation under German law. After applying the relevant laws to sections 6a, 6b, and 6c of said contract, I hereby order you to comply with *Señor* Horst Beller's instructions regarding any and all of Hacienda Toledo's expenditures. Failure to do so will give Deutsche Landesbank the right to foreclose your loan and take possession of the entire hacienda. You will also pay Landesbank a three-thousand-dollar fine and reimburse that institution for the cost of defending itself against your frivolous suit."

Henning battled the urge to slump in his chair. His pain was no one else's business.

He'd never heard a dying man's last breath but felt sure it would sound much like Uncle Alfredo's sigh before he asked, "Now do you believe Benavides was bribed?"

"I still don't understand why. Landesbank didn't gain anything."

"Except the satisfaction of telling you what to do whenever they like.

And with typical German thoroughness, they even arranged for you to pay the court costs along with a fine to cover Benavides's bribe."

In California Henning had recovered stolen gold from six armed Mexican bandits. As a merchant in San Francisco he'd thrived despite cutthroat competition. His guano business on Altamira Island had outlasted a ruthless adversary and withstood bombardment from a British man-of-war. He'd prospered during the Spanish blockade of Peru's guano islands. He'd thrived in the nitrate business despite a tidal wave and a war between Peru and Chile. In the Chiriaco Valley he'd outlasted Emiliano Cabrera and built the world's largest agricultural empire.

But he'd been under Horst Beller's scrawny thumb for years, and was now there more firmly than ever. For the foreseeable future, Beller would decide what he could and couldn't do, even though he paid the man's salary. And Henning would continue wasting time on worker complaints, ordering seed, and other trivia.

Weaving through packed spectators Henning politely acknowledged attempts to console him. Outside, his new driver was polishing Toledo's carriage and Martine was reading. Women and *cholos* weren't welcome in Peru's courts.

Seeing Henning's scowl, Martine closed her book and folded her hands. Henning sat beside her, shoulders drooping.

"Aren't you going to remind me I would've won if I'd bribed Benavides?" he asked as the carriage lurched forward.

"*Dios mío,* no," Martine replied. "It breaks my heart to see you penalized for your honesty. But maybe this will convince you to work less and appreciate life more. And please don't tell me you enjoy work more than anything else. How could you possibly know? That's all you ever do."

CHAPTER THIRTY-NINE
RUBBER BARONS

Martine had been up two hours when Henning joined her downstairs. She was surprised to see him. These days he seldom summoned the energy to get out of bed early.

At birth, his life expectancy had been forty years. He was now a robust sixty-seven, but roused himself from despondency only once a month, when Landesbank's mortgage statements confirmed that Toledo's quadruple payments were bringing *Herr* Beller's departure date closer.

"It's time to stop looking forward to life after Beller," Martine said, joining him as Chabuca served his breakfast. "You need to live in the present."

"I've decided to start an outside business to accelerate the repayment of our mortgage," he replied with a trace of his former enthusiasm.

"Where will you get the money?" she asked.

"I can borrow it if I find something promising."

For a week Henning slept at Uncle Alfredo's and strolled Cortéz's rundown docks talking with ships' captains. Finally, one described an opportunity that triggered his interest.

Sitting on the screened porch's sofa back at Toledo, he told Martine, "I'm going to look into Brazil's rubber business."

"I'll go with you. Spending time where we honeymooned should do us good." Flirtatiously she peeked over the tops of her eyeglasses. "It's been too long since sparks flew between us...the romantic kind anyhow."

Next morning, Henning bought tickets to Brazil and gave Uncle Alfredo a power of attorney. That afternoon he had Alcalino take over his remaining duties at Toledo.

"His zest for life came back the way bubbles suddenly appear in champagne when you pour it," Martine told Chabuca that night.

On Saturday Henning and Martine left for Manaus, a thousand miles up the Amazon River. Standing at the rail as their ship steamed away from Cortéz, he touched her shoulder and said, "You can come back whenever you want."

"Not without you," she replied. "We've already spent too much time apart."

******

The sky was dark as Henning and Martine disembarked on one of Manaus' unique floating docks. A British engineer's answer to fifty-foot fluctuations in the Amazon River's height, these were secured to pilings with loose-fitting, horseshoe-shaped brackets that let them rise and fall with the water.

"Manaus has the richest per-capita population on earth," the hotel bellboy told them.

Roaming through town the next morning Henning stopped asking Martine's opinion of the stone mansions. Some had stood in Europe before being taken down, brought across the Atlantic, and reassembled. She found such opulence obscene so close to the misery of the surrounding shantytown.

Rubber was used for balls, erasers, flexible tubes, and tires for bicycles, wheelchairs, and carriages. It was also the perfect coating for rainwear, boots, and electric wire. Manaus' rubber barons had a monopoly that produced immense profits. They ate Argentine beef and drank French champagne. Their clothing came from Rome and Paris and was sent to London for dry cleaning.

Despite the sweltering heat, their mansions had fireplaces made of stone from Spain and Portugal. One eccentric had four, none ever used, all large enough for him to stand inside with outstretched arms. He had also covered his downtown office walls with Brazilian currency, which—due to the ravages of inflation—was cheaper than wallpaper.

Manaus' centerpiece was the *Teatro Amazonas* opera house, lighted by two hundred crystal chandeliers. Under construction for years it was finally ready for an opening-night concert starring the world-famous tenor, Enrico Caruso.

Henning bought tickets and took Martine. The *Teatro's* driveway was paved with a mixture of rubber, sand, and clay to dampen the sound of arriving vehicles. Inside its lofty blue and gold dome, a mosaic created the illusion that the audience was seated under the Eiffel Tower. It was the perfect place and its intermission the ideal time to meet rubber barons.

******

For a week Henning researched the rubber business while Martine enjoyed the Meeting of the Waters, six miles from town. From its riverfront cafe she could see pink dolphins and watch the chocolate-brown Rio Negro join the yellow-gray Rio Solimões, forming the Amazon River. The contrasting waters flowed side-by-side until currents and eddies mixed them, creating the yellowish brown that would eventually stain the Atlantic Ocean for hundreds of miles.

When back in Manaus, Martine sat in their room rather than be depressed by the natives' inhuman living and working conditions. They'd been lured to town and tricked into signing one-sided contracts. Those who ran away were tracked down and mutilated as a warning to others. It broke her heart to see men with one hand or foot begging in the streets.

She missed Toledo, Chabuca, the workers, her trees, and horseback riding. Compared to the Valley's wide-open vistas, Manaus—surrounded by impenetrable jungle—was a claustrophobic prison. She hated the humidity, the stench of mildew, and the acrid smoke from never-ending fires that liquefied raw latex.

"I can't stand seeing you miserable," Henning told her in their room after two weeks. "We're going home."

Reaching that decision, he'd changed his mind many times, but in the end empathy for Martine had outweighed even his need to be free of Beller.

"Don't return to Toledo to please me," she said, avoiding his eyes. "If things get so bad I can't stand them, I'll go home. We can survive being apart."

"It's time for us to do better than survive," Henning replied.

"In Manaus you've been full of purpose and happy. At Toledo you'll be haunted by the opportunity you left behind."

"Brazil's monopoly won't last. If they haven't already done so, Europeans will smuggle *seringueira* seeds and plant them where the trees can be better cared for and the latex more easily collected." He put on his raincoat. "I'll be back with our tickets."

"You're not the same man I married," she teased.

And Martine wasn't the woman he'd married. She'd proposed to him motivated by a desire to save Toledo—without any sign that she loved him. But now she was prepared to stay in a place she hated rather than see him unhappy.

When he returned, Martine wore a sheer nightgown. Her clearly visible abdominal scar had faded since he'd walked in while Chabuca was bathing her after the traumatic loss of their child. And her body had added appealing curves.

"I thought we'd celebrate your choosing my happiness over the world's best business opportunity." She raised her hand to stop his response. "No more nonsense about Manaus being doomed. You could make a ton of money in the years it'll take for smuggled *seringueira* seeds to grow into rubber-producing trees."

"Speaking of trees…" He slapped his palm against his stomach. "Do you think the sap still rises in this dried-up old trunk?"

"It hasn't been *that* long," she protested.

As Martine backed into the bedroom, sunshine came through an opening in the clouds. Passing through water sliding down the windows, it projected undulating patterns on her body.

"Race you to the bed," she challenged. Going backward in high heels, she got there first.

Afterward, Henning asked, "Would you like to go dancing?"

She stared in silent disbelief.

"The best part of old age," he explained, "is that I no longer worry about what anyone—except you—thinks of me."

CHAPTER FORTY
BELISARIO'S SECOND DEATH

For twenty years people had enviously told Henning he never seemed to age. No one said that anymore. He moved slower and tired more quickly. Sunlight that had once tanned him now left him dry and puckered. The skin on his arms was so thin it tore. His voice was huskier and his eyes less luminous. And furrows on his forehead suggested sorrows and regrets.

"I spend too much time wondering if I wasted my youth," was all he dared tell Martine. Revealing more would remind her of the son they'd buried before he was born.

Henning's childhood hadn't instilled a sense of family. And after going to sea he'd been too busy to develop one. But now, watching others enjoy sons, daughters, and grandchildren, he knew his life lacked something essential.

In the year since he and Martine returned from Manaus, Toledo's finances had deteriorated. A worldwide depression reduced the demand for sugar and livestock. Beller couldn't have prevented that, but his tightfisted policies worsened its impact. He also stopped Henning from updating the boilers and crushers, then from building a private dock so his sugar could bypass Cortéz's expensive, antiquated port. As a result, declining profits had forced Henning to reduce his mortgage payments to the minimum.

"Our loan would be down to half and Beller would be gone if he'd let me modernize," he told Martine at dinner one evening.

She left the table.

Returning with the now-familiar map she asked, "Why don't you look for *Don* José's treasure? Uncle Alfredo thinks it's worth at least as much as we need to send Toledo's keeper of the purse back where he came from."

She unrolled the parchment, then put the meat platter on one edge and the gravy bowl on the other.

"Only *Don* José could read that without a key," Henning grumbled.

"Take another look."

"Why? I memorized every detail years ago."

******

Chinese coolies on the guano islands had grown pea pods and ginger so they could preserve their style of cooking in their new homeland. After the guano was gone, some opened restaurants on the mainland, introducing soy sauce and flash frying to their new homeland. At first, their clientele had been limited because they had a reputation for cooking anything that moved. But fashionable families now had Chinese cooks. And Martine had hired Juan Li.

"You've never eaten tastier food," Henning told Belisario as they sat near the fireplace in Toledo's living room. Pegs above the mantle held Henning's Colt Paterson rifle, purely ornamental since he'd bought his lever action Winchester.

Henning had Chabuca serve dinner on the coffee table between them because Belisario had palsy and didn't want Martine to see his hand tremble as he ate.

Losing a forkful of oriental peas with flat pods, he groused, "I've reached the age where strangers automatically pick up things I drop, as if I were an old lady. Ever wish you could put the mind you have now in the body you had at twenty?"

"Ever since I was twenty-one." Henning's grin pulled one side of his mouth higher.

"Speaking of days gone by, thank you for convincing me to send my stallions to your livestock station. If you hadn't, they'd have sired fewer than fifty foals among them."

After using those stallions on Toledo's Indian mares, Henning had sold hundreds of their offspring and—over Beller's protests—had shared the profits with Belisario.

"By the way." Henning handed over a *Lima Correo*. "Andrés de la Borda wrote a very complimentary article about your horses."

"Wasn't he the reporter who took us to a witch doctor when Sultán raced Goliat?"

"One and the same."

After reading the article twice Belisario said, "According to this, I'm a celebrity."

"You are. I've heard breeders from Tumbes to Tacna discuss your bloodline for hours."

"No one would've heard of me if you hadn't used my sires on your Indian mares. That's the only reason I'll leave anything behind when I die."

"You're forgetting Antonio," Henning said.

"Despite everyone's suspicions, including yours, I didn't father Antonio."

"Then why did you let people think…"

"Because that's what Encinas wanted."

"Why?"

"She had her reasons."

******

Months later Belisario succumbed to a heart attack. Former neighbors forced from the Valley by Emiliano Cabrera came from as far as Ica to see him laid to rest between his wife and son in Toledo's family plot. Too tall to fit in with Jaime Arrieta and the other pallbearers, Henning followed the casket to a freshly dug grave.

The gloomy mood was enhanced by an overcast sky and a violinist who played Chopin's haunting funeral march, head back, eyes closed. At the graveside Martine's pupils shone brightly as she read the inscription Henning had composed for Belisario's headstone.

> We loved him for his Virtues
> And were blind to his Faults.

During the ceremony, Henning remembered the first time Belisario had died. On that afternoon, ten years earlier, Henning had arrived at the horse-breeding farm and found the employees mourning.

"*Don* Belisario passed away last night," a stable boy told him.

Shocked and saddened he went to the house and knocked, intending to offer condolences. Someone half-opened the door, grabbed his arm, and yanked him inside. As his eyes adjusted to the dark interior he saw Belisario grinning wickedly.

"Everyone thinks you're dead," he exclaimed, elated.

"I know," Belisario said, nudging the drapes aside with one finger and peering outside. "I wanted to see what effect my death will have. So far, I'm pleasantly surprised."

"How long are you going to play dead?"

"Long enough so everyone has time to tell Encinas how much they'll miss me," Belisario had replied.

Ten years later Henning stood near Belisario's grave until the guests left, then poured water on the bonfire he'd built so people could warm their hands. As the glowing coals went black, he tore up a handful of knee-high ryegrass and whipped the stalks against his leg as he paced to and fro.

"I should have given Belisario more of my time," he finally said.

"It's too late to do anything about that, but you can help another friend who needs you." Martine removed her hat and shook her hair until it tumbled down around her face. "With Belisario gone, Encinas is alone. Antonio married a German lady and won't be coming home."

******

Encinas answered the door at the horse farm, crying, a handkerchief crumpled in one hand. She touched his arm, then waved him inside.

Composing herself she said, "Thanks for coming."

They'd met in their teens and were still friends though now of an age attained by few. If they weren't friends already, neither would have noticed the other on a street. Their history was what held them together.

Henning shrugged off his jacket. After hanging it and his hat on pegs near the door, he went back and forth with Encinas while she brought afternoon tea to the dining room table.

"I miss Belisario," she said, sweetening his cup with two teaspoons of sugar. "He was awfully good to me, especially after Antonio left."

"I regret that Antonio and I didn't find time to get together again after our dinner in Cortéz. What's he doing these days?"

"It's a long story, best told when I'm less emotional."

"Martine asked me to invite you to dinner."

"Thank her, but I'm not ready to be with people."

"You're shivering."

"Age changes everything. Remember how I used to walk around half naked in that chilly little cabin near the House of Smiles?"

She put her coat on and Henning lifted her hair so it wouldn't get caught under the collar.

Later when he left, he missed Belisario even more than when he'd come.

******

The next day, Henning returned to the horse farm after an early morning downpour. Encinas was in the yard watching birds feast on worms as they lay atop the saturated ground in the morning sunshine.

"I was so sure you'd come," she greeted, "that I brought an extra chair outside."

"What made you think I'd be back?"

"You have a question you couldn't bring yourself to ask yesterday."

A crow filled its beak from a puddle, then threw its head back and swallowed.

"You're right," Henning said. "Two months ago Belisario told me he wasn't Antonio's father. I couldn't help remembering what happened in the cabin we shared on the ship that brought you here from Iquique."

That brief rekindling of their romance had ended before they reached Cortéz, where both felt no regret but no desire to continue.

"Back when you were pregnant, I wondered if it was my child," Henning said. "But Antonio's birth date meant he couldn't be mine—not unless you'd carried him twelve months."

"I lied about his birth date. He's yours."

He met her eyes then looked away. Antonio had been born in Lima while Henning was at his nitrate mine. He had accepted the birth date given, as had everyone with the exception of Belisario who'd accompanied her to Lima and taken care of her after the birth.

"In fact," Encinas continued, "you're a father and grandfather. Our grandson is eight. I've never met him, but Antonio's wife was very appreciative when I sent Antonio Junior a ticket to come here for the summer. I think she and Antonio Senior consider the boy inconvenient."

"If I'd known Antonio Senior was mine, I would have helped you raise him."

"As a boy, he resembled that photograph of your father in his cavalry uniform. I thought you didn't want to acknowledge him."

"Now that you mention it," Henning said, "he did look like my father. I didn't notice at the time and am ashamed you had to raise him without my help."

"You helped a lot. To mention what comes to mind, you paid for the specialist who delivered him, provided the house where he grew up, brought food when *Don* José's well went dry during the Chilean occupation, gave me an extremely generous salary, and paid his tuition."

"But I didn't give him the attention sons deserve from fathers."

"You shouldn't feel bad about that. You didn't know he was yours."

Angry with himself—not Encinas—Henning stood and began pacing. "I should have known he was mine. When I think back, it's obvious he suspected I was his father."

"If he did, he never said so. You may have been misled by his inborn sadness."

When Henning returned the next day a beaming Encinas answered his knock.

"This morning," she greeted him, "Martine's Uncle Alfredo brought me a letter from Antonio. Our grandson is coming to visit."

In April, Toledo's telegraph operator brought Henning a message from Uncle Alfredo.

'Encinas's grandson arrived,' it read. 'You can pick him up at my house.'

The telegram protruding from his shirt pocket, Henning hurried to the vehicle shed.

"I'm going to Cortéz," he told Javier Vega, his driver.

"I'll get your carriage ready," Vega said. "Shall I drive you?"

"That won't be necessary, thank you."

"The *señora* is visiting the Arrietas. Where shall I tell her you went?"

"To pick up Encinas's grandson."

******

With Encinas beside him, Henning drove the second half of the horse farm's U-shaped driveway, looking forward to the coming day but braced for disappointment.

"I hope Antonio Junior speaks Spanish," Encinas said, excited and happy when they reached the main road. "Otherwise he and I can only converse when you're there to translate."

She rambled on until they reached Cortéz's outskirts, then fell silent.

"What is Antonio Senior's profession?" Henning asked, finding her silence awkward.

"He's in the Prussian cavalry. Incredible, no? He never met your father, yet pursued the same career in the same army. He said his heart took him there, but I credit your father's blood."

Henning liked Antonio Junior immediately and even more during lunch at Uncle Alfredo's. Pleasantly shy, the lad said little while they ate, but enough to show intelligence and passable Spanish. Blond, thin, and tall for an eight-year-old, he resembled Henning as much as any photograph. But unlike either of their fathers, the boy was full of joy.

During dessert, he cleaned every trace of caramel *crema volteada* from his bowl.

"Would you like to scrape the dish where that was cooked," Alfredo asked.

"That would be bad manners," the boy replied.

"Not if you do it in the kitchen. Come with me."

After Alfredo and Antonio left, Henning whispered, "He's a ray of sunshine in a world that's been dark for too long. How can his parents consider such a lovely boy inconvenient?"

"An accident of nature, I suppose. Some people are born without the prescribed number of fingers or toes. Others don't have normal emotions." Encinas shifted uncomfortably in her chair. "I hope Alfredo hasn't noticed how much Antonio resembles you."

Leading the way to the door, the boy tripped over his travel trunk in the entry hall. He took three quick steps to regain his balance and looked back, clearly hoping no one had seen.

"I'll carry this," Henning offered, picking up the trunk. "Can you please open the door?"

Once Antonio Junior was seated in the carriage, Uncle Alfredo complimented him on his manners. Embarrassed, the boy crossed his legs and slid both hands between them.

During lunch Henning and Encinas had done everything they could to make their grandson comfortable. Evidently they'd succeeded. On the drive to the Valley he sat between them, swinging both feet and chattering in a language he'd probably used only with his father.

At the horse farm Antonio was fascinated by the nearby Indian ruins.

"You can explore them if you like," Encinas told him. "But they're old and very important. Please don't touch or climb on anything."

"He's surprisingly grown-up," Henning said, watching the boy slowly and carefully enter the centuries-old ruins. "You can already see his respect for those ruins."

"He's had a lonely life," she replied. "Children like that often mature early."

"Does he remind you of his father?"

"He reminds me of you. Antonio Senior is as cold and self-centered as you described your father. Antonio Junior, on the other hand, has your pure heart and uncomplicated nature. But he's more open and spontaneous."

"You know all that five hours after meeting him?"

"All that and more. He's been extra kind to me. Even though he doesn't know I just lost Belisario, he senses that I need comforting."

"Have you noticed how often he stifles his laughter?"

"I imagine he learned that from his father. Or maybe he noticed how serious you are."

"I laugh."

"But you do it in a cold-blooded monotone, like an English aristocrat— not like you really mean it. If you'd show your emotions as strongly as you feel them, it would be a huge favor to Antonio Junior and everyone who loves you."

CHAPTER FORTY-ONE
SO NEAR YET SO FAR AWAY

Martine was at Elena Murillo's house in Cortéz. They'd met at the Valley's convent while helping nuns educate orphans. Having recently won an award for her poetry, *Señora* Murillo was preparing for a reading at Lima's *Teatro Municipal*. While Martine helped her, Henning spent an unforgettable week with Antonio Junior.

On the day Martine was to return, Henning called on a retired Englishman, Cecil Aubrey, who lived on the Valley's outskirts. Aubrey had brought horses, hounds, and foxes from England rather than give up hunting. From his latest litter of puppies, Henning bought a black and tan male with long ears, a high-domed forehead, and large brown eyes.

Making this purchase without consulting Encinas was risky, but she might say no and would forgive him for not asking. And if she didn't want to take care of a puppy, he'd pay a stable boy to do it.

Antonio Junior was on Encinas's lap when Henning arrived. Staring at Henning across the top of *Beauty and the Beast*, she recited the words from memory while their grandson followed the print with his finger. When her words varied from the text, Antonio gently corrected her.

After Henning set the puppy on the ground Antonio sprang to his feet and dashed down the steps, then dropped to his knees. Forepaws against the boy's chest, the puppy licked his face.

"He's yours," Henning said.

"How did you know I like dogs?" Antonio asked.

"Because I did at your age."

"Did you have one?"

"Only for a few days," Henning replied sadly.

"What's this dog's name?"

"You can call him whatever you want."

"Tahbert. That's my other dog's name, but he's only imaginary. I won't take Tahbert in the ruins. He won't know he should be careful."

Baying, Tahbert bolted after a squirrel with Antonio Junior scrambling to keep up.

Encinas touched Henning's arm.

"I received a letter from Antonio Senior's wife this morning," she said, voice lifeless. "He was killed while training to go to Venezuela. Forgive my tears. I used to read *Beauty and the Beast* to him."

Henning's chest thumped and his throat constricted. Germany, England, and Italy had blockaded Venezuela after she stopped paying foreign creditors. When the United States objected, Germany intensified her military training. And for no better reason than that, Henning's ticket to Hamburg—bought yesterday—was useless. And his anticipated relationship with the only son he'd ever have was over before it began.

He brought chairs from the porch so he and Encinas could make sure Tahbert didn't go into the ruins.

"His mother doesn't want him back," Encinas said after a long silence. "When he's more comfortable here I'll tell him he's going to stay and what happened to his *papi.*"

"He'll be fortunate to be raised by you." Henning resisted covering her hand with his. "I'd like to be part of his life too, with your permission."

"Please. As much as possible without making Martine suspicious, take him along when you go places. He wants to know all about Toledo and loves being here."

Back when they'd met, Encinas had worn revealing dresses as dictated by her profession. Running Henning's water business, she'd dressed in frumpy clothes that wouldn't worry her customers' wives. Living with Belisario, she'd chosen conservative styles to please him. Free to be herself these days, she'd worn a dress as wildly colorful as Martine's rainbow eucalyptus trees. It had no doubt matched her mood before she'd read her daughter-in-law's letter.

"I wish I could correct the mistakes I made with Antonio Senior," Henning said.

"When people dream of reliving the past, they expect to use the wisdom they've accumulated since then. But if they'd known what they know now, they wouldn't have done what they regret. Don't start a relationship with Antonio Junior because you feel guilty. Do it out of love. And don't risk damaging your marriage by telling anyone you're his grandfather."

"I'd have told Antonio Junior already if not for Martine."

"We can't let Martine find out," Encinas insisted. "That would damage your marriage and end my friendship with her."

"Every time I start to confess, I remember Martine's uncompromising sense of right and wrong, and lose my nerve. But then I tell myself that she's always wanted children and might welcome Antonio as eagerly as you did."

"Don't make a decision we'll both regret," Encinas pleaded. "Please."

Long legs churning, Tahbert chased a squirrel into its burrow and stuck his nose in the hole. Behind him, Antonio bent over, panting, hands on knees.

Henning walked to a stand of cane and returned with a young, tender stalk. In Encinas's kitchen he chopped it into segments and sliced off their hard exteriors.

Delivering a bowlful to Antonio he said, "Chew these and spit out the pulp. The juice will give you energy so you can keep up with Tahbert."

"Thank you," Antonio said. "I love Tahbert."

The temptation to say *and I love you*, was nearly irresistible, but Henning decided to build up to that.

"Are you coming again tomorrow?" Antonio asked.

"Do you want me to?"

"Yes, sir."

Antonio smiled, tentatively as though wondering if Henning minded. Henning scooped him off the ground and felt two thin arms surround his neck with touching enthusiasm.

******

On Henning's best days he laughed easily and whiled away hours with Antonio. On his worst he sat brooding in his library. His life now contained everything he most wanted—success, the woman he adored, and a grandson to carry on with Toledo. But keeping all three seemed impossible. Withholding information from Martine in the past had always been a mistake. But he dreaded confessing to her after their relationship's dramatic turn for the better.

Perhaps instead of asking what would work, he should ask what was right. Being secretive in business was prudent. But being that way with his wife was wrong. He should admit he had a grandson and stop telling white lies to hide how he spent much of his time.

Or should he?

CHAPTER FORTY-TWO
DON HENNING

Early Easter Sunday, Martine found Henning seated in the library, staring out the window. When she returned with scrambled eggs and fried bananas he was grateful but not hungry. His food was still untouched when she brought coffee.

"No thank you." He forced a smile. "Maybe later."

"When I ask what you're doing these days," she said, sitting beside him, "you say you're getting ready for when Beller leaves. But that's not true, is it?"

"No. Let's go for a drive."

After Javier Vega brought the carriage Henning dismissed him and helped Martine aboard. Once underway, his small talk disappointed even him. They dismounted at the summit between the Valley and Cortéz. Hands on her shoulders he turned her toward the Valley and stood behind her.

"In my life I've done many things badly," he began.

"Nobody does everything perfectly," she said. "You're the only person I know who tries. I'll settle for that."

Clearly intended to encourage him, her praise had the opposite effect.

The panorama below had changed since he'd first seen it. Farmhouses and contrasting fields had been replaced by an ocean of sugarcane—a single, monotonous shade of green beneath a cornflower-blue sky. The only other color was the towering black cloud spewing from the smokestack at Toledo's refinery.

"That view was extraordinary," Henning said, "before Emiliano Cabrera and I ruined it."

"He would have changed it even if you'd never come. But under him, life would have been terrible for the workers, who—thanks to *Don* Henning—now live full, rich lives."

"I don't think of myself as a *Don*."

"You are one…in the truest sense of the word, which is why I love you."

Henning couldn't respond. Anything he said or did might ruin a perfect moment.

"That's the first time you've said you love me," he said matter-of-factly.

"I needed the push I got when you and Encinas began enjoying one another's company after Belisario's funeral. Nothing motivates a woman—especially one who's competitive—as much as jealousy."

"I'll never stop loving you," he said, raising her chin with his finger, "and I've never been unfaithful. But I do have a confession…"

"I already know," she declared, "that you and Encinas were once lovers and have a grandson who's your mirror image."

Henning felt as though his heart was shriveling.

"Don't worry," she continued, "I did what you always do. I analyzed the numbers, and they tell me Antonio Senior was conceived long before we married."

"How long have you known?"

"A few days."

"And you're not…angry?"

"Why should I be? These things happen when men and women fall in love and don't have a suitably suspicious chaperone."

Martine had grown up among people who were comfortable judging others' morals and didn't forgive lapses. Yet on what might have been Henning's blackest day, she had exonerated him as if it was easy.

"You'd have lots of grandchildren," she said, "if you'd married a young woman, as most men would have. I'm glad you have a little boy to steal your heart. Have you told him you're his grandfather?"

"Should I?"

"How else will he know what he means to you? Don't worry. I know you don't still feel romantic love for Encinas. And loving her the way you do doesn't leave less for me."

"Does romantic love fade," Henning mused, "because its essence is longing and we stop longing for what we have?"

"According to my only experience with romantic love, it matures into something better."

Wrapped in each other's arms, they kissed. The embrace lingered after their lips parted.

"If you're always there for Antonio Junior the way you are for everyone else you love," Martine said, "he'll be your best friend ever."

"Second best." Henning touched her cheek.

She stretched—unintentionally emphasizing her curves—then stepped up into the carriage.

Circling behind, Henning opened the cargo trunk and took out a rolled-up parchment. Before climbing aboard he handed it to Martine.

"*Don* José's map," she exclaimed. "Are you going to look for his treasure?"

"It'll give me something to do while waiting for Beller to leave. Do you think I should take Antonio if it's okay with Encinas?"

"Absolutely. You're not the sort of man who'll enjoy sitting around with his grandson on his knee. But he's young. Don't push him too hard."

"I won't. I remember what it was like when my grandfather did that."

Martine's head against his shoulder, Henning picked up the reins and clucked to the horses, then pivoted the carriage toward Toledo.

By the time they reached the valley floor, Martine was driving and the sun appeared to touch the horizon.

Studying *Don* José's map, Henning said, "Sultán must have often gone to where the treasure's hidden. If he were alive he might take me to it. At least I have a general idea of where to start. *Don* José once pointed toward Las Casitas Canyon while talking about his bank."

A flock of Martine's egrets glided in and landed in her trees. They were generations removed from the twelve that survived the voyage from Brazil.

"The best things in my life all came through you," she told Henning.

The corners of his mouth turned up.

"You have a marvelous smile," she said. "Please let me see it more often."

"I'll make sure you do."

EPILOGUE

When Henning reached Encinas' house, Antonio Junior and Tahbert were playing near the Indian ruins. Henning's tentative decision became final when the boy greeted him with an exuberant hug.

Kneeling to put Antonio down, he said, "I have something to tell you. Your father is my son and you're my grandson. That means I'm your *Opa*."

Though too young to appreciate the implications, Antonio was delighted.

"This shows where a treasure is hidden." Henning said, tapping the boy's head with José Geldres's rolled-up map. "Would you like to help me find it?"

The boy's eyes widened. "Before I came here, my father gave me a rolled up paper just like that one. The man who gave it to him said it's very important."

Antonio dashed to Encinas's house and went inside. At eight, Henning had been equally eager to please but infinitely more skilled at hiding his feelings.

The way you are is better than the way I was, he thought, watching his grandson return at top speed, head down, arms pumping.

Proudly Antonio handed Henning a rolled-up document.

"What is it?" Henning asked.

"I don't know. The man who gave it to my father said it should be given to his father. That's you, right? The man said this would be your reward for finding your son."

Henning unrolled the scroll and took his first look at the key to José Geldres's treasure map.

Verne Albright grew up in the American West. At age nineteen, he took his first of sixty-five trips to Peru. He returned sometimes for business but primarily for the pure pleasure of being there. "Finding a true calling is a miracle many people never experience," he says, "and Peru provided me with two. The first was Peruvian Paso horses, which I have promoted throughout the world. The second was Peru's rich history and culture, which provided material to feed a more recent passion, writing historical fiction set in that nation's fascinating past." Albright makes his home in Calgary, Alberta, Canada, with his wife and five dogs.

ACKNOWLEDGMENTS

I was blessed with an excellent team to assist and encourage me as I wrote the two-novel set composed of *Playing Chess with God* and *The Wrath of God.* Among those who contributed far above the call of duty were my good friends Mimi Busk-Downey, Henry F. Curry, Jr. M.D., Terry Ellis, Rhonda Hart, Lucille Rider, Babette Sparr, and Jan Swagerty; my creative brother-in-law, Charles Bazalgette; my exceptionally talented and sharp-eyed test reader, Tina Clavelle Meyer; my brothers--Deane, a very helpful test reader... Harold, generous with encouragement and suggestions...and Ralph, whose motivating support was always available when my spirits flagged or I needed help; my stepdaughter, Krista Weber, whose wonderful artistic instincts and tireless efforts were immensely helpful; my high school classmate, Kay Galbraith, who found time to help no matter how busy she was; my first editor, Michael Parrish, who passed away before the job was finished; my Rewrite Specialist Jean Jenkins (I'm sure few editors ever contribute as much to a book as she did to mine); and my Peruvian friend Robbie Watson, who said he'd help in any way possible and more than kept that promise. And last but not least, I'm grateful to my wife, Laurie, for putting up with me during those times when I was discouraged, crabby, and possibly even unbearable.

— Verne R. Albright

28299141R00200

Made in the USA
Columbia, SC
14 October 2018